The Gallup 14

THE GALLUP 14

A Novel

GARY L. STUART

The University of New Mexico Press Albuquerque

Second printing, 2000

Library of Congress Cataloging-in-Publication Data
Stuart, Gary L., 1939–
The Gallup 14 : a novel / Gary L. Stuart.—1st ed.
p. cm.
ISBN 0-8263-2133-X (alk. paper)
1. Anti-communist movements—New Mexico—History—Fiction.
2. Gallup (N.M.)—History—Fiction. I. Title.
PS3569.T8157 G35 2000
813'.54—dc21 99-050513

CONTENTS

AUTHOR'S DISCLAIMER

No lawyer worth his salt should write anything without making sure the reader knows the difference between the fact and the fiction of the writing. So here's the difference: This is, essentially, a true story. The context in which I tell the story and all of the dialogue is fiction.

The riot in Gallup, New Mexico, and the killing of Sheriff M. R. Carmichael occurred on April 4, 1935. It was a significant historical event in New Mexico. The trial of the men charged with his murder was a watershed legal event and an important marker in the cultural progression of race and labor relations in New Mexico. But the real story lies in the ferment and political intrigue that led to the riot, the jury's verdict at the trial, and the political conclusion to the saga of the "Gallup 14." That said, the reader must remember that this novel is not history, even by implication. This story is told with invented dialogue and imagined characters for the express purpose of avoiding history's limiting obligations and obtaining a different kind of truth—one that will endure and tell the story of Gallup in the greater context of New Mexico.

The two main fictional characters are Billy Wade and Mary Ann Shaughnessy. I created them, but there is a lawyer from Gallup who could have been Billy Wade, and there must be someone in Gallup who could have been his Mary Ann. The two main real characters are John F. Simms and J. R. "Dick" Modrall. They were adversaries in the trial in 1935 but became partners in 1937 and founded what is now one of New Mexico's largest and most prominent law firms. The ten men who were charged with Sheriff Carmichael's murder are lost in history.

The answer to the mystery of who really shot the sheriff and who killed the other two men that day is not only unknown, it's unknowable. I have included the newspaper accounts, the letters and petitions, the local opinions, the sworn trial testimony, and Bobcat's last word on the subject. Those readers who are interested in solving the mystery will be able to draw their own conclusions.

The eviction of Victor Campos by Senator Vogel is well documented in the files of the McKinley County District Court in Gallup. The arrest of Campos, Navarro, and Mrs. Lovato happened as reported in the story. The Gallup Riot took place in the alley behind the Sutherland Building between Second and Third streets on April 4, 1935. I have tried to accurately identify most of the men and women who were there that day. I placed them at the scene from the court records, from local and national press reports, and from information given to me in personal interviews.

While I have invented characters, created dialogue, and filled in missing gaps, I have nevertheless made an honest effort to accurately report what happened. The criminal complaints, search warrants, lineups, mass arrests, deportations, and kidnapping of the defense lawyers in Gallup are well documented in the official files of the McKinley County District Court. The widespread fear and influence of the American Communist Party and its National Miners Union are well documented by serious and respected researchers. The trial of the ten men ultimately charged with the murder of Sheriff M. R. Carmichael and the assault on Deputies Hoy Boggess and Bobcat Wilson took place in Aztec, New Mexico, from October 4 to October 17, 1935. The judge, the trial lawyers, and the witnesses in this story are real. I used a lot, but not all, of the sworn testimony given by the witnesses to tell the story of the trial. The names are factual, but the personal descriptions, dialogue, and disposition of the characters, both real and imagined, are all products of my imagination. I tried to make the testimony interesting by modifying the lawyers' questions. I am solely responsible for the arguments and attitudes of the lawyers. I created them as if I had tried the case (for both sides). The actual exhibits, affidavits, warrants, and court orders are accurate. They were excerpted from the official court transcript in the clerk's office of the New Mexico Supreme Court in Santa Fe. The case is officially reported as *State of New Mexico v. Ochoa* et al., 41 N.M. 589, 72 P2d 609 (1937). The letters, telegrams, and notes in the novel were copied directly from the originals on file in the various penal papers of four New Mexico governors in the New Mexico State Archives, in Santa Fe, New Mexico.

I have set the story in the format of a novel so that I could tell the real story in the context of the times. But all things considered, the story isn't really mine; it belongs to my hometown, Gallup, New Mexico.

PROLOGUE

Gallup, 1935

Gallup? What kind of a name is that for a town? No one gave it any thought when they picked the railroad paymaster's name for the siding alongside the track back in 1881. It was so small, it was lucky to get named at all. Railroad towns couldn't be too particular in those days. Even then, it was a better name than they gave weepy Winslow 120 miles down the track to the west. How embarrassing for a railroad town to have *slow* in its name.

I was one of six lawyers in Gallup in 1935, not counting the government lawyers and the judge. I was the youngest, the least experienced, and the only one close to Bobcat. Like everyone else, Bobcat called me Billy Wade and made it sound like my first and middle names, instead of my full name, like it really was. I was born in Oklahoma but raised, along with Bobcat, right here in downtown Gallup. Actually, I suppose I should speak for myself since Bobcat's "raising" took place more out of town than here. "Bobcat" wasn't only his name; it was his style. He got named that because no one messed with him. No one. He lived on the north side of the tracks but patrolled the south side the same way—fairly, right away, and without looking at your wallet or the shape of your hat. Hard hats, Stetsons, and old slouch hats were all the same to Bobcat. Looking back on it all, he was probably the best friend I ever had. How you spent your money wasn't his concern, but where you got it was. If you earned it, he respected you; if you stole it, he locked your ass up. Right away.

On April 4, 1935, the *Gallup Independent*'s entire front page was devoted to the riot and the killings in the alley, a half block from the county jail, between Second and Third Streets. It became a long and bitter story. The violence was predictable, or so some said. The heartache and the bitterness lasted long after the burials and the trials. Just like the tracks, the strike split off workers from bosses, renters from landlords, and friends from friends. The so-called Gallup Riot made my town famous, but all in all, we would have just as soon stayed quaint. Or quiet. Or whatever the situation was when people weren't getting killed over rent money. Gallup was then still part of the western frontier, at least as far as the dudes and the lawyers from back east were concerned.

Gallup was west of Albuquerque and east of Los Angeles and connected to both by Route 66 and the Santa Fe Railroad. Gallup was "new" even though it was founded before the turn of the century. Albuquerque was "old" but had an elegant name. At least the folks over there thought it was elegant because it had four syllables and ended on a high note. Just to get even, the railroaders, and everyone else in Gallup at the time, called it Al-burr-kirk.

Railroads were a big deal then. None of the railroad towns would have amounted to much if the men who drove the spikes had been interested only in reaching California. Of course, that's what they said they wanted—to reach California. But a lot of them stayed in Gallup. In time, it became clear that the rich coalfields all around, and under, Gallup were reason enough. Money talked every bit as loud then as it does now.

Gallup's main street, just like in all the rest of the railroad towns, became (you guessed it) Railroad Avenue. The men of the Atlantic & Pacific Railroad did the naming. The names they picked were plain and practical. Those names lasted for almost fifty years. By 1927 the A&P Railroad was long gone, the Atchison, Topeka and the Santa Fe was the big dog in town, and the good citizens of Gallup were trying to get used to calling Railroad Avenue "Route 66."

The next street south of Railroad Avenue was called Coal Avenue. They were parallel to each other in more ways than one. The not yet famous Route 66 ran from Chicago to the City of Angels out there in California. It ran right down the middle of Gallup, right alongside the railroad tracks. Which, you should know, ran right alongside, and sometimes right over, the Rio Puerco. All the kids, and most of the adults, called it the "Purkey." The Purkey was a dry river. Dry till it was wet and wet only when it rained. Then dry again. Kind of like the coalfields.

I don't mean to make it sound all that quaint. Fact was, the tracks, Route 66, and the Purkey split more than just the town down the middle. All three, in their own way, split the people, too. The tracks divided the town, the streets set the boundaries, and the Purkey became a place to hide the shame, and the evidence.

The coal strike in the winter of 1934 was about power, but the riot in the spring of 1935 was about pride. Both were in large supply for a railroad town.

Some said that's why this is Gallup, not the old Spanish city of Albuquerque and sure as hell not Win . . . slow. Gallup was already split down the middle by the tracks, Railroad Avenue, and the Purkey. When all those houses in Chihuahuaita were bought out from under the strikers, it was worse than fire in the pit. When it ignited, it nearly burnt the whole town to the ground. There were good men on both sides. Some died and some went to jail; the rest just let it go on by.

Long before the trial of the Gallup 14, the politics of New Mexico focused on the economic contributions from the coalfields surrounding Gallup. Four different New Mexico governors immersed themselves in the politics of Gallup. Governor Seligman declared martial law in Gallup back in August 1933. Governor Tingley was still dealing with the political consequences of martial law when the Gallup Riot occurred in April 1935. Governor Miles finished it all off when he received those handwritten letters from Juan Ochoa and Manuel Avitia in July 1939.

All four governors were running for reelection while the miners in Gallup were striking, rioting, or demonstrating. That sort of thing makes great yellow-rag press and politicians nervous. That's why all four of the governors who got involved with the mines and the miners of Gallup were politically petrified about the influence of the Communist Party and their so-called union in Gallup.

The National Miners Union won recognition by the miners in Gallup in the spring of 1933. The two major grievances were wage cuts and low pay for deadwork (that's union jargon for nonmining maintenance work). But everyone knew that what the men and women mining coal around Gallup really wanted was some small measure of control over their working lives.

So on August 29, 1933, the workers, all of whom were new members of the National Miners Union, formed picket lines at the five major coal mines in the Gallup vicinity. The strikers succeeded in a peaceful shutdown of all the mines. Around town, the NMU leaders were real proud of the fact that there was no violence and that 970 out of approximately 1,000 employees joined the union and stood on the picket lines.

That's when Governor Seligman stepped in. Although the strike was only on for one day and there wasn't a single act of violence, he declared martial law at 6:00 P.M. for McKinley County, New Mexico. He ordered the National Guard to surround Gallup. Not that it was all his idea, you understand. You see, the *other* union, the United Mine Workers (also known as the UMW) was real sore about losing the effort to organize the Gallup miners. John L. Lewis himself telegraphed Governor Seligman and offered his personal assistance. Mr. Lewis was kind enough to point out the ties between the NMU and the Communist Party. He went out of his way to offer the governor some advice on what New Mexico should do: "The policy ought to be for the mine operators in Gallup to make an agreement directly with the UMW and encourage a union which is committed to the upholding of American institutions."

John L. Lewis wasn't the only one to telegraph the governor that day. McKinley County sheriff Dee Roberts and several local mine managers also sent him a telegram, saying: "The condition is serious and beyond our control without bloodshed and probable loss of life and damage to property." The sheriff requested "immediate assistance." The governor's response—martial law—was justified in a letter he released to the people of New Mexico. He first noted that most of the unions (United Mine Workers, Big Four Brotherhoods, and the American Federation of Labor) had asked him to send troops. Their request was seconded by the American Legion Post at Gallup; the county peace officers, including the sheriff; the mayor of Gallup; and all of the prominent businessmen of Gallup, including the mine owners. The governor said he did everything possible to avoid sending troops, but "the appeals were so insistent . . . that I believed it best for me to act and act promptly."

The fall elections were coming up, the strike was still on, and martial law was still in effect in Gallup when Governor Seligman died of a heart attack on September 25, 1933. Now I don't mean to imply that Governor Seligman was acting without what lawyers (like me) call "legal precedent." He had plenty of that. In the last twenty-five years martial law had been declared three times in New Mexico—twice in Gallup and once up in the other coalfield in Colfax County. All three previous declarations of martial law were tied to coal strikes, and the last one, the one in 1928, was supposed to prevent a spread of the Industrial Workers of the World (IWW) organization during a "Wobblies" strike in New Mexico's rich coalfields.

Vice-governor Andrew W. Hockenhull succeeded Governor Seligman after his untimely death. One of his first official acts was to look into the ongoing strike in Gallup and the fact that the troops were still in town and martial law still in effect. Governor Hockenhull began his stewardship of the state with a political dilemma. The financial folks at the state capital were getting nervous at the cost of maintaining the troops in Gallup, which was approaching $80,000. On the other hand, the coal mines were paying a million dollars in taxes annually. Here's the dilemma: If Governor Hockenhull removed the National Guard and the mines closed down, the state would lose the tax revenue. If he didn't remove the National Guard, Gallup, New Mexico, would establish the record as having the longest period of martial law in the entire United States (except, of course, for the Civil War).

The governor appointed one of the leading lawyers in the state, Mr. W. A. "Bill" Keleher of Albuquerque, and a former governor, Merrit C. Meecham, to come to Gallup and try to resolve the strike. They gave it a mighty effort, but the strike went on. Bill Keleher might not have been able to stop the strike, but years later he included it in his memoirs. He managed to capture the dividing force between capital and labor—them and them that wanted it. Mr. Keleher described the business and professional men of Gallup as "ordinarily of good will and even temperament, [who] found themselves, willingly and unwillingly, engaged in last ditch commercial and political rivalry, battling and scheming in what appeared to be a life and death struggle over money or property."

You see, about all that stood in the way of settling Gallup's coal strike and getting the troops out of town was the fact that some of the union leaders had been jailed by Sheriff Roberts on charges of violating martial law. Governor Hockenhull pledged that those union leaders would be freed, more or less. The condition was that they leave the state of New Mexico. And so that's how they settled it. The men in jail verbally agreed to leave the state and to turn the NMU's operations over to "local" leadership. Those were the ones running the show when things erupted again in the spring of 1935 on account of the deal between Senator Vogel and the Gallup American Coal Company.

To understand the importance of that, you'd best keep in mind Governor Tingley's role in all of this. The Communist Party of America decided at about this time to get out of the union business. They dissolved the National Miners Union at the national level, but the Gallup local of the NMU survived—mostly because Governor Hockenhull wanted it to. But the voters replaced Governor Hockenhull, and Governor Clyde Tingley became our governor on January 1, 1935—to keep the peace, more or less. About three months later the Gallup miners decided that they either had to form a weak independent union, which would have cut them off from the Communist Party, or to make peace with their old UMW enemies. The Gallup NMU local met on the morning of April 3, 1935, to go over the amalgamation of the NMU into the UMW. It was agreed that the merger would take place in two days. Those boys could not have known what was about to happen the next day. What was going to happen on April 4, 1935, would change everything forever.

one

THE EVICTION

March 1935

Bobcat drank his morning coffee in a little café just this side of Chihuahuaita. He said it "Chee-wa-ita," and it sounded pretty close to the way it sounded in Old Mexico, where they talked real fast. Bobcat talked slow, like most of the men who gathered at the end of the day at the American Bar. He drank his evening bourbon and branch water there, ten blocks from Chihuahuaita—in the heart of downtown Gallup. The American Bar was run by Guido Zecca, who ran more than a bar in those days. Guido was widely respected for his political instincts and his business dealings. At the close of the business day you could hear the tinkle of the glasses by men who had spent part of their day two doors away in the Sutherland Building, where Judge Bickel held court. On Saturday nights you could hear the noise from the western band even if you were across the street in the Angeles Bar and Pool Hall—the bar frequented by most of the men from Chihuahuaita.

Every once in a while someone would take note of Bobcat's habit of drinking coffee in the morning at a Mexican café near Chihuahuaita and whiskey at night in the American Bar. Some said he didn't know where he belonged; others said that was just Bobcat. Bobcat's real name was L. Edison Wilson, but almost no one knew that. Even his family called him by the nickname that suited him like "Black Jack" suited General Pershing.

At twenty-seven he was one of the youngest deputies in McKinley County. Of course, that didn't mean he was a kid. Bobcat was never a "kid." He grew up tough and stayed that way. Sheriff Mack Carmichael and his undersheriff, Dee Roberts, liked him and respected him, but they didn't talk to him much. After all, a man called Bobcat wasn't expected to be much of a conversationalist. Most didn't know whether he was thoughtful or just quiet. What they did know was that he was no one to mess with, no matter which side of the bars you were on in the county lockup.

"Just what the hell do you mean, they're going to raise the rent and kick 'em all out?" Bobcat asked Deputy Hoy Boggess. "Hell, those men were brought here to break the strike of nineteen and seventeen in the first place. I don't know that it's right to take away their land now, when times are hard and the mines are down."

Deputy Boggess was a man who just did as he was told. The politics and the way everyone was carrying on about it weren't to his liking. He and Bobcat were alone in the jail that crisp April morning. There wasn't much to do but talk and drink coffee till Sheriff Carmichael and Dee Roberts showed up at eight o'clock sharp, just as they had done every other morning for the twenty years Deputy Boggess had been on the job in Gallup.

It was no fun telling Bobcat that the coal miners renting those cold-water shacks on the west side of town were liable to blow up. This deal that the Gallup American Coal Company had cooked up with Senator Clarence F. Vogel was dangerous, and heads were liable to get busted.

Bobcat was the best deputy that Sheriff Carmichael had, although Chief Deputy Dee Roberts would never have said so. It wasn't that Bobcat knew the law. He didn't. Dee Roberts knew more law than Bobcat and Sheriff Carmichael combined; it was just that Bobcat knew people better. At least he knew the ones who were most likely to come in contact with the law.

Bobcat was just shy of five foot seven and had a barrel for a chest and short tree trunks for arms. He had an easy way about him. He was comfortable out on the Navajo Reservation or in Chihuahuaita. Even though he was a *gringo,* he was welcome in Chihuahuaita. Gringos didn't live in the Mexican parts of town, like Chihuahuaita. And just now, that's where the law was likely to be needed or tested.

Dee Roberts, on the other hand, was a tall man with a strong face and a hard look. Most thought him fair but hard. His tolerance for radicals and malcontents was about the same as his tolerance for bad whiskey and mouthy women. The only time he went into Chihuahuaita was to serve someone with a writ or to drag some poor soul to jail. Even taking Bobcat with him didn't make him welcome.

Bobcat's social acceptance in Chihuahuaita was sort of hard to figure. Part of it was that he was of a size that allowed him to look everyone there right in the eye. The coal miners in Chihuahuaita were mostly small, with tight, sinewy muscles. Digging coal for a living made you that way. Their skins were dark, but their eyes were open to fairness. They could see that in Bobcat. They accepted him, but, like everyone else in Gallup, didn't mess with him. He knew all about cracking kneecaps and knuckle punches to the Adam's apple as a way of dealing with men who didn't see things his way.

When Sheriff Carmichael took a chance and signed him on as a deputy, he told Dee Roberts to break him in. The first thing that Dee told Bobcat was that the gun on your hip and the badge on your chest are a lot alike. One was there to make sure the other got respect. Sometimes it's hard to tell which was which. Try the badge first; if that doesn't work, the gun will.

The fact that Dee Roberts was "just" the undersheriff might have seemed strange to an outsider. Sheriff Carmichael was taking his turn to be sheriff of McKinley County. Dee Roberts had been the sheriff before him and would be again after this term.

New Mexico's two-term limit was a curious thing to easterners who thought that job experience was a good thing in elected officials. In New Mexico, experience counted just the same; it was just shared by men who understood one another.

First it was Carmichael's turn, and Dee Roberts would be the undersheriff. When it came election time again, Dee would run, win, and appoint Carmichael as his undersheriff. After all, the law said two terms per man, but it didn't say you couldn't work it out yourselves when it was your turn to be the sheriff. The ballots always said either Carmichael or Dee Roberts. Sometimes people wondered which one was calling the shots. Actually, it didn't matter. In the jail or out in the county, it was hard to tell who was the sheriff and who was the chief deputy. Either one caused men to look up and pay attention till they left. Bobcat, on the other hand, caused no stir. If you were minding your own business, so would he.

The latest strike would either get fixed or broken. It didn't matter to Bobcat which side won as long as both sides kept the peace. Gallup depended on the coal coming out of the ground, and no one could rest easy as long it was locked down in the pits and the coal diggers were facing the picket lines instead of the hoist lines.

The coal would still be there, but what with martial law and busted heads and all, there was no telling what might happen with this new deal. That new deal is not to be confused with FDR's New Deal. When a local big shot like Senator Vogel buys 100 acres of land right out from under striking mine workers, Gallup's new deal was likely to be Bobcat's bad deal. Like all the other cards dealt to him, he would play the hand and let the pot ride.

So Deputy Boggess was careful with Bobcat and answered up real quick when Bobcat hollered: "Damn straight I want to know who thinks they can pull a man out of his house after he's been there for nigh on to eighteen years. Just because you're a state senator doesn't make it right."

Deputy Boggess was older and more experienced than Bobcat, but he was, well, more fearful too. But then again, almost everyone was more fearful than Bobcat.

The *Gallup Independent* would confirm the rumor that night with a worrisome headline: "SENATOR VOGEL BUYS 110 ACRES IN CHIHUAHUAITA." Bobcat read the paper that night as he always did, with a little bourbon and branch water at the American Bar. Hell, now it was legal.

The *Gallup Independent* reported that State Senator Vogel bought the land and the houses (actually more shacks than houses) from the Gallup American Coal Company for an "undisclosed price." The purchase included "Chihuahuaita and the Henderson flats and plots on both sides of Highway 66 out by the cemetery."

I can vividly remember sitting with Bobcat reading the paper, along with the usual crowd in the American Bar. Other men in the bar were also reading the paper, and so you got some news with your eyes and some with your ears as the bar talk filtered through the small, smoky room. Too early for pool balls to clink and not late enough for Guido's radio to be cranked up behind the bar. So the conversations weren't exactly with one another as much as they were about the same thing. "It says here that our good senator didn't reveal the purchase price, but it runs to five figures." "What it runs to is bad news for those out on strike, that's for damn sure." "But doesn't he have a right to do that?" "If you got the money, you got the right."

The front-page article noted that "it was understood" that "Vogel plans to sell lots on the plot to present holders of homes on a monthly payment plan."

Bobcat didn't respond; as usual he listened more than he talked. The talk floated around and over him along with the smoke and clink of glasses. I could tell that the talk made his gut tighten up. My gut was telling me that the "monthly payment plan" would likely mean evictions at a time when this town was ready to blow.

Evictions out there in Chihuahuaita would be Bobcat's to serve. The Gallup Police Department would gladly duck that little job. Out of the city limits meant out of the city politics. Not that there weren't politics aplenty in McKinley County. Gamerco was out in the county. It was a town built by, run by, and owned by the Gallup American Coal Company. Since it was in the county, it was Bobcat's job to see that the law was there just like everywhere else in the county.

It was a perverse sort of thing that Gamerco had more deputies living in it than in the rest of the county altogether. That was because they had "special deputies" selected by the coal boss, Tom Dooley, and duly "deputized" by Dee Roberts on orders from the McKinley County Commission and the district attorney's office.

Hell, they argued, why do you oppose free deputies? The mine pays 'em, the mine gets to tell 'em where to patrol. As the sheriff put it, They're not our problem, but they're ours to call in when we need them.

Bobcat pondered those special deputies as he ordered his second and last drink of the day. His mind and his gut said that he would have plenty of help from the "special deputies" if he had to evict anyone in Chihuahuaita. That kind of help he could do without, no matter what the hell the county commission said.

Gallup was a fearful place in the spring of 1935. Every man and woman in town was in some way afflicted by the news that Chihuahuaita was being sold out from under the families that lived there. Back in 1917 another big coal-mining company, the Victor American Fuel Company, signed a labor contract with the United Mine Workers. Many thought that was a bad thing, although everyone had a miner in the family. Unions were back-east things. They weren't needed out here in the West—at least not at that time.

The bad news about Victor American's acceptance of a union for its workers was tempered by the good news about Gallup's other main business, the railroad. The railroad owners opened El Navajo Hotel. Just think of it. A spanking new hotel right on the track siding. The folks in Gallup mostly called it the Harvey House.

A month after the hotel was finished in 1923, the UMW organized Victor American's mines. A strike was called against the Gallup American Coal Company. That was the other big coal company in town, and they weren't unionized.

Hardly a month had gone by when the UMW brought in some so-called Austrians and tried to close down the power plant. That was an indirect way of hurting the mines, since the power plant had two coal-fired generators. If the power plant were shut down, no one would have electric power in town. That meant no water since the water system depended on electric pumps. Gallup didn't have backup oil-fired generators in those days.

The Gallup American Coal Company responded by bringing in strikebreakers from Mexico. In 1917 you could do that sort of thing. The strikebreakers didn't speak English, but more half the town spoke Spanish, so most everyone got along just fine. Gallup American Coal let their new workers put up adobe houses on the west side of town just this side of Henderson Flats. It became known as Chihuahuaita.

Before long, nearly a hundred families were living there. They paid a little ground rent, about ten to fifteen dollars a year, and stayed out of the union. With the combination of these non-English-speaking strikebreakers occupying Chihuahuaita and Gallup American Coal's owners convincing FDR's secretary of war to sit this one out, the strike was broken. The local politicians wanted intervention by federal troops, but that never happened. Gallup American Coal won that round by giving the men houses to live in while shutting the union out. Unfortunately for both sides, labor peace wouldn't last.

At the very start picket lines went up all over the north-side mines. The bigger mining companies had company stores and company houses. Some of them cut off credit. When that didn't work, they started eviction proceedings in Gamerco and Mentmore. The writs were filed in the McKinley County Justice Court, housed in the Sutherland Building just down from El Morro Theater on Coal Avenue. That JP court was run by a man who was called Judge Bickel to his face and "Bail-less Bickel" behind his back. The boys across the street at the Angeles Bar and Pool Hall on Third and Route 66 said it straight out: No bail, no *cojones*.

The evictions bothered some, but they weren't as bad as the embarrassment of having to call in the New Mexico cavalry to break up the crowds. That was a bad omen. But at least the houses in Chihuahuaita were left alone and the men went back down into the shaft, just as they had done every year since 1917.

Gallup would have gotten through 1933 just fine, even with the Depression and FDR's National Recovery Administration in town, if it hadn't been for the so-called National Miners Union. Thinking back on it now, it's hard to remember that the United Mine Workers was entrenched and working hard to bargain for fair wages out at Victor American Coal Company's mines. Who needed another union? Especially one that the assistant administrator of the NRA said was "linked to the Communist Party." Gallup was no place for communists in 1933 or any other time, for that matter.

You guessed it. Right smack in the middle of the 12th Annual Intertribal Indian Ceremonial, the workers walked off the job. They climbed out of every shaft at all of Gallup American Coal's mines around Gallup. The others followed suit, out of sympathy, I suppose.

There were two kinds of people in my little town in those days: the Anglo establishment and the Mexican coal diggers. Although the strike had been in effect for only one day and there wasn't a single act of violence, Governor Arthur Seligman declared martial law in McKinley County and ordered National Guardsmen to blockade the town. He later said that his decision was based on calls from the mine companies, local officials, *and* the UMW.

Martial law? Most people had no idea what martial law really meant. The few who understood the legal possibility of martial law for an American township could not have imagined how long it would last. As one of the six lawyers in town, I spent a fair amount of my time explaining just what martial law meant. Governors and presidents have the right to declare martial law whenever "an overwhelming public disturbance makes the civil authorities unable to enforce the law." For Gallup that meant that the New Mexico National Guard surrounded the whole town.

We were hardworking people, but we sort of took our freedoms for granted. We never gave much thought to legal terms like "*habeas corpus*" and "writs" and "forcible detainer." Gallup had been one of New Mexico's most important towns for almost forty-five years by then. No one had given two seconds' worth of thought to Article 1, Section 9, of the U.S. Constitution ("the privilege of the Writ of Habeas Corpus shall not be suspended, unless when in Cases of Rebellion or Invasion as the public safety may require It"). I looked it up for a lot of people that week. Almost all of them discussed it; quite a few of them cussed it. There were few answers. Who were the soldiers there to protect? People? Profits? A way of life?

We had our local sheriff and our local police chief, and they were all we needed before this. We didn't think we needed a full company of troops commanded by a bird colonel checking everyone in and out of town and threatening all of us with military jail if the curfew was violated. Right off the bat, the military commander hit my little town with a "mass gathering ordinance" that required a permit for all meetings of more than five persons. Needless to say, no permits were granted for the men of Chihuahuaita. The National Miners Union took to holding their meetings and so-called rallies across the Arizona border nineteen miles down Route 66 on the way to Win . . . slow. Back in town, the pickets were scattered down the roads leading to the mines, with no more than three or four congregating together.

John L. Lewis followed the situation in Gallup closely and telegraphed our governor and offered his personal assistance. Mr. Lewis pointed out that *everyone* knew that the damn communists in the National Miners Union were the instigators of all this. He argued for a policy in Gallup that would allow the mine owners to make a bargain with the UMW to "encourage a union that is committed to the upholding of American institutions."

Sure enough, the UMW offered membership to strikebreakers, and they signed up those who crossed the picket lines. That meant that instead of being labeled "scabs" they could claim they were union miners who choose to work. Hell of a deal. It was the Depression. It was the thirties. It was the time of the "red scare." Both the UMW and the mine owners heaped a bunch of discredit on the National Miners Union by adding racial slurs to red-baiting since the union's membership had a large Mexican majority. Our own paper, the *Gallup Independent,* referred to them as being from Old Mexico, just to make sure no one would be confused.

More than 300 troops came in and blocked entry on Route 66 east and west and on Route 666 north and Route 44 south. Blocking the roads was just part of it. The people of Gallup were more affected by the curfew than the roadblocks. Emotions ran high, and as a Vidal, one of Gallup's leading families, put it, we were "locked in, loaded for bear, and ready to blow."

August gave way to September and then on to October. Governor Seligman died of a heart attack. In the middle of November, I thought it would end when all sides seemed to reach an agreement. About 400 miners were then out on strike, and the companies agreed to rehire immediately about 100 of them. In return, our new governor, Andrew W. Hockenhull, promised that the remainder would be given jobs as soon as possible on new public works projects. The only thing that stood in the way of a settlement were the men in the McKinley County jail. It was no coincidence that they were the leaders of the National Miners Union who had been jailed for violating martial law.

It didn't help much here in town that American Communist Party publications all over the country were declaring the Gallup strike to be a victory for "the new proletarian spirit created by the Depression in America." What did help was that the two unions convinced the mine owners to raise the pay from $4.48 to $4.70 per day. As I said, the most pressing problem was the rehiring of the men out on strike. The mines gave a pledge of guaranteed work, and the unions sacrificed many of their other demands. The promise of employment to a lot of those men was never fulfilled. It would play heavy in the minds of the people in Chihuahuaita a year or so later.

Martial law lasted longer than anyone thought it would. Winter hit hard that year, and the troops still surrounded the town. Curfews and checkpoints and search warrants became everyday things. The governor even said the week before Christmas, "We cannot keep the troops in Gallup forever." But it seemed like he was going to. On January 31, 1934, it finally stopped. Martial law was lifted, and civil law returned at 8 A.M. Bobcat had his usual morning coffee just about that time just this side of Chihuahuaita. Everything was back to normal. Sort of.

Bobcat stood in front of Dee Roberts's big quarter-sawn oak desk, looking down at the mess of paper. That seemed preferable to sustaining Roberts's steady gaze as he waited for more.

"I told you all I know," Bobcat said. "My friend Emiliano lives there. He said his dad has them all paid up, although that isn't true for everyone out there. Anyway, he went to a meeting last night and heard that Vogel is going to put a high price on them. Everyone is afraid of eviction."

It had been thirteen months since martial law was lifted. Not everyone could go back to work. Some did and some didn't. Some hoists were full in the morning and some went down half empty. Some of the smaller mines settled on a wage plan, but the Gallup American Coal mines went from closed to open to closed again. The men went back down into the shafts when the troops left, but now they were staying home again. All in all, it was a time of getting by, not getting ahead.

Bobcat still had that gut tightening that last night's *Gallup Independent* had caused. "Goddamn hell, what's the matter with folks?" Bobcat thought out loud to the chief deputy. "Vogel doesn't need more money, Gallup American Coal doesn't need another strike, and we don't need to evict people who are out of work and are just getting by from day to day."

Roberts thought before he answered. Now, just when was it that what someone "needed" had anything to do with anything? This was what someone "wanted," and that always won out over what someone "needed."

Roberts knew that Bobcat didn't square with the strikers; he thought they ought to work just like everyone else. Sure, times were hard, but a job is a job. Why risk yours for one more damn dollar a day? Every mine around was paying almost five dollars a day. That was a damn sight better than no dollars a day.

So the men on the picket lines—Slavs, Italians, and Mexicans alike, whether from Gamerco or Chihuahuaita—were gonna be dumb shits in Bobcat's eyes even more now. They were out of work on purpose and about to be out of their homes, sort of on purpose. Besides, who in hell didn't know that there was a Depression going on? Bobcat wasn't an owner's man any more than he was a union man, but he did know that jobs were hard to come by everywhere.

He knew that the track yard just down the street from Bubany Lumber was full of hobos early every morning, that is, until the railroad dicks and their hired stiffs came in with the "morning newspaper." That was what they called the head-crunching sticks they used to clear out the railroad yard every morning. That was the routine, but not until after they had their own coffee at the White Café on Railroad Avenue.

Bobcat rambled on, although Dee paid little attention. "And even if it was our business, which it ain't, why in God's hell do the mine owners think that kicking the strikers out of their houses will get them back to work? A man fool enough to walk off a job in these times is fool enough to enjoy sleeping on the ground."

Roberts thought, That's just like Bobcat, getting good and pissed at the unfairness of somebody doing something they had a legal right to do. Even though he was an officer of the law and a direct damn subordinate of Sheriff Carmichael and Undersheriff Roberts, Bobcat's sentiments were well known: "Just because it's legal don't make it right."

Not that he said all that much about anything. He did let it be known that the strikers were dumb shits and that the mine owners had the law on their side. But as he said: "That didn't make kicking them out of their houses right."

As in small towns all over New Mexico, kids played together. It didn't matter that some lived in Chihuahuaita. The kids from the south side of town didn't know anything about strikes or work or politics. For them it was just play. For the parents it was different. They picked sides and pretty much stuck to their family groups. Back then you were family to the railroad or family to the mines. Even if you didn't work for either, you had family in one or the other and often as not both.

Whoever lost this round was likely to be poorer for it. And I don't just mean in a money way. The men who owned the mines lived back east (or Chicago; same thing). But the owners had managers, and the managers had foremen. The foremen were all deputized, and all had gold badges to prove it. That meant they had the law on their side. So if the court ordered evictions, the men who owned the mines could evict the men who worked the mines. It was as simple as that.

Most of the managers and foremen for Gallup American Coal lived out in Gamerco, but that was only four miles from downtown Gallup. The families who lived in those adobe mud houses and cold-water shacks and whose men went down into those warm-weather mines lived in Chihuahuaita. Chihuahuaita was in Gallup until it got in trouble. Then it was "out there."

The fact that they built Gallup twenty miles north of Francisco Vásquez de Coronado's winter camp when the conquistadors came through here 450 years ago was something we were proud of. We liked the fact that Santa Fe was only a half day away when the legislature was in session. The fact that Gallup had more money, more auto courts, more bars, and more sheep than any other town for 150 miles in any direction was downright chest thumping.

Gallup was mostly Hispanic, just like most of New Mexico. But we had a fair share of Italian, Irish, and Welsh families because they built the railroad. There were a lot of Slavs, a few Scots, a few Cornish Cousin Jacks, and a spattering of almost every other nationality. Lots of color, lots of passion, and our share of misery. We had ranchers and farmers and bankers and brothel operators. We had lots of traders and merchants, who claimed credit for making Gallup what it was. They understood that to make money, you had to sell your goods. Sometimes they forgot that every store in town was heated by coal and lighted by a coal-fired generator. A coal-fired electric plant pumped every drop of water. Everything came in on the rails, and most of what we sent out was by rail. Was Gallup a rail town or a coal town? In 1935 there was peace on the rails, but a war was about to break out in the mines.

Dee Roberts shuffled his papers while Bobcat fumed. "I know it's not right, but I'm only the undersheriff, not God, goddammit." Roberts often said things that Father Joseph up at St. Mary's Catholic Church would have laughed at before he declared it blasphemy. The irony of using God and goddammit in the same sentence escaped both Bobcat and his boss.

"I can't just go out there to Senator Vogel's house and tell him those people have a right to stay there after Gallup American has gone and sold the land to him, can I?"

Bobcat wasn't one to talk to or about Senator Clarence Vogel. Bobcat was half his age, and besides, he had never been properly introduced to him. That meant a lot to Bobcat. When Senator Vogel came in the office, he made his introductions to Sheriff Carmichael because he was in charge. Senator Vogel only dealt with the man in charge. Senator Vogel wasn't one to introduce himself to someone down the line, like a mere deputy, although he would talk to the undersheriff.

The fact that Bobcat didn't talk to or take any notice of Senator Vogel was unimportant, like a lot of things in Gallup, to Senator Vogel. Had he thought about it at all, it wouldn't have bothered him. Clarence Vogel was a man who spent all his time thinking about three things: paying the lowest price for what he bought, getting the highest price for what he sold, and upholding the "American way." That meant doing business with the Gallup American Coal Company. In other words, helping, if he could, to stamp out socialism and communism in New Mexico.

Like a lot of the men who were part of the political machine in the New Mexico state legislature at the time, Senator Vogel was a beefy man. His eyes and his eyebrows were bigger than most, and so he seemed to stare at you even when he looked away from you. His light skin sharply contrasted with the tans and browns of and the coal dust that was ingrained in the skin of those who worked the shafts. Senator Vogel's hands were connected directly to his forearms, as though he had no wrists at all. In addition to his title of state senator, he had a gold deputy sheriff's badge to put on when he needed a little more authority. He had an easy smile but a quick snarl. His way of talking to you was, like Bobcat's, right to the point. The difference was that Bobcat liked you as long as you didn't steal. Senator Vogel, while not a thief himself, sort of assumed everyone else did steal.

The next morning, across town, Mary Ann Shaughnessy read the *Gallup Independent.* As she read, she was reminded of the irony in its name. There wasn't all that much that was "independent" in it. It supported what was good for business. In Gallup that meant the Gallup American Coal Company. I agreed with her, at least privately, which is how we tried to keep our relationship.

The fact that she was a public school teacher and I was an up-and-coming young lawyer made us cautious. That is, cautious about being seen at the wrong time of the night (or morning) in either her little house on Aztec or my apartment up over The Style Shop on Coal Avenue. Dating was okay in Gallup, but it wouldn't do for people to wag their tongues about me leaving her house in the wee hours of the morning.

I thought she loved me but worried that she didn't. She liked that I was a man of the law but fretted about my relationship with Bobcat. She also worried about the fact that I was seven years younger than she was. As she put it once, "You and Bobcat are adolescents; I'm a thinking adult—why the hell am I involved with either one of you?"

Mary Ann Shaughnessy grew up in Albuquerque and, unlike Bobcat and me, pronounced it with all four syllables ringing clear in her best Irish accent. Of course, since she was only half Irish, her accent was a bit thin, but at least she didn't say "Al-burr-kirk" like everyone else in Gallup.

Mary Ann wasn't raised "Irish" any more than she was raised "Spanish." But she had solid claim to Spanish-Irish heritage since her mother, Maria Estafan, was born in Madrid and carried Spanish citizenship until her untimely death when Mary Ann was seven years old. Maria Estafan's father was the head of the Spanish consular office in Los Angeles and sent his daughter to study at the University of New Mexico in 1898. There she met and married Tyler Shaughnessy, a professor of anthropology. Their only child, Mary Ann, was raised by her academic father in an intellectually stimulating adobe on the banks of the Rio Grande. Mary Ann Shaughnessy grew up without learning Spanish or feeling "Hispanic," but she learned a great deal about tolerance, the world outside New Mexico, and liberalism.

Her father traveled a lot, and she became a very engaging part of his widespread intellectual circle after her mother died. Her moving to Gallup was not exactly what her forward-thinking father had in mind for her. Dating a lawyer who acted like a Republican and was seven years her junior was equally bewildering. Her father was now a professor emeritus who spent most of his time writing fierce articles and essays attacking capitalism or any viewpoint that could be labeled conservative.

The fact that she now lived in a small house just up the street from "downtown" Gallup didn't change how she felt. And she felt that these evictions weren't right. Evicting people to make a political point? Using the law of private property to break a lawful strike? Whatever would her father think?

Tall and striking at thirty-five, Mary Ann knew that her looks were important. But with her deep auburn hair, dusky complexion, and wide-set hazel eyes, she also knew she didn't look the part of a high school English teacher. It seemed that her cum laude degree from the university wasn't as important as the fact that she was one of the few unmarried "young" women in town. Of course, there were unmarried "girls" and unmarried "women" in Gallup. But her age and her looks seemed to demand that she marry, settle down, and keep her mouth shut, especially when it came to men's business.

She had a mind, just like the men in town, but most of them never gave her credit for that. Mostly they just gave her credit for high cheekbones and a wonderful view, from either direction, when she walked. To make my point, I once told her she was an "Irish lass with a Mexican ——." Even though I was smart enough not to finish the sentence, it cost me dearly, since she put me out on the street in the middle of the night without my shoes, coat, or the keys to my beat-up old Hudson.

"They have a right to stay as long as their rent is paid," she said to me over coffee and pecan rolls at her house. "No one can kick you out when you're paid up. I asked Wheaton Augur, and he said that was the law."

"Wheaton Augur? What in the world made you do a fool thing like that? He's not the mine's lawyer; he's not the union's lawyer. And besides, what were you talking to him for anyway?" Back in those days, the mere mention of my friend Wheaton raised my hackles a bit. After all, he had been sweet on her before she took up with me. Unrelenting and unfounded jealously were among my many faults as I mumbled, as much to myself as to Mary Ann: "Wheaton has no say in this."

"I didn't ask him. He just said it. I only talked to him because he was at our weekly Indian Ceremonial planning meeting at El Navajo Hotel. He's the only lawyer in town who's not on the mine payroll or the union payroll and so, just maybe, he's objective about this mess."

I sipped my coffee and ignored Mary Ann's delicious pecan rolls. "Objective or not, he has no say in it. You should quit talking about something that the Gallup American Coal Company has every right to do. That property used to belong to Gallup American Coal. Now that property belongs to our good state senator, Clarence Vogel. He can do whatever he wants with it. For your information, I talked to Mr. Glascock myself about this. Hellfire, Henry Glascock is not only the best lawyer in this town, he's the mine's lawyer. He said that the houses are company property and that the renters have only a month-to-month tenancy. That means that when they sold the land to Vogel, he can keep the same rent or raise it as he sees fit. If he raises the rent, they'll pay it or risk eviction."

Mary Ann thought a bit before she answered. She loved him in the dark of night but was often frustrated with him in the glare of morning. Bringing up Wheaton Augur was probably a mistake, but she did want to make her point about the poor souls living in those mud houses down in Chihuahuaita.

"Billy Wade, I'm sure you're right about the law and I have no doubt Mr. Glascock approves, but it's funny that he didn't say a word about this when Wheaton was talking at the Indian Ceremonial planning meeting." She paused, not wanting to start a real argument but not wanting to just drop the whole damn thing: "I'm perfectly aware that Mr. Glascock is the lawyer for the mines.

At least, he's the one for Gallup American Coal. But he's this year's Intertribal Ceremonial chairman, and it was at his meeting when Wheaton brought this up. He was worried that it might disrupt the ceremonial, and that would be disastrous for every business in this town."

"Yes, woman, I know that. Evictions would be bad. Bad for me. Bad for them. It would affect us all, but all I'm saying is it's Vogel's right."

I left, and Mary Ann sat at her little table, brooding over both the conversation and the evictions. As an English teacher and because she was her father's daughter, she was obsessed with recording her thoughts in diaries, journals, unfinished essays, and various other sorts of scribbling. She had an old leather-bound black journal her father had given her but couldn't place it at the moment. After fifteen minutes of searching, she found it hiding from her in plain sight on the top of the bookcase in her bedroom. The time spent on the search gave her the opportunity to pose, in her mind, the dilemma she perceived in the situation at hand. Since the *Gallup Independent* spoke for and to the business community, who would speak for and to the rest of the people of Gallup on such a subject? The subject was basic fairness, basic rights, and respect for poor people—even poor Mexicans. Should she take on such a task, or was she tilting at windmills like her father?

Putting it that way in her mind more or less forced the issue. She would write a journal, not a diary but a real, honest-to-God journal. She would focus on Senator Vogel's evictions and what they meant to the people of Gallup. All the people, not just the ones who lost their homes or the ones who profited from the deal. But who stood to lose the most? The poor families who were about to move in with relatives were first on the list—but they weren't the only ones. The rest of us—whose homes weren't threatened—might lose as well, she thought. You'd never see that in the so-called *Gallup Independent.* She got down the leather binder, took it to the kitchen, and began to write.

March 29, 1935
Gallup, New Mexico

Dear Journal:

It's my hope that in writing about what is happening in a town I have come to love, I'll give my town something it sorely needs right now: another voice. I'm not so presumptuous as to think that my voice is important, at least not more important than anyone else's. But I'm confident that someone (other than our local newspaper) needs to write about the evictions in Chihuahuaita. I hope my voice isn't shrill or consumed by property rights or economic status. I want to speak to the issue of whether the ordinary people of Gallup are being misled or deceived by the manipulation of one of our most important employers, the Gallup American Coal Company. I recognize the need for stability and, unlike my beloved father, hold no particular disdain for corporate America (or more particularly, corporate Gallup). I'm part of this town and have its interests at heart. But I think that people are more important than money, and I'm very concerned that money is creating the opportunity for disaster. Taking the homes away from a hundred families will put them in a position of desperation. Desperate people do desperate things, even violent things. Gallup has had more than its share of violence in the last few years.

The newspaper and Billy Wade are consistent in their lack of curiosity about Senator Vogel's purchase of what seems to be nearly all of Chihuahuaita. No one seems to know how much he paid or why Gallup American Coal chose this particular time to sell the property. Was it just to break the strike of the National Miners Union? Or was it a legitimate business deal with fair value being given? The lack of information coupled with the lack of investigation makes me uneasy. Unless someone steps in and attempts to mediate the efforts of the "new" owner (who is supposed to be a public servant) to evict everyone out there, they're liable to take matters into their own hands. They may be poor, but they have pride. They'll not likely just go away or give up their union. That seems to me the real aim of Gallup American Coal, to break the union. It's not like they needed the money. What they need are workers and maybe, just maybe, they think the way to get them is to break the union. If that happens, the men will be forced to go back down the shaft. If I'm going to find out the real reason for this deal, I'll have to be persistent and careful.

I don't know how or when this will be published. I guess if I'm honest with myself, I don't know whether it actually *will* be published. But that's my plan, and for now I'm sticking to it. I'll write again (as soon as I have something to write about).

The Gallup Intertribal Indian Ceremonial was Gallup's big deal. It all started with a local parade of Indian dancers back in 1920 and became the "Intertribal Indian Ceremonial" in 1922. It put Gallup on the map. Gallup was not only in the heart of Indian Country; it was a major stop on the Santa Fe Railroad's Indian Country Tours. People from all over the country were fascinated with the Wild West and the not so wild Indians who lived all around Gallup. Navajos, Hopis, Zunis, Apaches, and Utes came to the ceremonial to dance, trade, visit, and make a little money. Some of them came to drink, too; Gallup didn't outlaw liquor sales to Indians until December 9, 1933.

The ceremonial was unique because Indian traders from all the surrounding Indian reservations agreed to show the rugs and jewelry that they had encouraged the Indians to make. Each trading post encouraged distinctive design elements in the area's rugs, and the best of Navajo and Zuni turquoise and silver work was rewarded and recognized at the ceremonial in July or August. All this was jeopardized by the strike. The sale of the houses in Chihuahuaita made it even worse. Gallup had more than its share of riots and troops, but at least no one had been killed yet.

It's only natural that the mine owners thought they could break the strike by making it tough on the strikers. What better way than to make them move out of the company houses just before the ceremonial was to start? Gallup American Coal Company had houses in town, houses out at Gamerco, and houses everywhere else they had mines dug into the San Juan Basin. The ones in Chihuahuaita were out on the west side of town; that is, where a lot of the men on strike lived in the spring of 1935. Foremen and men not in the union mostly occupied the company houses four miles away at Gamerco. That meant that the ceremonial parade wouldn't be directly affected if there were turmoil in Chihuahuaita. That was because after the parade moved west on Coal Avenue, it circled back around and came east on Railroad Avenue. At First Street it would turn and cross the tracks and the Purkey and head on out to the ceremonial grounds on the north side of town.

Things would change if the turmoil moved back into town from the West Side and threatened downtown. Gallup couldn't afford trouble on Railroad Avenue or Coal Avenue. They were important to Gallup's commerce and its newfound economic base in the thousands of tourists who came to buy rugs and Indian jewelry and stay in the hundreds of rooms in our auto courts—which were a step up from the auto "camps" in the other towns along Route 66.

I stopped by the sheriff's office that afternoon to see Bobcat and get filled in on the story that was floating around town about some deputy getting his ass chewed out by the undersheriff himself. Everyone loved that. An ass chewing by Dee Roberts was a thing of beauty unless, of course, you were the chewee.

The fact that Bobcat and I were buddies wasn't strange in Gallup but might have been misunderstood back east or even in Chicago, for that matter. I'm as Irish as they come. My hair is cut close every week just like every other upstanding citizen's in town. I'm tall; Bobcat's short. My skin is absolutely pallid compared to Bobcat's weather-beaten hide. The law is important to both of us, although my views are a product of seven years of college and law school whereas Bobcat's views come from a ranching family and a deputy's job.

"Qué pasa, amigo," I greeted Bobcat with a grin. Bobcat was still on his first coffee of the morning.

"Que no," replied Bobcat. It was always the same. It didn't make any difference who asked who first what was happening; the other said nothing was happening. Like most New Mexicans, we saw this as good manners, not untruthful, even though it often was. This morning the strike and the rumor that the strikers' houses in Chihuahuaita were being sold were on the minds of both of us.

"So Roberts chewed you a new one, did he? A man your size can't take too many of those. Pretty soon you'll be just a nub."

As usual, I smiled when I joked about anything so serious as Bobcat's stature. It wasn't that five-foot seven was short in this part of the country. Mexicans weren't tall on average; Navajos weren't either; but for some unexplainable reason, every other deputy on the force was six foot or better. At six two, I towered over Bobcat. So it seemed natural to kid him about his height.

Some could joke with Bobcat about that and some couldn't. Those who could had best smile when they did it. As for those who couldn't, even a smile on your face wouldn't help. He would invite you outside no matter what. Now, if Bobcat invited you outside, two things were about to happen, and both of them were bad for whoever was dumb shit enough to accept his offer. He either kicked your ass or you backed off.

"No, he didn't chew my ass, but he sure didn't like what he heard. Undersheriff Roberts is an upstream man. This crap about kicking people out who are paid up on their rent is for downstream shit kickers. Dee Roberts isn't exactly a friend of the Mexican race, but he's a fair man and I've never known him to mistreat anyone."

I had no trouble with that. I knew that Roberts was something of a hero to Bobcat even if he did make life too simple sometimes. On the other hand, I tend to complicate things. That's why when I was a junior at Gallup High, the coach made me the quarterback on the football team. Simple guys, like Bobcat, played defense. We were on the same team and shared all our victories, but we got them in different ways. I tried to think of all the alternatives. Bobcat just knocked down whoever came at him. It was that simple.

I honed my instinct for complex things in college. That got me a Phi Beta Kappa key when my friend Bobcat didn't even realize it was Greek, much less an honor. I knew it was a complex thing when I heard about the decision to sell the land and the houses in Chihuahuaita to one of Gallup's leading citizens. Senator Vogel had a sharp eye for the dollar in everything. The sale was perfectly legal, but it was an open question, at least for me, about what could be done with the strikers who had built houses on the land over the last seventeen years. What about the legal doctrine of adverse possession? What about the tax issues? What about equity and fairness and unclean hands?

My inherent curiosity and my keen interest in arcane legal issues made me relish the complexity. Although Bobcat thought it was stupid, I was perfectly willing to pore over the casebooks and look for an answer, no matter which side sought my advice. Of course, it was unlikely that the Gallup American Coal Company would even think of asking me for advice. They got their legal advice from Henry Glascock, and he was as good as they come, anywhere in the state.

Could a new owner evict a month-to-month tenant before a new tenancy was created by the acceptance of a prior owner's agreed rental rate? Yes, that was hornbook law, but that didn't make it right. So did the tenant have any "equitable" remedies even if the "legal remedy" seemed doubtful?

The Socratic method of teaching law was still sitting softly in my mind as I talked about the simple side of all this with Bobcat. "That's the difference between simplicity and complexity—sometimes simplicity is wrong even if the legal principle attached to it is correct. Only by complicating the legal principle can you arrive at whether or not it was right."

Bobcat frowned and sort of grunted. Complex stuff wasn't very interesting. If it pissed you off, you knocked it down; you didn't study it, for chrissake.

"You're right about one thing," I went on. "Senator Vogel's land purchases down there in Chihuahuaita are irrelevant. But they might have some bearing on whether the ceremonial gets off to a good start this year. That's what Mary Ann says, and I'm sticking to it."

There was a time when Bobcat would have frowned at my lapse into legalese with words like *irrelevant,* but I had persuaded him that some four-bit words were necessary, particularly in the courtroom. Bobcat's courtroom experiences thus far were easy since he just told how and when he made the arrest. After he testified, Judge Bickel would typically ignore his testimony and rule however he damn well pleased. But Bobcat was thankful to me for teaching him some "evidentiary law" (as he put it) because there was bound to come a time when what he said in court was straight-out important.

"*Important* and *relative* aren't the same thing but are close enough for deputies," I said. Because I said it with a smile, Bobcat let it go.

"Well, can he do it or not?" Bobcat asked.

I thought before I answered. Was this the time to complicate matters? The easy answer to Bobcat's question was yes. The harder, I mean complicated, answer was no. That is, the answer was no if the evictees got some good legal advice in advance of being served with an eviction notice. Professor Ares at the Hastings College of Law could have secured a stay order from the court that would have prevented an eviction under these circumstances well beyond the time the mine owners wanted to pressure the strikers. That was what these evictions were really all about, anyhow. Pressure, not rent money.

In Chihuahuaita it was about pride, not money. To pose the legal issue in terms of pressure by the plaintiff (Senator Vogel) and pride by the defendant (Señor Campos) wasn't good legal analysis, but it certainly narrowed things down into the classic analysis of motive and opportunity. Of course, that's a criminal law analysis; this was a civil dispute, right?

"The simple answer is yes, they can. Do you want the longer version or can I have a cup of coffee first?"

My answer wasn't what Bobcat wanted to hear. He would have liked to be able to go into Dee Roberts's office in a few minutes and tell him that Billy Wade said the eviction would be illegal. Simple as that. If your rent was paid, you had a right to stay in your house. If you had the money to pay for next month, they had to take it. Even Bobcat knew that kind of logic wouldn't hold up for long. After all, you couldn't stay in a rental house forever.

But he wasn't worried about forever. He was worried about right now. Besides, nobody in the sheriff's office had any interest in anything that was long term. They wanted to stop trouble before it started. The way to do that was to let this strike work itself out without kicking the striking workers out of their homes. Maybe the workers were being dumb shits, but the sheriff's office didn't need women and kids on the streets while men were on the picket lines.

"Besides, I'm not their lawyer," I said. "If I were, I'd be hard pressed to come up with a remedy that Judge Bickel would buy. He knows where the business bread is buttered. He enjoys his share of the jelly, too."

For Bobcat, as always, it was simple. Could they kick them out and would Judge Bickel allow it or not? "You know, Billy Wade, going to Hastings Law

School didn't make you smarter, just harder to understand. Can you just answer a simple question?"

"Sure," I said. "What's the question?"

There were about a hundred small adobes and shacks in Chihuahuaita. The Mexicans who had been brought in by the mine owners to break the 1917 strike had built the homes. The new workers more or less thought they were buying those homes by paying the "ground rent" of ten to fifteen dollars a year.

A lot of them walked the half mile to the Southwest Mine, where they went down the hoist every morning. The Southwest Mine and the Gallup American Coal Company were separate, competing mining companies. But they had one common interest. Here's how it worked: Southwest collected $1.50 a month from the paychecks of its workers who lived in Chihuahuaita and turned it over to Gallup American Coal Company. As a favor, I suppose.

In addition to employed miners, Chihuahuaita had a sizable bunch of unemployed miners, who had been blacklisted by the mines for striking or associating with the National Miners Union or, worse yet, the old and nearly forgotten IWW. They got a little federal relief, but it didn't go far. As for citizenship, well, some in Chihuahuaita were "US of A citizens"—but there was a large percentage of Mexican nationals, too.

While the evidence was sketchy, somehow it got out that Senator Vogel, who never did disclose how much he paid for the 110 acres he bought, intended to kick most of the people out. He started the process by passing out sales contracts that gave the people of Chihuahuaita the choice of either buying their lots for ten dollars a *month* or abandoning the houses and getting out. Houses of similar size in other parts of town sold for about $25, but Senator Vogel wanted $150 for the ones in Chihuahuaita.

That wasn't the worst of it. The sales contracts had a clause that allowed the good senator to treat a failure to make a monthly payment as a forfeiture of all earlier payments, clear back to 1917. The people of Chihuahuaita needed someone to speak for them, and the National Miners Union, communists and all, stepped right up. The people of Chihuahuaita first offered to just keep on paying the same "ground rent," even though most thought they had been *buying*, not renting. Senator Vogel said *nada.* As it turned out, *no más* would have said it better—about half of them signed the contracts knowing full well that they could never make the payments.

You see, that's the way things had worked for eighteen years—from 1917 to

1935. The miners who lived in Chihuahuaita had missed their payments to Gallup American Coal lots of times. But the company never evicted anyone. Now, eighteen years after it put these families in Chihuahuaita, it sold the land to Senator Vogel—who changed all that. A new owner and a new strike. That was a bad combination.

Senator Vogel took a few people who missed their payments to court to make his point. Gallup's local justice of the peace cited two men for contempt on account of they were contemptuous, I guess. But everyone knew that it was old (Bail-less) Bickel who was contemptuous, of the National Miners Union, that is—and their communist members, too.

Neither attribute set very well in Judge Bickel's court in those days. In his capacity as a private citizen and businessman, "Mr. Vogel" evicted tenants who were behind on their rent. As a legislator "Senator Vogel" took it one step further: he offered a bill in the legislature in Santa Fe to make evictions easier, quicker, and final. On the other side, the NMU offered an anti-eviction bill. All the debate and fuss proved to be too late to prevent what was about to happen. The idea was to put a little pressure on without letting things get out of hand. Trouble was, no one thought it through.

Gallup had money, opportunity, and a pleasant summer climate. So it naturally attracted good lawyers. Some made good judges; others made good money. All of them made life interesting, except maybe to the Roberts brothers and Bobcat. For Bobcat, they just made it more complicated. He understood the difference between being a lawman and a lawyer.

It became the job of Harris K. Lyle, Esq., to explain the law to Judge Bickel. He filed an application for a common law writ of eviction in favor of Senator Vogel and against "numerous and sundry illegal possessors" of the land Senator Vogel had bought from Gallup American. The first legal writ he filed specifically named one Victor Campos.

The application for the writ against Señor Campos provoked an intriguing comment by the judge. "Now, Harris, you know that the common law of possessory interests in real property isn't something that comes up very often in my court. I've read your application for a writ, and it says that the land in Chihuahuaita was initially titled in the name of the Gallup American Coal Company. But now it's titled in the name of our good senator C. F. Vogel, Esq. Is that the sale I read about in the *Gallup Independent* the other day?"

Lyle's response was legally predictable. "Yes, Your Honor, I perfected the title two days ago. As you can see in our application, we have legal title to the land;

unfortunately we do not have possession. That's why we are seeking an eviction order based on forcible entry and detainer by Mr. Victor Campos." Title was one thing; possession was another. But why confuse the judge? Especially when the judge you had not only didn't know the law, he didn't even suspect it.

The law was clear that the possessor of real property had rights to the property that were good "as against the whole world," except those of a lawful titleholder. Like all laws, this one had exceptions. Anyone in actual possession of a piece of real property had the common law right to build and live in a structure on the property as long as the titled owner didn't object. That was the legal predicate Lyle intended to use to convince Judge Bickel that title prevailed over possession.

Harris argued in his forcible entry and detainer action that "Gallup American Coal, the prior title owner, had no objection from 1917 to 1933 to the 'tenants at sufferance' living on or possessing the houses they built on the land. However, the new titled owner, one C. F. Vogel, does object and has asserted to you, under oath and pain of perjury, that the tenants, specifically Victor Campos, are forcibly holding the property to his detriment. I therefore respectfully plead for a writ of eviction based on the aforesaid forcible entry and detainer."

Now Judge Bickel was no stranger to reversal by the district court. He didn't like being reversed—it tended to affect his insurance business, which he also ran out of the same building in which he conducted his justice of the peace business. So he asked, remembering something he had read somewhere about the doctrine of adverse possession, "Is it not entirely possible, Mr. Lyle, that the tenants at sufferance in Chihuahuaita can lawfully claim title by reason of adversely possessing the property since 1917?"

"With respect, Your Honor, the doctrine fails in this instance. As the court surely knows, for one to hold real property and acquire title adversely, his possession must be (*a*) actual and exclusive, (*b*) open, visible, and notorious, (*c*) continuous and peaceable for the statutory period of fifteen years, and, most importantly, (*d*) hostile and adverse. It is the last element that fails here. In this case, the tenants at sufferance, including the first name on the writ, Mr. Victor Campos, never claimed actual ownership. None of them ever claimed lawful title or asserted the right of possession, as opposed to 'title,' against Gallup American Coal. None of them ever even asserted or tried to assert 'color of title' by way of any instrument purporting to be a conveyance."

Judge Bickel seemed in a mood to quibble just for the sake of quibbling. "Are there no leases or rental agreements to review? How has the former owner dealt with this issue for these past seventeen years?"

Mr. Lyle's answer was the same one he gave over drinks last night at the American Bar. "The former owner was in the business of providing housing for the men who worked in their mines, Your Honor. But Senator Vogel is not in the business of providing housing for miners; indeed, he is not in the mining business at all. It is no concern of his how Gallup American conducted their landlord relationship with respect to this property. He was under no duty to inquire of the seller of the property as to their leasehold practices. He's a respected member of the legislature and a man in the business of developing business and residential property. His first step in developing this particular plot is to deal with a few men down there in Chihuahuaita who may believe they are in lawful possession but who, in the eyes of the law, are nothing more than squatters."

The argument prevailed for three reasons. First, Judge Bickel didn't know any better. Second, Harris Lyle had Senator C. F. Vogel with him in court, and last, no one was there to object. Writs in forcible entry and detainer actions were typically conducted *ex parte;* that is, with only one side present in court. Since there was no objection to the issuance of the writ, Judge Bickel did as expected: he signed a writ against "one unlawfully holding possession of the afore described property." Of course, it wasn't "one" but over a hundred such writs that were issued. It was his misfortune that Victor Campos was the "one" named in the *first* writ of eviction. In fact, Senator Vogel had no intention of serving *all* his writs. A few would suffice to convey the message. As Bobcat would put it later, the message was: "Go back to work and you can avoid a writ of eviction; stay on the picket line and you can look for a new home." To everyone's misfortune, the special deputies from Gamerco were eager to serve the first writ, and they selected Victor Campos as a suitable man to "get the message" and "spread the word."

Victor Campos had built his house in Chihuahuaita himself. He made his own adobes in the traditional way of his native country, and he inset the windows and the doors the way they look in Old Mexico. Because of that he agreed to put his name on the lease that Senator Vogel gave him to sign. The fact that he couldn't read wasn't of any importance. He didn't know that the gringo contract contained a clause that permitted eviction without legal notice. What did he care for the law? He, like everyone else in Chihuahuaita, thought he owned the house he had built and paid for over the last seventeen years.

Victor Campos had been out of work for almost nine months. He attended the NMU meetings and went to church. Both did their business in Spanish, which was good because Victor had no English. He was active in the union and in his church, but neither one was much help when he wasn't rehired. When the mines reopened last year, most of the men with his seniority were rehired. He was not. Some said it was because he was on the picket lines too much.

Since he was out of work, he was home the morning the special deputies came to serve Judge Bickel's order of eviction. Judge Bickel had appointed several mine guards as special deputies. They had their official writ in hand with its official-looking red seal of the State of New Mexico embossed on it. All Victor Campos could read was the "Mexico" part of "New Mexico."

They nailed the order of possession on the door to Victor's house and removed the bed, an armchair with a broken leg, and the coal stove to outside, where they unceremoniously left them in the dirt. All the other people in the neighborhood watched in quiet sadness. The mine guards with the special deputy badges told Victor the house was no longer his, and they left him with his furniture in the dirt on the street.

Two people came to his aid, Esiquel Navarro and the town's most fired-up woman, Lugardita Lovato. Navarro was a strong leader in the National Miners Union and had been one of the most vocal rank-and-file leaders on the picket lines for years. In other mining towns he was called "Euesibo" but in Gallup he was called "Esiquel." Lugardita Lovato, or "Mrs. Lovato," as even her friends called her, had a huge chest and a huge appetite for trouble. She was a woman to be avoided if you wanted to keep your peace. Esiquel Navarro came to Gallup from Old Mexico because, as bad it was here, it was worse there. Some days here he actually worked, but now they wouldn't let him down in the mines.

Navarro was a man almost impossible to describe or remember if you saw him only once or twice. He looked like everyone else in any crowd. Medium, average, just the same, about like that was how everyone described him. He had a face that looked round from a distance and oval up close. His mustache was black unless you looked close and saw the flecks of gray. His dark eyes had a way of lighting up in the sun but were hard to see under the brim of the felt hat he always wore, even inside, unless there were women around. But his nondescript looks belied his fiery defense of the oppressed and the unemployed. He was a believer. He had taken the "oath," along with many others, in Kitchen's Opera House a year ago.

Gallup's only photographer, Mr. Mullarky, photographed that oath-taking ceremony. There in the middle of that print stood Navarro, flanked by the men and women who joined him in taking the oath of allegiance to the American Communist Party. The taking of the oath was not at all like promising to tell the truth in a court of law. It was more like promising to give your life to a philosophy that was as foreign to most of the men and women in the room as was the English language. Even the physical aspects of the oath taking were different. In a court of law you were asked to raise your hand. The American Communist Party asked you to raise your fist. And you didn't just raise it, you clenched it hard. The Mullarky photograph captures the lack of understanding and emphasizes the anger in that smoky, cold room in Kitchen's Opera House on Railroad Avenue in Gallup in 1934.

In many ways, the labor pool in Gallup was an army of dispossessed, unskilled, and perennially unemployed foreign-born men who dug coal because it was all they could do. Very few of them knew of Marx or believed in the inevitable success of industrial unionism. They just wanted to feed and clothe and house their families. But one or two, like Navarro and Juan Ochoa, were committed and dedicated. They had read the books and heard the speeches. They bent their own lives to the cause of labor and moved not from job to job but from fight to fight. They lived lives of acquired insecurity and accumulated grievance and wrong. So for them, the cloudy deal between the Gallup American Coal Company and Senator Clarence Vogel was just another step by bosses who trampled on what little the workingman had to call his own—his house, the one he built with his own hands.

Navarro and Lovato waited till darkness fell and quickly tore down the boards nailed over the front door and moved all of Victor's stuff back inside. Victor was there but didn't do all that much. Mostly he kept guard. He was convinced that someone was watching them. He was right. Within an hour, all three were arrested and taken to Sheriff Carmichael's jail.

Mrs. Lovato was released, of course, on her own recognizance. She wasn't a miner. She wasn't a member of the National Miners Union. Campos and Navarro were guilty on both counts. They were on strike, and they were union members. And Navarro had taken the oath.

They were taken directly to jail. First thing next morning, Sheriff Carmichael sent a deputy over to Judge Bickel's court to get a commitment order. This was a written order, with a place on it for the justice of the peace to fill in the statutory bail set for the particular crime charged against the defendant. But as usual, Judge Bickel didn't attend to small procedural details in his court. Judge Bickel didn't endorse bail on the commitment order. "Bail-less" Bickel acted true to form.

The sky was bright but the mood was dim in the Spanish-American Hall on April 3, 1935. Even though only men worked the mines in those days, women were in the union and went to the meetings. The men and women of the local National Miners Union weren't all "Spanish Americans." While some liked to think so, the so-called Spanish Americans weren't "Spanish" at all. They were one step removed from Spain. That step was Mexico. But they didn't think of themselves as Mexican Americans either. Mostly they thought of themselves as Mexicans, so we did too, whether or not they were U.S. citizens.

They weren't the only ones who dug the coal beneath the streets of Gallup. Other miners came from all over Europe. Yugoslavia, Austria, Wales, and Italy all sent their sons to the American coal mines as well. So the crowd that afternoon in the Spanish-American Hall was both clannish and mixed. Although no one took an actual count, it was later reported that fifty to a hundred were there. The National Miners Union had a local "Unemployed Council." This group was supposed to help those on the picket lines and those blacklisted when the lines were down. The NMU had little money and virtually no respect from the *gringo* part of town. Its members were long on passion but short on planning.

"So, didn't I tell you they would try something?" The harsh voice matched the deeply lined face of the man doing the talking. Juan Ochoa was at ease in Spanish or English. He had been born in New Mexico but had lots of relatives in Old Mexico. He was more or less the chairman of the meeting. Like the others, he was a member of the National Miners Union, and like the others, he had taken the oath last year at Kitchen's Opera House. He was a miner for sure, and he had the coal look in his dark skin and the coal feel when he shook your hand. His hand didn't feel dirty, just gritty, like calloused chalk. Like all miners, he worked to scrub and scrape the dust of the pit off every pore of his body.

Strength and darkness were what you thought of, if you thought at all, when you first met him. Mostly you just said something like, "Hello," "Nice to meet you," "Heard about you," and so on. Then you waited while he talked.

Leandro Velarde and Manuel Avitia were there too. Both were well known, but for different reasons. Leandro was cross-eyed and angry—all the time. Manuel Avitia was happy—all the time. He was from Durango and had little English. You'd call Leandro lean and Manuel squat. Manuel's pockmarked face made him easy to spot in a crowd. Leandro's wandering left eye and Manuel's pockmarked face were to become markers later on—in the trial.

Most miners weren't talkers. Most miners worked the shafts and coal rooms in silence because breath was hard to come by deep underground. Most miners were so tired after being hoisted out of the 1,000-foot-deep shafts that they saved their talking for their wives and kids. Juan Ochoa was different. He was a miner who always talked, no matter where he was. He talked about justice and class and rights. Some said he was a communist, but he never said one way or the other. He just said he was here because he believed in the National Miners Union and went wherever he was needed.

Juan said: "I'm telling you all something. No one can be sure whether Senator Vogel really did pay Gallup American for the land our houses are on. For all we know, they just gave him the land so they wouldn't have to face a court action if they raised our rent. We're a union, and we have lawyers too, *que no?*"

Not to argue, but to inquire with respect, someone said: "But this man, Senator Vogel, is supposed to be a man of respect. He makes *las leyes* up in Santa Fe. Why would he help the mines unless he really wanted the property? Why would they give him something for nothing? Are you saying that this man has no honor?"

"I don't know the man or whether he has honor. I do know that he is after your house, and yours and yours. What are you gonna do when he comes and points his finger and says: *Y usted también?* He can do that, you know." Juan translated for Joe Bartol: "Hey, Joe, he won't say, 'And also you' to you because you don't live there. But he'll point at me and Leandro and Rafael; *usted también.* When he does, man, we're fucked. He makes the laws, but they're *gringo* laws and are not for the workingman. His business isn't the law. His business is buying and selling land. That's why he's perfect for this thing that they're trying to do to us. Señor Vogel's main business may be land, but he gets it through *gringo* politics. He's part of the law, as far as I'm concerned. We have to stand up to this *gringo* senator, but we have to do it under the law."

Leandro Velarde said, "Hey, the man *is* the law, and he has Carmichael and the Roberts brothers and their big guns on his side. *Cómo grande es su arma*?"

"So what?" countered Juan, trying to keep everyone calm. "There has been no need for guns."

But Leandro wasn't in a mood to be calmed. "What do you think he's going to do? He'll get the law and their guns on us, and we have nothing but our pride and our *pica dientes.*"

Everyone laughed. *Pica dientes* were Mexican toothpicks, although *gringos* often got it wrong and translated it as ice picks.

Juan Ochoa continued to talk to the men in his quiet, reassuring way. "Senator Vogel is either in this for the money or for the power. If he's in it for the *dinero,* he'll raise our rent enough to make him a nice profit. If he's in it for the power, he'll raise your rent so high, you can't pay. Either way, his action will give Gallup American Coal what it wants. They want to break you. They know that less than ten percent of their workforce lives here in Chihuahuaita, but they know that the real strength and the leadership of our strike and our union is here. If they can split you up and make you think about the wrong things, then they can break this strike."

"What do you mean, the wrong things?" asked Agustin Calvillo, the oldest man there. Calvillo was born in Jalisco, Mexico, forty-five years ago. Unlike the others, he didn't come to Gallup to work the mines. He came to work on the railroad and became a miner only when he lost his railroad job. Calvillo was a big imposing man who wore his drooping black mustache proudly. The mustache and his icy-black eyes made him fearsome when he frowned and charismatic when he smiled. Chihuahuaita wasn't his home now because he had found a rental house on the North Side for his wife and six children

Calvillo's parents lived in Chihuahuaita. Their house wasn't a shack, although he knew some might call it that. It was adobe and snug, not like this drafty old shack used for strike meetings. "What my father and all of the other older men are worried about is keeping their houses and staying where we are. It's his home, you know."

As always, Juan carefully chose his words. "Of course it's his home, but the main thing here is to keep the strike going no matter what. Gallup American Coal will bargain with us only when they know we got real staying power. If everyone starts to worry about this house or that house, then we lose momentum and power. We have got to stick together on this. Those who are evicted can move in with those who don't live in company houses. Our fight is over where we work and how much they pay us, not over where we live."

Juan Ochoa was more or less in charge. Most of the time he wished it was less. He sensed that this meeting might get out of hand but still proposed that several of them go to Sheriff Carmichael and ask to see the two prisoners, Campos and Navarro. Someone at the meeting reported that Jeannie Lovato had already been released. Someone also said that Bail-less Bickel would never let them out. They had to do something. Trouble was, the something some wanted was trouble. They said they wanted Navarro.

"What do you mean, you want him?" Juan asked over the hum of disjointed talk.

"*Por favor,* Mr. Big Shot," responded Solomon Esquibel, "I mean we should take him and set him free. You know those *pendejos* did him wrong when they arrested him. *Aiee,* they could arrest Señor Campos; it was his house. But Navarro is an innocent man. We should have him, not them."

Most didn't want trouble; they only wanted to stay in their homes. Twenty or thirty of the men there didn't live in Chihuahuaita and so didn't have to worry about their homes. Those who did knew that what happened to Victor Campos was about to happen to them. Maybe they wouldn't have a "Navarro" to help them in the dark of the night. So maybe they should help this man Navarro, *que no?*

"What makes you think he will even talk to you?" someone shouted out. The fact that the question was posed in English was part of the problem. Many of the men and women there could speak only Spanish. This meeting was about more than just the jailing of Campos and Navarro. This was about how the people of Chihuahuaita were being treated by the sheriff's office.

"He will talk to me. He's not that bad. We can talk without shouting all the time, you know." Juan Ochoa sounded more confident than he really was. He knew that Sheriff Carmichael was on the side of the mines because he was the law. The law always sided with whoever was boss.

But he thought he could at least talk to the man. Sheriff Carmichael had no history of hating any man, no matter where he came from or what he did. Juan knew that one of his deputies, Bobcat Wilson, even had friends in Chihuahuaita. Juan didn't know Bobcat himself, but he had seen him taking his coffee there in the only restaurant that catered to men from Old Mexico and New Mexico, side by side, sometimes at the same table.

"Hey, man, who do you want to go with you?" It wasn't so much a question as a demand. Solomon Esquibel was a man with fire in his belly. Whether it was caused by drink or by passion was not known or important. He was so dark he was almost black, like the coal he dug, not brown like the others. Some said he was a mestizo; others said he was a "black Mexican."

Juan wasn't close to Esquibel; no one really was, but he said, "How about you?" Talking in English to Esquibel was respectful to the *gringos* who were standing with them, even though they didn't live in Chihuahuaita.

Esquibel didn't have such respect. *"Tontería del gringo"* was how he thought of the Slavs and the Scots, whose skin whitened up on Saturday night when a week's worth of coal dust came off in the tub. His skin was as dark as his mood—all the time.

"Okay, man, I'll go with you," Esquibel said disgustedly. "How about taking a *gringo* with us so the sheriff won't spit on us?"

The hall went quiet for a minute. Juan thought: Shit, we don't need no fucking trouble among ourselves. Why does he have to call someone a *gringo* when they're only here because they have the same problem as us? He was silent for a moment, hoping that Solomon would let it go.

"Go by your fucking self, man; what is your problem?" The booming voice of

Joe Bartol cracked through the room. Joe Bartol was a man who everyone knew but few liked. He was the *gringo* equivalent of Solomon Esquibel. Joe Bartol was a miner, and he was a union man through and through.

His wife, Julia Bartol, was committed to the social ideas of the communists, and Joe was committed to the working class. Together they could organize and agitate with the best of them. Joe was big and looked like a man designed to keep Julia energized. Julia was even bigger but lacked the booming voice of her husband. Whereas his was loud, hers was shrill. He looked directly at you; she looked past you.

More by default than anything, it was agreed that Juan Ochoa, the voice of reason; Solomon Esquibel, the man of action; and Joe Bartol, a true union man, would go see the sheriff.

The next hour was spent more or less talking about what the "committee" of the local Unemployed Council would say or do when they got to the sheriff's office. It was only three blocks away, but everyone knew that it was another world. Jail was a thing to be feared and ashamed of unless you really believed in unions and social justice. Or unless you were worried about losing your home. Then maybe jail was worth risking.

They made up a list. First of all, the representatives were to ask to see Campos and Navarro and take them some fresh tamales. Jail food was no damn good for anyone, particularly an innocent man, right?

Then they were to ask the sheriff just exactly when he would take the arrested men to court and get him to say how much bail would be so that the others could raise it. And third or last or whatever, the representatives were to make sure that the sheriff knew that no one wanted trouble.

Esquibel had to have the last word. "And we want Navarro," he snarled.

Juan Ochoa had the only car that would carry all of them to the jail. Leandro Velarde rode over there with them but said he would stay in the car. Too many might seem like a crowd. They wanted to be friendly, but they were there to learn what was happening. If they could find out what they needed, they could arrange for others to join them and show support for Navarro.

As it turned out, they didn't need their list of things to ask about. Sheriff Carmichael was there but not interested in any list. Bobcat Wilson was there and would have listened, but he wasn't in charge. It was just as well that Undersheriff Roberts wasn't there. One former mine guard in the room was enough.

Carmichael sat behind his big oak desk, wearing his wide-brim felt hat, and locked his jaw at them. He listened to them, but he didn't really hear what they had to say. As usual, he was a man of few words. "No. This is a jail, not a social hall. We let in relatives sometimes, but you men aren't related."

"Señor Carmichael, can you tell us when these men will go to court and how much bail will be set?" Juan Ochoa used a respectful tone because he thought it would get an answer, not because he respected Carmichael himself.

It was not so much that he disrespected him, either. Like most Mexicans, he thought the law was for the *gringos,* although he was glad Bobcat was there.

Bobcat started to answer Juan's question but was cut off by the sheriff. "They will go to Judge Bickel at nine in the morning, but I cannot be expected to guess their bail. If you are so interested, come to court and find out. It's a free country."

Bobcat wished that Sheriff Carmichael was inclined to be a little more helpful. This Juan Ochoa was a slick one but was showing good manners. Esquibel was sullen as usual, and Joe Bartol was itching to say something. Why couldn't they just wait till tomorrow? Bobcat figured that the sheriff would at least talk to them. Instead Carmichael talked at them. There was no call to sass them. Carmichael acted like they ought not to even come into the sheriff's office. *Qué pena!*

It was a free country, even for agitators like Bartol and troublemakers like Esquibel. But that didn't make no never mind to Carmichael. He said his piece and turned back to his paperwork. And he turned his back on them. They knew they were dismissed. It was a short meeting, but a lot happened. Trouble wasn't very far away when men quit listening to one another.

They were back fifteen minutes after they left the Spanish-American Hall. Juan told everyone what had happened in a few short words. "The sheriff was there, but he was in no mood to talk. Campos and Navarro will go before Judge Bickel tomorrow at nine o'clock."

"But what about the bail, and what about letting them go tomorrow? What did they say about that?" asked Leandro Velarde. He had decided to walk back to the hall when some special deputies told him to move on. "No loitering around here, Mister . . ." He didn't hear what they called him but knew it wasn't flattering.

"Hey, Leandro, *amigo,* I just told you. Carmichael was in no mood to talk," Juan said, more patiently than he felt. They should have let us see Victor at least, he thought. But to tell Leandro, or anyone else for that matter, would do no good. It would just make trouble.

Joe Bartol couldn't seem to just talk. He had to talk loud. "Justice. What do you think that is? Is it just a name for what happens when some judge makes a ruling? What about our world right here in Gallup? What about the real world—the one where lawmen with guns and badges put poor people in jail for standing up for themselves? Campos was facing eviction for no legal reason, and Navarro only tried to help him. Is that a crime? If it is, there is no justice."

Even though everyone listened to Bartol, he talked pretty much above them. They understood more of what Leandro Velarde had to say. In particular, Mrs. Concepción Aurelio always listened to Leandro. He was a friend of her daughter and had been to her house many times. She came from a long line of miners and railroaders. She knew about the troubles that the men who worked on the tracks had, whether the tracks were on level ground or 600 feet belowground.

Because he was her daughter's friend, she remembered Leandro's words of a few weeks ago: "Get ready. We should go to the house of Victor Campos. And then to the court. Be prepared. Let the officers take their guns; we don't need anything but toothpicks."

Of course, like many in the crowd, Leandro sprinkled Spanish phrases liberally through his English sentences. What he actually said was: "We don't need nothin' but some *pica dientes.*" They got the little joke; his point was that no one should bring a gun. He wanted a protest, not a gunfight.

The last thing Juan Ochoa told them after reporting that they were not allowed to see Victor Campos and their friend Navarro was: "Hey, we should go there and show we're standing by our people. But don't give them any chance to make things worse."

There had been a lot of big talk at the meeting, but he wasn't worried. "We need to be there to show support. Losing our houses is one thing. Don't do anything stupid. You could lose more than your house. Remember, *su vida es más importante que su casa.*"

two

THE RIOT

April 4, 1935

"Goddamn, there better not be any goddamn trouble this morning," Bobcat said, as much to himself as to the other deputy. Deputy Hoy Boggess listened and nodded as he checked the rounds in his .45 Smith & Wesson double action. He put three cartridges in each of the half-moon clips and snapped them into place. "And while you're at it, you'd best hope no one else has one of them goddamn hog-leg shooters like that. Hoy, I don't know why you carry that weapon. Those clips would drive me nuts. They're a goddamn mystery to me."

Actually it wasn't so much a mystery as a curiosity. Sheriffs and their men bought their own weapons, and everyone had their preferences. But Deputy Boggess was the only lawman in the county to pack the military version of the Model 1917 .45 Smith & Wesson double action. In the first place, at two and a half pounds it was too big to carry comfortably, unless you had a good holster. Hoy did not. Second, it had a tendency to shoot low. That could be compensated for if you were a dead shot (like Dee Roberts). Hoy wasn't.

Dee preferred a single-action Colt. He had several but mostly holstered a .38 caliber that was light, fast, and plenty powerful. He didn't spend all day cleaning and checking it either, like Deputy Boggess.

Just as well, thought Bobcat. God help us if Hoy ever has to pull that hog killer; more than likely he'll shoot himself or one of us.

They had heard there would be a crowd that morning when they took the prisoners down to the justice court to be arraigned on breaking and entering charges.

I had no official business at the sheriff's office that morning, but I had heard about the meeting yesterday at the Spanish-American Hall and I wanted to hear how Bobcat and the other deputies were preparing for the "crowd."

There was some tension in the air on account of that little meeting yesterday when that Ochoa guy and the two others from the union stuck their unwanted noses into the sheriff's business.

"So you didn't even let them see Campos and Navarro," I said when Dee Roberts left the room.

"No, we did not. Besides, it was Navarro they seemed to be interested in, and he's a shifty one. Mack told them straight out, they weren't relatives and they damn sure weren't lawyers, so they had no cause to see the cells or who we got in them."

"My friend," I said, "sometimes giving a man what he wants will keep him from taking what he wants. All they wanted was to see Navarro. Now you have to worry that they might want to take Navarro."

At about that time, Sheriff Carmichael and Dee Roberts walked back in and put an end to our conversation. They knew me, but they gave me a pretty wide berth. I was a defense lawyer and sometimes made their arrests difficult with all that shit about due process and probable cause. As soon as I left, Bobcat and Hoy went to the back of the jail and brought Victor Campos and his little buddy Navarro out front for the trip to court.

Sheriff Mack R. Carmichael was a miner's lawman. As a former mine guard, he understood the hard life of the miner, but he was never one of them. Knowing their life but not living it was a definite plus. Going down into the shaft to arrest someone was one thing; going down to dig coal was another. Besides, you never wanted to get too close to someone you might have to bust—or too close to a man who didn't behave. In either case you might have to lock his ass up. So keep your distance. That was Mack's rule.

The sheriff knew most everyone in town—miners and merchants, organizers and agitators. And because he knew every mine owner and pit foreman in town, he also knew Juan Ochoa, at least by sight. Ochoa was a friend of the workingman, and that made him suspicious, at least in the eyes of the Gamerco coal bosses. For his part, Sheriff Carmichael was unsure about Juan Ochoa—was he just an organizer or a goddamn agitator?

While Carmichael didn't much cotton to unions, he was downright hostile to agitators. Folks said that Juan Ochoa was a decent but committed man. In Carmichael's mind, the difference was organizers did their work peaceable like; agitators always looked for trouble. So when he heard about the meeting that Juan Ochoa and a few dozen others "like him" held at the Spanish-American Hall, he pondered the difference between those who organized workers and those who agitated for trouble.

He had two men in his jail. He wanted them arraigned and out on the street without trouble. Navarro was a known troublemaker and a real agitating son of a bitch. Victor Campos was just a man caught up in the times. He lived in the wrong place and had the wrong friends. But in a day or two they would be back out. Goddamn. Why did Bickel keep locking men up without setting bail? It was a damn nuisance for him.

If Bobcat and Hoy were nervous, they didn't let it show to the sheriff and his undersheriff. Mack and Dee were hardheaded, hard-jawed men of the law. It was their job to put those who violated the law in jail. How long they stayed there wasn't their affair. They just took them to court and let the lawyers and the judges do the rest.

There wasn't much of a crowd, but some men were sort of lollygagging about down there on Coal Avenue in front of the Sutherland Building, where Judge Bickel held court every Monday morning. Leastways that's what Roberts said when he drove by there on his way to the jail.

The trip to court was uneventful. They walked Campos and Navarro down the block in two separate groups. They went down Second Street a half block to Coal and then another half block to Judge Bickel's court. There was a small group in front, but you would hardly call it a crowd. It seemed peaceable like.

No one said much other than, "*Qué pasa,* Navarro."

"Estoy bien," he replied as they entered the door next to a colored glass window that blocked part of the view of the front room of the court.

Some looked at Campos, but most seemed to focus on Navarro. Maybe it was because Navarro was the kind of man who attracted attention. He was a quick, easy mover. He looked like he was nervous, even when he was silent. Victor Campos smiled even when being escorted down the street, but Navarro just looked about everywhere at once, without stopping to look at anything.

Bobcat was in back and looked at the little group to see who was doing the talking. Sure enough, it was Juan Ochoa. I wish he wasn't here, thought Bobcat. But this will be over in a few minutes and we can get these *hombres* bailed out and gone.

An hour later they were still sitting on the bench in Judge Bickel's court when they heard the first sound of real anger from the crowd out front. The small group had grown, and they were downright pissed about being kept outside. He looked out the colored glass of the small window by the front door.

Bobcat hoped that Ochoa was gone, but there he was, standing and listening. Only now it was, by God, a huge crowd. Goddammit, he thought, why in God's hell didn't Judge Bickel get on with it? No good could come of making men wait to see what they didn't want to see in the first place.

A crowd is a funny thing. Some came because the word was out that Senator Vogel would be there in court. Some came because they were at the meeting at the Spanish-American Hall the day before. Some just were passing by and stopped to see what was going on. This crowd was getting nasty. Probably more than a hundred had gathered by now.

It was a typical April morning in Gallup—cold. Some wanted inside, either to listen or to get warm. Dee Roberts put Bobcat and Deputy Boggess next to the front door to keep the crowd out. "They got no business here unless they're related to the prisoner or have one of them goddamn press badges. Relatives and reporters only, you hear me?"

Bobcat knew that Roberts was speaking for Judge Bickel, who talked to the sheriff and the undersheriff in his little office in back of the courtroom itself before he started the first case of the day. He called it his "chambers," and that always got a snicker from most folks. "Chambers" seemed to be the kind of thing you'd find in a whorehouse that had those little alcoves with curtains on them.

They could hear Judge Bickel up there on his bench, but it wasn't easy. The crowd outside was getting noisier, and there were some bad sounds coming through the colored glass window. Bobcat took it in stride, but Hoy started snapping and unsnapping the lock-down strap on the tear gas canister he had brought from the jail. That didn't make anyone feel better. It was sort of like a tic. Snap. Unsnap. Snap. Unsnap.

Finally Dee Roberts leaned over and held Hoy's right wrist. "No need to worry, Hoy; Judge Bickel will get to our business soon enough."

Well, thought Bobcat, it'd best be sooner. Those *hombres* outside might not be so sociable in another hour or two.

Just about that time the crowd started some serious cursing, serious, that is, for a crowd that included women and children. "Hey, *cabron,* what the fuck you think we are out here, *peónes?*" A small rock cracked the colored glass, and everyone tensed up inside.

Senator Vogel and his lawyer, Harris K. Lyle, were having second thoughts about even coming to the arraignment. They had no part in it, as the only thing that was supposed to happen was the entry of a plea to the charge and the setting of bail.

Sheriff Carmichael was worried but didn't show it. Dee Roberts was the same as always: confident and ready for whatever came his way. Like Bobcat, he rarely felt fear. Unlike Bobcat, he sort of enjoyed confrontation. For Bobcat it was part of the job, but that didn't mean you had to like it. Dee Roberts probably would have quit the job if things were always easy and no one got out of line. His job was to put troublemakers back in line, one way or the other.

As time droned on, there was more than a hum coming in from the street. Funny thing about crowd noise—it can be real nice like in a crowded theater or a dance hall. Barroom crowds can be fun, but this crowd was no fun. This was a serious bunch, but the judge and the district attorney didn't seem to be getting it. They went on with their regular Monday morning court calendar just as though no one was out in the street.

Hoy Boggess kept looking up at Judge Bickel, who kept looking at the district attorney and the federal officer who had the first case of the morning. None of it made much sense to him, and it didn't seem to make much sense to Judge Bickel. Finally he said he had heard enough, ruled on the case, and then called the case of *State of New Mexico vs. Victor Campos and Esiquel Navarro,* for breaking and entry on premises owned by C. F. Vogel. By way of understatement, he asked: "Is everyone ready?"

The civil writ of eviction Judge William H. Bickel issued on behalf of Senator C. F. Vogel necessitated a criminal charge because those evicted didn't stay evicted. Going back into Campos's house was, technically, breaking and entering. That made it necessary for the district attorney of McKinley County to charge Victor Campos and Esiquel Navarro in criminal court. The formal charges weren't actually filed until an hour before the arraignment. The arrests of Campos and Navarro were accomplished without the benefit of an arrest warrant and before the filing of a criminal charge against either man. Bail wasn't set for either man. Gallup eventually followed the law, but not always at the right time.

The single charge ascribed to the defendants was wrongful and forcible breaking and entering of a certain house. The language of the formal charge described Mr. Campos's going back into his own house as "a willful deed committed without lawful justification or excuse, which unreasonably disturbed the public peace and tranquillity."

Of course there was more to the formal charge than this, but it was legalese for ignoring a state senator and being a member of a suspect group that might be advocating the overthrow of the government.

The district attorney believed the defendants to be dangerous to the good people of Gallup and therefore insisted on criminal charges against the men involved, but he was confident that Mrs. Lovato meant no harm and dropped the charge against her.

"Mr. Navarro, I see you're here without counsel. Do you have a lawyer?" intoned Judge Bickel over the racket of the crowd outside. As he waited for the answer, the judge was thinking about more important things like, Lawyer or not, I've waited too long and the boys outside are pissed and I'm going to get this case the hell out of here.

"No, Judge, I don't have no lawyer and I can't get one in jail, so could you set me some bail so I can get out?"

That drew an interruption from the prosecutor, who wanted the case to start with Campos, who did have a lawyer. "Your Honor, Mr. Campos's lawyer can speak for both of them, at least for purposes of a plea and bail, and we can get this case off your busy calendar." Like the judge, the prosecutor wished he hadn't delayed things so long with the last case, but how was he to know the crowd would turn nasty?

Just who were these two beaners anyway? A simple B&E was all that was on the docket sheet he picked up in the office on his way to the usual docket call on Mondays before Bail-less Bickel. Now here he was, in the midst of an angry bunch of out-of-work miners who were acting like this was an important case.

"Mr. Navarro, the court cannot proceed with your arraignment and will not take a plea on your charge until you are properly represented by a lawyer. If you cannot afford a lawyer, the court will appoint one for you. You will have to fill out the forms and give them to the clerk. That can be done later. As for the other defendant, Mr. Campos, I see no need to proceed with his plea since both are charged with the same violation. I will set bail at a nominal sum for both defendants, but that cannot be done until the afternoon calendar. I'll endorse it and send it to the jail at 1:30 P.M. today. That's all we need accomplish. The sheriff will no doubt want to get the prisoners back to jail for processing so they can be released this afternoon."

It was clear to those in court that Judge Bickel was speaking to the crowd, but of course they couldn't hear him. What they could see through the colored glass on Coal Avenue was Sheriff Carmichael and his men getting the prisoners up and moving to the rear of the courtroom.

Bang! The sound was sharp and jolted everyone into attention. Everyone looked at the rear of the room, where the venetian blind was still shaking as it snapped up into position. Someone had hit the glass by the door so hard, the blind snapped up.

Sheriff Carmichael decided that Campos could wait in the small holding cell till they got Navarro back to jail. They could come back for him on a separate trip. Navarro was the agitator, and it looked like he was the one that nasty crowd out front was interested in. So he put Campos away and moved Navarro to the rear of the court.

The rear. That seemed to be what Navarro was trying to signal to the faces pressed up to the plate glass out on the sidewalk. Navarro guessed that Sheriff Carmichael was planning on skipping the crowd in front and was going to walk him out the back and down the alley to Second Street. The jail was just up the alley and across the street; he would be back in his cell in three minutes flat.

Someone in the crowd hollered, *"Regresar en salvar!"* and twenty or thirty men ran to Third Street and headed south to the alley. The sidewalk was a mixture of concrete, dirt, and gravel. The sound of that many men running, like a pack, was ominous, but there was more to it than just the sound. Somehow the wind pushed ahead of the crowd and carried the smell of excitement, of anger, and of fear.

As the crowd reached the alley, the ones in front could see someone starting to come out the back door of Judge Bickel's office. Ignacio Velarde and Solomon Esquibel were leading the pack. Along with them was the big man with the black hat, the black mustache, and the black look in his eyes. He had a club, but he didn't raise it; it was carried level to the ground and moved from side to side as he took ever longer strides to get from the street to the rear door of Judge Bickel's little courtroom.

Fred Montoya was the first deputy to step out into the alley. He gulped, flinched, and stepped back inside. Sheriff Carmichael moved to the front, and he and Dee Roberts grabbed Navarro between them and moved through the doorway out into the alley.

Bobcat and Hoy Boggess followed right behind. Four men with guns, and Navarro.

The alley was about sixteen feet wide, with back doors on both sides. It was mostly houses on the south side because they fronted onto Aztec Street, a residential street. The buildings on the north side of the alley were businesses and had little space in between—except for the vacant lot on the east side of the justice court. Since the crowd was coming from their right, the sheriff and his men pushed their way east, toward their jail and safety, for them as well as for the prisoner Navarro. Bobcat and Hoy Boggess were closest to the crowd and were between them and the prisoner, Navarro, held on both sides by Sheriff Carmichael and Dee Roberts. Of the four of them, only Boggess seemed to be aware of just how close the crowd was. He could smell their anger, and they could smell his fear. Those closest to him could see with sharp clarity how the deputies elbowed and hampered each other, reluctantly turning to resist the crowd as it slowed their forward progress to their jail.

The deputies could feel the continuous stir of men, women, and children getting out of the way. The short silence as the two groups of men faced each other gave way to a steady, ponderous rumble like the sound of Navajo wagons crossing the plank bridges across the Purkey. The lawmen braced against the elusive weight of the crowd and moved on down the alley.

As the crowd surged in, a dark and forbidding man shook his fist and shouted, "Now you'll see it, *desgraciado.*" That may mean "unlucky" in the dictionary, but Bobcat took it for what it was. Hunker down, lawman: "We're here for Navarro." As it happened, they didn't get him. No one did. A sharp *crack,* vaguely like that of a .22 but different, startled the crowd. They seemed to push forward and then lean back, like there was a strong wind blowing. The smell of tear gas was suddenly overpowering; the sense of panic, even more so. Navarro burst loose and then on through the crowd just as the first shot was fired. The odd, almost eerie sound of the tear gas canister became a part of the thrust of the movement of the crowd and the deputies. The crowd rushed backward to the west, and the deputies picked up the speed of their march to the east.

Bobcat heard a louder pistol blast, saw Navarro run and the sheriff fall. All in the space of two or three seconds. The crack of the shot was surprising, but the gushing of blood from the head shot the sheriff took was absolutely terrifying. Bobcat struggled and for a few moments was completely helpless, tossed under trampling feet, smothered and squashed under struggling bodies. As he reached for Navarro, he felt rather than saw him move on up the alley. Drawing his gun, he felt and heard the blasts of other guns, but they seemed far away. Hoy buckled next to him as something or someone came crashing down with a mauling weight. Even as he dropped to the rough stones in the alley, Bobcat could hear the last shots, smell the blood, and feel its splatter, hot but oddly refreshing.

As Dee Roberts looked to his left at the sound of the first shot, another rang out. The sheriff was hit again as he fell to the ground. Dee had heard a hissing sound just before the first gunshot, but it was lost now in the hail of bullets all around him. Dee felt a bullet whiz by his cheek so close, he felt the wind of it as he drew his gun. He heard the soggy *puck* sound the missed bullet made in the telephone pole to his left. At first he thought he was alone in the crowd, but then he realized that Bobcat was still standing, but stooped over, like he was hit. Hoy was down and bleeding. Hoy's blood splattered on Bobcat and in seconds began to mix, from the outside to the inside, with Bobcat's own blood, now gushing from the gaping shoulder wound.

Dee Roberts was struggling with his own weapon. Something was wrong. He couldn't get it to fire at first. With his left hand he fanned the hammer of the single-action .38 and hit Solomon Esquibel with the first shot.

As Bobcat spun to his left, he felt the burn and was jolted by the second bullet blasting into his right lung. "I'm shot," he cried. As he fell he saw the claw hammer come out of the crowd and slam Hoy Boggess again and again. He thought he saw the flash of a blade or a pick; he couldn't tell for sure. He seemed to be firing, but maybe it was just the firing at him that he heard.

Hoy was still trying to unloose that big .45 hog-leg from his back belt when he hit the ground, three or four feet from Sheriff Carmichael's twitching body. What Bobcat didn't know at the time was that Deputy Boggess actually threw the first punch, so to speak. As they came through the door, Hoy could see the crowd in front of him, on the other side of Sheriff Carmichael. He thought he saw a gun, but no one else did. He had a tear gas canister in his hand, even though Sheriff Carmichael had told him to put it away just before they came through the door. He thought someone was reaching for the prisoner. He had ahold of Navarro with his left hand and was intent on drawing his gun. So it seemed logical, at least to him, at least then, to hurl the tear gas canister into the crowd. Trouble was, the tear gas didn't disperse as much as it infuriated the crowd. Those in front saw Hoy throw the gas, and one of them had a claw hammer. Getting hit in the head with anything is gonna give you a bad day, but a claw hammer will mess up your whole year.

All in all, some fifteen shots were fired. Dee Roberts emptied all five rounds from his single-action .38 Colt. Some said that Bobcat fired twice after he was hit, but others doubted that. Hoy Boggess later said he used Bobcat's gun to fire twice into the crowd before he lapsed into unconsciousness. Sheriff Carmichael never fired his gun.

As quickly as it started, it was over. Fierce-eyed men with guns were coming into the alley from both ends, fearful of enemies, but there were no enemies, only bodies. The remaining few in the crowd of onlookers seemed as bewildered as the newly arrived men of the law. None seemed to comprehend the bloodied, dirtied shirts of the deputies or the blown-up unrecognizable face of Sheriff Carmichael visible in the brown pool of his own blood. The stillness of his body matched the stillness of the crowd.

Two dark-skinned men in the crowd died, one right away and the other a week later at St. Mary's Hospital. Everyone assumed that it was Dee Roberts who got them. He thought so too. Direct or ricocheting bullets hit at least six other men and one woman. The cries, the smell of open wounds, and the fierce burning of the tear gas were at first overpowering and then almost an understatement. When the dust settled, the smell of revenge became overpowering.

Sheriff Carmichael was dead at the scene. Everyone assumed that someone in the crowd had shot him. Dee Roberts thought so too. That is, he thought so until it was pointed out that the two he shot were the only ones with guns, and he killed them both.

That was a problem, since he shot them just as Bobcat got hit in the chest with a .45-caliber bullet and Hoy Boggess was felled with a claw hammer. Then he remembered that Hoy's gun was lost in the melee. When they find Hoy's gun, they'll find Mack's killer, he thought.

When they dug a .45-caliber bullet out of Sheriff Carmichael's shoulder at his autopsy and compared it with the .45-caliber bullet they took from Bobcat's lung at his surgery, it looked like someone shot the sheriff and Bobcat with Hoy's gun. The question was, Who? And where was Hoy's gun? When the gunfire let up and the dust settled, his hog-leg .45 was gone. And so was Navarro.

Gallup had itself a hell of a mess to deal with. Every lawyer in town, including me, spent the rest of the week in one way or another dealing with the riot. About an hour after the ambulances carried the wounded out of the alley, a blast on the fire siren summoned the American Legion and the Veterans of Foreign Wars into action. Gallup took on the look of an armed camp as special deputies (mine guards) equipped with shotguns, rifles, and pistols filled streets. Warrants were signed and arrests were made—lots of 'em. Hundreds of houses were ransacked as the lawmen looked for a Model 1917 .45 Smith & Wesson—all that turned up were piles and piles of communist literature. Up in Santa Fe, Governor Tingley assured a group of demonstrators that "only the guilty need fear punishment." While Sheriff Roberts was rounding up more than a hundred men and women, Governor Tingley sent a telegram to Governor E. C. Johnson of Colorado. Governor Johnson had faced some similar problems in his state, and Governor Tingley requested details on his method of concentration camp and deportation of aliens. The telegram read:

COPY OF WESTERN UNION TELEGRAM

APRIL 4, 1935

GOVERNOR ED. C. JOHNSON

DENVER, COLORADO

PLEASE GIVE ME DETAILS REGARDING YOUR METHOD CONCENTRATION CAMP AND DEPORTATION OF ALIENS ON RELIEF.

CLYDE TINGLEY, GOVERNOR

SEND PAID

CHARGE GOVERNOR

Funny how a telegram *from* a governor gets answered right away, particularly when it's *to* a governor. Governor Johnson telegraphed his reply back that same afternoon just about the time that the roundup of aliens and other radicals in Gallup was moving into high gear:

POSTAL TELEGRAPH

THE INTERNATIONAL SYSTEM

DENVER COLO. 949A APRIL 4 1935

HON. CLYDE TINGLEY, GOVERNOR

SANTA FE, NEW MEXICO

BECAUSE OF TREATIES WITH FOREIGN COUNTRIES DEPORTATION MUST BE VOLUNTARY WHICH WOULD BE EASY TO WORK OUT IF FEDERAL RELIEF AGENCIES WOULD COOPERATE BY WITHHOLDING OR THREATENING TO WITHHOLD RELIEF WHICH THEY WILL NOT DO EVERYONE ELSE INCLUDING FOREIGN CONSULS AND IMMIGRATION DEPARTMENT COOPERATING WE ARE NOT MAKING ANY HEADWAY JUST NOW

ED C JOHNSON, GOVERNOR OF COLORADO 1002A

That sort of thing seemed to be justified since the large group of defendants sitting in jail that day asked Carl Howe to speak for them. Mr. Howe wasn't a lawyer, but he was active in the local Communist Party in Gallup. He was also the spokesman for the International Labor Defense League in New Mexico and had lived in Gallup since 1933. In the next three months well over a hundred people were sent out of the country by the Immigration and Naturalization Service at the request of the governor of New Mexico.

The man who first tried to figure out who shot the sheriff was the McKinley County coroner, Dr. Travers. He did the autopsy. He did it the way he hated to—with an audience. He would have much preferred to do it alone, and he would have preferred to wait a few hours. He had done hundreds of postmortem examinations and was long past the idea that the body on his examining table was a human being. Nevertheless, he thought the family had a right to see the deceased before he did his cutting.

Dr. Travers said he would explain what he found as he went along, even though he knew that the new sheriff (Dee Roberts) and the district attorney (David Chavez) weren't interested in the details. They wanted to know the answer to just one question: Could the autopsy tell them who shot the sheriff?

The first thing the coroner did was to look at the head wound; actually it was a face wound. "Look here, Sheriff Roberts, you can see the tattooing right here above the nose."

Dee didn't want to look at his lifelong friend's blown-up face, but he did. "Sheriff Carmichael never had no tattoo, Doc, I can tell you that. What in hell are you talking about?"

"Tattooing is caused by gunpowder embedded in your skin when someone shoots you at short range. If you look close with this glass, you can see the projectile gunpowder right here. That cannot be wiped off. It tells me right off that whoever killed our sheriff was standing no more than three feet away when he fired on him. And he wasn't much closer than that either because there's no soot present."

"Soot, you mean like from a stovepipe or what?" chimed in Mr. Chavez.

"No, Mr. Chavez, I mean soot from gunpowder. Is this your first autopsy?"

It was his first and, he hoped, his last. He didn't want to be here any more than Dee Roberts did. But as long as he was, he thought he'd best get it straight. Judge Otero had ordered him to be present and expected him to report back quickly—even though the judge would get the autopsy itself straight from the coroner's office.

Three men dead, six men and one woman in the hospital, and pretty near fifty-five men and women locked up in less than two hours since the bloody battle in the alley. Those were surefire reasons for Judge Otero to make everything a priority. First on his list was to find out who shot the sheriff.

While Doc Travers was making clinical notes at Carmichael's autopsy, Mary Ann was writing in her little black binder.

April 4, 1935

Dear Journal:

My purpose in starting you was a simple one. My plan was to record the events and circumstances surrounding the eviction of those pitiful people in Chihuahuaita. I don't even know them. A man I hardly know, our local state senator, started their evictions. Now I'm sure I don't want to know him.

That was my "plan" until this morning. I never thought I would write to you (or anyone on the face of this earth) about the death of a man I know and the possible death of another man who may be as close to Billy Wade as I am. Sheriff Mack Carmichael was killed this morning, and Bobcat Wilson, his deputy, was shot twice. Billy Wade says Bobcat probably won't make it.

I feel so helpless because I love Billy Wade. That's not the way love is supposed to be. Love is being able to help whoever you love. But I can't help Billy Wade because Bobcat, his closest friend, is lying on a white starched sheet, looking as white as it is, gasping for breath and holding on to life as fiercely and as silently as he does everything else. From the news at school this morning, someone tried to free a prisoner who was being taken from court to jail and all hell broke loose. I know that's not very descriptive, but I've heard so many different versions from so many people that it's probably the best anyone can do right now. In fact, "all hell broke loose" was what our principal, Mr. McDonald, said in the lunchroom. Apparently he heard about it during second-hour homeroom from Abby Gonzales (who heard it from her father, Frank). The first wild story we heard was that a bunch of radicals were waving banners and shouting things because of the evictions in Chihuahuaita. We heard that they shot dozens of people. Everybody is blaming the union that has the coal miners out on strike. But then someone said it was a riot that started when the deputies opened fire on the crowd. That seems equally unlikely. Sheriff Carmichael and Bobcat aren't the kind of men who "open fire" on anyone. They're the kind of men who defend themselves, but I cannot believe they would shoot into a crowd of people, even angry people. Particularly Bobcat, who has friends in Chihuahuaita (according to Billy Wade).

The paper is already out, and the ink is hardly dry on the ugly big headline about Bobcat and Mack. The story is predictably sketchy, but that's to be expected. I do hope they decide to really go after this story and report the truth about whatever it was that happened. Billy Wade tried to go down to the jail to get something for Bobcat, but Second Street is all blocked off from Aztec to Coal Avenue. They did let him through, but he said it was hard because there are troopers and mine guards all over the place. No one seems to expect any more trouble (as though we didn't have enough already).

My innate suspicions are probably getting the better of me, but I wonder if the prisoner was one of those who was resisting the evictions. Madam Journal, I started to write to you about the evictions. Maybe I still am. Maybe this unspeakable tragedy is actually another chapter in the eviction story. Oh, one other thing. They said that a man by the name of Navarro was the prisoner and that he's still loose somewhere in town. Someone at Harshman's garage heard the people in the alley chanting, "We want Navarro," or something like that. I'm sure Billy Wade told me last week that a man with a name like that was arrested by Bobcat for resisting the eviction of some friend of his in Chihuahuaita. If that's really the case, then there's a connection between the evictions and the killing. God, I hope it's only one killing. I'll feel so sad for Bobcat's family and Billy Wade. Damn, why do people love money so much? But there I go again, asking a question that might not be relevant. Was it money that's at the core of the evictions? Maybe not; maybe it was more complicated, like breaking a labor union. Of course, come to think of it, that's about money too, isn't it?

First things first, as Billy Wade put it on the phone from Rehoboth Hospital this afternoon. Let's pray for Bobcat now; you can investigate later. He didn't mean it in a cruel way, but it hurt anyhow. I should be thinking about Bobcat's life, not how he got where he is.

I must sign off for now and meet Billy Wade. He'll need me tonight.

three

THE CHARGES (QUE SÍ!–QUE NO!)

April and May, 1935

The men and women of Gallup could hardly believe what had happened in their little town. Labor strife had been a way of life for years, but this time there were dead bodies all over one of the most traveled alleyways in Gallup. Everyone else was mad or scared or both. We could hardly believe it—we all thought things would get back to normal in a day or two. We never thought this would make our little town notorious.

The official court record on what became known as the "Gallup 14" case was duly noted on the criminal docket of the New Mexico First Judicial District, McKinley County, No. 1299. Actually, there were four separate criminal dockets on the case because it kept changing. It started out as case number 1299 because that was the official criminal complaint that Gallup's brand-new sheriff filed as his first official act on the morning of April 5, 1935. Undersheriff D. R. "Dee" Roberts became Sheriff D. R. "Dee" Roberts the instant Sheriff M. R. "Mack" Carmichael died. Like in a lot of western towns at the time, the men mostly had two formal initials in their name but went by nicknames. The women just had names, no initials and no nicknames.

Mack and Dee weren't just men who worked together; they were the best of friends. Dee took Mack's death awful hard, and he vowed to put the men who did it in the death house. That more or less explains how Dee was able to do something I argued was "legally inconsistent." Everyone thought it just plain strange. Dee shot and killed the man who shot the sheriff; then, first thing next morning, he filed a formal complaint against the man that he had just killed, charging him with killing the sheriff.

The conundrum was, How could you swear out a murder complaint against a man you had shot and killed the day before? But that's just what Dee did first thing on the morning of April 5, 1935. In fact, there were two different legal papers filed that morning. In the first one, Sheriff Roberts swore out a warrant for the "arrest of Solomon L. Esquibel & Ignacio Velarde for the murder of M. R. Carmichael on the 4th Day of April 1935, in Gallup, New Mexico." The boys at the American Bar allowed as how you'd have to go to the boneyard to arrest Solomon Esquibel. The other one, Ignacio Velarde, was in the hospital with Dee Roberts's bullets still in his back. In the second legal paper, Sheriff Roberts swore on his oath that "the following did unlawfully, knowingly, willfully, and feloniously murder M. R. Carmichael on the 4th Day of April, 1935, in Gallup, New Mexico." The complaint went on and on. It listed the names of thirty men and women who Dee Roberts thought were "involved" because someone had spotted them on Coal Avenue in front of the JP court or out in back in the alley "at or about" the time of the riot. It didn't seem to matter to Dee. If he heard you were there or anywhere near there, he put your name down. That is, if your name either ended with a vowel or he thought you were an agitator or a communist.

The first two names on the list were those of Esquibel and Velarde (even though they misspelled it as "Andrade"). Seeing as how Dee Roberts shot them because he saw them shoot the sheriff, it made sense for their names to be on the list. But most of the rest on the list were suspect just because someone thought they *might* have been there. Arguably, they were "suspect." However, the formal complaint categorically accused them of premeditated murder, and Dee Roberts swore it to be true. He didn't swear that they *might* have killed the sheriff because they were there; he swore they did do it, in fact. There seemed to be no doubt in his mind.

As it turned out, there were six names on that first list of thirty that made it all the way to the courthouse for the trial. These six were Juan Ochoa, Joe Bartol, Serpio Sosa, Manuel Avitia, Willie Gonzales, and Leandro Velarde. Four more would stand trial, but Dee hadn't yet heard that they were there.

That afternoon Dee and every deputy he could find, every city policeman he could muster, a sizable number of mine guards from Gamerco, and several New Mexico state policemen descended on Chihuahuaita and rounded up fifteen people for murder. By five o'clock, Dee and Assistant District Attorney C. R. McIntosh were in Judge Luis Armijo's court with a motion to "transport prisoners." Dee actually filed the motion, not the district attorney. The motion urged the court to allow transportation, asserting that fifteen people had been arrested for murder in the first degree and that "it was necessary for the public welfare and safe custody of the prisoners that they be transported to the State Penitentiary in Santa Fe."

And so early the next morning, Judge Armijo ordered that fifteen of Chihuahuaita's finest citizens be locked up in a railroad car and shipped to the state pen up in Santa Fe. Ochoa, Velarde, Bartol, Sosa, Avitia, Gonzales, and Velarde were among the first bunch to go.

Every one of them, except for Joe Bartol, stayed there for the summer. Joe posted his $7,500 bail. The rest were locked up until they went to trial up in Aztec in October 1935.

One of the many arrested that day was a black-eyed young señorita named Gutierrez. She was transported to Santa Fe along with the rest because she admitted being the daughter of Basilio Gutierrez, one of the National Miners Union leaders. She was also kin to Solomon Esquibel, the man Dee Roberts shot in the alley the day before. Lupe Gutierrez insisted that she wasn't even in the alley that morning. It didn't change anything. Her biggest problem was that she was kin to both the boss of the union and the man who, according to Dee Roberts, killed the sheriff. When Lupe finally got to court up there in Santa Fe in front of Judge Otero, he listened to what the lawmen said about her and the speculation that she *might* have been in the alley that morning. He was about to bind her over for trial with the rest when he thought to ask her age. When she said fifteen, he said, "Turn her loose."

None of this was a secret. Not here, not in Santa Fe, and not in Los Angeles or in New York. Every big city paper in America was following the story. Not that they much gave a damn about Gallup or even that it had lost its sheriff. The big story was about the mass arrests and the connection to unionism and communism, which some thought were the same thing.

But no one in town could ever have guessed how much of the world's attention was about to be focused on little Gallup, New Mexico. The sun had hardly set before the first big-shot lawyer stepped off the train from Los Angeles. District Attorney Chavez would later call this big-shot lawyer *"una pendejada."* And a bloody nuisance he was, too.

I sat beside Bobcat in that aseptic-smelling room at Rehoboth Hospital, five miles east of Gallup. Bobcat wasn't talking, as usual. But this time he wasn't talking because he had four bullet holes in him. Two were caused by the bullets going in, the third by the one bullet that came out. The other was still in him. I wasn't sure I was supposed to be there as Bobcat's lawyer, but that's what I told him. I was there as his friend, but in fact, I was pretty helpless in either role.

Old Doc Pousma allowed as how it was too early to take the bullet out. He said it was in a dangerous place. "Besides, he might die before we even try, in which case there's no need to bother with it." I bristled at that and was glad none of the Wilson clan was around to hear it. But come to think of it, it would have made no difference to Bobcat one way or the other. He would have agreed. He had what you might call a fatalistic view of life. He also had a short view on doctors.

Bobcat was one of the few white men who not only spoke Navajo, he thought in Navajo. The Navajo way was to accept your fate and avoid medicine men if at all possible. Bobcat wasn't what you would call important around Gallup. Lying there in that hospital bed, in the whitewashed room with white curtains and a pale-looking cross on the wall, he looked small and ready to die.

The fact that my best friend might well die was clear but vaguely incomprehensible to me. The fact that the law was starting to run amok in town was also weighing me down. I was anxious to talk to Bobcat to find out what really happened. As it turned out, I wouldn't really know for another fifty-two years.

The *Gallup Independent* had lots of rumors but was short on facts. Sheriff Dee Roberts had lots of suspects but was short on evidence. All told, the law had already rounded up over a hundred people (men, women, and a few juveniles) and placed them in jail for "protective custody."

Many of them couldn't speak English, none could afford bail, and only a few had any idea what kind of trouble they were really in. The feeling around the courthouse was that most would either be convicted or deported (preferably both). Our sheriff was dead, and two of his deputies were badly wounded in the shoot-out. Sheriff Mack was well thought of, Hoy Boggess was at least thought of, and Bobcat, well, Bobcat was someone nobody messed with. With Mack dead, Hoy beat up real bad, and Bobcat about to die, feelings were running high.

That's why I was hoping to get to talk to Bobcat that morning before the International Defense League's main lawyer, Mr. A. L. Wirin, got to town. The telegram I got last night asking me to meet Mr. Wirin at the train depot was both exciting and a little unnerving. I wasn't exactly in tune with the International Defense League, and Bobcat was damn sure no communist. For chrissake, I wasn't even a liberal. Why did they want me to meet Mr. A. L. Wirin? He's a lawyer with a big rep, and I'm a lawyer with hardly any reputation at all. Why doesn't he want to talk to Mr. Denny or Mr. Glascock?

I sat there for two hours, and Bobcat never said a word. He was semiconscious but not talking. So I left and went by the high school to talk to Mary Ann. Miss Mary Ann Shaughnessy's ninth-grade English class was just getting out, and she didn't have homeroom duty until after lunch. So we went for an early lunch down at the Chocolate Shop. We weren't hungry, at least for food, but that would have to wait until the sun went down. So we settled for burgers and fries, with extra grease, and Nehi grape soda.

"Billy Wade, what in the world has happened? The teachers' lounge was empty this morning. No one showed up on time. Seems to me like everyone in school has a friend or a relative who's either locked up or is out looking for someone *to* lock up. Has Dee Roberts gone completely mad?"

"Whoa, slow down!" I held up my hands. "I can't keep up, as usual. You're forgetting that Mack Carmichael is dead, Bobcat is about to die, and the morgue has two bodies in it, not to mention the six others who have bullet holes in them that weren't there yesterday. What did you expect Dee to do? He's investigating; that's his job."

"I expect you and every other lawyer in this town to insist on the due process of the law." Mary Ann faced me with fire in her eyes. "Everyone is saying at school that these arrests are being made without warrants and, what's worse, on the basis of suspicion, not proof. Surely that's not the law. Can he just arrest people and send them in cattle cars to Santa Fe because he thinks they were in the alley yesterday? This is America, you know."

"Look, I'm sure that Judge Armijo isn't allowing arrests without probable cause. I'm also sure that arrest warrants are being used. Dee's madder than hell, but he's a man of the law. Now, what do you want for lunch?" As I said that, our knees touched under the bench and we both wished it was dark and we were somewhere else. "We could just crawl under the booth and skip lunch," I added.

She said, "You stop that, or I'll slap your wrist with my ruler, which I always carry right here in my purse."

We spent the next twenty minutes munching the toasted buns that flopped over the edge of Miss Rita's great hamburgers and nearly hid the fried onions and green chili. As we finished up, I said, as casually as I could muster: "By the way, I'm meeting a big-city lawyer from Los Angeles this afternoon. I expect he'll be representing most of the people who are locked up in Dee Roberts's jail. I have no idea why he wants to talk to me."

While it was true that I had no idea who hired Mr. Wirin or why he was coming to town, Governor Tingley certainly did. That same day Wirin, the big-shot lawyer from Los Angeles, wrote to Governor Tingley:

Honorable Clyde Tingley, State Capitol
Santa Fe, New Mexico

Dear Sir:

Unless you, as chief executive of the State, speak out clearly and fearlessly in favor of civil rights and constitutional guarantees at once, the State of New Mexico will follow in the footsteps of North Carolina and Alabama, and Gallup will become another Gastonia and Scottsboro combined.

The wholesale imprisonment of workers under charge of murder merely because they were present at the scene of a shooting is reminiscent of Gastonia. Today at Gallup the Scottsboro case was re-enacted: ignorant Mexican Workers facing execution were denied the constitutional right to counsel. They were induced to waive preliminary hearing and denied a continuance. Surely you will not tolerate such defiance of the constitution. The International Labor Defense of Gallup joins with me in this protest.

Very Sincerely Yours,

A. L. Wirin,
Attorney-at-law
1022 Civic Center Building
Los Angeles, California

Gastonia? Scottsboro? They didn't sound like New Mexico towns and didn't mean a hell of a lot to the folks in Gallup. Mr. Wirin announced he was in league with the so-called International Labor Defense of Gallup. Sometimes it called itself the ILD. The ILD was the International Legal Defense affiliate of the Communist Party of America. They banded together and sent postcards from almost every state in the union demanding the immediate release of the Gallup Fourteen. Governor Tingley received tens of thousands of these postcards. The front side of the postcard had the slogan on it that would ring throughout New Mexico for the rest of the summer: FREE THE FOURTEEN GALLUP MINERS. The backside of the card said:

To Governor Clyde Tingley and
Attorney General Frank Patton:

I (We) vigorously protest against the attempt to send to the electric chair ten innocent Gallup Miners, who are held on a frame-up charge of first degree murder. I further protest against the attempt to railroad four innocent workers to jail on a framed-up charge of aiding a prisoner to escape.

I further vigorously protest against the action taken by the Labor Department in its approval and support to the State of New Mexico in its attempt to arrest and deport 90 Gallup workers.

I DEMAND:

The immediate and unconditional release of the ten innocent miners, who are held for first-degree murder, those held for aiding a prisoner to escape, and all of those held for deportation.

Name: ______________________________

Address: ______________________________

CIRCULATED BY THE GALLUP DEFENSE COMMITTEE

P.O. BOX 204

DENVER, COLORADO

Every day from early April through the end of June 1935, Governor Tingley's office received letters, postcards, and petitions demanding the prisoners' release. Some of them came from individuals, like this one:

Dear Governor Tingley,

Is justice dead in our Courts and are all police cowards—with their brutal beating of unarmed working people? In Gallup one was killed and seven wounded.

Carmichael was killed with one bullet—so the charge that 55 miners are guilty of murder is ridiculous and you are unworthy of your high position if you permit such things in your state.

The answer of course is that the police and courts are under the influence of the employer interests and not truth and justice.

It is for you to point the way to decent treatment of all citizens, rich or poor, residing in your state.

It shall be understood we are watching what you do.

Cordially,

Anne C. Kennedy

About all Mrs. Kennedy got was a curt *"esa pinche mujer"* from the governor's right-hand man. A letter from the Workers School in San Francisco dated

April 15, 1935, warned our good governor: "The workers of America are awake to the increasingly drastic methods being used to reduce their condition to abject misery and starvation." The letter from the International Labor Defense in Milwaukee, Wisconsin, was more blunt:

> Deputized gunmen attacked the workers who protested against an eviction that was engineered by the American Coal Co., and . . . we demand the immediate disarming of the fascist bands of the American Legion, who differ in nothing from Hitler's Brown Hordes, and the punishment of the actual murderers.

Of course, not all the telegrams that Governor Tingley got were against the lawmen in Gallup. Here's one he got when he was back in Washington, D.C., talking to the secretary of labor about the situation on April 23, 1935:

> COPY OF WESTERN UNION TELEGRAM 1935 APR 24
> HON CLYDE TINGLEY=CARE MAYFLOWER HOTEL WASHDC=
>
> STRONGLY URGE THAT YOU SEE SECRETARY OF LABOR AND HAVE HER UPHOLD THE ACTION OF IMMIGRATION OFFICERS NOW WORKING IN THIS CITY ON DEPORTATION OF ALIEN COMMUNISTS STOP PROPER ACTION BY SECRETARY OF LABOR AT THIS TIME WILL RID THIS COMMUNITY OF A MENACE THAT HAS CAUSED ENDLESS TROUBLE TO LAW ABIDING AMERICAN CITIZENS
>
> VINCE JAEGER EXALTED BPOE LODGE 1440

Right on schedule, the Santa Fe Chief pulled into the depot in front of El Navajo Hotel. The steam whistle shrieked and the steel wheels screamed to a stop. After the black-suited conductor hopped down and placed the step-down stand on the concrete, Mr. A. L. Wirin stepped off the train.

I was about twenty feet away under the *viga* and *latilla* overhang in front of the station, but Wirin spotted me and came right over. "Mr. Wade, I presume?"

"Yes, sir, that's me," I said, almost reluctantly. I didn't want to start this off with any false impression of being overly impressed with big-city lawyers and immediately thought I should have skipped the "sir" in my opening salutation.

"Where can we talk?" A. L. asked, without further formality.

"Well, my office is a block and a half, or we can have coffee here in the hotel coffee shop—whatever you like."

"Your office, please. I'm not sure how safe we'll be in public."

What an odd thing to say. Of course we were safe. This was Gallup, not Los Angeles. But as soon as I thought it, I blanched. Here I am meeting a communist lawyer, the day after what might have been a communist riot, and he's telling me that we might not be safe. Shit, he's probably right.

As we were collecting his bags and sending them on into the hotel, Wirin and I watched as dozens of armed men (some in uniform, some not) loaded several groups of prisoners into the last car on the train bound for Santa Fe. All were intent on their business, but one or two looked over at me and the well-dressed stranger. Their curiosity was returned by Wirin, who said that his office had sent him a telegram on the train, saying that the "deportations" had started.

"They're not being deported, Mr. Wirin; they're being detained for their own safety in Santa Fe."

"Make it A. L., please, and I'd like to call you Billy. But let me ask you, what legal basis can possibly exist for transporting citizens to the penitentiary before they have even had a confrontational hearing or an arraignment in a court of law?"

"Most folks hereabout call me Billy Wade, my whole name, as though it were just my first name, so I guess that's what I'm mostly used to. As to your question, there's no legal basis, but the point is that the prisoners are safer up there than they are here. Feelings are real high around here."

"The point is, my young friend, that even in New Mexico, the constitution protects the workingman from the oppression of the capitalist-controlled officers of the law."

For the second time today, I bristled. I was young, but I wasn't yet and might not ever be Mr. A. L. Wirin's friend. I didn't need a lecture on constitutional law to tell me that moving these people was dangerous but necessary. To change the subject, I asked as we walked up Second Street how Mr. Wirin came to be here so fast, seeing as how the riot just happened yesterday.

In his most lawyerlike tone, A. L. responded: "Well, now, we don't really know that it was a riot, do we? But to be more responsive, my sponsoring organization, that is, the International Defense League, was contacted yesterday within an hour of the firing of the shots, and I was asked to come here posthaste and assume responsibility for the defense of those who will surely be convicted unless a massive intervention occurs."

I knew of A. L. Wirin by reputation but not exactly what he did for the IDL.

"Are you an employee of the International Defense League or what? I guess I'm not sure what it is, come to think of it."

"Actually, I'm general counsel for the American Civil Liberties Union in California, but our office is often contacted by the International Defense League to work on cases of mutual interest. You know about the Sacco and Vanzetti case, I presume. That's one where both organizations worked for the defense of the workingmen charged with crimes they didn't commit. This case might be the same. That's why you'll see a sense of urgency in what we have to do over the next few days."

As we reached the corner and waited for the traffic, A. L. went on: "I believe the first call was from a Mrs. Julia Bartol. Do you know her?"

"I don't know her to speak to, but I do know of her. I understand she and her husband, Joe, are very active in the labor movement and have been instrumental in organizing the National Miners Union. Maybe you can satisfy my curiosity on that. Is it part of the Communist Party or not?"

Rather than being put off by the question, A. L. seemed flattered to be asked. "The National Miners Union was initially a subset of the American Communist Party, but it has moved on to have its own identity as its membership has grown. Some are party members, but some are not. The American Communist Party also established and funded the International Defense League to defend the rights of workingmen to organize and join a union other than Mr. John L. Lewis's United Mine Workers. But to get to your precise question, the National Miners Union is not entirely controlled by the party any more than the United Mine Workers is entirely controlled by the mine owners. But there are more capitalists in the United Mine Workers, just as there are more communists in the National Miners Union. I would be pleased to be more comprehensive over dinner, if you would be so kind as to join Mrs. Bartol and myself, and perhaps others."

I avoided answering the dinner question by announcing that my office was just there, up over the bank on the corner of Second Street and Coal.

"Isn't it near here that those men were shot?" asked A. L.

"Well, the riot occurred in the alley back of here, but things started right down there about half a block," I said as I pointed west on Coal past the American Bar on down to Judge Bickel's court. "One of my best friends, a deputy, was shot and may die. In fact, I'd best beg off for dinner and check on him in the hospital."

As we climbed the stairs to my second-floor office, A. L. asked, "Has your friend told you who shot the sheriff? Wait, before you answer that, I guess we had best talk about our relationship because I wouldn't want to compromise any confidential relationship you might have with your friend, the deputy. Are you representing his interests or that of his family, or is it just a social relationship?"

I let that go and ushered Mr. Wirin into my office, where I got right to the point. "Mr. Wirin, I'm not sure why your office asked me to meet you, but I hope you understand that I have a lot of friends who are not fond of your National Miners Union, and I wouldn't feel comfortable in undertaking representation of a group based on political ideologies that are radical or foreign based."

A. L. didn't appear offended and responded in a direct and friendly voice. "We had only a little time to seek out local counsel, and we quickly learned that there are no lawyers in Gallup active in party affairs and none who are likely to ascribe to our political ideologies. No, my young friend, we do not expect you to share our passion for the workingman; we seek only your counsel on local procedure. You will not be asked to sponsor our position, just to assist us in clearing the way to the courthouse so that the men who will no doubt be bound over for trial can get one that is as fair as can be had under racially charged and politically motivated circumstances. You are aware that your Sheriff Roberts is engaged in, as we speak, a massive violation of the Fourth Amendment in a thinly disguised effort to seek out and identify members of the Communist Party under the ruse of seeking evidence on the whereabouts of a certain gun allegedly lost by one of the sheriff's deputies at the scene of the shootings."

Although I was now more uncomfortable than before, I didn't mean to sound angry, but I'm sure I did. "Jesus H. Christ, man, you just got here ten minutes ago, the riot just happened yesterday morning, the investigation is barely begun, and no one has been charged, even though warrants have been issued. It seems to me you're jumping to lots of conclusions based on lots of rumors from people who are of questionable veracity. That's not how I practice law, and I'm not at all sure that I can be of any assistance to you on 'local procedure,' as you put it."

I hadn't intended to make a speech, but A. L. Wirin seemed to expect it. He paused and waited for me to continue, so I did. "Bobcat Wilson is as tough as mule hide, but he's shot up and may die. Sheriff Mack had no politics to speak of, and he's dead. Sheriff Dee may have close connections to the mines, but he's a man of honor and he is *not* out there arresting people on a ruse."

"Mr. Wade, I'm not the enemy; I'm just a lawyer looking for local counsel. Tell me what you know about the missing gun."

"I can tell you what the boys over at the American Bar were talking about last night. As I understand it, the gun that they're looking for is a unique weapon, and there's good reason to believe that someone in that crowd may have copped it off old Hoy as he was clubbed to the ground. The thinking is that it was used to kill the sheriff and wound my friend, his deputy. That will all get sorted out and proper procedures will be followed. Besides, it's not clear to me just what your role is in this. Has one of the men who are under arrest retained you to defend him?"

Wirin looked thoughtful and waited a full minute before he responded. When he did, his words came out measured and calm. "Billy Wade, I owe you an apology. I assumed you had no passion for my politics, but I was wrong in my assumption that you lacked passion for the situation you and I are in. To the contrary, you are just the right lawyer I need to assist me."

I took a deep breath myself. "Mr. Wirin, we've been here five minutes and don't seem to be talking about the same case. Why do you think I'm the right lawyer?"

"Because you will question my every move, and that will ensure good legal positioning. You will make sure that I am objective in assessing the strength of the opposition, and that is always important in a case like this. Most important, you know and respect the men who will build the case against my clients, and that knowledge will be invaluable in building a defense to keep them out of the death house in Santa Fe based on their ideology and their race.

"As for who has retained me, I can only tell you that there are, as we speak, hundreds of committees all over this country, seeking dollars to support the representation of those already arrested and on their way, in cattle cars, to your state penitentiary in Santa Fe. Will you assist us? You don't have to like us or join in our beliefs; we ask only that you make available to us your able legal counsel and that you share your long-held beliefs and knowledge of Gallup and its people."

I stared at Mr. Wirin and said, in as measured a tone as I could muster: "Mr. Wirin, I really have to make a quick phone call. Could I just ask you to have a seat out in the waiting room? Miss Susan will get you a cup of coffee, and we can continue this in a minute or two."

Wirin went out, and I made my pretextural phone call. I called Mary Ann, knowing that she was supervising her homeroom students and couldn't take the call. Billy Wade, Billy Wade, what the fuck are you doing, I thought. My ethics and my instincts are telling me that I should undertake this because maybe he's right. This might become a first-class witch-hunt because money and property are at the bottom of it. But on the other hand, how can I take a case that might put me in a courtroom where Bobcat, if he lives, will be on the stand?

Could I ever cross-examine him? What if his testimony hurt one of my clients? Whoa, Nelly. I don't even have a client; all this guy is asking is a little help on local procedure. I can do that and cross the cross-examination bridge later.

Those thoughts took a few minutes to bounce around in my head. A. L. Wirin waited patiently in the outer room. I expect he guessed that I needed time more than I needed to make a phone call. When I buzzed Miss Susan to have him come in, he smiled and waited for my answer.

"A. L., I'm still not sure why you need me, but at least for now, I'll give you what help I can."

A. L. Wirin looked genuinely pleased and held out his hand to seal the bargain. "Thank you, Billy Wade. You won't be well paid, but we won't embarrass you."

As though he had read my mind, he added: "And you won't have to face your friend in court. When the case gets to court, I'll try it."

Sheriff Roberts looked at Assistant District Attorney C. R. McIntosh with that hard stare that so many had faced since yesterday's shooting. From his side of the desk in the McKinley County Court Building, McIntosh wondered how Dee could be so matter-of-fact about killing two men and losing his best friend in a gun battle.

"What difference does it make that the bastard's dead? That doesn't change what he did. He killed Mack, he damn near killed Bobcat, and he tried to kill me. I want him number one on the charge or the information or whatever in hell you call it."

McIntosh thought over his answer because he was facing that hard stare and wanted to sound supportive as well as legally correct. "It's called a criminal information. We have to file that or else convene a grand jury, and that will take a week or so. I'll file it based on your sworn complaint. But Dee, I just wanted you to know that listing Solomon L. Esquibel as the first name on the information will strike Judge Otero as odd. Mr. Esquibel is dead, and we don't normally charge dead people with crimes.

"Incidentally, your sworn complaint doesn't include Navarro. Since he was the focus of everything and is now a fugitive, shouldn't we be naming him in the information as well?"

Dee Roberts had already had this conversation with his brother Bob, so his answer was ready. "Navarro is a long-gone little turd. He's probably across the Rio Grande by now and we've seen the last of him. Good goddamn riddance. I'll hear that chant 'We want Navarro' for as long as I live, and if I ever catch the little turd, I'll bring him to trial on the arrest warrant that Senator Vogel swore out. But he was in my jail when those redbirds had their conspiracy meeting and he was in my custody when they shot Mack and Bobcat. So I didn't swear him out on the murder complaint. Do you think we can tie him to it somehow? If you do, then add the little turd's name to the list; it don't make no never mind to me. I'd settle for getting the rest of his kind back across the Rio Grande as long as we get the shooters. Navarro may be a turd, but he wasn't a shooter. Those are the ones I want on the list. The shooters."

"We'll do it your way, at least until Judge Otero tells us otherwise," responded McIntosh.

But Dee wasn't quite through. He said: "The record should be clear starting today that every last man and woman in that alley is going to pay for what they did, one way or the other. And while we're setting things straight, between you and me I don't care one goddamned bit whether they're Mex or Slav or any other damn thing. They're communists, and we're going to get them out of our town before they start another riot and kill more lawmen. Now, what more do you need of me this morning? I've got warrants to serve and I'm going to find Hoy's gun if I have to rip down every goddamn shack in Chihuahuaita."

McIntosh took a deep breath before plunging into what he knew was a sore subject. "That reminds me, Dee, what's the story on Hoy's gun? Why do you think that it was used on Mack?"

"I don't know that for a fact today, but I do know that hog-leg gun of Hoy's was one of a kind. He had it on him when they clubbed him down. He never fired it, but it had a real different kind of sound, and I believe I heard it just as Mack was dropping to the ground. I figure maybe one of those little red bastards scooped it up and blasted Mack with it. Anyhow, it's missing, and it's important evidence because when we find it, then we can tie whoever has it directly to the scene of the shooting. So even if it wasn't the murder gun, it's damn important."

McIntosh always enjoyed the colorful jargon of the sheriff and his deputies, but "hog leg" as a description of a gun wasn't all that clear. "Why was Hoy's gun called a hog leg?"

"Well, that was what Bobcat called it more than the rest of us. Bobcat allowed as how it was about the size of a hog's leg. Hoy never did have a holster for it; just stuck it in his waistband. Bobcat said more than once that Hoy was more likely to shoot himself just getting the damn thing out than he was some criminal. Thing is, that could have happened in the alley yesterday. Hoy was clubbed right out of his mind, and Bobcat was next to him when he got all shot up. Maybe Bobcat's prediction came true, and Hoy's gun ended up blasting both Mack and Bobcat."

"Sheriff," Assistant District Attorney McIntosh said in his most serious voice, "if that is what happened, then it could be Hoy himself who was responsible for Mack's death."

"Now wait a goddamn minute, I didn't mean Hoy did it; I meant that it might be Hoy's gun. I'm sure that if it was, it was in the hands of one of those little brown commies in the alley. They were there to free Navarro and shoot the lawmen that was guarding him. That's what they did, and when I find Hoy's gun, I'll prove it."

Dee Roberts was, as everyone knew, *qué mucho hombre!*

The die was cast in Gallup the day after the shooting of Sheriff Carmichael. Assistant District Attorney McIntosh filed his criminal information on April 5, 1935, listing the same thirty citizens in the same order as the complaint that Sheriff Roberts had filed the day before. During the next three days Chihuahuaita was turned upside down with deputies and lawmen of all types looking for evidence, suspects, communist literature, and, of course, Hoy's gun.

On April 8 Sheriff Roberts filed a second complaint in which he swore under oath that eleven men "unlawfully, knowingly, willfully, and feloniously murdered M. R. Carmichael." His petition to the court requested that this new list of eleven men be "arrested and dealt with according to the law." The eleven new names on the growing list of suspects were men who had three things in common. They were out-of-work miners. They belonged to the National Miners Union. And they lived in Chihuahuaita. Some of them might even have been in the alley the day of the riot, but that was somewhat beside the point.

Gallup had itself a real conspiracy, and the law was hard after it. Judge M. A. Otero dismissed three men from the criminal information on April 22; three days later, he dismissed one more. This last one was just a bit ironic because it was Victor Campos. After all, it was Victor Campos's house that started this whole thing—Navarro was helping Campos, and now Navarro was nowhere to be found. So neither of them was charged with finishing what they started.

Judge Otero took charge, and it didn't please everyone. He seemed to be taking seriously the motion for change of venue. That motion was based on the assumption that the people of Gallup couldn't give the men who killed our sheriff a fair trial. Like the rest of the lawyers in town, I knew he would have to take it seriously. But feelings were high, and that made for bad decisions.

While that motion was pending, Judge Otero cleaned up the official record a bit. He dismissed case numbers 1299, 1300, and 1301 because the DA and the sheriff kept filing new papers on more and more people. He also ordered that Joe Bartol be released on bond. The NMU put up the $7,500 in cash for Mr. Bartol's bail. Most everyone in town said it was because he was a Slav, not a Spanish American. In fairness, he was the main organizer for the union. It was rumored that his wife, Julia (who had also been arrested), brought in those "fancy-schmancy" lawyers from Los Angeles and New York.

Mr. A. L. Wirin went to Santa Fe on April 7 in the company of Mrs. Bartol to take part in the *habeas corpus* proceedings before Judge Otero. Wirin didn't ask me to accompany him. Judge Otero was holding those hearings up there because Gallup, along with Santa Fe and Aztec, made up the First Judicial District. In addition, all the men and women subject to the motion had been transported by cattle car from Gallup to Santa Fe.

The most serious allegation in the *habeas* petition was that the arrests in Chihuahuaita were made with substantially more force than the situation warranted. While the actual number of men and women arrested jumped around a lot depending on whom you were talking to, there were at least sixty-eight men in the pen up there in Santa Fe. A fair number of them were bruised and bloody from the beatings by the armed so-called special deputies that Sheriff Roberts deputized to serve his warrants. In fact, it got so bad later on in May that the attorney general of New Mexico, Mr. Frank Patton himself, joined in with our district attorney here in Gallup and filed a legal paper called an "affidavit of judicial bias." They charged in their paper that our very own Judge M. A. Otero "cannot, according to the belief of each of said attorneys . . . preside over the same with impartiality." Imagine that: a Spanish-American judge cannot be impartial in a trial of Spanish Americans in Gallup.

Shortly after that, on June 4, 1935, the defense lawyers and the prosecutors filed a joint stipulation saying that they could not agree on a new judge for the case. That meant that the chief justice of the New Mexico Supreme Court would make the choice. His choice was Judge James B. McGhee from Roswell, New Mexico. For his first official act in the case, Judge McGhee signed an order to arraign the prisoners on the morning of June 4. His order listed nine of the ten men who would go on trial (Juan Ochoa, Leandro Velarde, Agustin Calvillo, Manuel Avitia, Victorio Correo, Gregorio Correo, Willie Gonzales, Rafael Gomez and Serapio Sosa). He didn't mention the tenth man (Joe Bartol) because he was out on bail. The rest were still in the penitentiary.

These ten men became known as the "Gallup 10," which confused folks since the national press insisted on calling the case the Gallup 14. Right after he arraigned those men, Judge Otero granted the defense motion for a change of venue. Mr. Wirin was hoping for a move to Albuquerque or Santa Fe but didn't get it. Judge McGhee moved the trial to Aztec, New Mexico. Aztec was in the same judicial district as Gallup but had fewer Spanish Americans and hardly any communists. It was mostly a white community of farmers and ranchers who took life as it came to them—hard and cold. As far as I was concerned, the prosecutors couldn't have got a better venue for a trial like this one. I told A. L. that in the last conversation I ever had with him.

I was still having doubts about my decision to help with the defense of whoever ultimately got charged with the murder of Sheriff Carmichael when David Levinson called me from Santa Fe. Mr. Levinson was on "assignment" from the International Defense League from his law office in Philadelphia. As the phone call progressed, I thought that the only thing more pompous than an LA lawyer was a Philadelphia lawyer.

"Yes, Mr. Wade," Levinson said in a fast, East Coast sort of way, "I will be assuming the role of lead counsel for the forty-eight men and women imprisoned here for their political beliefs. I must say, I get an entirely different picture of New Mexico from the press and the people of Santa Fe as opposed to what passes for journalism in the *Gallup Independent*. What do you know about Judge McGhee?"

I was finding this conversation as troubling as my first meeting with A. L. Wirin. Where did these guys get off, rolling in here from LA and Philadelphia and God knew where else and crapping on Gallup like it was the Deep South or something? As an Anglo in a Hispanic state, and certainly a Hispanic town, I felt not only welcome but genuinely at home.

"You know what, I think maybe you guys are making too much of the fact that the defendants in this case are Hispanic and the judge is an Anglo. Judge McGhee has a good reputation and is considered fair by everyone who comes before him. He has tried many a man and treats them all the same, no matter whether they are here as New Mexicans or here from Old Mexico with lots of vowels in their names. As for the press, I won't make excuses for the *Gallup Independent* because they haven't got very much of this case right so far. But it seems to me that they do express the point of view of lots of people here—Spanish, Mexican, white, or whatever color you can think of. Whoever shot the sheriff and blasted the deputies ought to be tried for it. If they did it and if it was premeditated, then it's a capital case, brown skin or not."

After another ten minutes of telephone sparring, Levinson hung up. I assume he went back to the fascinating matter of race relations in New Mexico. He told me he had picked up several "intriguing papers" at the University of New Mexico in Albuquerque. He also had a stack of recent bills that were rammed through the state legislature, one of which was Senator Vogel's bill making it easier to evict tenants.

Taken as a package, I was starting to think that this was more about money than skin color. But for him, the racial and political angles were far more suitable. He and Wirin wanted a political statement to be made in this trial that would establish the rights of the workingman. The racial or political mind-set was far easier to attack than the mind-set of simple greed, or fair profit, for that matter. I turned my mind back to the agenda that someone had prepared for the meeting of the Gallup Defense Committee set for this coming Thursday, May 2.

By the time May 2 arrived, Julia Bartol, Katherine Gay, and Ida Ruth Estaban had all been doing their part to make sure that the Gallup 14, as they still insisted on calling the case, was kept in the national limelight. That evening those three women waited on the siding for the Santa Fe Chief to arrive from Santa Fe by way of Albuquerque. They would have stood out in most crowds but were easy to spot in Gallup. They were sternly dressed but in a fashionable sort of way. Tailored dresses, new coats, and very different hats. Different from one another, that is, not different from other women at the station. It was as though they consulted one another before selecting their hats du jour.

Mrs. Bartol was larger by half than either of the other two. The other women weren't just slim; they were trim. It occurred to me that they were so serious about organized labor and politics that food had little attraction for them. Mrs. Bartol, on the other hand, clearly enjoyed food for the body as well as food for thought.

These women had the responsibility of making sure the press had sufficient material to keep this story alive and on the front page. The party newspaper, the *Daily Worker,* had been running regular feature articles, and several New York daily newspapers had picked up the cause. Even the Associated Press stringer in Albuquerque was passing on their daily releases about the oppression of the striking miners by the mine owners in the Gallup coalfields.

The rally last week in New York's Central Park was very successful. It was reported that 7,000 "citizens" attended. Most of them dropped money in the hats passed by the party faithful. It was amusing to Julia Bartol that most New York women would have found life in New Mexico unbearably common but would still come up with dollars to support the grand cause of the party. She wanted to make sure this money was properly spent. It should go to lawyers they could trust to carry the message. That meant none of it could be spent on the likes of me or anyone else in Gallup. It should also go to the investigators from Philadelphia and Chicago so that the real facts of fascism, racism, and greed could be brought out in the trial. If there was anything left, it should, of course, be used for living expenses of the families of the men charged.

These weighty matters were being discussed in whispered tones in the lobby of El Navajo Hotel. The three women were waiting for David Levinson and Robert Minor, another International Defense League lawyer, to arrive. Then they would all go to the eagerly awaited meeting of the Gallup Defense League.

Robert Minor looked out of place with David Levinson, a pompous International Defense League lawyer from Philadelphia. Mr. Levinson's obvious good grooming sharply contrasted with Minor's almost slovenly appearance. Levinson's tie wasn't quite as jaunty as A. L. Wirin's (who had just arrived), but it was bright and expensive looking. Levinson's East Coast fedora and his long-stick umbrella looked out of place against Minor's workingman's cap and his rumpled raincoat. Levinson and Minor were about the same size, but where Minor slouched, Levinson seemed to puff out. All in all, it was clear that Levinson wanted to look important (even if he wasn't) and Minor was oblivious to what he looked like (which he thought was unimportant).

The three women had much in common with the three men. All of them were smart, educated, and dedicated. All six were the kind of people who you might not notice on a crowded Santa Fe street but who would stand out in a Gallup bar. Like the men, the three women smoked cigarettes but didn't expect any of the men to light theirs. This was a highbrow crowd; no doubt about it.

On this chilly May evening, the room was one of the best Gallup had to offer. The lobby of El Navajo Hotel was elegant in its depiction of Indian art and artifacts. The furniture was what would later become known as Southwestern—massive, dark oak, leather covered. It seemed to fit right in with the Navajo rugs generously spread throughout the room. But it wasn't a place where one could count on privacy. Open rooms rarely gave people who talked in secret any comfort.

The big clock on the south side of the lobby, facing the tracks out in front, struck a chime at a quarter past the hour. Minor looked at his pocket watch to check the accuracy of the local clock, without thinking that this was another sign of his East Coast superiority.

The brightly lit room contrasted with the now full darkness outside. No trains would be coming in until tomorrow, so the crowd was just what was left over from the dining room. The meeting of the Gallup Defense League continued for an hour or so in the lobby.

"Mr. Levinson," asked Mrs. Bartol, "how's the fund-raising going back east? I mean, are we going to be able to get enough money to mount the defense out here?"

Levinson knew she meant well but didn't want to talk about such things in a public dining room. He assumed that Julia Bartol had a car, considering her position and the fact that she was the only one who actually lived in Gallup. He asked: "Mrs. Bartol, would it be possible for us to speak with more privacy in your car?"

"Well, yes, of course, but my old Packard is pretty well caked with clay from my trips out to Gamerco. But if you aren't too picky, we can sure continue this in the car."

Levinson thought she was entitled to the facts about the fund-raising effort. He also wanted to pass on some recent intelligence from Philadelphia. "No, I'm not picky. In fact, this whole town seems to be covered with clay dust, although your permanent sort of wind keeps it moving. I don't mind a little dirt if it will give us a bit more privacy."

A. L. Wirin had retired to his room to work. Katherine Gay demurred, and so did Ida Ruth. So Bob Minor and Levinson escorted Julia Bartol out to the west side of the hotel to the parking lot facing the tracks on one side and Route 66 on the other.

A few minutes after they got into the car, Levinson noticed two cars pull up and stop somewhat to the rear and on the left side of Mrs. Bartol's Packard. They just sat there for about five minutes with their engines running. He took them for "spooners" at first. Just as the reconvened car meeting was winding down, three new cars pulled in beside them at great speed and slid to a stop on either side and in back of Mrs. Bartol's car.

Levinson had sat in the backseat so he could talk to both Mrs. Bartol behind the wheel of her car and Minor in the front passenger seat. He wasn't looking at the rear of the car. Mrs. Bartol was the first to see the men jump out of their cars and run the few feet to hers.

Even the fact that Gallup had been under martial law for weeks could not have prepared them for the sight of men wearing hoods over their heads with holes cut out for eyes and mouth. The masks came down to the shoulders of each man, and what Mrs. Bartol's group could see of the clothes below that told them nothing.

The men seemed to be talking to Levinson when they said: "Come out, you son of a bitch, and keep quiet."

Levinson frantically tried to find the lock button on the driver's side rear door, but it didn't matter. The passenger side door jerked open and he was dragged outside by a man fifty or sixty pounds heavier than he was. The first blows seemed to virtually rain down on his expensive hat as he heard Minor shout, "Help, police! Help, police!"

What happened next was documented in the twenty-five-page affidavit that Minor and Levinson filed with the U.S. Attorney's office two days later—the day they left town for good. Levinson and Minor were dragged out of Mrs. Bartol's car and stuffed into the backseat of two cars with the hooded men. They were beaten up and driven out onto the Navajo Reservation near Tohatchi to a place called Coyote Canyon. After a little more banging on their heads and a clear instruction that "you sons a bitches better get out of here and never come back," they were left to fend for themselves. They spent the bitter-cold night in an abandoned hogan and were found the next morning by a man named Bene Tohe. Tohe took them to the Indian hospital at Tohatchi.

The first call Levinson made from Tohatchi was to the office of Governor Clyde Tingley in Santa Fe. Somewhat to his surprise, the governor took the call after his secretary explained the situation. Levinson reminded the governor of their conversation just a week ago in his office; Governor Tingley was surprised but not shocked at what had happened to the easterners. That's the sort of thing one might expect over there in Gallup. It's a rough place, he said. Governor Tingley tried to sound calm. "Stay there; I'll send a state police car and some armed guards out to get you."

At the hospital in Gallup, Minor and Levinson were poked and prodded and photographed to confirm their injuries. As things turned out, it didn't matter much. The state police wondered why the Gallup police didn't show much interest in the kidnapping, but in the end, neither seemed to care very much.

Two days later Levinson and Minor went back to the Indian reservation with their new state police escorts and four newspapermen. Mr. Tohe met them at Coyote Canyon. With his help they backtracked to the point where their kidnappers dumped them.

Somewhat to the surprise of the state police, they found several hoods left behind by the abductors, along with Levinson's hat and a noose of rope. Close by were Mr. Minor's sunglasses and the belt of his raincoat. All of this was examined by the state police but given over to Levinson's custody for the trip back to Gallup. When they arrived in Gallup, Assistant District Attorney McIntosh appeared at Levinson's room at El Navajo Hotel and demanded that he relinquish custody of all items found in the desert to him.

Facing the assistant district attorney, Levinson said: "Well, Mr. McIntosh, we both know the law. Our abduction occurred within the city limits of Gallup, but we were illegally transported against our will onto an Indian reservation. That act invokes the jurisdiction of the federal government and the Mann Act. It is our intention to give our evidence and our testimony to the United States Attorney in Santa Fe. That is consistent with my conversation with Governor Tingley."

McIntosh knew the law, but he also knew that it was important to control this matter and keep it in local hands. The case against the men who killed the sheriff depended on local control. The damn fools who tried to run off these buttinski lawyers could really screw up the works. With this in mind, McIntosh laid it out for Levinson. McKinley County has jurisdiction—give me the evidence or I'll lock you up.

As it happened, the jurisdictional crisis was averted because Judge Otero arrived back in town that very Sunday afternoon and they delivered the evidence to him in his chambers. He impounded everything and turned it over to the custody of the court reporter, Mr. Bennage.

The next thing Levinson and Minor knew, their state police guards were told to withdraw. Levinson called the governor but was told that he could no longer justify a police detachment now that they were back in town and no longer in danger. Governor Tingley told Levinson that Officers Dean and Irish would be happy to escort him and Minor to Santa Fe. Governor Tingley made it real clear. They should both come to Santa Fe and stay there or leave the state altogether.

Mr. Minor and Mr. Levinson returned to Santa Fe in fear for their lives. At the end of May they made arrangements to go to Philadelphia, where they negotiated with Colonel William J. Donovan of the Donovan & Leisure firm in New York City to take over as lead counsel in the Gallup 14 case. With that accomplished, Levinson closed his book on Gallup and its police establishment. Levinson's last act was to tell his friend A. L. Wirin that he, too, should leave New Mexico.

A. L. Wirin could scarcely believe what was happening to the fine team of lawyers and investigations put together by the ACLU and International Defense League for the Gallup 14 case. He couldn't blame Levinson and Minor for leaving, but he still didn't understand why the governor's escort had been so abruptly withdrawn.

When Levinson called him, Wirin called the governor. Wirin publicly reported the governor's resolution: "Mr. Tingley told me that his hands were tied and that he felt he had a duty to the people to see the case tried without outside agitation. I asked him if my life was also in danger, and he said that he couldn't comment other than to say that New Mexico had the right to charge its own and to defend its own."

Governor Tingley made it clear that if the out-of-state money was withdrawn, the local courts would appoint counsel for the defense since the men charged were as poor as Job's turkey.

Wirin swore that Governor Tingley more or less promised him that if he withdrew from the case, the governor would use his influence to see to it that those men had the best legal talent available. He proved to be a man of his word.

four

SIMMS AND MODRALL

New Mexico in the thirties was certainly not short of talent in the lawyer department. That's one of the reasons I came back here to practice after three years in San Francisco. We had a small population, but we had big vistas, a fair amount of money, and a long history of attracting some of the best lawyers in the country.

John F. Simms was at that time a shining example of how good the state's trial lawyers were. A graduate of Vanderbilt University Law School, he began his law practice in Albuquerque in 1913. He was appointed to the New Mexico Supreme Court in 1929 and served two years as an associate justice. But for John Simms, the pit of the court was preferable to the bench itself. He resumed his private practice in Albuquerque in 1931 to get back into the courtroom he so dearly loved.

New Mexico also picked good men to prosecute cases. Our attorney general, Frank Patton, was first rate, and his chief deputy, J. R. Modrall, was considered a crackerjack trial lawyer. Gallup could also take pride in itself because David Chavez, our district attorney, was no stranger to the courtroom. Unlike some DAs in other small towns, Chavez wasn't merely a politician; he was a stand-up lawyer.

Hugh B. Woodward was the man picked by Judge McGhee to serve as co-counsel for the defense. He was a former U.S. Attorney and had prosecuted a large number of major cases. But this was his first time in defense of a major capital case. He and John Simms were a good team, although Judge McGhee might not have always agreed.

John Simms easily guessed why his old friend A. L. Zinn, the chief justice of the New Mexico Supreme Court, insisted that he come to Santa Fe on such short notice. As he drove north from his law office in Albuquerque he pondered the not so mysterious message left with his secretary: "John, you should have stayed on the court. Then you could have appointed someone else to take on the defense of the biggest case New Mexico has ever seen. Get on up here as soon as you can."

There was only one case his old friend could have in mind. Chief Justice Zinn had an ironic connection to the Gallup 14 case. As a resident of Gallup, he was elected to serve in the New Mexico state senate. He was also the district attorney in Gallup for eight years before being elected to the New Mexico Supreme Court in 1932.

Like everyone else in New Mexico, he had been following the case in the newspapers. In addition, the remarkable pretrial proceedings were causing great controversy among the trial lawyers of the state. As best he understood it, a great deal of money had been raised back east for some high-priced legal talent, but the folks over in Gallup hadn't taken kindly to outside lawyers butting in their business.

As he passed the Placitas turnoff and headed north to Santa Fe, he thought about how he could avoid the appointment as defense counsel. The challenge of defending such an important case was tempting, but he wasn't inclined to take the case if what he had been hearing about it was true. It was one thing to defend a murder case and quite another to take on some political cause that seemed to enamor the so-called elite society in Santa Fe.

The ride up the Rio Grande valley was just the place to mull over what he knew about the case. Earlier that morning he had stopped by the University of New Mexico library and asked for a collection of recent newspapers on the Gallup 14 case. It was being called that because, although hundreds of men and women had been arrested and imprisoned within a day or two of the riot, only eleven men and three women made it through the preliminary hearings. The papers repeated the essential facts about the McKinley County sheriff being shot in what seemed to be crossfire in an alley.

He had followed the early coverage but didn't keep up with it once it seemed to become so political. Reading the *Gallup Independent* made him think the case was open and shut. Reading *The Santa Fe New Mexican* made him doubtful. Reading the *Daily Worker* made him laugh because they seemed to be reporting on an entirely different case. Actually, he was surprised that the University of New Mexico even had copies of the *Daily Worker.* Communist newspapers weren't exactly common reading in New Mexico. In fact, like most everyone else, he was surprised at all the connections there seemed to be between the union activity in Gallup and the communist movement in more "liberal" parts of the country.

He knew Frank Patton and J. R. Modrall to be first-rate men, even if they were trying to put your client in the electric chair. So he was prepared to take it on if, and only if, he had a solid man at his side and if the high-paid out-of-state help would step aside.

He parked in front of the white stucco building and walked up one flight to the private chambers of the members of the court. Chief Justice Zinn occupied a corner suite for his chambers in the majestic old Supreme Court building in Santa Fe.

"Make yourself to home, John. As you can see, I haven't changed things much since you moved out."

John Simms looked around at what once was his office and smiled to himself. It was very different now that he was a working lawyer again. His office in Albuquerque out on Fourth Street was pretty tame compared to the trappings of the highest court in the state. The paintings on the walls were different and the framed certificates had different names on them, but everything else in this beautiful room was almost the same.

"I suppose you've guessed why I asked you to come up here," the chief justice said. "Judge McGhee wants to appoint you as lead counsel for the defense and Hugh Woodward as your co-counsel. I told him I would talk to you about it. Frank Patton is assuming personal control of the prosecution, although he will rely on J. R. Modrall and David Chavez for a lot of the work. The defense seems to be mostly big-city boys from back east, and they could turn the trial into a national spectacle if we aren't careful. Will you take the case?"

As usual, John Simms paused before answering. His ability to assess both the legal significance and the political consequences of most situations had served him well. "First, is there anything to accept? The men who were bound over already have lawyers, although I'm not sure where things stand after that fracas over in Gallup involving the man from Los Angeles—Levinson or something like that. I've also heard the barroom rumor that the famous Colonel Donovan is coming in from Wall Street to lead the defense for something called the International Defense League, which might be connected to the American Communist Party. Anyway, if that's all true, why is Judge McGhee going to appoint anyone to the case?"

The chief justice's answer was crisp and to the point. "John, these men are indigent and entitled to appointed counsel at the expense of the state. Colonel Donovan won't show, although he's got some youngsters out here spending the money raised in the rallies back east. I have assigned the job of trying the case to Jim McGhee. As you know, he's a fine man, and the folks in Roswell can spare him for a week or two. As a technical matter, the trial judge must appoint the defense team in a *pro bono* case, but I've been in close touch with him about the case because this is so important for everyone. The bottom line is that these men are New Mexicans. The governor and this court want New Mexico to defend its own."

"Your Honor, I'm flattered to be considered, but I have a lot of questions and will have to sit down with Frank Patton and Dick Modrall before I can give you an answer. My questions go to the merits of the case, so I really ought not to bring them up with you. Would it be all right if I got back to you tomorrow?"

"Of course, John; take whatever time you need, but please remember that there's a lot more involved here than just trying another murder case." The chief justice leaned back in his padded leather chair and frowned. "This is a conspiracy case, and there are some unique legal questions involved. It'll be fine if you take a day or two, but we really need to make sure that these men are properly defended before things get out of hand. I'll call Jim McGhee and tell him we've talked and you're considering it. Give my best to Anna."

As he walked down the hall past the offices of the other justices, Simms could see many of the people he had worked with during his two years on the Supreme Court. While he missed the intellectual challenge, he didn't miss the isolation and the long hours spent poring over legal briefs. When you're a member of the state's highest court, no one asks you to lunch and no one makes small talk or passes on rumors about lawyers. That was one of the many reasons he decided to leave the bench and go back into the courtroom as an advocate, not a referee.

All in all, he was happy with his decision to return to private practice, although this Gallup case might give him pause to reconsider his decision. He was intrigued over the chief justice's description of the case as a "conspiracy" case. Maybe the prosecution was going to use New Mexico's rather unusual felony-murder statute as the primary prosecution theory. If it was up to me, he thought, I'd try it as a straight murder case, but then again, maybe they're a little short on evidence.

He left the Supreme Court Building and walked across the mall to the AG's office. He might as well see if Frank was in and could spare him a few minutes to talk about the case.

"John, it's nice to see you," Frank Patton said with that perpetual smile he wore for all public occasions. "What brings you back to Santa Fe? Are you reconsidering your decision to leave the court?" Frank Patton was a good lawyer, a better politician, and one of the best at knowing every piece of gossip and rumor that surrounded the bar and the judiciary. He was a solidly built man with bright but somewhat narrow eyes. He made it a point to look right at you, almost through you, when he talked to you. If you were on his side of the case, that kind of attention was comforting, but if he was against you, his focused glare tended to make some folks nervous.

John thought the anteroom to the New Mexico attorney general's office wasn't the best place to get into his business, so he said: "Well, I'm just a working lawyer now, trying to make ends meet. I thought if I came up to the capital city of Santa Fe, I might just scare up a case or two. There's one in particular that I'd like to ask you about if you have a few minutes."

Frank's focused gaze faltered a bit, but he quickly recovered and said: "By God, I have a feeling that you've been across the mall, conversing with your replacement on the Supreme Court. I have a sneaking suspicion that he's pushing you to take on the defense of New Mexico's biggest case. Let's go into my office and talk about my plans to prosecute those boys from Gallup."

After they were seated, Frank got right to the point. "John, you should know right from the get-go that I intend to convict those boys whether you're in the courtroom or not. Good as you are, not even you can save them from the electric chair for the killing and maiming they did 'for the cause' over in Gallup. This is by-God New Mexico, not Russia, and we follow the rule of law here."

John thought, That's a pretty strident position for the AG to take straight out of the box. Maybe this was a case that really needed defending after all. "Look, I take your point about this not being Russia, but don't you think we ought to give those boys a trial before we strap them in the chair? Maybe the lawmen over in Gallup got some innocent men mixed in with the bunch, or maybe the hysteria over all this Communist Party stuff got in the way of proper procedure. I only know what I've heard about the case, and I haven't decided to take it on yet. What can you tell me about the evidence? What are your plans for the felony murder statute? Are you going to try it as a straight murder case, or is it really going to be tried on a criminal conspiracy theory?"

"I'll be happy to jaw with you about the case in general terms, but I'm sure you understand that I can't be very specific until you're here in the official capacity as a defense lawyer." The AG met John's gaze directly. "But let's not stand on ceremony. Here's how I see the case coming down."

Frank Patton went on and on about the strength of the case against the ten men finally bound over for trial. He explained that there were actually two cases set for trial before Judge McGhee. The main one was against the ten men directly charged with the murder of the sheriff. The other one was a companion case against four other people who were there at the time of the killing but were charged only with aiding the prisoner, a Mr. Navarro, to escape.

Frank Patton's overview of the case took more than an hour to relate, not counting the many questions that John put to him as he told his side of it. In fact, all things considered, John got more out of Frank by just asking "about" the case. Had he been here officially as a defense lawyer, Frank might not have been so forthcoming. Of course, they would have to work out the exchange of evidence and the delivery of exculpatory material, which the prosecution was legally and ethically bound to turn over to the defense before the trial of any case. But that could wait.

"So you're going to try it with Dick Modrall and David Chavez?" John asked. "I know Dick pretty well; I can understand why you want him on board. Tell me about the DA over in Gallup. I know him by sight but have no trial experience with him. Is he a straight shooter?"

"Yes, sir, damn fine man," the AG replied. "He knows the case, and he's worked hard to keep a lid on the emotions in Gallup. The victim was well known and well respected, so the emotions ran pretty high on this one. In addition, the deputies who were beat up and shot up were local men with big families over there. In particular, this 'Bobcat' Wilson, who was shot twice in the riot, will make a strong witness, and David Chavez knows him well. If you take it all in, I'd say this case is about to be nailed down real tight. Your reputation as a winner might take a bruising here. Maybe you ought to pass on this one and let the boys from back east take the hit."

"No, Frank, you've done a good job of explaining just why I have to step in on this one." John Simms stood and nodded thoughtfully. "First off, those boys have rights, and we all have to work hard to see to it that they get a fair shake. Besides, I like the odds on this one. To hear you tell it, first-degree murder convictions are a foregone conclusion. Those kinds of odds are pretty tempting. If the case comes out your way, it will be because you have all the evidence. If the case comes out for the defense, I might be a hero. Either way, it seems like a case that needs defending since you have it all wrapped up in a conviction package with a death-penalty bow on it."

"Well, John, have it your way," Frank replied.

The first thing John did after leaving Frank Patton's office was to stop back by Chief Justice Zinn's office to tell him that he would take the case. That done, he used the hour and a half it took to drive back to Albuquerque to give his newest and biggest case some serious thought.

First on his mental list of things to do was call Hugh Woodward. Assuming, that is, that Hugh got the same sort of arm-twisting from the chief justice as he did. Those boys were up for capital murder; they ought to have at least two "local" lawyers on their side since the prosecution team was about as good as New Mexico had to offer.

So the battle lines were drawn. Getting a stand-up lawyer like John Simms in the case would change things. Not just because he was a lawyer who had a way with juries. I told the crowd in the American Bar that John Simms wasn't a New Mexican by birth, but he had lived here for twenty years and was as New Mexican as a Tennessee transplant could get. He was just what the doctor ordered to make sure that this trial was fair and square. I tried to explain that otherwise there might have been a lot of high-minded talk about the rights of the workingman but not such a close look at the actual evidence. With John Simms in the case, the prosecutors had their work cut out for them. I thought that was a good thing, but the boys in the bar had their doubts. They wanted a fair trial, but they also wanted a conviction.

As for the local prosecution team, Chavez and McIntosh, like most everyone else in town, they thought the outside influence of the National Miners Union was to blame and tended to paint every member with the same guilty brush. On the other hand, the prosecutors from Santa Fe were more or less students of the law and looked at the case as a textbook felony-murder case.

Attorney General Patton and his chief deputy, J. R. "Dick" Modrall, knew that conspiracy was very entertaining for the newspapers but pretty hard to prove in the courtroom. They also knew that the felony-murder rule made sense to judges and folks familiar with the law but was often looked at askance by ordinary men on the jury. I say men because, of course, women didn't sit on juries, particularly in cattle country like Aztec, New Mexico. Needless to say, that rubbed Mary Ann the wrong way.

Aztec was a good deal for the prosecution, given their local politics—extremely rural and conservative. Gallup was a long, 140-mile drive south of Aztec, but the miles weren't as important as the politics. Aztec was in high grass country—a beautiful river, big ranches, and no coal mines. That meant there were no unions and, for damn sure, there was no National Miners Union. The people of Gallup and Aztec did have one thing in common, though—we all thought that the NMU was made up entirely of radicals and communists.

For another thing, most of the miners, even those not in a union, were foreign born, while the people up in Aztec and all through San Juan County were mostly native-born Americans. Of course, some were of Spanish or Mexican descent, but they weren't thought to be from "Old" Mexico. They thought of themselves as New Mexicans and didn't take to causes and such.

To add to the mix of difference, there had been no strife, no riots, and no martial law in Aztec (or anywhere else in San Juan County). That fact alone made it seem like a good place from a prosecution standpoint to try those "radicals" and a good place to get out of, if you were for the defense.

But then again, the defense might like Aztec men on a jury if the state stuck with its conspiracy theory. Country people generally thought you ought not to make everyone responsible for the acts of one or two. If you did something yourself, then you ought to stand up for it, but if you just happened to be along for the ride, so to speak, then maybe you ought not to have to answer for the driver. In other words, the conspiracy theory might not fly so well in a conservative place like Aztec. Back and forth, that's how the bar talk went.

The law requires something called a bill of particulars when the state accuses people of crimes. In this case the state alleged in its bill of particulars:

> First: The Defendants were then and there present, procuring, counseling, aiding, or abetting an unknown person in the perpetration of a felony (an assault with deadly weapons, to wit, pistols, clubs, and hammers), upon M. R. Carmichael, Dee Roberts, Hoy Boggess, and E. L. Wilson, thereby and thus resulting in the killing and murdering of the said M. R. Carmichael as aforesaid in the Information and original bill of particulars.
>
> Second: The Defendants, while engaged in the perpetration of a felony, to wit, aiding or assisting Esiquel Navarro, a prisoner, in escaping or attempting to escape from M. R. Carmichael, Dee Roberts, Hoy Boggess, and E. L. Wilson, who were officers having lawful custody of Navarro, resulting in the killing of M. R. Carmichael.
>
> Third: The Defendants did knowingly combine and conspire with themselves and others and did unite with unknown persons for the purpose of committing a felony, to wit, the escape of Esiquel Navarro, resulting in the killing of M. R. Carmichael.

The prosecutors were quite satisfied with their bill of particulars, but for ordinary folk, a lot of questions weren't answered in that "bill." Mary Ann and I spent long hours debating the importance of legal nuance as posed against the need for clarity. My suggestion that lawyers understood the language of the law was hardly acceptable. As I later learned, she penned a strident critique of the prosecutors' bill of particulars in the wee hours of the morning after I left her apartment.

June 9, 1935

Dear Journal:

Billy Wade is gone, but his tired defense of the law and its so-called bill of particulars is still glaringly with me. There is much about Mr. Chavez's bill (why is it called that, anyhow?) that is ridiculous. For example, the first part said the defendants were all present when the felony was being done with pistols and clubs. How could anyone possibly know that? Were they all there? Did they all have pistols or clubs? Did that actually "result" in the killing of the sheriff?

With the exception of the "radical" press (that is, the *Daily Worker*), no one seems to be asking questions—like what about the ones with clubs and no pistols? No one suggests that Mack Carmichael was clubbed to death. So what difference does it make if one of them had a club? Those not caught up in the politics of it all should be more concerned with who shot Mack, not who might have had a club.

The second part of the bill of particulars says that the defendants were helping Navarro to escape and that "resulted" in the killing of our sheriff. Seems like those are two different things. What if you tried to help Navarro escape and had no thought of killing anybody, least of all the sheriff? Did that kind of act really "result" in the killing of the sheriff?

The third part of that bill just carries on and on. It's unbearably long because it claims the defendants conspired with themselves "and others" to let Navarro escape, "resulting" in the killing of the sheriff. What confuses me is what, exactly, is this case going to be about? Is the state going to try to prove that one of these ten men actually fired the gun that killed Mack Carmichael? If that's the case, does that help the others who didn't actually fire the gun? Or are they just as guilty because they were there in the alley with whoever actually shot the sheriff? If that's the case, do they have to actually agree in advance to kill him, or is it enough to decide in advance to do something else, like help Navarro get free? What if you had no thought of anyone shooting anyone and you were just as surprised as the deputies when the gunfire went off?

Let's say your only idea was to help Navarro or, at least, to show your support for him. Can that alone make you a candidate for the death penalty? That makes the location of the trial very important for a reason no one seems to want to talk about. All the defendants, except Joe Bartol, speak Spanish. One or two of them can converse in English, but the whole trial will have to be translated so that the defendants will know what is being said about them. Up in Aztec, it isn't too likely that anyone on the jury will be a Spanish speaker, so how will anyone on the jury know what the translators are saying? And if it turns out that none of the defense lawyers speak Spanish, how can they be sure the translators are saying the same thing as the witnesses? It's not just a racial matter; it's language, custom, culture, and a whole variety of issues that a jury in Aztec might not get.

Now, here in Gallup, my lovely new adopted hometown, there are lots of Spanish speakers. Even those of us who don't speak Spanish still understand a lot of words. Everyone eats the same hot food, and everyone has someone in their family who is at least a little bit Spanish. There are other things that we have in common with Aztec, but they might not help if the fairness of a trial is the objective. For example, when Sheriff Roberts began his roundup on April 4, 1935, in Gallup, he said he was going to "arrest everyone connected with the radical movement here." At least, that's what the *Gallup Independent* quoted him as saying on that date. The *Gallup Independent* and the *Farmington Times Hustler* both devoted most of what was in their papers to the labor strife, the aftermath of the riots, and the roundup of the radicals.

I know I am beginning to ramble, so I will cease and desist (as Billy Wade might put it). Good night, Madam Journal.

While the number was reported very differently depending on which newspaper you read, it was undisputed that Sheriff Roberts brought a large number of men from San Juan County to help in the roundup. The prosecutors denied any connection, but the *Farmington Sentinel* reported on May 17, 1935:

> The State League of Young Democrats met here this week to map out a program to combat the growth of communism and allied movements in New Mexico. At a banquet given by the League, Saturday night, Dave Chavez, Attorney General Patton, and R. C. Charlton, Adjutant General, spoke on the menace of the growth of communism.

That sort of thing was bound to make the defense lawyers a mite nervous. The Gallup prosecutor and the Santa Fe attorney general just happened to be asked to speak at an anti-communism banquet to the very folks who were likely to sit on the jury in a few months? Not even the town fool thought that was a coincidence. Politicians would rarely pass up a chance to make a speech to red-blooded Americans. So if it helped their reelection and the case at the same time, why not?

As if that wasn't enough, there were several news stories in Aztec and Gallup about the formation of a secret, militant organization called the "United American Patriots," which appealed to "red-blooded Americans." All such were invited to join the organization for the "purpose of combating communism." All you had to do to join was send your request to Box 414 in Aztec, New Mexico. They would take it from there. This God-fearing, America-loving, red-blooded organization ran an advertisement for their little group in the *Farmington Sentinel:*

> Do you want to make America FREE of all foreign entanglements? Do you want American Ideals, Traditions, and Sentiments preserved? America today is the last stronghold of Citizen Controlled government in the world. It is time for America to wake up and take charge of her government or that "Government of the people and for the People" will perish from the earth. COMMUNISM MUST GO!
>
> Do you know that less than 80,000 communists, who were armed, took over Russia with her population of 160,000,000 and now rule with an Iron hand? IS THERE ANY DANGER TO THE UNITED STATES OF AMERICA?
>
> It is estimated on good authority that more than 500,000 communists, Atheists, and other brands of radicals are in America today. They interlock and are well financed and in many cases are well armed. They operate 460 subversive and diversified cells. They all advocate the destruction of our Government. THE UNITED AMERICAN PATRIOTS ARE HERE.
>
> They strike like lightning and are being organized very rapidly and very secretly. They maintain their secret service throughout the entire nation and have their hands on the very pulse of America and an ever watchful eye on every movement of the American Communist Party, as well as on every movement those undercur-

> rents with which the average American citizen is not familiar. THE VOICE OF THE PEOPLE MUST BE HEARD!
>
> Are you a red-blooded American? Does the Constitution of the United States of America mean more to you than just a mere scrap of paper? Do you believe in the principles of the Christian Religion? Do you believe in protection of the home and of American womanhood? This organization is nonpartisan and nonsectarian. Your politics and your religion belong to you. What we want is manhood! And be sure it is American! For further particulars, write box 414, Aztec, N.M., and we will arrange for a personal interview.

There were 2,592 qualified voters in San Juan County, but only about 800 of them were eligible to actually serve on a jury. The defense offered proof that every one of them was sent copies of the advertisements, and a fair number of them went to the political rallies that the prosecutors were holding throughout San Juan County in the summer of 1935. All in all, it didn't look good for the defense as the summer changed to fall and the leaves started to drop in Aztec.

Hugh Woodward was experienced and smart but practiced law in a fairly relaxed fashion. He was polite but casual about court formality. This was a trait that would get him into trouble in Judge McGhee's courtroom. But for John Simms, Woodward was just what he needed to help balance out the defense team: a New Mexican who had no biases or prejudice. His trial experience as a former federal prosecutor would be very valuable on this case. It was likely that a conservative jury up in Aztec would readily accept him as a New Mexican and therefore give him, as well as Simms, the benefit of local trust and confidence.

Of course, neither of them was "local" to Gallup; they were from the big city of Albuquerque. The closest thing they had to "local" counsel from Gallup was in the person of Mr. Wheaton Augur and me—more or less. But I was still fearful that Bobcat would become a central figure in the trial. Even though I had never actually met Mr. Simms, I wrote him a short letter, telling him that I simply could not be a part of the courtroom team when the case was actually called for trial. Mr. Simms called me and graciously agreed that I could stay in the background and, perhaps, attend the chambers arguments without sitting at the counsel table or being directly involved in the actual trial of the case.

Wheaton Augur had been in the case for some time, having been appointed by Judge Otero the week after the shooting. He had assisted Wirin, Levinson, and Minor until they decided that their lives were more important than this particular case. When that happened, the International Defense League turned the case over to Donovan & Leisure of New York, New York. In time Donovan & Leisure would become one of America's leading law firms. The firm's founding partner, Colonel J. Donovan, had agreed to lead the defense but had yet to make an appearance in New Mexico in the case. He had sent two junior lawyers from his Manhattan office, but they had little to say and even less to do in the case.

John Simms and Hugh Woodward traveled to Gallup for their first look at the scene of the riot almost five months after it had occurred. Although they knew each other fairly well, they used the trip to go over what seemed to be the most pressing problems for the defense. "So, Hugh," Simms said, "we're meeting with Billy Wade. I got a short note from him and called him back to calm him down some. What do you know about him?"

"Not much, but what little I do know makes me think he's okay and should be easy to work with." Hugh Woodward shrugged and glanced out the car window. "He's been in Gallup for several years and has a nice little practice, but he's not at home in a courtroom and hasn't had much criminal experience. He assumes that you'll take the lead in the courtroom and is ready to back you up however you think best, as long as he can stay out of the courtroom."

"Well, that gives us five lawyers to defend ten men. I expect the odds to be fairly even since our friends the prosecutors are planning on having at least four trial men in the courtroom."

"John, you're counting those two fellows from New York in our five," Hugh said with a wry look. "I know we're more or less stuck with them, but I expect they'll be pretty useless to us when the jury gets picked. They seem well intentioned, but they take their marching orders from New York. We have to concentrate on New Mexico law and New Mexico justice if we're going to save those boys from the chair. As I see it, you and I will do the jury work, Wheaton will back us up, and the fellows from Donovan & Leisure will back up Wheaton. Anyhow, that's how Wheaton sees it based on their participation thus far. We have about three months to get this case laid out, and I don't expect to see those New York fellows until a week or two before trial. That's when the out-of-state press will descend on us again."

John Simms let the five miles go by in silence as they passed the beautiful red rocks just east of Gallup. Like many others, he wondered why they put the town where they did when five miles east would have made Gallup one of the most beautiful towns in the state. He'd heard it had something to do with ownership of the land by the railroad. Did the AT&SF really own those magnificent red rocks?

"I expect you're right; I've read the transcript from the preliminary hearings in Santa Fe," he said at last.

"I suppose we should start with the physical evidence," Hugh said. "You've read the file; what do you think they really have?"

"I suspect that Frank Powers, the ballistics man from El Paso, has given them hard evidence, but they sure were cagey about it at the prelim," John replied. "When do you suppose they're going to provide us with the ballistics report? They'll tick off old Judge McGhee if they try to play games with that sort of evidence. He's not inclined to put up with any 'hide the pea' stuff."

"You're right." Hugh nodded. "I'm real interested myself to see their hard physical evidence. I noticed that they introduced a lot of photographs and a club or two but only one gun at the prelim. The testimony wasn't complete by a long shot. My guess is there were a couple dozen shots fired, at least four bullets recovered from bodies, and lots of guns confiscated in the first few days after the riot. Why do you think they're being so damn secretive about the guns? Makes a fellow think maybe they don't have the gun that fired the bullets they took out of Sheriff Carmichael. Do you suppose we could be that lucky?"

"It's not just luck," John said firmly. "Seems pretty clear to me. They don't have the gun. They looked long and hard for it, and they issued a dozen search warrants for it. If they had it, it would have been Exhibit Number One at the prelim. They no doubt have a plan to deal with it, but they don't have it or we would have already seen it."

"Well, damn my hide, John, you must be right." Hugh sounded excited. "Why didn't I think of that? Of course they don't have the gun. That probably explains why they're so all fired up about their conspiracy case, too. If they had the gun, they wouldn't have to rely on conspiracy law to get the conviction."

"No, they need the conspiracy theory and would use it even if they had the gun," John said. "In fact, if they had the gun, it would make the conspiracy theory even more important. Dick Modrall knows damn good and well that even with the gun, they can't convict all ten of those boys. They have to tie in the men who didn't have the gun somehow, and there're only two ways to do that. They can connect them to the actual shooting and call them aiders and abettors, or they can establish a conspiracy and then connect the defendants to it with collateral evidence. With or without the actual murder weapon, we have to face a conspiracy trial and they have to try to tie in all the defendants to the actual shooter, whoever he was."

"So," Hugh said as they passed through the hogback cut a couple of miles east of downtown Gallup, "what chance do we have of beating their conspiracy case?"

"Well, now they have to worry that the jury might think one of the deputies shot the sheriff in the heavy cross fire that took place right after that tear gas bomb went off. If that happens, they still might get a conviction on the basis of the felony-murder rule, but that's a tough sell without the actual murder weapon. So they can win with or without the gun, but they might end up with less than they want. Frank Patton told me that first day I talked to him that he intended to fry those boys. He can only do that with a solid first-degree murder conviction."

"So you don't think the conspiracy theory will work for the death penalty but might get them second degree and a long prison term? Aiding and abetting is different from conspiracy, although most jurors never get it straight. Even a well put together conspiracy case might only net them second degree. That's not what the prosecution is after in this case."

The discussion continued on into Gallup. We met in the coffee room at El Rancho for our first "real" defense conference.

John Simms began the meeting with the topic that he and Woodward had discussed for the last hour of the ride from Albuquerque. "Well, now, Mr. Wade, Mr. Woodward and I have been talking about our defense, and we agreed that the best way to start is to discuss what we think the prosecution has by way of physical evidence. In particular, we think the guns collected by the state will prove to be important pieces of evidence. Do you think that makes sense?"

I thought before I answered. After all, I was the junior man here. I felt a little bit intimidated by the presence of a former Supreme Court justice and a former United States Attorney. Between the two of them, they had tried more cases than all the lawyers in Gallup had ever seen, much less actually tried. I knew that I could hold my own in Gallup, but this was a real change in how the defense had been handled up to this point.

Wheaton Augur and I had been given small assignments and had done most of the interviewing of potential witnesses, but the International Defense lawyers hadn't thought to ask us about real strategy or tactics. To be honest, I was a bit surprised that the eminent men picked by the Supreme Court to defend the case were even vaguely interested in my advice on tactical plans.

"Mr. Simms, I'm sure that your experience in cases like this gives you insights that I could never match. I know a fair amount about what our clients have to say about what happened, but I don't know very much about the physical evidence that Dee Roberts and David Chavez have been collecting. I expect I know some more about the guns because of my friend Bobcat Wilson, but as you know, he hasn't really talked to anybody about what happened."

"Well, sir, that's something I'd like to talk to you about," Simms said softly. "Does your friendship with Deputy Wilson affect how the prosecution might handle this case? I noticed that he never did formally appear in the case and that your name isn't on any of the early defense motions or notices in the court file. I did hear from someone, probably Frank Patton, that you were helping out the man from Los Angeles, A. L. Wirin."

"I don't know what my friendship with Bobcat means to the prosecutors." I shrugged. "He knows about my limited role in acting as local procedures counsel, and I'm sure he told his boss, Dee Roberts, about it. He and I have never really talked about what happened. That isn't because I'm a lawyer or because I was helping Mr. Wirin; it's more because Bobcat doesn't seem ready to talk to anybody about what happened. I can tell you that I didn't go to the preliminary hearing in Santa Fe because I wasn't asked to, but I was just as glad because they had Bobcat up there and we all thought he would be called as a witness. For some reason they decided not to put him on, but I expect he'll be called front and center when the real show starts up in Aztec in October."

"Thank you, Mr. Wade. While you're at it, why do you think the state didn't call Deputy Wilson as a witness at the prelim up in Santa Fe? Surely he's a crucial witness in the case. He not only was lined up right behind the sheriff at the time of the shooting; it sounds like the same man, or at least the same gun, might have shot him.

"Well, Mr. Simms, Bobcat speaks Navajo like he was one and always stands up for Indians and Mexicans alike. His family is part of the establishment in Gallup. Bobcat has had his share of brawls and bare-knuckle solutions to differences of opinion. He comes from a political family, but he just isn't the kind of man who talks very much. You pretty much do it his way or you back off. It may be that his view of things is a bit different than that of someone else on the prosecution side; I really don't know. I do know that he'll say it his way or not at all. That's another reason I wouldn't want to cross-examine him. It would be a waste of any lawyer's time trying to get Bobcat Wilson to say something different than what he believed to be the truth."

"Yes, that's helpful for us." John Simms looked at me closely. "Do you think his health had anything to do with the decision?"

"I'm not sure. As you know, he was severely wounded and damn near died. I don't think he was ever really well enough to testify, but he's tough as a twenty-five-cent steak. If he was asked to testify, he would never let his wounds get in the way of giving his evidence."

Hugh Woodward chimed in: "They didn't really need Mr. Wilson at the prelim anyway. They had Dee Roberts and Hoy Boggess, and all they needed was enough evidence to get our clients bound over. Putting Bobcat on would have been overkill. Besides, they might have thought he wouldn't make a good witness. He's said to be short on talk and long on action, if you know what I mean."

John Simms pondered the situation a bit. "What do you think Deputy Wilson would do if you asked him what he knows about the guns collected by the law here in Gallup? Will he cooperate with us at least that far?"

"Sure. He's a straight shooter, no pun intended. If the prosecutor will allow an interview, Bobcat would feel ethically bound to tell you truthfully whatever he knows about the case. He has his enemies, mostly men he's locked up, but no one ever said he's not an honest man. I don't think David Chavez will allow it, though.

"Well, fine. Thank you, Billy Wade. Now, to get back to the physical evidence. The court file indicates that Judge Bickel issued fifty or so individual search warrants. Most of them were sworn out by Deputy Bob Roberts, whom I gather is the brother of Sheriff Dee Roberts. Deputy Hoy Boggess attested to the rest. What is most interesting about these warrants is that they seem to be seeking guns and ammunition at addresses all over Gallup. There are specific houses listed, but the only specific gun identified by type is a Model 1917 .45 caliber Smith & Wesson. That's the one carried by Deputy Hoy Boggess at the time of the shooting. What happened—did he lose it or what? Did this happen during the shooting or afterward? And more important, why are there no returns of service on any of the warrants? Surely after searching what amounts to half the homes in Gallup, they found something."

Hugh Woodward took the pause in Mr. Simms's commentary as a chance to put the question a little more bluntly: "Or is the local practice here in Gallup not to file a return on a search warrant after it's executed and served? That fits in nicely with the railroad job the radical press says is going on over here."

"No, sir, that is not the case," I said quickly. "David Chavez is pretty much a stickler for the rules, so I have no explanation for why the court file doesn't contain any returns on the search warrants. It might be that they never found anything listed in the search warrants. I went over the same file myself. It seems to me that if they had found Hoy's gun, they would have marked it in evidence up in Santa Fe at the prelim. They didn't. So I sort of thought they never found it. They sure busted into a lot of homes to come up empty-handed."

"Billy Wade, are you aware of Frank Powers ever coming to town in connection with this case?" Simms asked quietly.

"No, I don't know that one way or the other. I mentioned his name to Mr. Wirin, but I don't know if it was ever followed up on."

Simms and Woodward looked at each other. Without saying so, this told them a great deal. The boys from out of town hadn't been smart enough to ask their local counsel about the man who likely would prove to be a critical witness if this case turned out to be one that involved ballistic evidence.

Frank Powers was considered the best in the business, at least in the West. Any guns or bullets found as a result of the search warrants would likely have been turned over to him in person. With Mr. Powers's reputation for detail, it's likely he would have come to Gallup in person from his office in El Paso just to collect the evidence directly from the lawmen. That way the official chain of evidence could be kept intact in case the judge got fussy with it at the trial.

Both Simms and Woodward brought me up to date on the legendary Frank Powers. They intended to draft a motion to force the state to produce his report first thing tomorrow.

While the new legal team was building the defense, the newspapers and the labor groups around the country were almost frantic. There was a national sense that much was wrong in Gallup and, by implication, the entire state of New Mexico. The so-called Writers and Artists of New York, National Committee for the Defense of Political Prisoners, had told Governor Tingley on April 26, 1935, that the prosecution was based on the "flimsiest evidence under antiquated statutes." You will recall that one of the strikers killed in the riot was named Solomon Esquibel. His name was nationally prominent solely by reason of his death. Governor Tingley got the following petition two months before the trial of the Gallup Ten:

Santa Fe, New Mexico
August 8, 1935
To Governor Tingley, New Mexico

A DEMAND

Whereas, The State Relief Administration in Gallup, New Mexico, is showing definite discrimination against the families of the ten political prisoners held on framed-up charges of murder in the State Penitentiary,

Whereas, the food orders have been so severely limited that these families are without food,

Whereas, the family of Agustin Calvillo has had no food for four days, and the youngest baby is dangerously ill,

Whereas the family of Juan Ochoa is also without food,

Whereas the relief officials of Gallup have repeatedly shown themselves to be the agents of the Gallup bosses, determined to force the working people of Gallup into submission, adding starvation to the long list of acts of terrorism against the workers, particularly the families of the ten defendants,

WE DEMAND that these people be given food, wood, and rent orders *at once.*

WE DEMAND that all discrimination cease *immediately.*

WE DEMAND that the relief officials responsible for this situation in Gallup *be removed at once.*

Solomon Esquibel Branch
International Labor Defense
Jane Erwin, Secretary

Thousands of letters, postcards, and telegrams continued to flow into New Mexico. Most of it came from unions like the United Ukrainian Toilers Organization, the Cleveland Council of Optical Technicians, and the Kalamazoo Cultural Club. Governor Tingley did what any red-blooded American would do with such things: He offered all of it to J. Edgar Hoover, thinking that it "might be of some value to him."

It wasn't just local politicians who were are all fired up. U.S. Representative Vito Marcantonio of New York moved to have the House of Representatives hold its own investigation, but the House voted him down 270 to 30. Someone told Mr. Simms that was voted down because we hadn't even had the trial in New Mexico; there was no reason to start the lynching in Washington yet.

five

THE BATTLE IS JOINED

October 1935

Mary Ann squinted at me and asked, in her most challenging tone: "And why, pray tell, do you think I should *not* go to Aztec for the trial? Is it just your standard New Mexican attitude about uppity women, or are you really worried about what I might find out about this whole ridiculous mess?"

As usual, Mary Ann's questions were put in such a way as to defeat any rational answer before it was given. Consequently, I did what I usually did when Mary Ann did this to me. I ignored her question by asking one equally unfair: "Do you want to go up there just to stir up trouble for yourself at Gallup High? Or are you really trying to pick a fight with the town council, the mayor, the chief of police, and every lawman and lawyer in town?"

"I have spent most of the summer trying to understand why ten men are facing the death penalty when the men who killed Sheriff Carmichael are dead. I could understand it if the charge were something other than premeditated murder, but since no one actually saw any of these men with a gun and since some of them might not even have been there, I just don't understand it. And besides—"

"Wait a minute, woman, who have you been talking to? I read the same papers you do and I've talked to more of the men who were actually there than you have, and I sure don't remember anyone saying that none of these men had guns or they weren't there. Of course they were there; they were all identified at the preliminary hearing as being directly involved. I expect there'll be lots of testimony up in Aztec that directly puts each one of them at the scene in a position to do harm to Carmichael. Maybe it was one of them who shot Bobcat. You know how I feel about that—it's why I'm watching from the sidelines."

"Billy Wade, this trial is not about who shot Bobcat." Mary Ann was fuming.

"We both know that. Bobcat is a victim and somebody nearly killed him in that alley, but he can't or won't say what happened until he is called as a witness at the trial. I would think you'd be glad that I'll be there to hear it firsthand. What's really important here is the press is doing a terrible job of covering this trial. They either think it's a totally baseless charge that is motivated entirely by politics or it's a waste of time and the men should be taken straight to the electric chair without bothering with a trial. I want to know exactly what happened and I want to write it down so that my students and anyone else who has no ax to grind in the matter can read an unbiased report. Would you like another cup of coffee?"

This discussion had been going on for over an hour now, and we had drunk more coffee than we wanted. "No thanks, I suppose I ought to get on home. But I didn't know you intended to actually publish your journal of the trial. I thought it was just for your benefit."

"Well, it is for my benefit." Mary Ann nodded vigorously. "But the more I think about it, the more I think it might be fun to publish it. I guess maybe it's the frustrated author in all English teachers. Maybe it will be really awful and I'll be embarrassed to show it to anyone. Then I'll treat it as a diary, not a journal."

"You know there'll be an official court reporter up there and the press will descend on Aztec like locusts." I just couldn't fathom why she wanted to do this. "Lots of people will be writing up every word that's said. Have you thought about how hard it is to write up stuff like legal testimony?"

"I'm sure you're right, but I don't intend to write down the actual testimony," Mary Ann said. "I'll try to write the essence of what happens without repeating every word everybody says."

"That's what the press is supposed to do, Mary Ann," I repeated patiently. "That's their job. The court reporter will take down verbatim testimony and the reporters will take down what they think will sell newspapers. So is your journal or your diary, whichever it turns out to be, going to be somewhere in the middle?"

Mary Ann took some pleasure in the implied admission that it was okay for her to go and smiled as she answered: "My version will be, hopefully, a balanced interpretation of what is important about this trial. By the way, did I tell you the principal seemed to be really pleased I was going to do this and said to take whatever time I needed? He got one of the teachers out at Rehoboth to cover my class for the whole week. You don't think it will take any longer than that, do you?"

"I'll tell you one thing, sweetheart, John Simms is a master in the courtroom." She really seemed determined to do this. "The trial will take as long as he thinks he needs to get his points across to the jury. That might take a week; it might take a month. But however long it takes, it'll be entertaining, to put it mildly."

Saturday Night, October 5, 1935

It's all over but the shoutin'. At least that was what the boys down at the American Bar believed. Like everybody else in town, they were talking about the trial that was scheduled to start Monday morning up in Aztec. On the one hand, they were pissed off that those red bastards weren't going to get what was coming to them right here in Gallup. On the other hand, they were cocksure that the men of Aztec would do the right thing. By that they meant fry 'em.

Not that it was completely unanimous. Nothing ever said in the bar run by Guido Zecca was agreeable to every other man in the bar. There was plenty to disagree about even though the end result of the trial wasn't in dispute. It was agreed that every last one of those agitating, ungrateful outsiders ought to get a fair trial and then go straight to the electric chair. What they didn't agree about was why they couldn't have the trial right here where the murder was committed. The witnesses were all here. The bodies were buried here. The law was here. Why wouldn't it be fair to try them here?

The naysayers allowed as how maybe, all things considered, it was better to move the trial up there in cattle and farm country. There was no agitating up there. They did have a fair number of Mexicans and Spanish-speaking folks, but they were the "right kind." By that, of course, they meant real Americans, not Russians or some other communist, anti-Christ assholes.

And another thing, Aztec had sent a fair number of men to Gallup to help in the roundup of the radicals right after they killed Sheriff Carmichael and did great bodily harm to Hoy and Bobcat. They were conservative men who loved their country. Surely they would make short work of whatever bullshit defense those *Albuquerque* boys tried to throw up against the prosecution.

Of course, all this was being discussed without the benefit of hearing from Hoy or Bobcat since neither of them seemed to be around much anymore. Dee Roberts and his brother Bob stopped in on occasion, but neither talked much about what would happen once the trial got started.

This was my last night in town before the trial began since I planned on driving up tomorrow morning with Bobcat. But as usual, like the other town lawyers, I tended to complicate things in the American Bar. Over a cold beer I allowed as how the men on trial were entitled to the benefit of the doubt since no one had *proved* a damn thing yet.

Two blocks away, it was a lot more complicated. You will remember that some of the men charged in the case spent the morning of the riot in the Angeles Pool Hall on Coal Avenue, directly across from Judge Bickels's court. There, just like in the American Bar across the street and only two doors away from Judge Bickel's, the main topic of discussion was the trial. Of course, a lot of the discussion was in Spanish and their view of how fair the trial would be a damn sight different. As it stood, though, both groups agreed on one thing: the boys on trial would likely be found guilty on all counts.

The crowd in the American Bar called it justice (if the mines go under, so will this town!). The crowd in the Angeles Pool Hall called it *gringo* justice (*deje de o se pone ausente*). That pretty much says it all. The mines versus the working classes; there's no way to avoid it except by making one do what the other won't. Give up or get out. *Que pena.*

While most everyone in town was talking about the trial, most of them didn't intend on traveling up to Aztec to actually see it. Other than the official witnesses and the families of the defendants, Mary Ann and I were about the only ones to attend just to watch.

I spent the morning reading *The Aztec News* and was amused that the main story about the trial included a little gossipy item about Judge James B. McGhee and Sam McCue, the sheriff from Chaves County, who, it said, spent their mornings fishing together. I expected the defendants might see that as a little too cozy, considering the trial was about killing one sheriff based on the testimony of another one. The paper also made it clear that the lawmen up there expected trouble of some sort. Judge McGhee told the court staff and Sheriff McCue that "these defendants were not to be railroaded, and no trouble was to arise during the trial." So they built a bull pen of live electric wires around the jail itself and hired special guards to be on duty day and night. They also did something never done before in a courtroom in this state: they searched every person entering the courtroom for arms. Suspicious-looking persons loitering around the courthouse were to be "immediately investigated."

Mary Ann and I went to the San Juan County Courthouse early Monday morning. The courtroom itself was up on the second floor and had room for eighty-five spectators, not counting the chairs out in the aisles or the spaces needed for witnesses. Obviously space would be limited for this trial because sixteen lawmen were supposed to be inside the courtroom at all times "just to keep order." As the trial progressed we would find that the folks in Aztec dealt with the turmoil as best they could. They certainly didn't relish the thought of having a trial that really didn't involve them in their sleepy little town.

James McGhee looked like a judge. Graying hair cut short. Gray eyes, spaced well and accented by large bushy eyebrows that could, if you watched real close, give away his mood. When furrowed, they signaled trouble. When relaxed, they signaled serenity and a comfort that made you relax. At least until he spoke. He had a voice that inherently commanded authority.

He was a man of average intelligence but seemed to know more than most. He rarely expressed doubt and announced his decisions like he carried himself: upright, with purpose, and with ultimate confidence. Not a man to dispute, that's what they all said about the honorable James B. McGhee.

"Come on in here, gentlemen; we won't stand on ceremony given the room we have here." Judge McGhee was standing in the doorway to the small anteroom between the judge's chambers and the courtroom itself. The lawyers were standing uneasily together in the cramped space with the court reporter and the bailiff.

As the lawyers filed through the door, Judge McGhee took the opportunity to introduce himself to the two who he didn't already know. "Mr. Brick, Mr. Thayer, welcome to New Mexico. You've come at a fine time; we are about to harvest the apple crop up here and I am told there are none better, even in your home state of New York."

Dick Modrall thought as he overheard this exchange that what our good judge might be telling these young lawyers from the big Wall Street firm of Donovan & Leisure was that the lawyers here were every bit as good as those in New York. For their part, Messrs. Brick and Thayer took the greeting at face value, although they were a bit taken aback at the doorway greeting. They had expected one of the other defense lawyers to introduce him once they were inside the judge's chambers and to move their admission to try the case in a formal manner. New Mexico is not New York, lesson number one. More to follow.

As they filed into the judge's chambers, the lawyers, like lawyers everywhere, looked at the available seats not for comfort but as a matter of tactics. Experienced trial lawyers knew that this first "seating" generally established the place where each would sit in all future chambers proceedings. After all, one didn't take someone else's chair for fear of giving offense. Some judges had better hearing on one side or the other and occasionally forced the issue on which side of the judge's desk was best. If there were only two lawyers, then both would sit directly in front of the desk, but this wasn't possible when each side had several lawyers. You wanted to sit with your side so you could whisper strategies and comebacks if necessary. And most important, you wanted to be on the side where the outside windows were since judges tended to look outside while keeping one ear on the arguments.

In the old but soundly built courthouse in Aztec, the windows in the judge's chambers looked out to the east with a point or two down south. Thus it was a most pleasant morning sun that streamed in through the somewhat uneven glass. The space below the windows was mostly bookshelves, but most were empty of books, although there were briefs and copies of pleadings from bygone cases strewn throughout the room. Of course, this room was normally occupied by the judge elected to sit in San Juan County, but he had been asked to hear matters in Roswell while Judge McGhee heard the Gallup case here in Aztec.

As if on cue, John Simms said as everyone settled into their chairs: "Your Honor, now that you have recognized Mr. Brick and Mr. Thayer as relative strangers among us, I would like to move their admission on the record based on—"

Judge McGhee interrupted: "And good morning to you too, John, but you cannot do anything on the record until we have a record established."

With that and with a smile on his face, he said to his court reporter: "Let the record reflect this is Cause Number 1302 on the criminal docket of the McKinley County District Court with venue having been settled here in San Juan County by my prior order. Today is Monday, October 7, 1935, and we are present in chambers to resolve whatever pretrial matters are at issue before we begin the trial. Gentlemen, would you state your appearances please, for the record."

While it probably escaped most of the others, John Simms and Dick Modrall had the same thought at the same time: Judge McGhee was not simply announcing the formal start of a chambers proceeding; he was giving fair notice that the "record" in this matter was his to make. He was in charge, and everyone had best remember that.

Trial protocol established the order of speaking. The side with the burden of proof went first. In a criminal case the state had a very high burden and therefore went first *and* last. Frank Patton stood and said: "Judge McGhee, it is my pleasure to formally present the prosecution to you. Appearing with me throughout this trial will be my chief deputy, Mr. J. R. Modrall. The McKinley County district attorney, Mr. David Chavez, and his chief deputy, Mr. D. W.

Carmody, will assist us. We expect Mr. C. T. Smith to join us directly; as you know, he is also from Gallup and serves there under Mr. Chavez."

"Thank you and welcome to Aztec, Mr. Patton. I'm sure we will have a fine, orderly trial with solid men such as you have gathered to present this case for the state. John, I cut you off before, so I will turn to you now to introduce the defense men."

"Your Honor, it is my pleasure to inform the court that Mr. Hugh Woodward and I will be assisted in the defense of this case by Mr. Wheaton Augur of Gallup and by two fine fellows from back east. May I present Mr. Francis A. Brick, Junior, and Mr. Walter N. Thayer the Third, both of the New York bar. These men are in good standing before the bar of New York, and I would ask you to admit them to try this case with me *pro hace vice* if the court please. Now, Mr. La Follette is also part of the defense team and is, as you know, an Albuquerque lawyer. He has been specially retained *only* to represent the interests of the defendant Joe Bartol. Mr. Brick and Mr. Thayer will join Mr. Augur, Hugh, and me in representing the collective interests of the other nine defendants, which I would like to put on 'your' record, if the court please. Those other nine defendants are Juan Ochoa, Leandro Velarde, Agustin Calvillo, Manuel Avitia, Victorio Correo, Gregorio Correo, Rafael Gomez, Willie Gonzales, and Serapio Sosa. At the court's pleasure, we will argue the matter of our renewed request for a trial continuance."

Judge McGhee tensed a bit at the impertinence of mentioning a pending motion before he had called for it on the record but let it go for the moment. "Yes, thank you, John. Do I take it you and Hugh are vouching for the character of these men so that I can admit them *pro hace vice?* Well, mighty fine. Hearing no opposition from the state, I will order the admission of Walter Thayer and William Brick to this court for the limited purpose of appearing as trial counsel for the defendants in this case. Now, does the state have any motions before I take up the renewed request for a trial continuance by the defense?"

"If it please the court," John Simms began, knowing that Judge McGhee was a stickler for both formality and good manners, "we are mindful of the court's prior rulings denying our requests for a new venue, but we find the present circumstances require that motion be renewed. If the court is still inclined to try the case here in Aztec, then we move for a continuance of the trial to deal with the prejudicial matters that now jeopardize the defendants' right to a fair and unbiased trial. As the court is well aware, all defendants except Joe Bartol have been incarcerated since April 5, 1935. These men are not likely to get a fair trial here for two reasons: First, the total population in San Juan County is

14,367 and the qualified voters' number about 2,592. We are told by the clerk's office that the total number of persons qualified for jury service is about 800. Judge, within twenty-four hours of the arrival here of the defendants day before yesterday from the prison in Santa Fe, pamphlets were delivered to most of the homes and ranches in the area that were highly inflammatory and calculated to arouse resentment, prejudice, and ill will against the defendants. We believe that the jury pool has been antagonized and prejudiced. I have two of these pamphlets here for you and will have them marked as exhibits to our motion. These two pamphlets are over eleven pages long. You can see for yourself that the first one has the most misleading headline I have seen in some time. Please take a few minutes and read it. We have had it marked as Exhibit 1 to our motion to continue the case."

Judge McGhee lost his patience after reading the first two pages of the eleven-page document. "Now, John, you know that I can't consider a newspaper article, if you can call it that seeing as how it is patently ridiculous, as evidence of any sort. I'm surprised you would even offer it. A lot of these pages have to do, supposedly, with the 1933 strike over in Gallup. How can that possibly be relevant to your motion to continue?"

"Judge, with all due respect, it is quite relevant. The men on trial are all miners, they were all on strike in 1933, and they were made scapegoats here because of that. Briefly stated, Your Honor, the strike down there in Gallup was to enforce their right of collective bargaining supposedly guaranteed them under Section 7a of the NIRA. This pamphlet, true or not, accuses the mine owners of getting the National Guard to come to Gallup to break the strike. The pamphlet says, true or not, the mine owners tried to split the solidarity of the workers by building up the United Mine Workers as a rival union to the National Miners Union, which won the 1933 strike."

Judge McGhee tapped impatiently on the desk. "John, I find it hard to believe that you would think I would put any credence in this sort of thing. I will not continue this case or move the trial from here just because some radical organization, maybe communist for all I know, wants me to."

"But Judge, this pamphlet says men were beaten and third-degreed. Women were taken to lonely places, terrorized, threatened. Drunken armed men made indecent proposals to young girls. Little children were called out of school and forced at the gunpoint to say their parents were "communists." Sixteen men and four children were jammed into two small jail cells and kept there all day and night. Altogether over 600 workers and their families were victims of this "roundup." Two hundred were at first charged with murder. Then the number was reduced to forty-eight. Now, you and I know that those numbers might be a bit exaggerated, but the fact is the jury pool has no doubt read this stuff, and I'm not sure there's anything we can do to bring them around to fairness after reading this kind of stuff a few days before this trial was to start."

Simms tried to retake the high ground in the argument by directing the judge's attention to the second pamphlet. "Judge, just take a look at Exhibit 2 to our motion. It's even more odious than the first and shows even more clearly that the venue here in San Juan County has been poisoned."

Judge McGhee took in a deep breath as though he wanted to hold his temper along with it. "I do not need to read this thing again. As you may have guessed, I was given a copy of these insidious documents by the court staff upon my arrival in Aztec yesterday. I take your point that these eleven pages are important to the case, but I cannot ascribe any particular motive to whoever saw fit to pass out this stuff. On the one hand, this may have been prepared and distributed in the misguided belief that the men of San Juan County will find sympathy with the cause of the unemployed and striking miners down in Gallup. While I have no particular expertise in labor matters or social unrest, for that matter, I can see that the factual basis for this document is strained to say the least. This stuff might make it awkward for the people in San Juan County to hear this case, but who's to say that will change if we put this trial off for a few months or even a few years? Now, you've attached to your motion the affidavits of some local men who support your belief that the jury pool is tainted. I have read those affidavits. Does the defense have any additional matters that they wish me to consider?"

"We will stand on our motion and the affidavits before you," Simms said.

After hearing briefly from the state in opposition, Judge McGhee denied the motion with the vigor and decisiveness that would come to mark all his rulings during the course of the trial. It seemed obvious that he favored the prosecution's side of this issue since he nodded as they made their points: It is the state's position this trial will be tense no matter when it is tried. It will be possible, but not necessarily easy, to pick a jury that has not been unduly affected by this sort of pretrial posturing by unknown parties or forces. The best thing for the men on trial and for the rest of New Mexico is to get this case tried to a final verdict.

Judge McGhee turned to his court reporter and ruled: "I find from the affidavits and testimony that the motion is not well taken. I will see that you get a fair and impartial trial. I will not let a juror sit if he has an opinion. If he has an opinion that will take evidence to remove, we will remove him immediately.

What else do we have before we call the first venire panel into court for *voir dire?*"

Dick Modrall glanced at David Chavez before responding to the judge's question. "Your Honor, the state moves to add Mr. L. E. Wilson as a trial witness. We seem to have overlooked him when we put together our witness list. Mr. Wilson did not testify at the preliminary hearing, but we would like to call him as a trial witness."

Hugh Woodward seemed to sense something but nevertheless said: "No objection by the defense."

"Well, now, let's try to keep that up," the judge observed. "I believe that all witnesses who have relevant evidence should be called even if someone forgot to add their name to our witness list. Motion granted. If there is nothing else, let's go out into the courtroom and the clerk will call the venire panel for *voir dire.*"

"Actually, there is one other matter that requires the court's attention before we pick the jury," Woodward said somewhat reluctantly. He knew he had to try but also knew his chances of convincing the judge were damn slim. "Judge, the defense is entitled to know which legal theory the state will rely on before the case is opened. As it stands now, we still don't know how they intend to prove that the crime of murder was committed. The charging document in this case is the criminal information drawn up by Mr. Chavez and Mr. Carmody. As you know from our argument about their bill of particulars, the state has at least three and possibly six different legal theories. It is just plain unfair to the defense to make us start a capital case without knowing which trial theory is going to be relied on by the state. They conflict with one another; at least some of them do. I believe the law requires the state to elect a legal theory before the jury is picked; otherwise, we have no way of defending since we cannot guess at which theory they will argue at the end of the case."

Judge McGhee knew well that Hugh Woodward was a former U.S. Attorney for the District of New Mexico. He was a first-rate prosecutor turned defense lawyer and a scholar as well. Combined with John Simms, a former justice of the New Mexico Supreme Court, the defense included the two men many thought were the two best trial lawyers in the state. But nevertheless, they were already beginning to try his patience. Judge McGhee thought: They ought to quit this posturing and try the damn case. "Mr. Woodward, you are plowing old ground here, and I might say that your furrows are none too straight. When you made this argument before, I asked you to apprise me as to whether there was any precedent to support your position on election of a trial theory. You had no case to cite then, and I did not hear one from you this time either. I believe the state is entitled to charge the defendants with alternative theories as long as you have fair notice of all their theories. That does not mean I will let them argue all of the theories at the end of the case or that I will charge the jury with the law on each one. That will depend on how the evidence shakes out on the witness stand. I have read all of the charging papers and have reread a fair amount of the testimony from the preliminary hearing. Their evidence on conspiracy seems a mite thin, and their evidence on the actual shooter was confusing at best. But they have a right to present all the evidence they have because they have given you boys on the defense fair notice. One could argue that they run the risk of confusing the jury, but that is for them to assess. Your motion to require election of a legal theory just doesn't carry water. I will expect you to reargue this at the end of the case so that we do not end up with inconsistent jury instructions. As you know, I have already told the prosecution that this case could be presented to our jury as a straight murder charge based on their ballistics evidence as to who shot the sheriff. But till we get all the evidence in, they do not have to elect which theory to argue in the end. Motion denied, and before anyone brings up something else at the last minute, you are excused. Join me in the courtroom in five minutes for *voir dire*."

Monday, October 7, 1935

In the courtroom, Mary Ann and I watched the faces of the families as they waited for their men to come in. The lawmen waited for the lawyers, and the reporters seemed mostly interested in themselves. But everyone was on edge as they waited for the judge. This courtroom took on a lifelike form as "it" waited for Judge McGhee like an anxious movie theater waited for the raising of the curtain. Come to think of it, the entry of the judge presents a scene much like the beginning of an eagerly anticipated movie—both venues are structured in a traditional way and both signal the start of something either enjoyable or terrifying—depending on where you sit.

All of the characters in this courtroom seemed serious and impervious to human frailty; all, that is, except for the ten forlorn men who filed in, deputies attached, and sat on the defendants' bench. They appeared helpless, like children among adults. I don't mean they were childlike; quite the contrary—they had tight jaws and narrow eyes. Children in similar settings are always wide-eyed and inquisitive. These men looked as though they knew the end of this movie and dreaded getting there.

Courtrooms are public places, but unlike parks or museums, they don't lend themselves to casual conversations. The crowd, as it awaited the entry of the judge, occupied itself with a constant insectlike hum of noise; not small talk but not conversational either. The lawyers talked to one another, and the jurors looked away from the lawyers. The crowd in the back of the courtroom seemed to ignore both the lawyers and the jury. For the most part they sat quietly and stared intently at the backs of the heads of the defendants. It seemed to me as if they were looking for guilt or innocence in the shape of the nape of the neck or the rigidity of a man's shoulders. The court reporters busied themselves with their inks and steno pads, and the bailiff and the clerks engaged in the kind of make-work that they hoped would make them look important while they waited for the entry of the judge. It was as though this courtroom was his, not the citizens of Aztec's, not the defendants', in a way both impersonal and imperative.

Mary Ann and I sat together. She looked around the courtroom and said quietly that she felt slightly smothered by the lack of emotion on the defendants' bench. The room was stale with tradition and social authority but not the kind the Spanish-speaking defendants were used to. That night she told me how demoralized she felt as she looked at the officious, many-armed, impersonal power of the prosecutors and the lawmen and the court staff. The prosecutors looked ambitious; the jury looked like the kind of farmers and ranchers who feared violence and were scared of the taint of radicalism that drifted toward them from the defendants' bench. The press were busy with their notebooks but seemed avid in their attempts to see the faces of the defendants or at least the sides of the faces.

The families of the defendants were scattered throughout the right-hand side of the public pews, but the defendants rarely turned to look at them. When they did, the look on their faces was more of a grimace than a smile. Little wonder, since they were waiting for their first look at the judge who was about to take total control of their lives. When the court stage seemed fully set, the jury firmly boxed, and the lawyers at proper attention, the bailiff rose in anticipation of the entry of the Honorable James W. McGhee.

The *voir dire* took all day. *Voir dire* means, more or less, to tell the truth. Everyone in the judicial system expects that the veniremen will be truthful when they are asked downright personal questions about their secret thoughts and their prejudices and fallacies. That's a nice theory. Like most judges, Judge McGhee used the process of *voir dire* to ask questions of the jury to see who might be fair. Lawyers use it to ask questions of the jury to see who might go for their side. The press sits in the back and listens real close to see who might be talkative about things after the trial. And of course the relatives and friends of those on the venire panel listen up to see if the answers are, in fact, by God, truthful. So *voir dire* is a fair name for the process in a loose sort of way.

In this particular *voir dire,* Judge McGhee asked all 274 of the men who had been drawn by the jury commissioner to state their names, ages, line of work, and local address if they had one. Naturally, they weren't all physically in the jury box since it was too small to hold them all. Most of them were down on the grassy area under the cottonwoods in front of the courthouse. They would have to be called upstairs one by one. The ones in the back of the courtroom could hear their name as the clerk called it out. The bailiff summoned the rest of them by shouting out the window. Extra chairs were spread out over half the room. For a while it was hard to tell the veniremen from the rest of the people in court.

That is, except for the defendants themselves. They didn't look a bit like any of the veniremen. The defendants were all dark skinned (except for the Slav, Joe Bartol), and they all looked bewildered, whereas the veniremen merely looked uneasy. The defendants all looked at the interpreter most of the time, while the veniremen looked at whoever was talking at the time.

Even though the veniremen didn't look like the defendants, they sure enough looked like they were all from the same place. The farmers and ranchers who made up the jury panel looked just like you would expect them to look. Most of them lived out in the county, although there were a few townsfolk spread out among them. No coal dust or railroad cinders on these men. They were weathered and serious looking. All in all, they looked sort of hard to convince. Trouble was, they looked hard to convince to both sides. In a case like this, that could mean a long trial and a hard decision.

Judge McGhee asked each man a series of questions and got a whole boatload of no's. Not a one had ever laid eyes on any defendant. No one admitted to having actually "read" any of the pamphlets about "saving the Gallup workers." Only a few had gone to the political rallies attended by the prosecutors, and none of them had been to Gallup to look in the alley behind Judge Bickel's court. That's the way it went until he got to the two questions that started the veniremen scooting out the rear door: Do you have an opinion about the guilt or innocence of these men here on trial? Do you have any strong feelings about the death penalty?

This was the largest number of men ever called for a jury trial in Aztec. In fact, it was the largest number ever called for a jury anywhere in this state.

Judge McGhee declared thirty men unfit for jury service that first morning.

Most of them were booted for admitting they had a strong opinion on the case or admitting they could not abide the death penalty. As each one would say something like that, Judge McGhee, in his stern but slow way, would say: "Mr. Juror, you are excused."

Not all of them walked out on account of opinions about the defendants or the death penalty. For example, one Bruce Walters was worried about circumstantial evidence and allowed as how he would have to have direct evidence to convict, and it would have to be very strong. The defense seemed to like this and even got this fellow to say he wanted powerful direct evidence and "none of the circumstantial brand." He was excused for cause. Some of the *voir dire* was downright amusing. A Mr. George Leming got his name called out of the second-story window since he was one of those down on the grass in front of the courthouse. He rushed up and took his seat out of breath, and before they could ask him any questions, he announced that he had sat on a homicide case once before. To sort of balance things out, he told the judge that he was a farmer and a rancher, that he had three children, and that he was a veteran of the World War and had served overseas. Turns out, he made it onto the jury and was the only one who had any real serious jury experience in the past.

Some of the questions asked were more or less foolish. For example, the state asked several times if any of the men on the panel had prejudice against "subjects of some European monarch." One of the reporters from Denver commented that he probably meant the Duke of Alburquerque. Along this line, the defense lawyers harped on the prejudice that some folks have against Spanish Americans and other aliens. The state came back with a statement like, "So, you would go into the jury room with an open mind, is that right, sir?"

Every one of the possible jurors was asked about the pamphlet that someone was spreading about to save the so-called Gallup 14. Charles Bolton was a good example of what most of 'em answered: he said he had seen one in a barbershop but "did not pay any mind to it."

I don't mean to imply that all the answers were in the negative. Some of the men answered yes once or twice during the forty minutes it took Judge McGhee to *voir dire* this panel. Some of them knew about the actual murders and had heard of Sheriff Carmichael or Bobcat Wilson or Dee Roberts. Some had a little experience with the law, both for it and against it. Most had read the newspaper accounts, but none allowed as how it made a big impression on them. Several reminded the judge that they were planting in the spring at the time of the riot, cultivating, watering, and weeding all summer and just now finishing up the harvest. The farmers, that is. The ranchers spent the spring rounding up, branding, and moving their cattle to the railhead. But farmer or rancher or town man, they all had one abiding hope: they said they sure hoped this wouldn't take long.

After he finished his questions, Judge McGhee called for the lawyers to exercise their strikes. That woke up the courtroom. It seems that both sides sort of took it for granted they would get to ask their own questions of the venire panel after the judge was through. He said no, he didn't think that was necessary as he had covered most all of the things that go to making up a fair and unbiased jury panel. After a noisy (although you couldn't make out their words) conference at the bench, the judge gave in a bit and said he would ask some follow-up questions just to satisfy everyone.

Judge McGhee took another half hour, and everyone learned that none of these men belonged to a union. None of them owned a Model 1917 .45-caliber Smith & Wesson double-action model revolver with two clips making up the revolving part of the pistol. None of them worked as deputies or guards or such; two of them spoke Spanish, and none of them belonged to the Communist Party. This last question was asked with a straight face, as if any of them would have dared to speak up if they were. It wasn't clear which side wanted this last group of questions asked, but it sort of proved the judge was right when he said he would ask their questions for them; that way, neither side got painted with a negative bad brush right off the bat.

At five o'clock on Monday afternoon, October 7, 1935, the judge announced that they had a jury. It was made up of "twelve good and true men." Just in case you're interested, the men on the jury were Filemino Lujan, J. W. Norton, Sabino Chavez, Ernest Wall, Curt Steiner, A. F. Rinehart, W. I. Whitney, Joel Kohl, Rudy Ferrari, D. C. Hamblin, George Leming, and E. P. Ralston. All were ranchers or farmers; not a coal miner in the bunch. They were put in the box, and they all raised their right hands and took an oath to "well and truly try" this case. That would remain to be seen.

This trial was making a lot of "firsts" in New Mexico. It was the first trial to have that large a jury panel. It was the first trial in which the jury was sequestered (more or less locked up) in a church basement. Aztec had only one hotel, The American Hotel, and it had only fourteen rooms. Every last room was taken by the prosecution to put the witnesses and the state policemen up. As for the jury, they were told they would have to spend the trial down in the basement of the church, but that wasn't too bad, all things considered. They wouldn't have to troop out to one of the three public restaurants for meals. Their meals would all be home cooked and brought in to them three times a day. They even moved in a piano for them to play during recesses in the trial.

Right after the *voir dire* part, the judge called for the evening recess. He admonished the jury to keep mum among themselves and not to let anyone approach them as they went back and forth from the church to the court. He told them they would all come back first thing the next morning for opening statements by the lawyers.

While I didn't know it at the time, the next ten days were to become the most intense learning experience of my professional life. I can't really put the experience into words, but I can tell you this: What passes from the witness stand to the jury box doesn't always come out the way the lawyers want it to or the judge, for that matter. The verdict of a trial jury is far more than a collection of the individual views of the jurors themselves. It's a composite of their emotional attachment to the case. Whether it's good or bad is not the point. I learned that a jury verdict is like a great banquet. It exists despite the best efforts of the cooks and servers and master chefs. It's what is left over after the straining and sifting of evidence and often bears no relationship to the recipe used to cook up the case in the first place.

six

DO YOU SWEAR TO TELL THE . . .

Tuesday, October 8, 1935

From his high-backed seat up on his bench, Judge McGhee greeted the solemn men at the two tables in front and at the long bench on each side of the courtroom. "Gentlemen, our jury has been sworn, and the charges have been read and the pleas recorded. I have asked the state to have all its witnesses here this morning so we can swear them all in at once. Are they all here?"

Attorney General Patton rose and said that most of them were, and he waved his hand to the state policeman at the rear of the court. In a few minutes some forty to fifty men and women were ushered into the courtroom and given a mass oath by the judge. Then he told them all to be sure not to discuss their testimony in the case with anyone except the lawyers. He then excused them and said, "Now, none of you can stay in the courtroom during the trial except for the ones who are physicians or lawyers and, of course, the chief investigator for the state, Mr. Martin. The rest of you will have to wait outside until you're called for your testimony."

Among the crowd were the lawmen from Gallup: Sheriff Roberts, his brother, Bob, and Deputies Bobcat Wilson and Hoy Boggess. They didn't look pleased at being excluded from what they saw as "their" trial.

"Are we ready to start this trial?" Without waiting for an answer, he more or less ordered: "Fine, Mr. Patton, are you going to open for the state?"

The bench closest to the jury was filled with lawmen, the one on the other side of the courtroom with defendants. The lawyers sat in front at the two tables with the wicker-back chairs. Their tables were covered with books and official-looking documents and writing pads. The defendants had nothing to write with or on. The lawmen were there to guard the prisoners, but they didn't need anything to write on since they had nothing to write about. Their job was to make sure that the jury knew they were safe from the prisoners.

The public part of this public courtroom was filled to capacity. Two rows were reserved for the press and one row for families of the defendants. The prosecution had half a row reserved, although no one was there now. The balance of the room was made available on a first-come, first-serve basis. About half of these seats were taken up with interested onlookers and thrill-seeking gawkers. The pressmen and -women who were eased out of the two reserved rows grabbed the other half up. The press also gathered in the hallways and on the large front porch of this wood-frame building that normally sat quiet and serene year after year. It had not, up to now, ever held more than fifty people at any one time. Today there were over two hundred, with more on the lawn, looking in the ground-floor windows (although no part of the actual trial could be seen since the courtroom was up on the second floor).

This was Frank Patton's first chance to speak to the members of the jury since up to now, Dick Modrall had done most of the talking to them. Of course, all that had happened so far was the selection of the jury. Mr. Modrall announced the peremptory and for-cause challenges. Patton was the highest law enforcement officer in the state, and he intended this to be a plain statement of the case. He knew Judge McGhee well and knew he wouldn't countenance any "argument" in the opening statement. The argument of the case would come at the end. This was just the time to "state" the case. So he started out with the easy facts and tried real hard to keep any emotion out of his voice. He had his statement all typed up, and he read it slowly and carefully to the jury. As he did so, he stood real still, three feet away from the jury rail:

"A few days before April 4, 1935, Esiquel Navarro was arrested down in Gallup on a charge of housebreaking. He was confined in the McKinley County jail to await a hearing before a JP. On April 4, 1935, a hearing was set for Navarro. Sheriff M. R. Carmichael and his deputies took Navarro to Judge Bickel's court for that hearing.

"The night before the hearing a meeting was held, and some of the defendants in this courtroom attended the meeting." At that moment Patton looked over at the line of defendants on the bench behind the defense table for the first time. He didn't dwell on any of them and didn't seem to look at all of them.

The best English speaker was Leandro Velarde, and he sat on the end next to Juan Ochoa. They seemed somewhat animated but only when compared to the other defendants. The others seemed immobile but were keenly intent on the voice of the interpreter in the middle of the courtroom, who said in Spanish whatever was said in the courtroom in English. It seemed to some that Frank Patton looked only at Velarde and Ochoa when he talked about "the meeting."

After that short look over his shoulder at the defendants, Patton continued: "The next morning a large crowd gathered at Judge Bickel's court. The hearing was continued to enable Navarro to obtain a lawyer to represent him. Because there was a mob in front of the court, the officers attempted to take Navarro out the back door of the court to return him to jail."

Hugh Woodward burst out with the first objection of the trial. He was a large man with a courtroom voice, and he boomed from his cane-back chair: "Objection. We object to the use of the word 'mob,' Judge. That's argument, and it's prejudicial."

Judge McGhee didn't look pleased. He didn't like lawyers interrupting each other during opening statement, and he didn't like lawyers making objections while seated in their chairs. Proper courtroom decorum was important. But he knew the objection was proper and said: "Sustained. Perhaps, Mr. Patton, you should select another word."

Patton seemed perturbed but promptly apologized. "Of course, Your Honor, I will substitute the word 'crowd' for the word 'mob.' "

Turning back to the jury and continuing to read from his prepared statement, Patton said: "The crowd of people that had been in the front had moved to the back to the alley. The trouble started almost immediately. As a result, or the result of some preconceived plan, the prisoner escaped."

With a wave of his hand in the general direction of the defendants, he continued: "The defendants were present in the alley and actively engaged in aiding and abetting an assault on the officers. During that assault Sheriff Carmichael was killed by means of a pistol fired from the hand or hands of some of these defendants or by someone who was present in that crowd. At least two other officers were wounded."

With that, Patton seemed to lose his place momentarily. After an awkward moment he continued: "That's what happened, gentlemen, and we will prove every word of it right here from this witness stand. Thank you for your attention."

The defense was prepared for a long trial and had assumed that a long opening statement would be delivered by the state. When Patton resumed his seat after barely ten minutes before the jury, the defense table buzzed with whispered conversations.

Simms stood and addressed the court. "Your Honor, I wonder if we might have a five-minute recess to confer on the advisability of reserving our opening statement until the close of the prosecution's case?"

Thinking it unlikely that they would pass on the opportunity to address the jury early in the case, Judge McGhee nevertheless said: "I do not want to get into the habit of delaying this trial by short recesses, but I suppose your request is reasonable given the celerity of the prosecution's opening. Five minutes, gentlemen. Members of the jury, I will ask you to remain in the courtroom for this brief recess. These lawyers can step out into the hall and gab a bit, and then we will be back in here to continue the trial. Don't make any decisions yet and don't talk about what has happened this far in the case. I will be telling you that over and over as the case moves on."

Without waiting for the bailiff to announce his leaving the bench, Judge McGhee stepped out of his chair and through the door directly behind his bench. It looked like part of the woodwork. You only realized it was a door when the judge came in or out.

Out in the hallway Simms, Woodward, and Wheaton Augur burst into comment all at once. " 'Celerity'—my, oh my, what a wonderful little word," mused Wheaton. "Wherever do you suppose he got onto that one?"

"I expect he used it because he wanted to send a signal to us that the jury wouldn't get," said Simms. "That was the shortest opening I've ever heard, and it tells me something real important, but I'd like to hear from you-all first."

Hugh Woodward was quick to respond. Augur was just as quick to defer. Wheaton had no real grasp for tactics like this and was glad that Simms and Woodward were in the lead on this case.

Woodward, with the confidence of a former prosecutor, said: "John, they're still unsure how the evidence will shake out and are holding back on their real theory because of it. If they were certain of their witnesses, we would have heard direct reference to hard evidence. For damn sure, if they had the ballistics on the murder gun, they would have nailed it down right then and there. I'm starting to think that the famous Frank Powers didn't wrap this case up for them after all."

Simms listened but shook his head in a questioning manner while he analyzed Hugh's thesis. "Well, you might be right, Hugh, but even if you are, it doesn't help us make the decision on whether to give our opening statement now or to hold off till they rest their case. Seems to me that they might have trouble placing some of our men at the actual shooting by someone other than Dee Roberts. If that's their problem, then we can't commit to a defense plan till we know the strength of their eyewitness testimony. Placing our men at the scene is one thing; attributing shooting to them is something else altogether. So it seems to me that whether their case is shy on ballistics or on eyewitness finger-pointing, we'd best hold up on the opening statement. Agreed?"

Establishing a pattern that would last throughout the whole trial, Woodward agreed, Augur deferred, and Mr. La Follette simply listened without appearing to reject or accept the proposition before the defense "team." As for the young men from Wall Street, they weren't expected to comment and so did not.

After the judge returned to the bench, this time with a proper announcement by the bailiff of, "All rise. His Honor, Judge McGhee, presiding," Simms announced: "The defense will reserve its opening statement for the commencement of its case as soon as the state has given its evidence to the jury."

Disguising his surprise well, Judge McGhee said: "Thank you, Mr. Simms. The state may call its first witness."

"Your Honor, the prosecution wishes to call Dr. P. L. Travers to the stand," said David Chavez, looking relieved to be finally getting this case out of the conference room and into the courtroom. As is always the case, everyone craned their necks to the back of the room to see the witness, whoever he might be, enter the courtroom.

Ironically, everyone but the defendants knew Doc Travers on sight. He was a well-known physician in western New Mexico, but his regular practice didn't include miners, who had little English and even less money.

Dr. Travers took the oath and assumed the witness stand with the same ease he attended bereaved families after a surgical death. He looked calm and collected even though everyone around him was on edge. He looked at the defense table and nodded to Wheaton Augur and then to the prosecution table, where he nodded in a familiar fashion at Chavez and Carmody. He then turned his attention to David Chavez, the district attorney for the First Judicial District.

For his part, David Chavez also waited for Dr. Travers to settle in so that the jury wouldn't be distracted and would focus in on this important if somewhat dry testimony. "Dr. Travers, our jury would kindly appreciate your stating your qualifications to practice medicine. Would you please state your education and your medical training as well as your current practice?"

At this point John Simms rose and began to speak before the witness could begin his answer. "Your Honor, the defense is perfectly willing, in the interest of saving time, to stipulate to Dr. Travers's qualifications and training and will say on the record that he is qualified to offer expert medical opinion on the work he did in this case."

"Very well, Mr. Simms," the judge noted, "we will dispense with qualifying the good doctor. Dr. Travers, you may proceed with your testimony without stating all your degrees and such, although I am sure it would have been most interesting."

"But Your Honor," Chavez interjected, "we believe the jury will benefit from knowing just how well trained and how experienced Dr. Travers is and would like to have him explain this to the jury so that they will know he is, indeed, an expert."

Judge McGhee was somewhat unkind in saying: "Mr. Chavez, the defense has stipulated; I have ruled. Move on."

"Very well, Your Honor. Dr. Travers, did you perform an autopsy on the body of one C. R. Carmichael in Gallup, New Mexico, on or about the fourth day of April of this year?"

Once again, in anticipation of evidence that wasn't helpful, Mr. Simms offered his assistance to the court. "Your Honor, we have stipulated to the written report of Dr. Travers's autopsy on Sheriff Carmichael. Perhaps we should have a bench conference with the possible goal of stipulating to all of Dr. Travers's purported testimony, and he can be on his way back to Gallup, where his patients, no doubt, are awaiting his attention."

Using his hand to motion down the rising David Chavez, Judge McGhee said with a wry smile: "Well, now, that is kind of you, but the state has a right to offer testimony in support of the written autopsy report, and I may have some questions of my own for Dr. Travers after his examination by the state. Mr. Chavez, you may proceed with your examination."

"Yes, I did the autopsy at Rollie Mortuary in Gallup on April 4, 1935. As noted in my report, the first thing I did was to extract a .45-caliber bullet from the sheriff's shoulder wound. You see, I thought this was important because . . ."

Dr. Travers spent another thirty minutes on the witness stand but only managed to make three points clear to the jury: The bullet he extracted from the sheriff's shoulder wound was the one marked in court as Exhibit 3. The sheriff's other wound was from a bullet, which entered his cheek and went out through his neck; it was not recovered. The official cause of death for Sheriff M. R. Carmichael was "bullet wounds." As the doctor put it: "His death was caused as a result of bullet wounds. I would make it plural, bullet wounds. Both of them."

On cross-examination, he admitted that the entry wound for the bullet marked as Exhibit 3 was "four or five inches in the axillary line below the arm and came out at the top portion of the shoulder." That single point seemed to please the defense so much that they declined to ask any further questions.

David Chavez seemed surprised at the brevity of the cross-examination. He was reviewing his notes and didn't realize the witness was finished. Judge McGhee recognized his inattention and said kindly: "Mr. Chavez, your witness has been released; do you wish re-direct or will you be calling another witness?"

"Your Honor, the state calls Dr. Richard Pousma to the stand." And once again necks craned to the rear to watch Dr. Pousma mosey up to the witness stand. He was an affable man with a large protruding stomach and the kind of smile that put his patients at ease. But he wore no smile today. He was dressed in his best doctor suit, but it was plain that he was uncomfortable in a courtroom setting. Where Dr. Travers seemed relaxed and even eager to testify, Dr. Pousma seemed reluctant.

"Will you state your full name for our record, please?" Mr. Chavez asked.

At first the doctor seemed not to hear and then answered so quickly that his three names all seemed to blur together: "My name is Richard Hedtema Pousma."

"Thank you, Dr. Pousma, now tell the jury where you practice medicine."

"I practice at the Rehoboth Mission just east of Gallup. I have been the primary physician there for many years. You might say I have devoted my life to caring for our Indian brothers, both physically and spiritually."

With this, Chavez turned and spoke directly to John Simms: "Will the defense offer the same stipulation with respect to this medical witness? It will shorten my examination."

John Simms followed the same two rules of courtroom etiquette in place throughout the country. He never addressed his opponent in open court and he never addressed the court without standing first. He rose and said to the judge: "Your Honor, I will be most pleased to offer the state a similar stipulation. The defense will accept the avowal of the state that this man is a licensed physician and that his medical opinions are based on his medical education and training. However, we hope that our cooperation does not suggest any license on the part of the doctor to offer opinions not specifically called for by the state or us."

As if on cue, Judge McGhee turned to Dr. Pousma. "Doctor, the defense has generously stipulated to your credentials as a physician and to your expertise in medical matters. But since you are not often seen in courtrooms, let me take this opportunity to caution you to limit your testimony to the specific question asked of you by one or the others of these lawyers here. It is not helpful if you decide to blurt out something that you think medically interesting but that I might have to rule is legally inadmissible. Now, sir, give us the best answers you can. You may proceed, Mr. Chavez, and the record will reflect the stipulation of counsel establishing the expertise and qualifications of Dr. Pousma."

"Doctor, were you in your hospital on the fourth of April, this year?"

"I was."

"Did you attend to gunshot wounds that day?"

"I did."

"Whose wounds did you attend to?"

"Bobcat's wounds."

"That would be Deputy L. E. Wilson, a man also known as Bobcat?"

"Not sure about the L. E. part, but I knew him as Bobcat. He was a deputy for sure."

Dr. Pousma wasn't on the stand as long as Dr. Travers but managed to make as many points for the state's case. He had extracted a .45-caliber bullet from Bobcat Wilson. It was marked in evidence as Exhibit 4. He confirmed that Bobcat had been brought to the Rehoboth Mission hospital in "great agony." He described the bullet as having gone through the upper part of the lung, broken the fourth rib one-inch from the spinal column, and dropped down to the level of the ninth rib, where it was extracted twelve days after the riot. The operation was very dangerous, and no one expected Bobcat to live through it because the bullet was lodged very close to the spinal column.

The cross-examination wasn't just short. It was pointed. John Simms asked: "Bobcat Wilson didn't die, did he? He was right here this morning, wasn't he? Sworn in at the same time as you, right, sir?"

"Yes, sir."

This time Simms looked squarely at the jury and said: "Got well?"

Dr. Pousma's answer was equally pointed: "Yes, sir."

That seemed to be just what Simms wanted, and he closed his examination of Dr. Pousma with: "Well, thank you very much, Doctor, you have been most helpful. That is all I have for this witness, Your Honor."

Judge McGhee took out his large gold pocket watch and popped the lid; he seemed to study it for a long while and then said: "Well, it's too early to quit, and we want our jury to hear as much of the case as we can before supper time. Do you have another short witness we can put on for about an hour or so, Mr. Chavez?"

David Chavez seemed puzzled at the question, as though it had never occurred to him that they might quit for the day since it was only three o'clock. "Yes, of course, Your Honor. The state will call John Kilner."

Mr. Kilner was the city surveyor for Gallup. He testified regarding the maps and drawings that would be used in the trial to depict the alley running between Second and Third Streets to the rear of the Sutherland Building and the

Odd Fellows Hall. His testimony was entirely mechanical since all he was really doing was laying the foundation for the eyewitness testimony that was coming up. He introduced the big wooden model made by Mr. William P. Henderson of Santa Fe. The model was four by six feet in size and over a foot high. It portrayed everything to scale, including the buildings, alleys, fences, and telegraph poles, all in color as they looked on the day of the riot. Some of it was made of clay, and all of it was very realistic.

On cross-examination, Mr. Kilner clarified that there were actually two ways you could reach the alley behind Judge Bickel's court. Just east of the Sutherland Building was a vacant lot that ran from the alley to Coal Avenue. Just west of the Sutherland Building was the office building where Judge Bickel held court. Mr. Kilner admitted there was free access through the vacant lot on the east side or up Third Street to the alley on the west side.

When Mr. Kilner left the stand, Judge McGhee announced that they would take the midafternoon recess. After the break, David Chavez announced: "Your Honor, the state will call Gregorio Romero to the stand. Good afternoon, sir, will you tell the jury your name and your place of residence?"

"My name is Gregorio Romero, I am fifty-nine years old, and I have lived in Gallup for about twenty-nine years."

The prosecutor wanted to capture the jury's attention after the last three technical witnesses. He asked: "Did you know the Velarde brothers down there?"

"Yes, I know Leandro, who's sitting over there on the bench with the other defendants. I also knew his brother Sena, God rest his soul."

"You said Sena—was that short for Ignacio?"

"I guess it was; we all just called him Sena."

"Did you know any of the other defendants in this case?"

"Sure, I knew some of them, including the one on the end, Mr. Joe Bartol."

"Did you know these men as a result of your job?"

"Well, maybe. I'm the manager of the Spanish-American Hall in Gallup. I already told everyone about the meeting that took place at the hall back on April 3, 1935. That was the day before the trouble in the alley."

As it turned out, Mr. Romero couldn't identify Juan Ochoa; he said Sena Velarde rented the hall. He couldn't identify Agustin Calvillo; he said he knew the other defendants by sight, but they weren't there at the meeting "the day before the trouble."

When Simms said, "No further questions, Your Honor," the prosecutor made a quick decision not to re-direct his witness. He motioned the witness off the stand and said: "Next we would like to call Patricino Chavez."

As Mr. Chavez was escorted to the witness stand by the bailiff the jury could see his nervous look at the long bench where the defendants were sitting. Everyone wondered if this was going to be a witness who would finally have something to say about the shooting of the sheriff. His nervousness made him anticipate the questions. His answers sounded like he was reading from a script. It was as if he ignored the questions and just gave the answers that had been planned for him.

"I am fifty-seven years old. I have lived in Gallup for more than fifteen years. Sure, I was there at the meeting at the Spanish-American Hall on April 3, 1935. I guess there were about fifty or sixty men at the meeting. The ones I saw there were Juan Ochoa, Leandro Velarde, and Joe Bartol. Juan Ochoa was the chairman of the meeting. Sure, Juan spoke a lot at the meeting. But I never heard Joe Bartol say anything there. At this meeting it was agreed by all of us to name a committee so we could know the results about the prisoner Navarro. He was in jail, and we wanted to find out why. The committee included Leandro Velarde, Joe Bartol, and a Negro by the name of Cutoff. Bill Cuton. The committee went to the sheriff's office. That's all I know, as I told him [pointing to someone at the prosecution table] before."

Woodward looked at Simms as David Chavez announced that was all they had for this witness. Simms shook his head; Woodward smiled, nodded, and said, without getting up from his chair: "We have no further questions for this man, Judge."

Woodward's casual approach in the courtroom irritated Judge McGhee, but he let it pass and turned to the prosecution table and said: "Well, fine, call the next one."

"If it please the court, we will call Hoy Boggess." When the attorney general of New Mexico rose to make that announcement, it caused a wide stir in the courtroom. Even the men at the defense table seemed to sit up a little straighter in their chairs. The audience went alternatively noisy and then quickly quiet as they anticipated not only an eyewitness to the shooting but also a man who was assaulted during the shooting. Now we're getting somewhere, they thought. They were half right.

Mr. Patton began his direct examination with the usual: "Tell these good men on the jury your name, your age, and where you live."

"My name is Hoy. Hoy Boggess. I live in Gallup, and, what else, oh yes; I'm thirty-seven years of age. Did you want to know how long I've been there?"

"Yes, thank you, Mr. Boggess, or, I should say, Deputy Boggess," Patton said, more to the jury than to the witness.

This seemed to embarrass the witness because he said: "Well, I ain't a regular deputy. I have a commission, leastwise I did then. But anyhow, I been there for sixteen years."

"We'll come back to that later in the trial, but right now we want the jury to hear your version of what happened on the morning of April 4, 1935, in Gallup. Now, sir, were you part of the sheriff's group of men on duty that morning?"

"Yes, I was. I helped them take the prisoner Navarro from the county jail to the JP court, and I was beaten up in the riot that took place when we tried to take the prisoner back to jail by using the alley behind the Sutherland Building."

Woodward interrupted without getting out of his chair at the end of the defense table: "Judge, we cannot object to this man's testimony unless he waits for a question to be asked. He's volunteering things that are not being asked about yet."

Before the judge could rule on this objection, Frank Patton jumped in. "Judge, we are only calling this witness at this time for the purpose of identifying the defendants under the statutes of New Mexico. This is a limited calling; we will recall him later on the factual events of the day, but I will caution the witness to restrict his answers to the questions that I put to him."

Judge McGhee frowned again at both Woodward and Patton and said: "Well, get on with it, then."

The attorney general returned his focus to the witness and said: "Were you on duty at the jail the day before Navarro's hearing?"

"Yes, sir, I was there when that committee came up and demanded the release of—"

Again Woodward reacted. "Now, Mr. Attorney General, I thought we just dealt with this. You said this was statutory identification only and—"

Judge McGhee interrupted and made his displeasure real clear: "You two had best stop talking to each other. Your remarks are to be directed to the court from a standing position." Turning to the witness, he said: "Mr. Boggess, I want you to answer whatever question one of the lawyers puts to you, but you seem to want to add something else. That can only come in evidence when you are asked about it." Turning his frown to the prosecution table, he said: "I will give you a short recess so you can caution your witness or you can proceed, Mr. Attorney General."

"Thank you, Your Honor, but I believe we can finish this part up quickly, and we will meet with the witness before he is recalled. Now, Mr. Boggess, we are only going to ask you about who was there and what, generally, was the subject of the meeting. Let's start by asking you simply to identify the men who came to the jail the day before the shooting."

Boggess identified Bill Cuton, a Mrs. Trujillo, and the younger Velarde boy.

"What was the subject of the meeting at the jail, as you understood it?"

"Well, they said that they demanded the immediate release of Navarro, and Mr. Carmichael rejected, saying he couldn't do that."

Mr. Patton seemed surprised and followed up with: "Was that it?"

"No, then they asked the sheriff when the trial would be. Sheriff Carmichael told them the trial would be the following morning at nine o'clock. Sheriff Carmichael said it would be at Judge Bickel's courtroom."

"Did you hear any of the defendants in this courtroom say anything to Sheriff Carmichael at this meeting?"

"No, but then this Mrs. Trujillo spoke up, saying that they would like to talk to Navarro, and Mr. Carmichael rejected again, saying that they would have plenty of time after the trial to talk to him."

Before Woodward could again object to the witness volunteering information, Frank Patton said: "Thank you, Mr. Boggess."

Woodward began his cross-examination from his cane-back chair, which squeaked a bit as he rocked it back and forth. "At the time of this meeting you have been talking about, you had Navarro as a prisoner back there in your jail, right?

"Yes, he was arrested and jailed some days earlier."

"Did he have a bond fixed at the time of his arrest?"

"I don't know, but I suppose he might of."

"Did you see it?"

"No."

"But as an officer of the law, you do know that bond has to be fixed on the warrant under the statutes of New Mexico?"

"I didn't know that."

Woodward paused, looked down at his writing pad, and said: "No more questions, Judge, but we'll want to cross him some more after he is recalled."

"Well," said Judge McGhee with a smile, "this is a good time for a break. Ten minutes." As the first row of spectators tried to get up, he was gone through his little door.

During the break, the prosecution hurriedly reviewed the status of their evidence thus far in the trial. "We've got both meetings in evidence, most of who was there, and their unlawful purpose," said the district attorney.

"Not hardly," replied Dick Modrall. "We have a foundation laid, but no overt act and damn few connections to the defendant group, except maybe Velarde. We got a start, but we need to caution our witnesses about jumping in with their own comments. It's not the facts I'm worried about. It's the conclusions they might come up with. We don't need a mistrial, and this judge isn't one to fool with."

You could set your watch by Judge McGhee. He said ten minutes, and he meant it. Half the courtroom was vacant when the bailiff rushed back in, out of breath, just to call out the "All rise for His Honor . . ." The judge darted in, sat down, and more or less interrupted his own bailiff with: "Call your next witness, please."

Already at a standing position, Mr. Chavez said: "We call Fred Montoya. How old are you, sir?" he asked when the witness was seated.

"I'm thirty-two."

Mr. Montoya went on to explain to the jury that he wasn't a regular salaried deputy, but he did have a sheriff's commission. He was working with Hoy Boggess on April 3, 1935, when some people came to see the sheriff about the prisoner, Navarro.

Montoya said: "Dominica Hernandez and Mrs. Anita Trujillo and Charlie Cuton came in. There were four of them. Charlie Martinez was the fourth one. Also, Perfecto Garcia was there, and Leandro Velarde, and Herman Velarde. Ignacio Velarde was not there."

Since very little new evidence came in through Mr. Montoya, Simms rose and addressed the court: "Your Honor, we will pass on this witness for the moment but might want to cross-examine him when he is recalled by the state."

Judge McGhee consulted his oversized railroad watch. When he snapped the lid closed, he turned to the jury and said: "Now, gentlemen, you are all sequestered, but sometimes it's tempting to talk to one another out of the court about what you heard here today. We all want you to keep an open mind. You can't let yourself be influenced by what anyone says who is not a witness in the case. So find something else to talk about over at the church till this case is finished. You'll have to skip the paper in the morning. Just keep an open mind. I'll see all of you in the morning at nine-thirty, but you lawyers had best come in a little early so we can talk about tomorrow's schedule."

With that, he spun his high-back chair around and disappeared through that disappearing door before the slow-moving bailiff could gavel them all to rise up for His Honor's leaving.

I spent the first evening with Bobcat and the second with Mary Ann. Bobcat's view of the first two days was simple, as usual. "I'll tell you all what happened—nothin'. Nothin' interesting, anyhow. About all they did was make an opening argument that was hardly an argument at all." To his way of thinking, the opening of a trial ought to be something like fire in your belly, like you took a shot of Guido Zecca's private grappa. Bobcat was particularly irritated that "the" attorney general didn't seem to know how to get to the gut of the jury right away so that the stage could be set for giving those red rascals the shock of their lives.

As Bobcat saw it, the defense sat on their hands and didn't even bother to give their opening. This, as you probably already guessed, caused our first argument of the trial. What was the defense doing? Were they playing it close to the vest and just waiting for a mistake, or was it just that they had nothing to say, seeing as how they must know their clients are goddamn guilty as sin?

And another thing, he said, "This business of stopping all the time so that the interpreter could catch up and tell it in español was a hell of a way to run a trial. If the AT&SF had of run their railroad that way, they would have only made it to Kansas by now and Gallup wouldn't exist." Like most lawmen, Bobcat had friends and relatives whose first tongue was Spanish. Most lawmen spoke some Spanish; at least they could cuss in it. What intrigued Mary Ann was the fact that the trial started off with the two docs who dug out the two bullets out of Sheriff Mack and Bobcat. On the one hand, it seemed a miracle that Bobcat lived, to hear Doc Pousma tell it. Her neat little notes reminded her that the bullet was within an inch of his spine, and it tore up a lot of his intestines getting there. That started the talk once again about why in the world Bobcat was so damn shy about the details of the shooting. Dee Roberts wasn't shy about his telling of it. Even old Fred Montoya was happy to regale any and all with his part.

So why was Bobcat so private about it? I reminded her that Bobcat wasn't all that public about anything. He might kick your ass, but he wouldn't go around bragging about it. Maybe this was just his way. Maybe he was saving it up for when it was more important, like when it would help to send "those red rascals to the death house."

"Billy Wade, you are succumbing to the base nature of the barrooms in Gallup. You don't really mean that, do you?"

"No, I'm just posing the issue in terms the conservative jurors here in Aztec might use."

"Getting back to the trial witnesses, the state seems intent on getting in evidence all those bullets that the doctors removed from Bobcat and Sheriff Mack. Why is that important?"

"I'm not sure, but it does raise again the speculation about just exactly which gun was used to gun down the sheriff. Hoy Boggess is still hopping mad about losing his, and as far as the defense knows, it never did turn up. Since the prosecution is so hot on getting those bullets in evidence, I'm curious as to how they're going to connect them to Hoy's gun if that gun was never tested. Dee had his and Bobcat had his and Fred wasn't armed that morning."

Bobcat fussed about the fact that the longest witness of the day was John Kilner. "Who gives a rat's ass about how wide the alley is or just how many feet it was from the *Gallup Independent* back door to the old post office? Goddamn it, killing occurred in the alley, and that was all that anyone on that jury needed to know."

Tuesday, October 8, 1935

Dear Journal:

Two days ago—Sunday, October 6, 1935—I came here to Aztec, New Mexico, to attend a trial. That's right, a trial. I am observing the trial of the ten men accused of killing our sheriff in Gallup last April. Although the trial began on Monday morning, nothing really happened until today. The judge and the lawyers wasted two precious days posturing and parading around the courtroom in a horribly inefficient process called "voir dire." After two days of inane questions and less than credible answers, twelve ordinary men were selected to sit on the jury. They might just as well have drawn numbers out of a hat (some man's hat, of course).

It was not the beginning I envisioned, and it seemed to disappoint everyone except the lawyers and the judge. Perhaps they weren't disappointed because they're used to such formality and lack of drama or action of any kind. There must be a reason for that, but it seemed to escape most of the rest of us throughout the day.

Judge McGhee seems to me to be a man very concerned about what Billy Wade calls "due process." I have heard Billy Wade go on for hours about how important it is that a person accused of a crime is given "due process of law." Since I'm not a lawyer, I'm not sure of everything that entails. But just from teaching high school civics, I know it starts with the basic idea that the trial has to be conducted in a way that is fair to you, not just fair to the lawyers and the jurors and the witnesses. In this trial the lawyers, jurors, and witnesses seem to be a lot more important than the ten scared men who sit, more or less ignored, behind the defense table. I say this because Judge McGhee says kind things to the lawyers, and the lawyers show great deference to the jurors. For their part, the jurors show great interest in the witnesses and seem curious about the crowd and even the court staff. But my point is that no one seems to care about or pay any attention to the men who are the defendants in this trial.

My impressions are probably quite unfair because they are based on only one real day of the trial (not counting waiting in an empty courtroom on Monday morning and the so-called voir dire for the rest of the first two days). Even with live witnesses today, we didn't get very far. It seems that due process has more to do with the way the trial is conducted than the way the men on trial are treated. Does that make any sense to you?

The process by which this jury was chosen was most strange. Rather than find out about how they really felt about these men and the crime they are charged with, the process called voir dire seems designed to find out about broad attitudes on high-minded subjects but very little about the real problems that will come up in this case. For example, they spent a lot of time asking for views on the death penalty, as though guilt was assumed and it was only the penalty that anyone was interested in. They also seemed to almost fixate on what the jurors knew from newspapers or some other source about the facts of the case. Of course, no one told the jurors just what the facts were that they might have read about, so it was like asking someone if they had read a book not yet written. Besides, what difference does it make what they have read? Isn't the real question how they feel about these men? All the men in the jury pool, or at least most of them, said they could be fair and open-minded. That's very nice and all that, but please, what did you think they would say?

None of the men picked for the jury seemed to know much about hunger, or sick children, or the despair of not being able to provide for your family. None of them seemed to be at all interested in the fact that the men on trial were there, in part at least, because of their political beliefs. In fact, the men picked to be on the jury seemed remarkably lacking in social conscience or a political focus of any kind. Is this really supposed to be a jury of one's peers? I guess they're someone's peers, but aren't they supposed to be peers of the men on trial, not the men who arrested them?

After the voir dire part, the attorney general made his opening remarks to the jury. He was introduced as the attorney general, and everyone seemed to be impressed with the title. Good thing he had an impressive title because his opening statement wasn't something to write home about. Believe it or not, he actually read a statement that was obviously written by someone else. He even lost his place at the end and just sort of sat down.

I have heard so much about John Simms from Billy Wade that I was very eager to hear his opening statement. You can imagine my disappointment when he announced that the defense would reserve its opening statement until after all the evidence was put in the case by the prosecution. But while I was disappointed, I kept remembering what a great lawyer he is, and so I started thinking about why he did that. There must be a reason. I just can't fathom it at the moment. Is the jury also spending this evening like me, trying to figure out just what the reason might be?

Maybe Mr. Simms thought the attorney general just didn't do much to start the case. Billy Wade says the state has the burden of proof on the whole case. Maybe the defense thinks they should just keep quiet for as long as they can. Maybe that's good legal strategy; I don't know. Maybe I should put myself in the shoes of the jury. Now, there's a thought. Can I really put myself in their shoes? Can I look at the case the way they are? Should I? These are weighty things, and I wish I had my father here. He'd know. I do miss you, Dad.

Back to the opening statement, or rather the lack of it, by Mr. Simms. I think it was a mistake. I was ready to listen to him right then and there. By thinking the prosecution didn't do such a good job on their opening statement and therefore waiting a few days, they're just telling me they don't know what their defense is to the case. After all, if these men are really innocent, then it shouldn't matter what the prosecutor says. What matters is what does the defense say. So why wait? As I said, if I was on this jury, I would want to hear just why the defense believes these men should be acquitted. I know they don't have to prove their innocence. To the contrary, they don't have to prove anything. But if the prosecution drops the ball that early in the game, the defense should pick it up and run with it, right?

After the opening statement fiasco the prosecution called three witnesses, two doctors and a surveyor. That took all morning, believe it or not. For almost three hours, the doctors told us about the bullet wounds in Sheriff Mack and Bobcat, including the gory anatomical facts. The surveyor told us about the alley between Second and Third Streets and all the boring geographical facts. I suppose this is what they call "foundation." I've heard Billy Wade talk about how important it is to have a "foundation" before evidence is admissible in a court of law. Even if it's important, does that mean it has to be boring?

We learned a lot about Sheriff Mack's fatal wounds but not about how quickly he died. Could he have seen the man who shot him? I would like to have known that.

We learned a lot about Bobcat's wounds and how he survived, but nothing at all about how he felt or what he said that first day at the hospital. Did he know Sheriff Mack was hit before him? Was the bullet that hit him the one that went through Sheriff Mack's face? Isn't this important? Why didn't anyone ask him?

However, to be fair, the medical testimony did make it clear that the bullets removed from Sheriff Mack and Bobcat were carefully preserved, and I sense they are important to how this case turns out. The doctors also made it clear that Sheriff Mack could have died as a result of either one of his wounds, and that could be important if he was shot by more than one person. It's curious that if this is the case, that is, two people shot him, the attorney general didn't bring this out in his opening statement. If this isn't the case, then why did he spend so much time getting the doctor to say that either wound could have killed him? Is it important or not? That is the question I'm left with.

It seems to me that if, God forbid, I was a lawyer trying an important case like this one, I would want the jurors to have answers, not questions, after the first real day of the trial. Perhaps tomorrow will be different.

Oh, I learned something else very interesting today that will make my self-assigned role as a journalist much easier. I was fascinated by the ease with which the court reporter took every single word down in shorthand in a little spiral notebook. So, since I was trying to keep track myself of the testimony of the witnesses as well as the judge's comments and stuff, I decided to ask her for a few tips after the trial. Well, she couldn't give me any, but she did tell me that she would be making up a typed transcript of every word uttered in the courtroom. It seems obvious to everyone that if these men are convicted, there will be an appeal; that's why she will make a typed transcript.

If they are acquitted, then there will be no appeal because the state can't do that. I didn't know the state couldn't appeal; I thought anyone had a right to appeal, but Billy Wade told me that the court reporter was right. It seems they can't appeal because the jury gets the last word on "innocence." But they don't get the last word on "guilt." If the jury decides these men are guilty, they have the right to ask the Supreme Court to check the record and see if there was enough evidence to sustain a guilty verdict. They can also appeal if they think the judge messed up somehow. Apparently in murder cases there is always an appeal from a guilty verdict.

Now, where was I? Oh yes, the importance of the court reporter's transcript. It means that I won't have to make this journal exactly accurate, if you know what I mean. I can concentrate on the important things, like how things feel and what's right and stuff like that. I can ignore things like facts and the actual words used by a witness and the legal rulings that Billy Wade defends so vigorously. Speaking of Billy Wade, I'm glad he's here. This trial isn't about justice or the law; it's about revenge and politics. I just hope I can record my thoughts well enough to be able to explain to my students what really happened up here in Aztec.

Of course, that assumes something really is going to happen. So far, the prosecutors (and there sure are a whole bunch of them) have put on six witnesses (all men, wouldn't you know), and none of them have said a word about the shooting in the alley. The doctors talked about wounds and bullets, and the surveyor talked about feet and inches. The other three were officers of the law, but they seemed to be afraid to talk about the real story here. For example, they didn't say anything about fear or pain or dying. Not a word about the passion of political belief or the despair of losing your home or the gnawing feeling of helplessness that comes from being out of work for a long time.

I wonder if the defense team of lawyers (all men, too) is going to do anything to humanize this case. I hope they don't leave it up to me. Good night, Madam Journal.

Postscript—Is one allowed to write postscripts in a journal? If so, well, here goes. (If not, I'll edit this out later.) This journal began as a sort of commentary about my town, my views of it, and my sense of the larger picture of how Gallup is treating itself (and being treated) over the ordeal of the sheriff's death and the trial of those ten forsaken men in the courtroom. But I'm feeling somewhat introspective, as though this journal and the compulsion to write in it needs to hear from me about me. Does that make sense? Do I need to talk to myself as well as my students and whoever else in the world might read this? The thought of writing about my insecurity is unsettling. Maybe postscripts aren't allowed for good reason. I'll sleep on it.

seven

HOY'S GUN

Wednesday, October 9, 1935

The lawyers and their clients were ready in the courtroom for the start of the second day of the trial. Judge McGhee came to the side door in the courtroom and motioned his bailiff to come into the hallway. "Get the lawyers and have them come see me in chambers for a minute."

A call to chambers was usually not something to cheer about during a trial. More than likely, someone was about to get chewed on. With Judge McGhee, that was rare because he was a gentleman's judge all the way. Nevertheless, he did have his standards.

As the lawyers took their previously picked chairs, Judge McGhee said: "Now, men, you are all experienced trial lawyers, and so you've disappointed me some with your bickering among yourselves yesterday. I trust we won't see any more of that. I also trust that you know that objections to evidence are to be made on your feet. I do not cotton to sitting objections. It looks disrespectful to the audience and makes you look bad to your jury. But I don't want to make too much of it. What I really wanted to find out was how we're doing on timing and scheduling. It seems like you boys covered a lot of ground yesterday, and I am surely grateful for that. Are we going to run out of witnesses today, or have you got enough lined up?"

Modrall spoke for the prosecution. "Judge, we did indeed move rapidly yesterday, and that makes me happy as well. Our second witness this morning will be a lawyer. So you know he might not be all that quick, given the lawyer's natural predilection to verbosity. Besides, Mr. Lyle is about the only Gallup lawyer not involved as trial counsel, and he needs to be heard from just to stay in business. I think he'll be our longest witness of the day."

Since they were in chambers without the court reporter or other court staff,

Judge McGhee loosened up a bit. "Well, damn. Here I was giving you all some attaboys for getting seven witnesses on in one day; now here you go calling a lawyer to the stand. That might get you an awe-shit if he takes up the whole afternoon."

The lawyers returned to the courtroom in good humor but put on their adversarial masks as soon as they got to their respective tables.

"All rise, His Honor, Judge Edward E. McGhee, presiding in the case of the State of New Mexico versus Ochoa and others," intoned the bailiff as everyone scrambled to their feet while the judge opened the little door, stepped in, and sat down. The oak floors creaked and the bottoms of the cane-back chairs squeaked as everyone tried to quiet down at once. As that was happening, Judge McGhee set the tone for the rest of the trial.

"Good morning, gentlemen of the jury, counsel, and all you good folks in the audience. We're going to start the testimony in just a moment, but I thought it best to make sure something is straight in your minds. These men here are on trial for their lives. Since not all of them speak English, we have to have an interpreter translate the testimony for them into Spanish. That slows things down a bit, and I noticed yesterday that some of you started your own little conversations during the translation. While I'm sure that nobody meant anything by it, I also saw a snicker or two during the day. Now, as I said, these men are on trial for their lives. There is nothing funny about the fact that what happened down in Gallup resulted in the death of three men and the incarceration and possible execution of ten others. So you all get your snickering done outside the courtroom. If I hear one rude sound from any of you, I will clear this courtroom. Now, Mr. Patton, is your next witness ready?"

The lawyers for both sides very much appreciated the judge's comment. All of them found it somewhat awkward to put a question to the witness, get an answer, and then wait for the translation into Spanish before moving on to the next question. But they understood how important it was that this trial be conducted in a way that no one could say New Mexico wasn't fair to its defendants, whether or not they were citizens.

The lawyers had been a little embarrassed yesterday when someone in the back rudely snorted or grumbled, suggesting that the translation was either not necessary or not accurate.

The other thing they liked about Judge McGhee's start-of-the-morning comment was that it showed, as if there was ever a doubt, just who, by God, was in charge in this courtroom. Judge McGhee wasn't worried about Dick Modrall or

John Simms, the two principal trial lawyers. But he didn't yet know what role those other men, the ones from back east, might be playing in this trial.

Frank Patton, responding to the judge's question, said: "The state calls A. G. Aldrich as its next witness. By whom are you employed, Mr. Aldrich?"

"I am a Deputy Special Officer for the United States Indian Service, stationed in Gallup, New Mexico."

"Are you a native of Gallup, sir?"

"No, but I have lived there for forty of my forty-seven years, so I might as well be."

"Are you considered a law enforcement officer, Mr. Aldrich?"

"Yes, but my jurisdiction is limited to tribal members and crimes or misdemeanors committed on all the different Indian reservations that surround Gallup."

The prosecution clearly had a more articulate witness to deal with at this point. The spectators sensed that this man might have some interesting testimony but were uncertain just how the U.S. Indian Service played a role in what all thought was a municipal problem.

"Did you have occasion to be in Judge Bickel's court on the morning of April 4, 1935?"

"Yes, sir, I was there as the case officer for the judicial proceeding that was scheduled to take place before the Navarro hearing that morning."

"How was it that your hearing was being conducted before a New Mexico justice of the peace?"

"That is a common question we get. You see, Judge Bickel was known to us as Commissioner Bickel. He held a dual appointment as a state justice of the peace and as a federal United States court commissioner. At my request he had scheduled a nine o'clock hearing on a check charge, a federal charge. I was there along with Mr. Albert, who was a federal Secret Service agent, and an Indian boy."

Allie Aldrich was the first of many witnesses for the state whose job was to identify the defendants as having been at the scene and to establish the danger posed to the lawmen by the unruly crowd. For reasons obscure to the jury and the audience but understandable to the lawyers, Chavez spent a laborious twenty minutes with Agent Aldrich establishing three points: One, the crowd on the street was noisy at first and became rowdy as time passed. Two, the lawmen were fearful for their prisoner and themselves. Three, he had no idea what happened after he left the court that morning.

"Thank you, that will be all, but the defense may have a few questions for you."

"Cross-examination, Mr. Simms?"

"Yes, thank you, Your Honor." Turning to face Mr. Aldrich and moving over toward the state's table, John Simms smiled at the witness and proceeded to establish a few little matters that Mr. Aldrich wasn't asked about by the prosecutor. Namely that Aldrich had been an undersheriff for McKinley County before he joined the federal service. He also established that the noisy crowd on the street was mostly women and kids and that none of them had clenched fists, were profane, threw anything, broke any windows, or did anything that he thought was mischief or misconduct.

"The state calls Mr. Harris Lyle to the stand."

Harris was a respected man who enjoyed a modest success as a mining lawyer. His primary emphasis was real estate law. As he walked from the anteroom to the courtroom Mary Ann reflected on how most of the state's lawyers seemed to dress alike. Starched white shirts, dark ties, even darker suits, and never a pocket-handkerchief. Lyle bowed respectfully to the judge as the clerk read him the oath.

As he took the stand I noted that his client, the Hon. C. F. Vogel, was in the audience. I wondered if he intended to observe the whole trial or only his lawyer's testimony. "Mr. Lyle," David Chavez said by way of introduction.

"Good afternoon, David." Mr. Lyle nodded cordially. Mr. Chavez covered the essential details of the land transactions that Lyle had handled for Senator Vogel. He was anxious to move to the issue of identification of the defendants. "Describe the scene as you arrived in court that morning, please."

"Certainly. Mr. Vogel came to my office, and we walked on down the half block to Mr. Bickel's office. As you know, he handles his insurance business as well as his judicial duties from that suite of offices. We got to court about nine-fifteen. Judge Bickel was holding a hearing involving Mr. Aldrich and a Navajo Indian."

"Was Sheriff Carmichael there at that time?"

"No, after we met in my office that morning, he went back to the jail to get Mr. Navarro; then I saw him again when he brought the man into the front part of Judge Bickel's court."

"I see. Who was with him then?"

"I'm sorry, do you mean who was with him in my office the first time we met that morning or when I saw him a few minutes later down at Judge Bickel's court?"

"I mean the second time, when you and Senator Vogel went to court for the Navarro hearing."

Lyle spent the next fifteen minutes making three simple points: First, there was no crowd in front when they arrived, but one gathered shortly after Carmichael got there with Navarro. Second, someone in the crowd shouted, "Goddamn Dee Roberts." Third, neither he nor Senator Vogel saw what happened in the alley when the gunfire erupted.

Hugh Woodward once again began his cross-examination from his seat at the defense table. Perhaps this was understandable given the ferocity of his first point: "Did I hear you correctly? Did you just testify that Sheriff Carmichael met you and Mr. Vogel just a few minutes before he brought Navarro to the court for the hearing?"

"Yes, you heard correctly. We met briefly to see if he needed testimony from Mr. Vogel at the hearing."

"Did you also talk about the trouble, expected trouble, that morning?"

"No, I knew nothing of that."

"All right, then, let's turn to the land transactions. I hand you Exhibits 22 and 23 and ask that you identify those for the jury."

I was very interested in Lyle's testimony about the land transactions and the legal maneuvering regarding the sale of Chihuahuaita, but I could see the jury getting bored with the detail. In essence, Harris Lyle admitted on cross-examination that Senator Vogel sued seventy-five different people in Chihuahuaita to get legal possession of the land that he held legal title to. One of the suits was against Campos, and when Campos balked, he filed a forcible detainer action against him. It was also Senator Vogel who arranged for the criminal complaint to be filed against Campos and Navarro. Harris also admitted that he knew that most of the people in the street in front of the justice court that morning were the ones he had sued for eviction from their homes in Chihuahuaita.

Lyle left the stand, and the judge called a recess.

After just a five-minute break David Chavez stated: "Your Honor, our next witness will be Mr. P. M. Griego."

As the witness took the oath from the clerk, Chavez noticed that this was a witness who spoke loud and distinctly. He even looked directly at the jury as he gave his name to the clerk for her record. Chavez decided to try to move a little faster on the preliminary matters, but as it happened, this was not the witness to jump ahead on. "Mr. Griego, as a longtime Gallup resident—" At which point the witness interrupted:

"No, sir, I live in Española now."

Acting as though nothing had happened, Chavez went on: "Yes, of course, I meant as a longtime resident as of April 4, 1935, the date I wish to discuss with you; you were living there that day, were you not?"

"Yes, I was, but I have been transferred to Española now."

"Where were you working that day?"

"I worked at Ellis Drug Company."

"Where is Ellis Drug?"

"It's right across the street on Coal Avenue," he said, pointing to the wooden model of downtown Gallup in front of the jury box.

Mr. Griego identified the two Correo boys and Rafael Gomez as having been in the street in front of the justice court. He described the scene but didn't seem to think anything was amiss. He said the crowd started to run to the corner and then down Third Street toward the alley.

"They were traveling pretty fast, kind of a trot. I heard some shots about two or three minutes after they left."

Jeez Louise, I thought. Two days of testimony, nine witnesses, and here, finally, someone admits that shots were fired.

David Chavez continued the examination. "I'll get back to the shots you heard, Mr. Griego, but first, tell the jury what you did when you saw the crowd running south on Third Street toward the alley."

Even with my limited trial experience, I groaned at this tactical blunder on the part of the prosecutors. It had taken them two days to get a witness up there to talk about the shooting in the alley; now that shooting was being relegated to second-class status in favor of yet more testimony about who was in the crowd. That seemed to me to more or less play into the hands of the defense since they were trying to establish that the whole case was really just an effort to charge men for being there, not for shooting the sheriff.

As it turned out, Mr. Griego knew very little more about where the crowd went or the shots he said he heard after the crowd went down Third Street. So Mr. Chavez passed the witness.

Judge McGhee looked puzzled but said: "Fine, it's your case to prosecute. Of course, the witness is subject to cross-examination. Who will be doing the cross?"

John Simms rose, and said: "Your Honor, if the court please, I will begin the cross."

"You may proceed, Mr. Simms."

"Mr. Griego, how long had you lived in Gallup as of April 4 of this year?"

"I had lived and worked in Gallup for many years."

"Did you work at the drugstore you mentioned for all of that time?"

"Mostly. In fact, I had known Judge Bickel for about twenty years, and I had seen people go over there to his office with cases and lawyers and witnesses many times. I had seen other crowds outside his office."

I looked around to see if the jurors caught that. Having a witness volunteer an important fact on cross-examination doesn't happen every day, even to big-time lawyers like John Simms. The next question posed to the witness was: "Did you have any understanding of why the crowd was out there that morning?"

"I didn't go over there to see why the women were making motions at the judge. I didn't hear any hollering out there."

Griego spent another ten or fifteen minutes on the stand but didn't volunteer any other helpful information for the defense. He finished his testimony by admitting that none of the defendants did anything that he could "criticize."

Simms said politely, "Thank you, sir, I have no further questions."

"Your Honor," David Chavez said, "the state calls Mrs. John Green as its next witness."

Mrs. Green took the stand hesitantly, as was expected of people not used to the formality of the courtroom. It appeared she knew the Gallup district attorney; she said "*Hola,*" to him as she was escorted to the stand by the bailiff after taking the oath from the clerk. Mrs. Green was severely dressed that morning, as if to attend a funeral. Her hair was pulled back and hardly visible under her small dark hat. She clutched her glasses in one hand and her purse in the other and struggled to get into the witness chair without being able to grab the rail in front of the witness box.

"Mrs. Green, how long have you been in Gallup?"

"I have been living there for twenty years."

"Were you there on March 29, 1935?"

At first everyone thought the district attorney had his dates wrong; up to now everyone had focused on April 4, 1935. But Mrs. Green seemed to know where the DA was going. "Yes, I already told you that."

"Look over there at the defendants, Mrs. Green, and tell the jury if you can identify anyone on that bench who you saw on March 29, 1935."

"Yes, I saw Leandro Velarde. I was talking to him at the home of Mrs. Concepción Aurelio in Chihuahuaita."

"And who else was there that day besides you and Mr. Leandro Velarde?"

"There were already four people in the house when I got there. Fred Rodarte and Concepción's father, whose name I do not know. There is another man they call Gueromo, but I don't know his name. Mrs. Aurelio was there, and so was Leandro Velarde."

"I see," said Mr. Chavez. He moved close to the witness stand to emphasize the importance of this testimony. "What did Mr. Leandro Velarde say there that day in your presence, Mrs. Green?"

"Leandro told them to prepare for the following day at eight o'clock in the morning, that they were to be ready at the house of Victor Campos." Mrs. Green stopped, as though she wished she didn't have to say what she had already said.

"Please go on, Mrs. Green; tell us the rest of what Mr. Leandro Velarde said there that day in your presence."

"He said to be ready and to let the officers take their weapons; that they didn't need anything else but a toothpick."

Sometimes courtrooms are so tense that the slightest bit of humor will cause the kind of laughter that seems irrational but serves to relieve the tension. This was one of those times as the entire audience broke out in uncontrollable laughter. But as they learned quickly enough, Judge McGhee would countenance no one laughing at a witness in his court. He boomed out in a voice louder than anyone thought he had: "There will be no more laughing. The next person who breaks out laughing will go out. We are not running a show for any spectators. If you can't control yourselves, retire at this time."

"Mrs. Green, please listen carefully before you answer this question," David Chavez continued. "Did Mr. Leandro say anything about Sheriff Mack Carmichael?"

"He said the first one they wanted to get was the deceased, Carmichael. You know, the first one they wanted to get hold of was Carmichael."

"Did he say why they wanted to get Carmichael?"

"Because he had a feeling against Carmichael and Carmichael had a feeling against him."

Recognizing an age-old tenet of trial practice wisdom, i.e., quit when you're ahead, Chavez did just that. Turning to the defense table he said: "Your witness, Counsel."

Contrary to the ferocious attack with which he started his cross on the last witness, Mr. Woodward waited a full minute before he put his first question to Mrs. Green. When he did, he sounded more like a traveling salesman knocking on her door than her cross-examiner. "Well, good morning, Mrs. Green; my name is Hugh Woodward. Could I ask you a few questions about that meeting at the home of, what was her name, Concepción Aurelio?"

Mrs. Green politely answered Mr. Woodward's polite questions. She explained that Concepción was not "her" name—it was "his" name, that is, it was the husband of Maria Louisa Aurelio. Her husband was a constable in Gallup, and she went to the sheriff's office to report the conversation she overhead because her husband *told her to.* She admitted that she didn't know much about the conversation going on at her friend's house but repeated that the Spanish word used by Leandro was *pica diente* and that she understood it to mean toothpick.

David Chavez unwisely elected to pose some questions to Mrs. Green on redirect examination. After explaining that she was of Spanish and German descent and that she was not from Old Mexico, she insisted that the word she used in the private interview with Chavez before the trial was *pica diente* and that it definitely meant tooth, not ice pick. The significance of the difference between toothpicks and ice picks was lost on the jury but seemed to be important to both sides. It was a controversy that would ultimately have profound implications for Mr. Leandro Velarde.

"Good timing, gentlemen," said the judge. "We will take our luncheon recess now. Let's reconvene at 2 P.M. and the jury will, of course, remember all my admonishments from yesterday."

During the lunch break the defense lawyers, like most everyone else, went to the homes of the people of Aztec. Both sides were being hosted in private homes because the only hotel in town was being used by the state police and the trial witnesses for the state. There were three boardinghouses in Aztec, but the large group of reporters in town for the trial had booked every one.

The home offered to the defense lawyers served them three meals a day. Lunch, like breakfast and dinner, was served family style. Since I was, at least informally, a part of the defense team, I took lunch with them. We didn't have a private room, but the family members seemed to ignore us. Hugh Woodward started off the lunch discussion by commenting that they had covered eleven witnesses in one and a half days. At that rate they might get through the state's list of forty-two people within a week or so. Most everyone agreed that the easy witnesses were being called first but disagreed on the wisdom of that.

"Sure, they have to lay enough foundation to set the scene, but I would have put a witness to the shooting on sometime this morning," said Simms.

Woodward, always the cautious one, said he thought they were going about it systematically and that did not bode well for the defense. "It's like building a wall, one brick at a time. Sometimes it's hard to tell what it is until it's too big to jump and too strong to tear down."

Simms enjoyed the analogy and used it to make his point. "Well, it seemed to me that Montoya and Boggess are more mortar than they are bricks. It's Dee Roberts and Bobcat Wilson that I'm worried about. Those men are coal-fired bricks for sure. They might have rough edges but will be hard to break nevertheless. I'm hoping we can chip away at the mortar. That wall will fall if that happens. But if they stack enough solid bricks on us, we'll have trouble getting through to the jury."

After the defense lunch, I met Mary Ann and we talked about the prosecution's case as we waited for the crowd to gather in front of the courthouse. I speculated that from the prosecution standpoint, Mr. Griego did little more than put the Correo brothers at the scene, but directly in the alley. Naming Rafael Gomez was helpful but not exactly penetrating evidence. Mary Ann wondered why they put so much emphasis on Mrs. Green. I said: "Their big hope of the day was Mrs. Green. She was quite important because she connected up their principal target, Leandro Velarde, to the breaking and entering of the Campos house back in March. I expect that David Chavez was quite pleased that she admitted Velarde wanted to get Carmichael. But a bad attitude isn't a crime; that nice lady also said that Carmichael wanted to get Velarde. Two steps forward and one step back."

"What happened between last Sunday and today to make her change from ice picks to toothpicks, Billy Wade?" Mary Ann asked dryly.

I grimaced. "That's what I hate about witnesses. No matter how careful you are in your pretrial interview, they always seem to piss backward on the stand. She obviously told Chavez *pica hielo* last Sunday, not *pica diente.* Today she says *pica diente* and acts like she never heard of ice picks, in Spanish or in English. But it makes little difference unless they tie in the stab wounds on Hoy with somebody's ice pick. Whether or not they can make that connection depends on Judge McGhee. If I were the prosecutor, I wouldn't take any bets on it. Judge McGhee seems pretty sharp, and John Simms is a great lawyer—he'll make the right argument to keep the connection out."

Mary Ann was bored with the evidentiary minutiae and changed the subject. "Who will they put on next? When will they get to the actual riot in the alley?"

"I have no idea, but Dick Modrall is a real stand-up lawyer. David Chavez is doing most of the examination of the witnesses so far, but I expect they're getting their strategy from Mr. Modrall. He'll get to the shooting and spill a little blood on the courtroom floor soon enough."

Back in court, the crowd anticipated the entry of the judge because the bailiff stationed himself right next to the disappearing door near the back of the bench. This time he got it right—he gaveled the judge into the courtroom and got it all out before the judge could slide into the chair. Of course, he said it so fast, no one could understand him.

"Who's next?" asked the judge.

"We recall Deputy Hoy Boggess, Your Honor," Modrall said.

Mary Ann leaned over to me and said: "Looks like there's about to be blood on the courtroom floor—they should watch where they step."

As I watched Hoy Boggess walk back up to the witness stand, I got the sense that the jury knew the preliminaries were finally over and that they would now hear from someone who smelled the smoke and felt the pain. This wasn't foundation testimony or conspiracy connection; this was *the* riot. "I remind you, sir, you are still under oath. Can I get you some water before we start?"

Hoy Boggess didn't look ready to start anything, much less the telling of the story that almost got him killed, but he couldn't say what he really felt, so he just nodded and waited for the first question. They had told him this part would be hard and that the cross-examination might get nasty. He had covered his fear as best he could and said he was ready for them, no matter what they tried to pull on him. As usual, his eyes darted about.

Bobcat once said: "Hoy ain't nervous; he's just quick." Today what he was most "quick" about was that someone might try to blame him for starting the riot with the throwing of that damn tear gas bomb. He looked over at the defendants as if to say: Well, goddamn it to hell, I had a right to defend myself, didn't I? I was sure that Hoy felt bad, not for those men, but for himself, knowing that he didn't acquit himself all that well in the self-defense department, what with losing his gun and all. Bobcat always said he should have got a holster for the damn thing.

"Now, Deputy, we are going to cover all that you saw and all that happened to you on the morning of April 4 after the hearing concluded regarding Mr. Navarro. This may take a while, so if you need to take a break, just let me know. Let's start with refreshing the jury on a few things. What time was it that you got to the jail that morning?"

Hoy said he got there a little before nine o'clock. Mr. Chavez spent fifteen painful minutes establishing that Charlie Massie, Dee Roberts, and Bobcat took Navarro to court and that Leandro Velarde was the only defendant he recognized in the crowd out in front of the justice court that morning.

Deputy Boggess seemed unable to relax and couldn't look anyone on the jury in the eye. He rambled on about the size of the crowd, the people who were there, and what they were doing before the "trouble" started. He was finally asked what he saw when the rear door to the alley was opened.

"There was a crowd all over the alley on both sides of the door, and there was just a little semicircle, probably seven or eight feet wide. There were possibly seventy-five or a hundred people there, and they were right up against the door on both sides."

"And then what happened, Deputy Boggess? Just tell the jury in your own words."

Hoy took a deep breath, mumbled something that no one caught, and continued: "And Mr. Roberts and Mr. Carmichael had the prisoner between them, and I followed right out behind the rest of the crowd. Mr. Wilson was ahead of me. The officers had to push by some of these people, they were so close. They had to push up against them in order to clear the way; they didn't stop, and they just walked right into them. We walked east toward the county jail."

Boggess appeared to be out of breath. Modrall took the opportunity to get him some water whether he wanted it or not. After pausing a moment for effect, he said: "Deputy, I want to direct your attention once again to the long bench where the defendants on trial are sitting. Tell the gentlemen of the jury which of these men you saw out in the alley that morning as you were escorting Navarro back to jail."

"When I came out that door into the alley, I saw Leandro Velarde, Serapio Sosa, Juan Ochoa, Joe Bartol, and Manuel Avitia."

Dick Modrall turned to the judge and said solemnly: "May the record reflect that an officer of the law has placed the five defendants just named at the actual scene of the crime charged?"

Judge McGhee acknowledged: "The record will so reflect."

"What direction were you all headed at this point?"

"We was walking east down the alley to a point where there's a telephone pole. Right about there," he said, pointing to the wooden model of the alley. "Some of the crowd had passed me, and some had already fallen in behind the sheriff and the prisoner, and Carmichael and Wilson were already ahead of me going east. That's when it started."

"Tell them," Modrall said, pointing in the direction of the jury.

"It was right then that someone called 'we want Navarro' real loud. There was no doubt they meant business."

Inexplicably Boggess stopped and looked back at Dick Modrall, standing at the prosecution table. "Go on, sir, go on with it."

"Well, okay, at that, almost in a flash, someone grabbed the prisoner. I don't know who that was. I turned, facing west, as the wind was blowing from the west, and I threw a tear gas bomb, which I had in my pocket. I figured if I threw the bomb west, the tear gas would take care of the biggest part of that crowd and stop them so we wouldn't lose the prisoner, but just as I released the bomb, that is, the tear gas, I was struck on the head and knocked unconscious, and I don't remember what happened then, of course, until I came to."

"Do you know, sir, how long you were knocked out?"

Boggess apparently didn't hear or comprehend that question and so just continued with his story.

"I was knocked down right around that telephone pole, within two or three feet. At the time I was struck, Leandro Velarde was on my right side, a few feet from me, and Manuel Avitia was running toward me. This prisoner that was killed, or this man that was killed, Esquibel, was that his name? Wasn't very far from me, just a short distance, and I've forgotten where the rest of the crowd was at that time. Just before I turned to the west, I saw Sheriff Carmichael and Dee Roberts and the prisoner Navarro."

Modrall knew this was important testimony, and he hated to interrupt the flow, but he also knew that important details might be lost if not heard in context. He interrupted Boggess and said: "Thank you, sir, I know how hard this is on you. Let's slow down a bit. Tell the gentlemen of the jury just exactly what position the sheriff and his prisoner were in the last time you saw them."

"Mr. Carmichael was on the right, or the south, side of the alley, the prisoner Navarro was in the middle, and Mr. Roberts, the undersheriff, was on the left. I don't know how long I was unconscious, but when I came to, I couldn't see very much. I heard Bobcat call, 'Come get me, I'm shot.' In fact, I heard him several times say the same thing, and I turned in the direction of his voice and walked up to him."

Modrall held up his hand to the witness and said: "Just so our record is clear, this was Deputy L. E. Wilson, also know as 'Bobcat,' who you are speaking of now?"

"Yes, sir, me and Bobcat met someplace between the telephone post there and Mr. Carmichael's body. He was already walking toward me, and he was in a stooped position at the time I came up to him. I took ahold of his arm and started walking east. We passed Mr. Carmichael's body there in the alley."

"Where was Undersheriff Dee Roberts at this time?"

"Dee was just ahead of the body. We just kept on going, and we got up to him. He said, 'Take Bobcat to the hospital,' so we continued on up to the alley to the sheriff's office, where I got a car and took Bobcat on out to the hospital."

"Excuse me, Deputy, but we're getting a little bit ahead of ourselves here. Tell us about Bobcat: Was he wounded when you first saw him, I mean, after you regained conscious from the blows you suffered, that is?"

"When I first seen Mr. Wilson, he was stooped clear over and would raise up occasionally. He was holding himself sort of in this manner, with his arm across his stomach, and as we walked he would raise up and then go down and bend over and stagger a little. As soon as I got up to him, I felt he was seriously hurt. I saw his wound a week or so later. He was shot right under the arm."

"Let us turn now to the matter of your weapon, Deputy. Of course you were armed, as you were in the service of the law that morning. What sort of weaponry were you carrying?"

"At the time I was in Judge Bickel's office, I had my pistol. I had it when I was walking down the alley. I did not draw it at any time. I had it when I was knocked unconscious, but when I came to, it was gone. I've never seen it since that time."

"Name the make and model of pistol, if you will."

"It was a .45 Smith & Wesson double action. It was a special model made for the army fifteen or twenty years ago or thereabouts. I didn't have any holster with me, so I had the pistol in my belt, back here. I had on a leather zipper jacket."

"What about bullets, sir? I trust your weapon was loaded."

"I had .45 automatic cartridges. There are clips made exactly for that type of ammunition to be used with my Smith & Wesson. The clips are in a half circle, two clips to a full load, with three bullets in each clip. These clips have little openings at the inner side of the chamber, and you slip your cartridges into those little openings. I had six bullets in my gun that day. You know it's customary in a double-action gun to carry a full load. As to the make of the cartridges, I think they were Western, but I really couldn't state definitely. They were automatic rimless."

"Let me show you an exhibit and ask if you can identify this for the jury, Deputy Boggess."

"This here is marked Exhibit 4. It's a bullet that I got from Earl Irish, state police. I gave it to Mr. Martin in Santa Fe. I got it on April 19 at the sheriff's office."

Simms rose at this point and said: "Your Honor, in the interests of time, we will stipulate that Exhibit 4 is the bullet taken out of Bobcat Wilson by the doctor at Rehoboth Mission."

When I heard that, I wondered why Mr. Simms was being so helpful. Then it occurred to me that this "stipulation" was just a way of slowing down important testimony. I guess the judge had the same feeling because he said: "Well, Exhibit 4 is already in evidence, and they already know where it came from, but your stipulation is accepted anyhow. Mr. Modrall, please proceed."

"Your Honor, that completes our examination of Deputy Boggess on the subjects just covered. But as the court knows, we are trying to present this testimony on consistent subjects. We will of course be recalling Deputy Boggess to the stand on other pertinent matters."

As Boggess started to leave the witness stand, the judge waved at him and said: "I'm sorry, Mr. Boggess, but I expect one of those defense lawyers over there will have a question or two for you. So just keep your seat. Who will be putting the questions from the defense to this witness?" he asked generically, but he looked directly at John Simms.

As visually predicted by the judge, Simms rose and started in on Hoy Boggess. "You didn't mention women or children out in front of the court that morning. You do not deny they were there, do you?"

"No, I saw women and children in the crowd in front of the court. They were mostly in the little entrance, or vestibule."

"And the weather, sir, it was clear, was it not?"

"Yes, the weather was good. It was clear."

"And every one of the many lawmen there had a gun in his possession, did he not?"

"All the officers had their guns on. The federal officers had theirs, and I had mine. Carmichael had his gun; Bobcat Wilson had his gun; Presley had his gun; Massie had his gun; I don't know about Fred Montoya or Jerry Garcia or Perfecto Garcia. Jerry Garcia is the jailer, and he usually has a gun on. So there were at least eight pistols in the room."

"Mr. Boggess, you testified at the preliminary hearing in this case, did you not?"

"Yes, I did."

"And I expect the state's lawyers have made that testimony available for you to read, have they not?"

Boggess looked even more worried than before and looked for reassurance at the prosecution table. He wondered if he had done something wrong by reading what he said the last time. "I read my testimony from the preliminary hearing. It was given to me by Mr. Chavez."

"Well, then, how do you account for the fact that at the preliminary, which was shortly after this occurrence, you didn't say anything about Leandro Velarde making any motion out in front?"

"I didn't know that I didn't."

John Simms looked sternly at Boggess and said: "I assure you, sir, you did not. Let me put it to you this way, Mr. Boggess, haven't you and the other officers discussed the question of what was necessary for the state to have a case?"

"Well, not the officers, but . . ."

"But what, Mr. Boggess? Please tell us."

"I never talked to the officers, but I have talked to Mr. Chavez. I don't recall him saying anything in particular about what was necessary to have a case."

"Let me take you back to your testimony at the preliminary hearing. Then you said, didn't you, that the last you remembered, Solomon Esquibel was walking past you alone?"

"I don't remember saying alone, because there was a crowd back there."

"Let me put another one to you, sir. You swore under oath this morning that Avitia was running toward you when you threw the bomb. How do you account for the fact that you didn't say that at the preliminary?"

"I don't know that I have anything to account for on that one."

"It is true, is it not, that the only one of the defendants on trial that you ever saw in the front of the office was Velarde?"

"Yes, that is so."

"And it is also true that every officer there either had a gun or a tear gas bomb on him that morning?"

"Yes, that's true."

"But you were the one who threw the tear gas bomb, and that was before you heard any shots or saw any act of violence by anyone, right, sir?"

"Well, I guess that's so."

"And you claim you didn't hear the explosion made by the tear gas bomb going off?"

"I didn't hear the explosion of the tear gas bomb I threw. The last thing I remember was that I threw it; then I was knocked out."

"Well, you do know what they sound like when they go off, don't you?"

"I had never practiced with one of those bombs."

"What were you trying to hit when you threw the bomb?"

"When I aimed the bomb, I aimed it to hit down into the crowd, as the wind was from the west."

"Were you trying to hurt these people or just scare them?"

"I figured it would probably act and come up stopping the biggest onrush of people. This is the first tear gas I have used in any trouble."

"Let me turn to the blows inflicted on you, sir. As you are under oath, you cannot say that any of the defendants struck you, can you?"

"No, sir, on my oath I cannot."

"As to the matter of your gun, is it true that it is still missing?"

"I have never seen my gun since that day. I don't know who got it."

"You told the jury earlier that someone shouted out something about Navarro, but you cannot attribute that statement to any of these men here on trial, can you?"

"Well, I already said I don't know who called out 'we want Navarro.' There's ten men on trial here; I can't say which of them said it."

"You cannot say that any of them said it, can you?"

"No, I reckon I can't."

"Any more than you can say that any of these men grabbed Navarro or acted in any way to free him, right, sir?"

"I can't say that any of the ten men grabbed Navarro."

"And on your oath, sir, you cannot say that any of them made a single hostile act or statement."

"No, I can't."

"Now, sir, let me remind you of some more of your testimony at the preliminary hearing. Even though you lost your gun while you were knocked unconscious, you claim that you actually fired several shots that morning with another gun. Whose gun did you use to fire on that crowd?"

"When I walked up to Bobcat Wilson, I got his pistol off him. I fired a couple of shots."

"Did you actually hit anyone or did you just shoot at them?"

"I shot. Well, I shot back into where I could see two people running into the crowd. I was still dazed from the blow, and I thought probably they were the prisoner or one of them was the prisoner escaping."

"So you, right after regaining consciousness and not knowing what had happened in between, you fired someone else's gun at two men you claim were running into the crowd? Have I got that straight?"

"Yes, these people were running away to the west."

"Bobcat's gun, which you claim you got off him while he was badly wounded, was an automatic, was it not?"

"Yes, I believe it was."

"And with that automatic, and suffering from the wounds you had, you then cut down those running people with that automatic?"

"I shot in the direction they were running. I don't know whether I hit them or not."

"Very well, sir. Let me move ahead to the days immediately after the shooting. You participated in the search of many homes in the Chihuahuaita section of town, did you not?"

"After this shooting affray, I swore out search warrants to try to find my pistol. There were quite a number of search warrants. I might have sworn out fifty warrants in one day."

"Did you know that in doing what you did, swearing that your pistol was in so many different places at the same time, that you were trying to evade the law?"

"I don't take your meaning."

"I mean, sir, that by swearing that your gun was in fifty different places at once that you were in fact evading the law or trying to evade the law and deprive these people who live over in Chihuahuaita of their constitutional rights and protection against unlawful searches and seizures."

"Well, I did what I was told to do."

"I have read your sworn search warrants, sir. Didn't you identify a man as being in the mob who was in fact not there at all because he was working in the Allison mine that day?"

"I ain't sure about that."

"Didn't you first estimate that six hundred people were there?"

"I don't recollect the exact number. There were probably hundreds, though."

"Didn't you identify forty-eight different people at the preliminary hearing, knowing that by doing so you were helping to charge them with a capital crime?"

"Well, in addition to the four defendants that I identified there in the crowd, I also saw Bonifacio Fernandez and Jack Barreras. I saw Ignacio Velarde, the one that's dead."

"But they are no longer charged, are they, sir?"

"No, I guess not."

"Your Honor, we are finished with Mr. Hoy Boggess."

To hear it repeated in the American Bar down in Gallup, the courtroom up in Aztec finally heard from the first witness in the case who can explain to the jury just what those red rascals did. It turns out that he was afflicted with a bad case of the "I don't remembers." Worse than that, what he didn't remember seems sort of important. Old Hoy says that so-and-so was there, but he don't remember that he didn't say that at the preliminary hearing. And, of course, they have to rub it in that the preliminary hearing was right after the shooting, when you ought to have a pretty good memory of what happened.

But even if he did remember more clearly what happened, it now looks like he just lost his grip out there in the alley and threw up a tear gas bomb before there was any real reason to do so. No act of violence had been committed. No one had done anything yet, but there he goes and lobs a bomb even though he admits he had never, not even once, practiced with one. Hell, he didn't even know what they sounded like when they went off.

Now, on the good side, he did name five of them as being right there at the shooting at the time all hell broke loose. And he did say that Bobcat was shot up real bad and the sheriff was shot dead. Everyone at the bar, as well as the few at the big table in the back, were in agreement that he ought not to have lost that gun. The defense lawyers sure jumped on that one. You'd think that he would of pulled his gun long before he threw a bomb. Come to think of it, his story for throwing it west on account of the direction of wind wasn't all that clear, was it? It seems likely that they'll have to call old Hoy back to the stand for some real "rebuttal" before the end of the trial.

Aztec, New Mexico
Wednesday, October 9, 1935

Dear Journal:

I am emotionally exhausted, but I forced myself to eat and will try to get the events of the day on paper. Today started out with a nice little chewing out by Judge McGhee. Of course, no one really knows, but the scuttlebutt was that he chewed on the lawyers when he called them into his chambers for their rude comments to one another in court yesterday. Then he chewed on us, the audience, for our rude chatting to one another while the translator was speaking up in the front of the courtroom. I felt bad because I found myself talking to that gossipy reporter from Denver too much. But I didn't feel bad for the lawyers; they deserved it (if they got it). The Denver man said they did. I wonder how he knew?

That federal agent for the Indian Service, Mr. Aldrich, was the first witness. I have seen him around town for years but was never quite sure what he did. About the only important thing he said was that the crowd in front of the court that morning was mostly women and kids. That must have been a different crowd than the one Deputies Boggess and Montoya saw.

The next witness was Harris Lyle. I know him fairly well. He goes to the same sorts of things that Billy Wade does, and we have seen him and his wife on social occasions. He seems pretty straightforward. I was a bit surprised when he said that he and Senator Vogel met in his office that morning *before* the hearing. I wondered why but Mr. Chavez didn't ask him anything about the purpose of the meeting. Later on, when Mr. Woodward cross-examined him, he said it was to see if Sheriff Carmichael needed Senator Vogel's testimony at the hearing. That made me wonder even more. Why would the sheriff need testimony? If testimony were needed, it would make more sense to meet with the district attorney, not the sheriff. But who knows, maybe the sheriff was going to talk to the district attorney. Am I making too much out of this, Madam Journal? Oh, I almost forgot. Lyle did describe the Navarro case as "our case." I guess he meant that it was Senator Vogel's case. Does that mean that Senator Vogel is going to testify? I certainly hope so. I'm still a little angry with the whole eviction mess, and I just know that it's the underlying cause of all of this. I don't mean that Senator Vogel really did anything wrong, but I have the terrible sense that he has no comprehension of the role he played in getting our sheriff and two other men killed. He was there in court this morning with Mr. Lyle. I looked at him but could not tell if he feels remorse or anger or anything at all.

As I looked at him, I noticed that the wives (and one grandmother) of the defendants carefully avoided looking at him. They're sitting in the back on the right side of the courtroom. Senator Vogel and Mr. Lyle were sitting on the left side, in the front row (wouldn't you know). In fact, I missed some of what Lyle was saying on the stand because I wandered off in my mind thinking about what those other women feel about Vogel.

The families sure did focus on the next witness—Mr. P. M. Griego. He used to work at Ellis Drug in town but moved up to Española. Of course, one doesn't really move "up" to Española from Gallup; its just that it's north of us. Anyhow, as I was saying, they watched him carefully because he was the first witness to describe the crowd—other than one of the law officers. He candidly admitted that most of the people in the crowd were women and kids. I got the distinct feeling, watching the women in the back of the courtroom out of the corner of my eye, that many of them were there that day. Mr. Griego said he had seen many crowds in front of Judge Bickel's court before and recognized this one as "being from Chihuahuaita." How did he do that? I've lived in Gallup for as long as he has, and I certainly couldn't tell a crowd of people, even Spanish people, as being from Chihuahuaita (as opposed to the North Side) or any other part of town. Of course, that was probably a point the defense wanted to make. No one is contesting that this crowd was there because of the evictions in Chihuahuaita. Did Senator Vogel get the point? I wonder.

The next witness was someone who lives in Chihuahuaita—Mrs. John Green. She was only referred to as "Mrs. John Green." That's typical of Gallup men, at least in formal settings. Don't they know she has a first name, just like her husband? She was obviously called to the stand for one single purpose—to incriminate Leandro Velarde. She caused quite a stir in the courtroom when she said that she was at someone else's home a week or so before the riot and heard Mr. Velarde say "he had it in for Sheriff Carmichael." She explained the meeting, but it wasn't clear to me what was going on. Apparently Velarde was asked about whether "they" (whoever they were) needed weapons to go to Mr. Campos's house. According to her, he said, "Let the officers take their weapons; we don't need anything but a toothpick." As she said it, it didn't make sense, but I do believe she is sincere. It's what she heard, but it wasn't what Mr. Chavez wanted her to say. It got very confusing because Chavez asked her questions, then Mr. Woodward cross-examined her, then Chavez asked her some more. All I could get out of it was that Mr. Chavez thinks the Spanish word she first used was the one for *ice pick,* but in court she used the one for *toothpick.* I tried to watch the jury a little, but they looked as confused as I was. Is this going to be a big point in the case? If it is, then it got lost because the audience actually laughed out loud when Mr. Chavez couldn't get her to change her words. That was when Judge McGhee gave us another stern little admonishment.

The only important witness of the day was Deputy Boggess. I swear, I do not know if that man is merely befuddled or is actually trying to evade the truth. To look at him on the stand, you fear he is about to burst. For example, he was asked a simple question in the beginning of his examination about people in the crowd, and he jumped right out and named five different defendants as being there. When asked if anyone said anything when the door to the alley was first opened, he immediately looked at the defendants and said: "Yes, they said they wanted Navarro." He volunteered that there was no doubt "they meant business." Of course, on cross-examination he admitted that he could not attribute that statement to any of the defendants, but that is certainly not the impression he gave on direct.

I tried to pay close attention to everything he said about his gun and how and when he lost it. Whatever happened wasn't clear to him, and he couldn't make it clear to us (the jury or the audience). At first he said he was knocked unconscious right after he threw that damn tear gas bomb. Later he said he walked some distance down the alley before he was hit. He said he had his gun in his belt and that he never drew it out from behind his back. It was a little vague, but apparently he had on a leather zipper jacket and the gun was stuck in his waistband in the back. Was his jacket zipped up? No one asked him. It was quite cold that day and windy. It's likely that he had it zipped up, but maybe not. Anyhow, he said he had it when he was knocked unconscious and it was gone when he came to.

On cross-examination he got very angry with Mr. Simms. That was understandable. Mr. Simms insisted on pointing out the several different ways his trial testimony differed from his preliminary hearing testimony. Billy Wade told me (on the phone again—wait till you see my bill) that this is called "impeachment." The word hardly does justice to what happened to poor Mr. Boggess at the hands of Mr. Simms. The point was very clear. Mr. Boggess met with Mr. Chavez sometime after last June and before this trial began. Mr. Boggess knew what needed to be done to make the case for the state. Apparently he didn't get the message last June, but he sure had it today. He just didn't realize that Mr. Simms would read his preliminary hearing transcript.

I'll be charitable and say that it's entirely possible that Mr. Boggess might tell his story differently every time he's asked about it. Consistency is not his strong point. I even felt sorry for him, up to a point. That point was when he insisted that he took Bobcat's automatic pistol from his holster and fired at two people who he saw running *into* the crowd. He admitted that he was dazed and he couldn't see clearly. What was he thinking? At first he said maybe it was the prisoner and someone else escaping. Even if that were the case, how could he just shoot into a crowd of women and kids?

I sort of lost all patience with him when he later said that he swore out about fifty search warrants when he was looking for his lost gun. Maybe it's just me, but I thought you had to be sure of something before you *swore* to it. How could you swear that your gun was in fifty places at once?

I'm tired. How can just sitting down all day be so exhausting? So I'll go to bed and hope someone else keeps track of whatever it was that I missed today.

Good night, Madam Journal.

Postscript. Well, I've mulled it over, as I said I would. Mulling is vastly overrated as a means of resolving things. Mulling just postpones, like putting watery ice chips back in the refrigerator. They don't melt, but they don't firm up either. I guess it's a little like limbo. Anyhow, I decided to postscript my journal because it seems like a nice little place to write to myself about just what, exactly, is going on in my so-called life. Here I am doing something I have never done (watching a trial) in a strange town filled with other strangers who are doing the same thing—writing down what we think is happening. From what I read, none of us is watching what the rest of us are watching. We see it so differently, depending on where we sit in the courtroom—and with whom. Billy Wade sits with me but makes me nervous. Do I really love him enough to spend the rest of my life with him? What will this trial do to our future, if we have a future, that is? Will I be able to abide his rigorous view that this trial is how things ought to be resolved when men die in alleyways where guns rule and reason wilts under the power of bullheadedness? I'm starting to wonder whether teaching English to rural high school students is the best long-term thing for me, and I'm becoming convinced that being a housewife, as comfortable as it would be with Billy Wade, is like having syrup without pancakes. Most of me wants more than that. *Adiós,* Señora Journal.

Reflecting on those first two days of trial, the backbenchers and stool-sitters in the barrooms of Gallup wondered why the judge thought he was so important that the lawyers had to talk *only* to him, not to each other. Some said it wasn't that at all; it was just the law's way of keeping order in the court. Others said it was just an exercise of power: you know if you can make the rules, you might as well make 'em in your favor. A sorry few said it was none of that; it was the capitalist way of keeping the workingman down, in or out of court. That last rationale escaped all but the agitators in the NMU.

The more interesting rumor around town was about the rift that seemed to be shaping up between Gallup's new sheriff, Mr. Dee Roberts, and my friend, the banty-rooster Bobcat. *Rift* might be a trifle strong, since whatever it was, it wasn't out in the open, where anybody could get their ears on it. It was more of a feeling than something you could actually chew on. Some said it had to do with the fact that Dee Roberts did all the shooting in the alley and was, more or less, the hero that day. But Bobcat wasn't a man to envy what others thought heroic. Fact of the matter was that Bobcat and Sheriff Mack both got hit about the same time; one died and the other nearly did. Bobcat surely knew that Dee Roberts's surefire draw and his keen shooting eye just might have saved him from a third, maybe fatal, bullet. But however elusive it might have been, this little tension between Sheriff Dee Roberts and Bobcat was making it hard for folks to pass judgment on anything.

On the North Side and in Chihuahuaita, they were all waiting for Bobcat to take the stand and tell just what he did in that alley in his own words. Not that they expected all that many words from Bobcat, but they did expect him to clarify a few things. For example, did he ever see that .45-caliber Smith & Wesson that Hoy lost track of during the shooting? If he didn't, what did he suppose happened to it?

In city hall as well as the county jail they were still looking for the gun, but the chance of finding it was looking dim. Some said they would find old Navarro a damn sight sooner than they would find Hoy's gun. Not that Navarro would have been all that hard to find. Most likely he was south of the border. If the truth be known, no one cared much now that the law had ten men to try (and fry) as soon as "they quit pissing around up there in Aztec."

The local lawyers made it clear that circumstantial evidence was as good as hard evidence in the eyes of the law. Most people accepted that abstract principle. But the people of Gallup wanted some hard evidence after two days of circumstances that didn't seem all that probative.

eight

DIFFERENT EYES, DIFFERENT VIEWS

Thursday, October 10, 1935

Over breakfast of eggs, green chili, chorizo, biscuits, and coffee, the prosecution team talked about the upcoming day. Dick Modrall and Frank Patton weren't as confident as the men from Gallup about their progress.

"We have to put Hoy back up there today," Dick Modrall said. "I'm hoping this will be his last day, but I do wish we had a little better control over his testimony."

David Chavez replied: "It's not his testimony that you don't like, Dick, it's the cross-examination."

"That's true enough." Modrall pushed away his plate. "Who can we put up there to follow him and take some of the sting out of the missteps he's sure to make?"

"Well, you know I'm not in agreement with your tentative decision to hold Bobcat until the end of the trial," Chavez said. "He's important and, unlike Hoy, he's a man of few words."

"Yes, I've noticed that." Modrall signaled the waitress for the check. "My problem is that his few words aren't exactly consistent with what most other folks say. I'm still not convinced that we need him at all. Why confuse what happened?"

"Hellfire, he wouldn't cause any more confusion than what we already got. As it stands now, we don't have anyone who can lay it out simple like."

Dick Modrall took it all in and said: "Men, when we put Dee Roberts up there, they'll understand just what happened. He's the man we want to close our case with. He can bring in a verdict just like he cleared out that crowd in the alley. He was a straight shooter that day and he'll be a straight talker when we call him to the stand."

"All rise for His Honor, Judge James B. McGhee, presiding over the case of . . ." The rest of the bailiff's call to order got lost in the shuffling. Judge

McGhee seemed to be in a hurry this morning. Maybe that was because it was nearly ten-thirty in the morning and the jury had been waiting in their little room for a long time while the lawyers hashed something out in the judge's chambers. "Call the next witness," he said as he straightened up the papers strewn about on his bench.

"We call Mr. Locorio Lovato," said David Chavez, rising to take the podium for the examination of this witness.

As Locorio Lovato was being called from the outer hallway, John Simms rose and asked for a conference at the bench. "May we approach, Your Honor?"

"Approach, one from each side," said the judge.

Simms started out in hushed tones at the bench conference. "Judge, this man is the husband of one of the defendants in the underlying case that was pending before Judge Bickel that day. I'm concerned that much of his testimony is secondhand hearsay, but it might be impossible to deal with if it comes in as part of the 'question,' if you know what I mean."

Waving off Mr. Chavez for the moment, Judge McGhee said, "John, I cannot rule on admissibility without hearing the specific question asked; you know that."

"Yes, of course, Your Honor, I'm not asking for an advisory opinion of evidence admissibility. But I think it's within your province to inquire of Mr. Chavez as to the general scope of this witness's testimony so that we do not risk a mistrial if he blurts out something that is clearly inadmissible."

Now Mr. Chavez jumped in. "Your Honor, we have no intention of seeking inadmissible testimony from this witness. We intend to ask him about what he heard in open court that morning and what he saw the man Navarro do."

Judge McGhee said: "Well, it seems to me that we have heard from several officers of the law about what they heard in the court that morning. Is what this witness heard any different than what we already have?"

"No, Your Honor, it's not different," said Chavez, thinking that this was a solution.

"Then it is cumulative and therefore unnecessary to offer it. Let's move on to what he saw Navarro do. Is that any different than what the others have said?"

Chavez realized he had walked into the judge's trap with the last answer and so hedged this one. "Well, it could be, Judge. You can never be sure. In any event, what he saw is not covered by the hearsay rule, and it's not cumulative since he's a different witness."

"All right, he can testify as to what he saw, but don't get us into any cumulative testimony about what is already in the record."

Chavez established that Mr. Lovato was a Gallup resident and that he was the husband of Jeannie Lovato—who was one of the defendants in the eviction hearing in Judge Bickel's court the morning of the riot. He briefly covered Lovato's tenure in Gallup since 1918 and moved to the central point. "Now, sir, tell our jury how long you knew Esiquel Navarro."

"I knew him for a long time; how many years, I can't say."

"Had he lived there as long as you?"

"No, not that long."

"At the end of the hearing, when they decided to continue the case, did you see Mr. Navarro make any particular motion of any kind?"

"No, he was just a man, not a lawyer."

"I didn't mean a legal motion; I meant a movement with his hands or his arms. Did you see anything like that?"

"Sure, he went like this." At that point the witness used his right arm to beckon the defense lawyers toward him.

"Did it look to you like he was asking them to come in or telling them he was going out the back door?"

"Objection, leading," said Mr. Woodward, without standing.

"Mr. Woodward, I have told you before, objections to evidence are to be made from a standing position. The next time you address this court, you'd best be on your feet. Objection sustained."

"To whom did he make this motion with his arm?"

"I don't know; maybe to his friends."

"Where were his friends?"

"Everywhere, I guess; he was a nice man."

"All right, sir, thank you. Oh, by the way, have you seen him since that day?"

"No, he's gone."

On cross-examination, Simms established that the only reason Mr. Lovato was there that day was because his wife had to be there. It was clear enough that this man wasn't an activist of any kind. "I have just one thing to clear up with you, Mr. Lovato," Simms said. "Can you tell us why you didn't mention this movement you remember Mr. Navarro made when you testified before about this case? You do remember your testimony in Santa Fe, don't you?"

"Yes, I remember going up there and them asking me all these questions."

"Well, why didn't you tell them about this movement by Navarro?"

"Because no one asked me."

Every trial needs a little humor, and Lovato gave the jury just what they needed. Even the grim line of defendants smiled at him when he left the stand.

Their smiles quickly faded when it appeared that another jailer was about to take the stand. Fred Montoya was coming in through the swinging gate that separated the pit of the court from the spectator area. As usual, it squeaked, and as usual, the bailiff looked down at the hinge as though it was squeaking for the first time. The jury looked at Fred Montoya without any outward display of emotion, but you could feel the antipathy throughout the room. Given that he was neither interesting nor informative the last time, why ever were they bringing him back?

"Let me begin by clearing up something from your earlier testimony," David Chavez said after the judge reminded Mr. Montoya that he was still under oath. "Were you a sworn deputy at the time of the Navarro trial on April 4, 1935?"

"No, not at that time. I had a commission."

"Were you directly involved with the return of the prisoner back to the jail from the justice court that morning?"

"Yes, the ones who were going to take Navarro back were Carmichael, Dee Roberts, Hoy Boggess, Bobcat Wilson, and me. Carmichael told me to open the door to the alley. So that's what I did." He paused to make sure every man on the jury got his point: He was the first one to start out into the alley.

"Well, sir, go on; tell us what you saw," Chavez said somewhat impatiently.

"First off, I saw Mr. Leandro Velarde and Ignacio Velarde and them others in the alley. Leandro Velarde was saying, 'Now you shall see it disgraced.' "

Chavez interrupted, so the interpreter didn't finish the translation for the defendants. "Hold on there, Mr. Montoya. Let's be clear about this. Are you sure that's the word he used, 'disgraced'?"

When Chavez paused, the interpreter said to the defendants: *"Ahora usted desaparece."*

Normally impassive, Leandro Velarde grimaced at this and slowly shook his head. Neither Chavez nor any of the other prosecutors was looking at him. It was just as well because his expression made Montoya's testimony all the more ambiguous. Did his facial rejection mean he didn't say "disgraced" or did it mean the translation was wrong?

Two men on the jury spoke Spanish, as did David Chavez. He jumped up and said: "Excuse me, Your Honor, but the translator is wrong. *Desaparecer* means 'disappear,' not 'disrespect.' "

Remembering the confusion with Mrs. Green over the translation of *pica diente,* Judge McGhee said: "Now, hold on here. Mr. Chavez, do you wish to challenge the accuracy of the translation?"

"Your Honor, as the court knows, I do speak Spanish. I challenge the translation, although I'm not sure there is a literal translation available. I'm led to believe that the closest English is 'disrespect,' which in Spanish is *desestimación,* and I would like to ask the witness for a clarification."

Turning to Mr. Montoya, Chavez said: "Now, Mr. Montoya, when you first heard the defendant Mr. Leandro Velarde speak in the alley that morning, was he speaking in Spanish or English?"

"He was using some of both, but he said the first part in Spanish. He said something like, 'Now you shall, or now you are gonna see it, disgraced.' I remember the 'disgraced' part."

Chavez paused, as he knew that he might make his own witness look foolish, but he could think of no other way to handle it. "Mr. Montoya, what is the Spanish word he used when he said 'disgraced'?"

Montoya did just what Chavez was afraid he would do. "I don't know the word; I just know the meaning of it."

"Very well, let's move on. Tell the jury whether Mr. Velarde said anything else."

All of us in the back of the courtroom hoped that Chavez would do what he said—move on—but instead he droned on with Mr. Montoya for another fifteen minutes. The only thing new we learned was that Solomon Esquibel was at the back door with his hand stuck in his jacket when the door first opened. That scared Fred, and he jumped back inside the courtroom. When asked why he did that, he said: "Because I wasn't armed at the time. There was no use for me to go out there and be shot."

John Simms rose for the cross-examination. "Mr. Montoya, you were a witness at the preliminary hearing before Judge Otero. At that time you swore under oath that the ones in front of Judge Bickel's court were Gregorio Correo, Victor Correo, and Rafael Gomez, but today you say it was Willie Gonzales, Manuel Avitia, and Juan Ochoa—why the difference?"

"Well, I can't remember every question they asked. All I know is what I saw."

"Let me refresh your recollection of what you swore then that you saw. You told Judge Otero that you saw the following people in front that morning: José G. Lopez, Vidal Rodriguez, Vicente Guillén, Felipe Baca, Victorio Correo, Rafael Gomez, Victor Campos. That is certainly a different list you gave Judge McGhee just now. Can you explain the difference?"

"No, I guess it just depends on who is asking the questions."

"All right. Let me ask you about a different matter. Were you the first or the last law officer to actually step out into the alley that morning?"

"I was the first one to open the door, and I was the last one to come out into the alley. The sheriff and the others and the prisoner were all going down the alley when I came out. They might have been about twenty or thirty feet from me—I'm not sure."

"So the sheriff and the others would have heard the same things you heard and saw the same movements you saw, right, sir?"

"I can't say for them what they saw, but Bobcat Wilson and Hoy Boggess went out before me. I opened the door before they went out."

"Well, then, if Leandro Velarde and Ignacio Velarde were out there and if one of them said what you said one of them said, Bobcat Wilson and Hoy Boggess would have both heard it, don't you agree?"

"I already told you I can't speak for them."

Simms looked at the judge when he said: "We have heard from Mr. Boggess, and he did not confirm your story. Perhaps when Mr. Wilson takes the stand, we will hear more about this word 'disgraced.' "

With the realization that he was being called a liar, Montoya said: "I know what I heard. I can't help it if *gringos* can't understand it." Pointing over at Leandro Velarde, sitting at the end of the defendants' bench, Montoya continued: "He said to me: 'Now you shall see what happens, disgraced.' 'Disgraced' is a bad word in Spanish with no literal translation."

"Thank you, sir. Tell me this: When he held up his right hand at you, that motion would have been seen by the others as well, right?"

"I guess so."

"And it is true, is it not, that there was nothing in his hand when he held it up?"

"He held up his right hand, but I didn't see anything in it. His fist was clenched."

"But surely, sir, you took these words and these actions as hostile, and therefore you told the sheriff about it to warn him, did you not?"

"I didn't tell the sheriff what Leandro had said because they were there also."

"But you said he said it to you in Spanish, right, sir?"

"He said it to me in Spanish."

"And Carmichael didn't speak Spanish, did he? So why didn't you warn him if you took his words and his actions to be menacing?"

"Because there was no time. After they went out, then Solomon Esquibel met me at the door and said: 'Move back; leave them to us alone.' "

"And so that's what you did, wasn't it? You left them alone?"

"Well, I already told you, he put his hand under his jacket when he said it. I knew he meant business."

"But you didn't see him take his hand out of his jacket. You never saw a weapon, and you were never in any danger, were you?"

"I didn't see him take his hand out or see any weapon. He didn't try to hurt me."

Turning toward the court, Simms said: "Your Honor, that concludes the cross-examination of this witness."

Disgraced or disappear? For the second time in the trial, language became important in understanding what happened in that alley. The out-of-state reporters were getting a lesson in "New Mexican" as a *language.* The Spanish spoken in all of rural New Mexico can be described as a sort of regional language made up of archaic Spanish, Mexican-Indian words (mostly from the Nahuatl), and a few indigenous Rio Grande Indian words. To add to the mix, you have to throw in some local vocabulary.

The way the Hispano in Gallup talked was more or less uniform all over the whole geographical area of New Mexico and southern Colorado—but not Arizona and not Texas. That's because our New Mexican language had survived by word of mouth for over 330 years. For the most part, this region was almost completely isolated from other Spanish-speaking centers; California, for example.

The professors at the University of New Mexico explained that our language was very different in morphology and syntax. "New Mexican" was an offshoot of the Spanish of northern Mexico. Most everywhere else in these United States, the language was either Castilian or derived from central or southern Mexico. You can understand it if you remember that New Mexico was an integral part of New Spain (Mexico) from 1549 to 1821. We were a part of Mexico from that year until 1850, when "New Mexico" became a territory of the United States.

Back east, the colonists were English speakers for the most part. But the colonists were Hispano in New Mexico throughout the seventeenth, eighteenth, and nineteenth centuries. Of course, those who established their *rancherías* along the Rio Grande acquired a few local Indian words. But that didn't stretch to the high desert in western New Mexico.

How was it that our New Mexican was so different from "Spanish"? It seems that the lack of continuous, day-to-day contact is the answer. All during the time of the "Conquest" (the sixteenth, seventeenth, and eighteenth centuries), there was damn little going on between Old Mexico and us. That's because we were far removed in one way (distance) but connected in another way (politically). There weren't many books or dictionaries, and our version of Spanish sort of stagnated. Or, some would say, blossomed into "New Mexican." Whenever folks couldn't recall the name of some useful article or even some deeply felt emotion, they would make up a new term; it became New Mexican, not Spanish. It didn't sound like English and it didn't translate into Spanish. The Hispanos in Gallup knew what was meant by *toothpick, ice pick,* and *disgraced* as long as it was said by one of them. If whatever *gringo* heard it didn't get it, well, *"Lo mismo es Chana que Juana."* Any one of those boys on that long hard bench up in Aztec would have known: "It doesn't make any difference."

"Your Honor, we recall Deputy Hoy Boggess to the stand."

At the mention of his name, even the jury seemed to collectively let out a not so quiet groan. Hoy Boggess was already in the courtroom but didn't seem to notice that the spectators were smiling as he walked over to the clerk's table. He started to raise his hand, but she told him: "No, that's not necessary. We already did that."

The judge looked over and said: "Take your seat, Mr. Boggess; you know just which one since you're becoming a regular around here."

As he took the stand, John Simms noticed that Mr. Boggess carried to the stand a blue-bound transcript, which he guessed was the direct testimony Boggess gave at the preliminary hearing. He rose and addressed the court. "Your Honor, I apologize to my honorable opponent for this interruption, but it appears that the witness has been supplied with some testimony as a matter of assisting his recall this morning. Might I inquire on *voir dire* if this appearance is a fact?"

"Well, no, you cannot. If the witness has been supplied with the testimony of himself, it's okay. If it's the testimony of some other witness, you can deal with it on cross-examination. Proceed, Mr. Chavez."

"Now, Deputy Boggess, since you've been recalled a number of times to help this jury understand what happened down there in Gallup, I hope I can say that you'll be able to go back to your normal life after today. The last subject we have to cover with you involves this exhibit." Chavez approached the witness and handed him a large automatic pistol. "Can you tell the jury what you know about Exhibit 25?"

"Yes, I can. This gun that has a tag on it, Exhibit 25, is the same gun that I took off Bobcat Wilson that morning. I believe I already explained what I did with it when I was on the stand before."

"And so you did, Mr. Boggess, but since the gun wasn't yours, now we want to know what you did with it after the events of April 4, 1935, were over."

To the surprise of everyone in the back of the courtroom, Deputy Boggess was somewhat succinct in his answers this time. He said that the gun in his hands was still loaded and it had the same bullets in it that he reloaded the gun with that morning after the shootings in the alley. I guess I was surprised at the fact that one of the exhibits in the case was a *loaded* gun, but no one else seemed to take notice of it. On cross-examination, John Simms cast some doubt on just how many shots were fired out of this gun. He got Boggess to admit that his testimony about reloading was based on his recollection that he only fired twice. If he was wrong about that, then he would be wrong about how many bullets he reloaded. But it was lost on the jury—they were plainly bored with this line of testimony or tired of Boggess, perhaps both.

The collective groan let out by the jury when Boggess took the stand was now replaced by a collective sigh. As I watched Hoy leave the courtroom I couldn't help but wonder if Bobcat was going to be as uncomfortable on the witness stand as Hoy was. I had tried to talk to him about the courtroom environment, but he just stiffened up and said, "Don't make no never mind to me. I got the truth, and that'll have to do it."

Judge McGhee looked relieved and said: "Well, now, just who do we have as our next witness, Mr. Prosecutor?"

"Your Honor, we will be calling Mrs. Elna Arcus."

The jury had been there in the box for two and a half days now and had heard from a dozen different witnesses. This was a name no one had mentioned before. As she walked to the stand, Elna Arcus smiled pleasantly at everyone. She had on her best dress and carried her best purse. Both were dark blue. They complemented her prematurely gray hair and the wire-rim glasses that perched on the middle of her thin but well-shaped nose. She was fifty but didn't look her age. She walked briskly and sat down quickly, as if to say: "I'm ready; are you?"

"Good morning, Mrs. Arcus," Frank Patton said as he moved his writing pad from the prosecution table to the small podium in the center of the courtroom. "Would you be so kind as to give us your full name and place of residence, please?"

Mrs. Arcus answered the usual background questions briskly and with an occasional smile at the jury. She explained that she felt unwell the morning of the trouble in Gallup and was lying on her davenport in her upstairs apartment next to the justice court on Coal Avenue when she heard a "commotion" out in front on the street. Fifty or so people were milling about, speaking in Spanish. She called her neighbor, Mrs. Wiler, who lived in the rear apartment, to come in, and they observed the crowd from her upstairs front window. They watched the crowd move down Coal Avenue to Third Street and then turn south on Third up to the alley. At that point they went to the rear apartment to see what was happening down in the alley below them.

"So your apartment did not have direct access to the rear of the building, is that right?"

"Actually there's a garage underneath the roof at the rear of Mrs. Wiler's apartment. It's right over the alley and right next to the back door to Judge Bickel's court or his office. When we got there, we could see the people start to come around from Third Street and come down the alley toward us. It was just two or three minutes after they left the front on Coal and ran to the back down the alley."

"This may sound odd, Mrs. Arcus, but are you sure that the same crowd you saw out in front was the same people who came around the back and down the alley?"

"It must have been the same mob of people."

Mrs. Arcus's recitation of what she saw was consistent with that of most of the other witnesses. The differences were brought out on cross-examination.

Hugh Woodward's first question on cross-examination boomed out across the room: "What did they have in their hands that you saw raised up in the air?"

Mrs. Arcus looked over at Woodward as though she was unsure who at that table was asking the question. "I don't remember seeing anything in their hands."

"You said you watched a small woman in the crowd. Can you tell us how many women were down there?"

"No, not an exact number. But there were women in the crowd, and they were doing a good deal of the talking."

"How about children?"

"There were children in front, but I don't remember seeing children in the back. There were no people in the alley until the crowd from the front came back there."

"That, madam, is an assumption on your part. You do not really know who was in the back, as you were looking in the front for twenty or so minutes, weren't you?"

"Well, yes, that's true."

"Thank you. Tell us what happened to the crowd when the tear gas went off."

"I don't know what happened when the tear gas went off because I was pretty much blinded by it myself."

"And it was at that point that you went into the house?"

"Yes, that is all I saw. Of course, I read all about it that afternoon. *The Gallup Independent* is right behind us, you know, right across the alley."

"Thank you, Mrs. Arcus. I have no further questions."

As she left the stand, Mrs. Arcus stopped near the last row of the spectator area and started to sit with another well-dressed woman. But the other woman got up when the prosecutor called out: "Your Honor, the state calls Mrs. Byron Wiler to the stand."

With that, the other woman pushed out of the row and moved forward to the clerk's small table to take her oath. But for the fact that her dress and purse were a slightly lighter shade of blue, it appeared at first that Mrs. Arcus was returning to the stand.

"Mrs. Wiler, can you tell our jury your full name and current place of residence?" asked David Chavez. He noticed how much the two women looked alike; maybe they were sisters.

Mrs. Wiler answered, as if she was reading his mind: "I am Mrs. Byron Wiler; I have lived in Gallup on the same floor, in the same building, and nearly for the same time as your last witness, but we are not related, even though everyone thinks we are."

Chavez couldn't help but comment: "Well, ma'am, you could have fooled me. Now, let us get on with telling the gentlemen of the jury what you saw that morning back in April with Mrs. Arcus. You heard her testimony, did you not?"

"Yes, I surely did, and I hope I do not have to repeat everything for you."

"No, ma'am, I think we can move forward some. But just for our record, you lived next door to Mrs. Arcus on the second floor of the Sutherland Apartments on the day of the shootings in Gallup on April 4 of this year, correct, ma'am?"

Mrs. Wiler confirmed the size, makeup, and direction of the crowd that morning. She volunteered the observation that ten or fifteen of them were carrying sticks. "I imagine that they were clubs of some kind," she explained.

"Did you see any weapons?"

"I saw a gun."

"Where was it, and who had it?"

"Right near the *Independent* building I saw this large Spanish fellow with a gun in his right hand. He was just standing there, pointing the gun toward the middle of the alley. I heard a shot, and from there I ran to the edge of the roof. I looked over just in time to see Mr. Carmichael fall."

"Who was with him when he fell?"

"I didn't see anyone with him when he fell. Then I heard another shot and I saw this large Spanish man; he turned around and fell on his face. He fell behind the *Independent* building."

"Could you see who he was firing at?"

"I didn't see him fire his gun; I only saw him holding it. I left then and went back into my apartment."

"And that is all you saw, ma'am, or is there something else you can add for our jury?"

"No, that is all I saw."

The cross-examination by John Simms was masterful and short. She couldn't identify a single defendant as being in the alley that morning.

There was a stir in the courtroom because as Mrs. Wiler left the stand, a large man in a police uniform moved from behind the prosecution table to the clerk's table. At first it appeared he was asking about something, and then David Chavez said: "Judge, we would like to call Chief Presley to the stand."

Gallup City Police Chief Kelsey Presley came from an old Gallup family and was well known in western New Mexico. His appearance on the stand promised to be interesting, as he not only was involved in the riot; he was directly responsible for the arrest of some of the men on trial. While he had friends in the courtroom, none of them were sitting on that long, hard bench behind the defense table.

"Mr. Presley, you are the chief of police in Gallup, are you not?" Chavez asked.

"I am."

"How long have you held that position?"

"More years than I want to count."

"Well, you need not do that; we are interested in your observations on the morning of April 4, 1935. Were you on duty that day?"

Chief Presley took fifteen minutes to set the scene and explain that he was there out of curiosity that morning. He saw the crowd in front and went inside the justice court to see what was going on. He identified both Correo brothers as well as Serapio Sosa, Agustin Calvillo, Rafael Gomez, Leandro Velarde, Manuel Avitia, Joe Bartol, and Juan Ochoa in front when he went inside. When he finished his identification of the defendants, there was a stir on the long bench occupied by the ten defendants. After three days of trial and sixteen witnesses, this was the first man to place Calvillo at the scene. Montoya had placed Avitia and Ochoa out in front, but only by way of impeachment on his preliminary hearing testimony.

"Now, sir, who did you see inside the office of Judge Bickel when you got there?"

Presley went on for another ten or fifteen minutes, giving his version of the events in Judge Bickel's court that morning before the shootings. He was asked about Navarro, the man on trial.

"Yes, as I told you earlier, just before they went out the back way, Navarro made some kind of motion toward the front door. He got up from the chair where he was sitting and took a step or two toward the west and just made kind of a motion like that. Carmichael grabbed hold of him and said, 'Come on here'; something that way. So Charlie Massie and I stayed at the front door while the rest of them went out the back. I stayed there quite a bit. I opened the door and started talking to the people, telling them there was nobody in there, but they were shouting and hollering, so they didn't understand, I guess, because they kept right on. After a few minutes I went outside and turned west toward the alley. I did this because I saw several men run across the street from the Cairo Theater, going south on Third Street, and quite a number of others leaving from in front of the door in front of Bickel's office. They started off kind of in a walk, then pretty fast, between fast and run; looked like they were in a hurry."

"Where did they go?"

"They ran to the corner and turned south down Third Street. I came out and followed them around because I thought there was going to be trouble. After I got around there, I met a lot of these fellows coming back."

"By these fellows, who do you mean?"

"Well, as I was running toward the alley, I met this man Agustin Calvillo running toward me and he had a club in his hand, and I took that out of his hand and I went on."

"Let me stop you there. What did you do with the club that you took away from the defendant Agustin Calvillo?"

"I held it in my hand for three or four steps and then threw it over the wall."

"Thank you, sir. Now I hand you State's Exhibit 24 and ask if you can identify that for the jury."

"This is the club that I took off Agustin Calvillo."

"Go on with your story, sir."

Chief Presley was a likable man, and the jury seemed interested in his testimony. He said he got to the alley just in time to feel two bullets whiz past his face. He avoided looking at the defendants as he methodically named off nine of the ten men on trial and claimed they were coming out of the alley as he was going in. Willie Gonzales was not named by the chief of police. He said he saw Avitia coming out with what looked like a gun in his hand. That caused him to arrest Avitia, but at the "moment" of arrest, he didn't have the gun. He saw a woman lying in the alley with a gunshot wound in her leg and identified the bodies of Sena Velarde and Solomon Esquibel. Lastly, he described Bobcat's shoulder wound and Boggess's bloody face for the jury.

As usual, Hugh Woodward could hardly wait to begin his vigorous style of cross. "How many officers were on your city police force back in April, Mr. Presley?"

"There are six police officers on the Gallup police force. Four of us were on duty that morning."

"Now, as to the front of the building that morning, no men were out there with weapons, were they?"

"I did not see any weapons on anybody when they were in front of Bickel's office that morning."

"No violence, no breaches of the law, no drunkenness, that sort of thing, right?"

"I did not see anybody making any breach of the peace, and I never considered arresting anyone at that time."

"Right, because if you had seen that, you would have arrested them on the spot, right, sir?"

"Well, yes, but the way they were pounding on the windows, some should have been arrested. But I didn't want to start something myself, so I let them go."

"When you saw the crowd run down Coal Avenue toward Third Street, you did not call your station for help, did you?"

"I didn't call for help from the police station because no one was there to call. We have some red lights that we can turn on and if the officers happen to be in the business part of town and see the lights, they know we need them, but if they're out of the business part of town, there's no way of calling them."

"That's right. You have those lights in the business district because Gallup is pretty much used to crowds in the downtown area, isn't that correct, Chief Presley?"

"I'm used to crowds of excited people in town. I thought we could handle them. I didn't see anybody fighting or making any assaults on anybody."

"Chief, you know the difference between the sound a gun makes and the sound a tear gas bomb makes, don't you?"

"I never heard any explosions of tear gas bombs. I had never heard one of those go off before, but I know gunshots when I hear them. I'm sure they were gunshots, but I don't know whether they were rifle shots or pistol shots. I don't think they were shotgun shots. I never detected any tear gas when I got to the alley."

"So as far as you're concerned, there never was any tear gas bomb. You didn't hear it or smell it, is that right?"

"As far as I knew, no one ever threw a tear gas bomb. I never saw any smoke or smelled any gas."

Mary Ann leaned over and whispered that maybe Chief Presley was in some other alley on some other day when there was no tear gas and no dead bodies. We tried to listen to the rest of his testimony, but I admit that he didn't sound credible after saying that there was no tear gas in opposition to every other witness who had taken the stand so far. He lost a little more credibility when he said he saw the woman with the gunshot in her leg but didn't try to help since he didn't know her. He finished his cross-examination by admitting that he took part in the roundup of people who he "thought might be implicated in the trouble." As he recalled it, they arrested "quite a number—maybe seventy-five or eighty." He also took part in the house-to-house searches for Hoy's gun and seemed perplexed at the interest of the defense in this issue. He ended with a smile and candidly said: "Nope, we never did find that gun."

Judge McGhee couldn't wait to adjourn for the day, and the usual admonitions to the jury were given in less than two minutes, following which the judge disappeared through his little door behind the bench.

Thursday, October 10, 1935

Dear Journal:

Well, today wasn't tiring at all. My bottom is sore, but I'm hardly tired. I don't know how men can sit all day on a wooden bench without feeling as sore-bottomed as I do. Of course, I'm speaking of the defendants in the trial, not the lawyers. The defendants (like the spectators) are on a wooden bench, but the lawyers are on cane-back chairs with little cushions on them; so are the jurors. I can't tell about the judge. He has a chair, and it has a high cane back, but from where we are, we can't see whether he has a cushion. I bet he does.

But enough of that. I guess I began with something so innocuous as benches and bottoms because I have bad news for you, Madam Journal. Nothing really happened today. They put on six witnesses (counting recalling Mr. Montoya and Mr. Boggess again) but mostly covered old tired subjects. Like, Who was there? How many people were out in the street? Who was in the alley, and what did they have in their hands? Frankly, I think the jury is getting fed up with the repetition of it all. I know I am.

That is not to say the day was a total loss. At least one witness (Mrs. Wiler) actually saw the man who shot the sheriff. At least she thinks she did. I happened to be looking at the juror on the top row seated closest to the judge when she described the actual shooting. He seemed sort of astounded that the prosecutor would ask for this testimony. If she's right, none of the men in the courtroom killed the sheriff. If she's wrong, she should never have been called by the prosecution. Either way, it got his attention. I'm going to watch him more often from now on, particularly when Dee and Bobcat take the stand.

The morning started out with Locorio Lovato. I don't know him, but he has kids in high school (none in my homeroom, though). Then they brought back Mr. Montoya for the second time and Mr. Boggess for the third time. We learned all about Mr. Montoya's wise decision to stay inside and avoid the bloodbath out in the alley and about Mr. Boggess's gun (the rare one he lost). I don't mean to be mean (my God, I'm an English teacher; why am I writing like this?), but he really is hapless. All I could think after he left the stand was, If the gun is that rare, why did Mr. Boggess have it? If he did have it, he shouldn't have stuck it in his belt. Why didn't he have a proper holster? Seems to me there are two possibilities here: either he lost it (if he's telling the truth) or he fired wildly (if he's lying). The latter means this case is tragic in more ways than I originally thought.

Now, Madam Journal, I admit to rambling on too much here. It likely upsets you, given my normal writing style (which I hope is good). But it sure is fun just to be able to put random thoughts down without worrying about my students or the recipients of my letters. The more I think about it, the more I think I'll just keep this journal for myself. But maybe I will publish it, as was my original plan. At least that was what I told Billy Wade, and I believed it when I said it. Who says you have to be decisive when you're out of town? I think I can be just as indecisive as the lawyers in this case are. Are they licensed to be indecisive?

It's becoming clear to me why the law allows the state to have lots of different legal theories about a case. Mr. Patton made it clear in his opening statement that the state had at least six different theories about what happened in this case. We have now covered three full days of trial, and they have called fifteen different people to the stand. They have offered lots of exhibits. And this much is clear. They need *theories* and lots of them because even they do not know what happened in that alley that morning. A theory is something that might or might not be true. On the other hand, a fact is not debatable. It either happened or it didn't. Here the prosecution doesn't know all the facts and therefore has to rely on different theories as to what might have happened. Mr. Woodward in particular seems to be agitated over this. He has argued that the judge ought to make them pick a theory and stick to it. I can see why they don't want to do that.

So far, we know that lots of mistakes were made and that Sheriff Carmichael was killed. I'm beginning to think that the most important issue in the case is whether his death was the result of those mistakes or was, in fact, premeditated murder. So far, the mistake theory is outweighing the premeditation theory.

If I'm right, there's another tragedy here, and that is the deaths of the *other* two men who were killed that day. I know this trial isn't about them and no one is charged with their deaths. But if Sheriff Mack died because his own men panicked or because he was hit in the cross fire, what about them? So far, no one has said they did anything wrong other than Mr. Boggess. It's frightening even to think about what happened if you make the assumption that Mr. Boggess isn't being truthful up there on that witness stand. I sort of believe him. I'm just not sure that even he knows what really happened.

Well, Madam Journal, tomorrow is another day. I do wish we had a list or something to tell who was up next. Like a batting order or at least who is scheduled to pitch. Can you imagine a baseball game where the batting team has no idea who will take the field until the batter is up at the plate and facing a pitcher he never heard of? If baseball can do it, why not the law?

nine

MARY ANN'S DOUBTS

Friday, October 11, 1935

After the now customary intonations about rising up, Judge McGhee looked out over the courtroom and said: "Well, good morning to you all. The record will show the presence of the defendants, their counsel, and the prosecution. Gentlemen of the jury, I take it you are all rested and ready for a full day of testimony. Before we swear in Mr. Porter as our next witness, I must say I was remiss in reminding you last night to stay away from the newspapers and the radio reports about this trial. I know that's real hard because that's all they seem to be writing about up here. Now, back home in Roswell, we're getting other news, but here in Aztec the whole paper is being devoted to this trial. You will be deciding this case on what you see and hear in this courtroom—what the papers say doesn't count. So that is why I will keep on reminding you to pay attention to what happens here and ignore what happens out there. Now, are you ready, Mr. Patton or Mr. Chavez?"

Chavez rose and took the witness. "Mr. Porter, good morning, sir. Please tell our jury your full name, age, and where you live."

"My name is Sherman Porter. I am thirty-one; I live in Gibson, New Mexico."

"Gibson is just outside of Gallup, is it not?"

"Yes, sir, it's about four miles north of Gallup."

"Were you in Gallup on the morning of April 4, 1935?"

"Yes, I was."

Sherman Porter was somewhat rare as a witness because he seemed very comfortable on the witness stand. He made eye contact with every juror and smiled at the judge and the bailiff. He almost seemed to engage them in a one-way conversation about driving south on Third Street and seeing the crowd of men and women running toward the alley.

"Could you tell if there was a leader or anyone who looked like he was in charge?"

"There was a tall fellow with a thin mustache leading. He was about two or three paces ahead of the whole crowd. He came to the alley and looked down it. He threw up his hands and hollered, and he motioned for them to go back the other way. Well, they stopped there, just for a fraction, just kinda checked theirselves, and at that moment there was a noise at the door and he hollered and motioned for them to come on. And then they all ran into the alley there."

"Then what happened?"

"After the door opened, I saw Carmichael step out. He had hold of a prisoner's arm; Dee Roberts had hold of his left arm. I could see that Bobcat and Hoy Boggess were close by."

"So you knew Deputies Wilson and Boggess?"

"Well, I knew who they were, but we're not friends or anything."

"What was the crowd doing?"

"The crowd was all standing around there and hollering and talking in very loud voices. Most of it was in Spanish. As they stepped out of the door, I saw Carmichael push this fellow with the long mustache and then they began advancing up the alley. The officers began advancing up the alley, and the crowd was rushing right in behind them. I recognized the man with the mustache that Carmichael had pushed away because I had seen him around Gallup before. This was the same fellow that had led the crowd up Third Street and had motioned to them to follow him into the alley."

"Let me interrupt you, sir, to make sure the jury is clear. The man with the mustache, is he one of the defendants on trial here today?"

"No, as I told you when you first interviewed me, he's not one of the defendants that is here in court."

"Now, sir, go on; what happened next?"

"After they advanced up the alley, they kinda, well, they had moved up past the door, and then I saw that fellow there pull this gun out of his pocket."

"Your Honor, may the record reflect that the witness is pointing toward the defendants' bench. Mr. Porter, will you tell the jury the name of the defendant who you are pointing to?"

"The fellow I'm talking about is a defendant and is here in court this morning. I don't know his name, but I can point him out."

"Your Honor, if I may be of assistance to the court," said John Simms, who had risen and was standing next to the defendant Porter seemed to be pointing to. He placed his hand on Manuel Avitia's shoulder and asked: "Is this the gentleman to whom you have been referring?"

"Yes, he is."

"Your Honor, the defense will stipulate that the witness had identified Manuel Avitia."

"Thank you, Mr. Simms."

"Your Honor, the state accepts the stipulation. Now, Mr. Porter, please go on. What did you see, if anything, Mr. Avitia do with the gun you just described?"

"I saw him pull this gun out of his pocket. He rushed right through what few people were in front of him toward the officers. Well, they had advanced approximately fifty feet, and there was a lot of loud talking as they were going up, and then I could see the heads of the officers and I noticed someone throw something. I couldn't tell what it was until it hit the street. It came over the heads of the crowd. It didn't hit anyone. It landed approximately across the alley from the rear door of Judge Bickel's office but closer to the side of the *Independent* building than the middle of the alley."

"Once it hit the street, could you tell what it was?"

"Well, just as that hit the street, it exploded, and just a fraction of a second after that there was a volley of shots fired. The crowd kinda swayed from one side to the other or seemed to go from one side of the alley to the other, and then they came running down the alley. This fellow here [pointing at Manuel Avitia, who continued to stare blankly at the heads of the defense lawyers seated in front of him], the same one with the pistol, came running toward me. He came running west down the alley, and he had this gun in his hand. He ran past me standing on the corner of the alley."

"What did he do then?"

"I don't know. I didn't pay him any more mind. That was when I glanced back up the alley and I noticed Dee standing up there with a gun in his hand, so I stepped around into the *Independent* office. Just as I got inside, they brought this here woman who was shot in the leg out of the alley into the *Independent* office. I got hold of her arm as she came through the door. At that time I noticed my little nephew opening the door of my car parked right across from there and he was going to get out, so I ran out the door and ran across the street over there and made him get back in the car."

"All right, sir, let me go back and see if I can clear something up. You have told our jury about hearing shots from the corner, but can you tell them who was firing those shots?"

Mr. Porter calmly explained that he heard about fifteen shots as he stood at the entrance to the alley. He went on to identify one other defendant—other than Manual Avitia—at the scene. That was, he said, Leandro Velarde.

John Simms rose for the cross-examination and began, as usual, with something that the prosecution failed to bring out on direct examination.

"Yes, I work for Gallup American Coal Company. I have worked for them for about sixteen years."

"Were you a guard for the mining company?"

"I was never a guard and never carried a gun for the company. I am a fireman at the power plant, which is actually located in town, in Gallup, I mean."

"How long have you been friends with the Roberts brothers?"

"I've been friends of Dee and Bob Roberts since I was a kid here in Gallup. I also know the chief of police, Mr. Presley, and I know Bobcat Wilson. I know Hoy Boggess. There's probably others that I can't think of right now."

"Let me ask you about the large fellow with the mustache who was leading the crowd up the street toward the alley. Did you see the man who was killed by the officers there in the alley that morning?"

"You mean, did I see that fellow dead? Yes, but he wasn't the big man with the mustache that was leading the crowd, if that's what you're getting at."

"And you never saw him again, I mean, since that time?"

"No, that's not the case. I never saw him any more that day, but I did see him on the street two or three weeks later after he was down from Santa Fe."

"Do you mean after he was down from Santa Fe or that you were down from Santa Fe?"

"I went to Santa Fe for the preliminary, but I didn't testify. I was summoned as a witness, but they didn't use me. I was subpoenaed down there. The big man I'm talking about was arrested and taken up to Santa Fe, but later I saw him walking around in Gallup. He's not one of the defendants. As far as I know, he's still in town, but I haven't seen him, so I don't know."

"Let me turn to Mr. Avitia. When you first saw him, was he standing apart or was he just a part of the crowd?"

"When I first saw Manuel Avitia, there was six or seven people in front of him and the rear door to the court. There was quite a few strung out behind him. But he was kinda by himself there. I saw him plainly, and I saw him pull out this gun out of his pocket. Just before he did that, the officers had come out with the prisoner and started east down the alley."

"How was he dressed?"

"He didn't have a hat on. I don't remember what kind of a shirt he had on, but he had a light tan coat, a sandy-colored coat. He pulled the gun out from his right side; I wouldn't say whether from his pocket or from his belt."

"You didn't see him fire the gun or do anything with it that was menacing to the police officers, did you?"

"When he pulled it out, he had it like this, and he started right through the crowd toward the officers."

"Was that before or after the explosion of the tear gas bomb?"

"I'm not sure."

"You didn't see anyone shot, did you?"

"I didn't see Carmichael shot."

"And, of course, you don't know who shot him, do you?"

"I don't know who shot him."

Simms continued to cross-examine Porter on other interesting but less significant facts. For example, he got Porter to admit that the only person he knew close to Carmichael at any time that morning was Chief Presley and that when he told Presley about Avitia having a gun, nothing was done about it. He carefully extracted an admission from Porter that Velarde never had a gun and never committed an act of violence that morning, as far as he could tell.

David Chavez asked for a few moments to begin his redirect examination. After conferring briefly with Dick Modrall, Mr. Chavez asked: "Mr. Porter, you described Avitia as being bareheaded and wearing a sandy-colored coat. Was there anything about him that was unusual, that caused you to be able to remember him so clearly here today?"

"Yes, he had kind of pockmarks on his face. I was standing right there looking at him, and there's no question in my mind that he was the one there with the gun."

"And is the gun marked as Exhibit 24 the one you saw him with?"

"I don't know; looks like it."

"Thank you, sir, that will be all."

Another ordinary citizen approached the swinging gates as Sherman Porter was escorted from the courtroom. They obviously knew each other, as they shook hands as they passed. The new witness's work clothes contrasted with the suit and tie worn by Sherman Porter. The clerk inquired as to spelling as Mr. Chavez informed the judge that the next witness would be Mr. W. J. Campbell of Gallup, New Mexico.

"And how long have you lived in Gallup, Mr. Campbell?"

"Nearly all my life."

"What do you do?"

"I'm a body and fender man. My shop, or the one I work at, is on Coal Avenue just two doors east of the JP court."

"Who owns that establishment?"

"I was working for Harshman and Benninghall that day."

"Does the shop face the street, that is, Coal Avenue, or the alley to the south of Coal?"

"I guess both. The rear end of the shop faced the alley and was two doors away from the rear door of Judge Bickel's."

"Now, sir, let me direct your attention to the fourth of April, this year, between the hours of nine-thirty and ten o'clock. Were you on duty that day?"

W. J. Campbell's testimony was somewhat the mirror image of Sherman Porter's, except that Mr. Campbell's view of the shooting was from the east end of the alley. He saw Sheriff Carmichael and his deputy, Dee Roberts, trying to walk prisoner Navarro through the crowd. He saw a man he couldn't identify strike out at Carmichael. When pressed for details, he said:

"I saw the three officers passing the window where I was at, and directly across I saw a man and lady standing on the corner of the *Independent* building. My attention was attracted to this man and woman when as I saw this man draw a pistol and raise it and shoot in the general direction of the officers. I was looking at him when he fired a shot. Then I moved over to my right farther to see what effect the shot had taken. I saw Mr. Carmichael falling. Just approximately at the same time, I would say simultaneously, there was another shot fired from down the alley, the direction from the west. But I couldn't see them at all down that direction."

"You said three officers; which three?"

"Sheriff Carmichael and those two deputies, Dee Roberts and Bobcat Wilson."

"Well, you have told our jury about what happened to the sheriff; now tell us please what happened to the other two officers."

"Then is when I moved back from the window to the double door where I was before. I saw Officer Bobcat Wilson and Mr. Dee Roberts pull their revolvers and fire."

"Are you sure about that? I mean, were all three officers there then, with the sheriff down on the ground and both Bobcat Wilson and Dee Roberts firing their revolvers?"

"Bobcat Wilson was there then, but when I first looked down the alley, I don't remember seeing him there. I couldn't see the prisoner at that time. I don't know what became of him. Carmichael was there, lying on the ground with his head toward the south."

"What about Dee Roberts?"

"I saw Dee Roberts fire at the man who fired at Carmichael. I saw that man fall. He landed on a little rise in the ground right there." Campbell pointed at the clay model of the alley and continued: "He wasn't in the alley; he was in the vacant lot."

Mr. Campbell finished his direct examination by failing to recognize any of the defendants as having been at the scene that morning. Chavez passed the witness, and Woodward took the cross.

"Did you own that place?" Hugh Woodward asked. At first the witness looked confused, as though one of the defendants was speaking to him. Then he realized that it was a lawyer sitting down at the end of the table.

"I worked at that shop for the former owner, and then I took it over; I was employed there for eight or nine months altogether. I'm unemployed right now."

"Did you continue to work there after the shooting that you told us about this morning?"

"Well, it's connected. I lost that job because I had to go to Santa Fe for the preliminary and I was there for nine days. But I didn't testify at the preliminary even though I was subpoenaed and kept there nine days."

Woodward rose from his chair and walked over to the witness stand. He paused and looked directly at the witness. "You did not see any man here do an act of violence of any kind, did you?"

"I didn't see any of these defendants shoot the sheriff, but—"

Interrupting him, Woodward said gruffly, "Thank you, you've answered the question. In addition to not seeing any of them shoot anybody, it is also true, is it not, that none of them even had a weapon. Right, sir?"

"Well, that's right, but as I was trying to say, I did see a shot fired in the general direction of one of the officers."

"All right, you said that. But none of these defendants fired that shot, did they?"

"No, the man who fired that shot is dead. I didn't see any of these defendants with a weapon of any kind. The only man I saw shooting at the officers was killed right there at the building. That's all I have to say on the matter."

I looked at Mary Ann to see if she caught this subtle little piece of lawyer luck. She smiled at me and nodded. Sometimes letting an adverse witness volunteer something is actually a good thing. Not often, but sometimes. But for Mr. Campbell's eagerness to volunteer his last point, this jury might have never heard an independent witness say that the man who shot the sheriff was himself killed at the scene. That was *not* what the prosecution wanted out of this witness, that's for sure.

Campbell left the stand and walked by the defense table without so much as a glance at the solemn group of men on trial. He did smile at the prosecutor and nodded reverently at Sheriff Roberts as he passed through the swinging gate to the public part of the courtroom. The next witness was called and sworn in, and we waited to see if this man could corroborate Campbell's version of who shot the sheriff.

"Mr. Burkett, thank you for coming up here. Tell the jury where you live and where you work."

Mr. Burkett told the jury that he was from Sanders, about forty miles from Gallup—"over on the Arizona side." He mumbled some but eventually got it out that he was at Harshman Motors that morning with Mr. Campbell when the shooting started. Jessie Burkett was a dour man who rarely smiled and seemed surprised at the apparent interest of the jury as they studied him on the witness stand. He was reticent on important details but almost verbose on trivial subjects. The prosecutor tried to get him to limit his rambling testimony to the simple facts of what he saw in the alley.

"Just tell the jury what you saw from that point forward."

"I saw that they hit that one man down there. I saw them hit this man and then saw him fall and saw a gun fall out in front of him."

"Who was the man who was hit?"

"I dunno."

"Who hit him?"

"Dunno that either."

"Was he off by himself; was he in uniform? What can you tell us about him?"

"I dunno who hit him. There were people near him, but I didn't know any of them. I couldn't say whether any of them was Anglo-Saxon or not."

"You say a gun fell out in front of him. What happened to it?"

"I saw a couple step over to pick this gun up. That's what I figured they were doing. He fell down kind of crossways of the alley and the gun fell out in front of him. I didn't see anybody pick the gun up. I saw them as they stooped over. Later I found out that the man I was looking at was Hoy Boggess. Leastways, that's what Campbell said. Well, I stepped back then, and right after that the shooting started."

"But you didn't see the couple actually pick up the gun?"

"No, they was starting to, but then everything got crazy."

"Did you see anyone actually use that gun; that is, fire that gun at any time that morning?"

"I saw one shot fired. That was Mr. Wilson. That was at the time that he got shot. I didn't see who shot Mr. Wilson, but I did see him get shot. I couldn't tell the general direction the shot came from. When he got hit, he flinched and then he fired a shot. He didn't go down. He stayed up. They was about twenty feet from me."

"What happened to the prisoner?"

"I dunno. I never saw him do anything."

The prosecutor seemed reluctant to turn over the witness but nevertheless said: "Your Honor, we pass the witness."

John Simms sensed that this witness might be almost as helpful as the last one. "Mr. Burkett, I have just two questions for you. Did I hear you correctly on your direct examination, that you do not know if *they* got his gun or not? It just looked like two of these people were going after it? Is that about it, Mr. Burkett?"

"Yes, that's pretty much it."

"Last question, Mr. Burkett. Sheriff Mack Carmichael was shot and killed, and Deputy Bobcat Wilson was shot and badly wounded. None of these men on trial here did that in your presence, did they?"

"I dunno if they did. Hell, I don't even know whether they were there or not."

"No more questions."

Mary Ann looked over at me as if to question whether I got the subtle significance of this little bit of good fortune. As it stood now, Bobcat was seen by two independent eyewitnesses to be firing away at the men who shot the sheriff, but neither witness placed any of the defendants anywhere near Bobcat or Sheriff Mack. Was this how the rest of this trial was going to go? The next witness called was Charlie Massie.

David Chavez knew that the rules of procedure prevented him from leading his own witness but sensed that both the jury and the judge might appreciate a little soft "leading" with Mr. Massie on preliminary matters, just to move the case on a little faster. The courtroom model of single-fact questions was a fair but somewhat inefficient way to present testimony. So he said to Charles Massie, when he was all settled in on the witness chair: "Mr. Massie, let me see if I can get you to the important part of your testimony this morning. You were one of the officers who was with Sheriff Mack Carmichael when they took Mr. Navarro to court on the morning of April 4, 1935, were you not?"

"I sure was; I was there mostly the whole time. I had a ringside seat, so to speak."

Charlie Massie was an infectious sort of witness. The more he talked, the better he liked it. It took a half hour to learn that he was on the "night force" of the police department and knew everyone in town. Unfortunately the only men he recognized out in front of the justice court that morning were Leandro Velarde and Manuel Avitia. He did see two others in the back alley after he got there, which was after the shots had been fired. Those two were Gregorio Correo and Agustin Calvillo. He was sure about the club that his boss, Chief Presley, took away from Agustin Calvillo. He described it as a piece of pick handle with a wire in the end of it. He then said it was Exhibit 24, which was the club that Chief Presley said he took away from Calvillo. It didn't have any wire on the end and didn't look anything like a pick handle.

Chavez sat down, and Woodward stayed down.

Contrary to his usual style of cross-examination, Woodward didn't begin immediately. Instead he just sort of looked at Massie for a few moments and waited till Massie looked over at the defense table. "Orderly crowd, wasn't it, Mr. Massie? At least it was orderly when you got there, right?"

"Well, yeah, it was orderly at first and then gradually got more excited."

It was short, but it wasn't pretty. Woodward's sarcastic style of cross-examination, while effective, was unsettling. Charlie Massie wasn't an educated man and wasn't used to sparring with lawyers about details that he thought were unimportant. Consequently he seemed to miss the points that Woodward was trying to make. He admitted that Hoy Boggess wasn't really a deputy sheriff but only held a "commission." He admitted that he wasn't really a police officer but only worked for the local merchants as a guard for the downtown stores. He admitted that he was trained to look at a man or a woman for the purpose of "sizing them up" but was unable to identify hardly anyone in the crowd of people there that morning. He did say that most of them were from Chihuahuaita and that "most of them trade and come to the picture shows and come back and forth to the courthouse all the time."

The balance of the cross-examination covered Mr. Massie's role in the roundup of men and women after the shootings. He had little new to offer.

Friday at Noon—October 11, 1935

Dear Journal:

My, my, we covered four witnesses this morning, and they were most interesting. I'm sitting outside, writing on the banks of the Animas River, eating apples and contemplating my freedom. That is both wonderful and disturbing because as I ponder the day, those men down there in the Aztec "bullpen" are pondering whether they have a life.

It's much easier for me to see now why lawyers love the battle of wits in the courtroom. There's no other forum where you have the chance to change another person's mind so many times during the course of the day. What I mean is, these four witnesses were all called by the state and all tried to offer evidence in favor of the state. But all four were vigorously crossed-examined and ended up offering evidence for the defense as well.

It was much like a good baseball game, even if you don't know the players in advance. One inning would be good for the state, and then the defense would have a good inning. Only it's not innings; it's answers, and the end result won't be losing the league pennant; it could cost someone his life.

For example, this Sherman Porter was a nice man with a good memory who said things harmful to the defense case. On cross, though, he was shown to have strong ties to the lawmen in Gallup and to the Gallup American Coal Company. He was a very good witness for the state against Avitia. But he helped the rest of the defendants.

Mr. Porter did not, in my opinion, take very good care of his five-year-old nephew by leaving him in a parked car at the end of an alley where a riot was taking place. He also didn't help the wounded people in the alley enough. But he did help the defendants tremendously by recalling that a large man with a big mustache led the charge down Third Street from Coal Avenue to the alley. He said that big man led the crowd right into the alley, where he charged at Sheriff Carmichael. Actually, it's not clear to me now—did he actually hit Carmichael or was it "almost"?

What was most important is this: The Mustache Man (I have to name him since no one else was able to do so) was the leader and the man most likely to have started the riot (other than poor Mr. Boggess). And get this, Mustache Man was actually arrested by the law enforcement officers and taken to Santa Fe for the preliminary hearing. But he must have been released and not charged because Mr. Porter saw him back in Gallup *after* the preliminary hearing. Mr. Porter was clear on this because he himself was subpoenaed to testify as a witness at the preliminary hearing. Incredibly, someone decided not to call Porter to the witness stand in Santa Fe. Can you believe it? *If* they had only called Porter as a witness, he would have told them Mustache Man led the charge and maybe the riot, too. Mustache Man would have been identified as the man who actually tried to strike Carmichael. That would have put Mustache Man on that long bench over there in the courthouse instead of free as a bird down in Gallup. I can hardly believe it.

Hardly anyone even blinked an eye at this testimony. Am I the only one who thinks this is important? After all, Mr. Porter isn't a lawman; he's just a citizen. He might have a slight bias in favor of the law. But even so, doesn't that make him even more credible? The next witness called by the state was another private citizen, a man named W. J. Campbell. He wasn't the most articulate witness to take the stand, but he was sure direct and to the point. He saw the man who shot the sheriff, and he saw the man who shot that man. But it wasn't any of the defendants, and he wasn't even in the alley. As Mr. Campbell remembers it, the man was in the vacant lot just east of the back door to the justice court. He saw *both* Bobcat and Dee Roberts pull their pistols and shoot *at* this man right after he fired at the sheriff. He wasn't sure who actually killed the man, but whichever officer it was, they should be able to confirm it when they take the stand.

Speaking of that, everyone is wondering when Dee and Bobcat will be called to testify. I'm not sure why they're waiting. Billy Wade says it's because you always want to close your case with a strong witness, but it seems to me that this jury is getting more and more confused with all this inconsistent testimony. At least I'm getting confused.

I can admit that, since I'm coming to the conclusion that this journal will be mine and I will not even try to publish it. That's partly because it's so, what—short, concise? "Meager" comes to mind. Meager things ought to remain private, don't you think, Madam Journal?

Getting back to Mr. Campbell, the defense made some points with him as well. He told the jury that Bobcat and Dee both fired and that even though he didn't see which one hit the man, one of them did. Most importantly, the unnamed man who was hit was the only man, other than Dee and Bobcat, who ever fired a gun in that alley—and he was killed. That was very good for all the defendants.

Right after Mr. Campbell, the state put on Jesse Burkett, who was right there in Harshman's with Campbell. In fact, it seems that Campbell and Burkett are friends and rode up here to Aztec together. I bet they talked about their testimony the whole way. It sure sounded as if they rehearsed it.

Mr. Burkett was a funny man with nothing funny to say. He saw poor Mr. Boggess get beat up and lose his gun. He saw a couple (I think he meant a man and a woman who were married or something) stoop over to pick up Mr. Boggess's gun, but then the gunfire started and he didn't actually see them pick it up because he was distracted. I thought that was odd. If it was Boggess's gun that was used in the shooting of the sheriff, how did it get fired before it got picked up off the ground in the alley? Of course, it could have happened and Burkett could be mistaken, but it's getting very curious over there in that courthouse. I wonder if the jury can see the inconsistencies. Or is it just me?

Oh, Burkett also confirmed Campbell's story that after Bobcat got hit, he pulled his gun and fired at the man who shot him. I can't wait until Bobcat gets on that stand. He must be a hell of a man (Billy Wade always says that) to return fire after getting shot in the chest and having the bullet lodge right next to his spine. Every time some witness talks about him firing or walking down the alley, I'm reminded of what Doctor Pousma testified to regarding his condition when he arrived at the hospital out at Rehoboth thirty minutes later—in mortal agony—near death—amazing!

The last witness of the morning was that Charlie Massie, the store guard who thinks he's a real policeman. He was definitely not interesting. I guess they have to call him because he placed more of the defendants in the alley, but I didn't think he was all that credible myself. I wonder how the jury saw him?

One of the reporters here from Texas told me today that the famous gun expert, Mr. J. Frank Powers, is in town and staying at the Aztec Hotel. He said that means the state is going to spring him on the defense tomorrow. Apparently he knows more about guns and bullets than just about anyone in the West. So that should be interesting, but what I'm trying to figure out is, how can he help them if they don't have the missing gun? Wouldn't he have to have that to test it? If he can't test it, how can he testify about it? Seems to me there are more questions than answers when it comes to the guns and bullets in this case.

Speaking of guns and bullets, there's also a man here from Denver who thinks he's a real smarty-pants on ballistics. He was talking down on the grass in front of the courthouse about .45s and rifling marks (whatever they are) and about Mr. J. Frank Powers. He has some books on guns with him and seems to be here just to listen to the testimony about the missing gun in this case. Tomorrow should be most interesting.

Good afternoon to you, Madam Journal, I'm getting to like you more now that I know you're going to stay with me and not go blabbing your big mouth all over town.

Postscript. Billy Wade argues with me over the smallest of things. Too small even to repeat. But it's not the content of the argument, it's the fact that we argue that's annoying. Annoying? Is that it, or is it something more? How can I love someone who annoys me? I do love him, and he does annoy me—it's like direct and cross-examination. One is supposed to inform, and the other is supposed change what you just learned. I love and am loved, but is that enough? Why do I feel like my love for him must be cross-examined to test its truth? Will we argue more or less after this trial is over? I'm getting the terrible premonition that the answer depends on what happens in the trial. These men seem innocent; indeed, they're presumed innocent. But if they're convicted, I know Billy Wade will say that the jury verdict was just and fair because that's how he sees the trial itself—just and fair. But even if he's right—these men, at least some of them, should not be here and should not have to face even a just and fair trial. Am I getting their ordeal mixed up with my future? What happens if they're all acquitted—Billy Wade will be just fine with that, but that's because he'll see it as the law at its best. I'm starting to think of an acquittal as the law merely recognizing the mistake of having a trial in the first place. Those are two very different things, and Billy Wade and I might spend the rest of our lives thinking differently about this and lots of other things as well. So I have to decide whether this trial is telling me more than I want to know about my future. Is it with Billy Wade, or should I be thinking about alternatives? Damn, I hate this.

Everyone in Gallup was surprised at the length of the trial. The trial went on and on, but the main point seemed to be getting further and further away. The men in the American Bar weren't all that thrilled with the way that the lawmen were conducting themselves. Seems that most, but not all, thought that putting Hoy and Fred and Chief Presley up there to lay it out for the jury was a bad move. Not that anyone in the bar claimed to know just how it *ought* to be done. No, planning wasn't part of the talk in the bar. Criticizing and complaining, that was what those boys did best.

That night after supper Mary Ann and I talked about how necessarily tedious trials really were. I said: "The prosecution must put on *all* the facts they have, even if some of them aren't all that interesting to either the jurors or the folks in the back of the courtroom, like us. They have to put on enough evidence to establish a *prima facie* case. That means that when the judge takes his 'first look' at the case, he says okay, you put on enough so that this jury can decide the rest. The prosecutors don't want him to take his first look at the case and say, you boys have been slacking off on the evidence so that the jurors would only have 'interesting' evidence. You should know better. Because you've been limiting your evidence to what is interesting, the jury doesn't have enough evidence on which to make a decision. Because of that, I'm going to have to throw this case out and dismiss the jury. They damn sure didn't want that kind of embarrassment, not to mention the lynching that'd likely follow. That's essentially why they're going slow and careful like. They're just putting up their *prima facie* case."

Bobcat was sitting with us for a spell after dinner, and he and I had another little disagreement about how things were going. Bobcat thought the defense lawyers were putting up a poor defense because they didn't make any big points or offer evidence of their own. As I put it, "That just goes to show how little you paid attention in our civics class in school. Let me remind you that the defense doesn't have to prove a damn thing. They don't have to call a single witness or offer one exhibit. All they have to do is poke holes in the evidence that the state is offering. And it seems to me that they're doing a pretty fair job of it. You see, at the end of the case they'll argue over and over that in this country, even if you're from the other side of the Rio Grande, you are by God fully presumed to be innocent until the by-God government proves you did it beyond any reasonable doubt. Now there's the key to the defense, as I see it. Reasonable doubt. Hell, except for Chief Presley, most of those boys up there on trial haven't even been mentioned by a witness, much less connected to the shooting of Sheriff Mack. If that jury is thinking fair and square, they have to be thinking that there's a reasonable doubt as to whether the state has any idea whatsoever who was involved at all, much less who actually did it."

Bobcat seemed to know what the boys in the Angeles Pool Hall down in Gallup were thinking. As you might expect, they had a much different view altogether. *Gringo* justice was still assumed to be the likely result. They knew about the so-called reasonable doubt standard and they knew how little real evidence had been put before the jury. It didn't matter, they said; it will be the same as always. The jury will decide that someone has to pay because a *gringo* sheriff died. That *hombre* is going to have brown skin, and his name is going to end with a vowel. It doesn't matter which *hombre,* just as long as they get someone. But they were encouraged about one thing: the *gringo* lawyers from Albuquerque were going after it, *que no?* The men on the long hard bench were getting defended just as though they were white and living on the south side of town. So maybe there's a chance after all. Bobcat told us what Paco, the philosopher and night bartender at the Angeles Pool Hall, had to say about their "chance": "You're fucking dreaming again."

That afternoon after lunch I sat on the porch of the old wood frame house where the lawyers from Albuquerque were living for the trial. We could just barely see the edge of the courthouse, down the street and on the other side of the Chinese elm trees that lined the blacktop street. "Are they heading in yet?" Hugh Woodward asked John Simms.

"No, I believe they're starting to straggle a bit. Seems like when we first started this trial, the public and those press boys lined up a half hour before court time. Now they straggle in right as the judge is taking the bench. I suppose when we finally get to the end, there'll be open seats in the gallery."

Hugh Woodward, always quick to respond even with his friends, boomed out: "John, they'll line up at dawn to hear your closing argument. Unless, of course, you want me to give it, in which case they'll be there at false light. Which reminds me, just what is your plan of argument? Are you going to concentrate on the obvious, like reasonable doubt, or are you going to come up with something novel, like they didn't do it?"

"Hugh, my friend, we have yet to hear from the two men who can put our clients in the electric chair, Bobcat Wilson and Dee Roberts. Until I hear their testimony, I'll not be planning any closing arguments."

"Well, you ought to get your wish soon. Mr. Patton and his fine bunch of prosecutors look to me like they're winding down their ordinary witnesses and building up for their stars, so I expect we'll hear from Deputies Wilson and Roberts soon enough. I rather doubt that you'll be calling them by those nicknames, Bobcat and Dee. Dee is all right, I suppose, but Bobcat sounds like a man you don't want to mess with, even on cross-examination."

With that, we walked the short block to the courthouse for the afternoon session.

ten

SWEET INEZ AND BALLISTIC SCIENCE

Friday Afternoon, October 11, 1935

Judge McGhee wondered to himself just where this case was going. It was of no consequence to him how the trial turned out as long as there were no legal errors and both sides did their best. But still, he viewed his role in criminal cases as more than just a referee. In a capital case, the role of the trial judge is even more profound. He has to act as the impartial conscience of the judicial system, just as the jury had to act as the impartial conscience of the community. It was their job to decide who was telling the truth, but he had to make sure the truth had a fighting chance to come out. So far, there had been little contest between the lawyers over the truth. That was because this was just the "fact-finding" part. Soon things would change, and he would start doing his job. He would have to move the case from "fact finding" to "law giving." In a case like this, it might not be the facts that decide guilt or innocence; it might be the law that he applied to those facts.

To that end he called the lawyers into his chambers at the start of the afternoon session and said: "Course, it's not for me to say, but my guess is that the prosecution is no more than two or three days from finishing up its case. I do not know and am not asking for any commitment from the defense as to whether it will call witnesses or stand mute, as is its right, at the end of the state's case. What I am starting to think about is the instructions that I will give at the conclusion of this case to our jury. I know that both sides have strongly held views of the applicable law. But as you men know, no meaningful decisions can be made until the evidence is all in. Be that as it may, I want you to be ready to advise me on which standard jury instructions you want me to give and which special instructions you think are appropriate no later than the day the evidence is all in. I will leave it up to you to figure that day out."

After they were all settled in the courtroom, the judge sensed the jury was anxious to get on with the case. It was as though they had heard from the important prosecution witnesses and were anxious to hear from the defense. But Judge McGhee dashed that hope when he asked: "Mr. Prosecutor, how many more witnesses will be called by the state?"

Dick Modrall answered: "We have eight or nine, Your Honor."

"That many? Who are they?"

"Well, Judge, we have three, perhaps four, more officers, three civilian eyewitnesses, a state policeman, and our ballistics expert."

"We'd best be getting on with it. Who is up first this afternoon?"

"I believe that Inez Lopez is here and ready to testify, Your Honor."

Inez Lopez was the fourth female to take the stand but without question the one who would be remembered the most by the men in the room. She was dressed in a simple dark dress that looked like it was the very best that she had. Her amazingly long dark hair framed a dusky oval-shaped face that defied description. Some would say beautiful, some striking, some angelic. Her walk was confident and purposeful, but it was her hands that caught the eye of every man in the room. She had the hands of a pianist, and she slowly clasped them in front of her on the rail as she faced David Chavez. She looked quite young, but few guessed just how young she really was. She gazed straight ahead as she settled into the witness chair but somehow seemed to look at all who looked at her. As she sat down, she inhaled, and the men closest to her, the ones on the jury, held their collective breath. For the remainder of the morning every time she took a deep breath, every man held his. She was both soft and crushing at the same time.

"Miss Lopez, are you comfortable? Can we get you a cup of water before we begin?" asked David Chavez as he moved close to the witness box. In doing that he became the envy of every man in the courtroom. Even Judge McGhee sat straight up in his cane-back chair.

"No, I'm comfortable, thank you."

"Just so our record is complete, would you be so kind as to tell the jury your full name and age?"

"I am Inez Lopez, and I'm sixteen."

With that, David Chavez turned to the judge and said: "Your Honor, given the age of the witness, I would like to inquire if the defense will accept my avowal that this witness understands the oath she has taken and is fully aware of the consequences of sworn testimony in a court of law."

John Simms rose and said: "Of course, Your Honor, we are happy to accommodate the state and stipulate that Miss Lopez can give competent testimony in this matter."

"Thank you, gentlemen. The record will reflect the stipulation, and the witness may proceed."

David Chavez turned back to Inez. The jury was still fixated on her, but she seemed to be troubled by some or all of the defendants sitting on the long bench to her left. She looked over there several times as though she was looking for someone she knew. The first question from Chavez made her uneasiness clear: "Now, Inez, you see the defendant Leandro Velarde there on the bench, don't you?"

She said "yes" in a voice that was distinct but very small. It was as much a whisper as it was an answer.

"I'm sorry, you'll have to speak up a little so the jury can hear what you have to say. You did say yes, didn't you; you do know Mr. Velarde?"

"Yes, I do know him," she said, only marginally louder.

"When did you last see him; before today, I mean?"

"It was the day of the shootings. That's when I saw him. Then they took him to Santa Fe."

"Mr. Velarde lived near you, that is, near your parents' house in Chihuahuaita, is that so?"

"Yes, our house is across the street from theirs. His wife lives there and so did he and his brother, before he died."

"How long had you known Mr. Velarde and his brother?"

"For five years or maybe even more; at least five years."

"How did you come to see him on the day of the shootings? Was it before or after the shootings?"

"It was just after, I think; I was there when he came home. Everyone was crying because of Ignacio. That's why we were all there. His wife was crying, and so was I."

"Now, we've talked about this in my office, but as I told you, you have to tell these men on the jury what you saw at the Velarde house that morning. When the defendant Leandro Velarde came into the house that morning and you were there, what did you see?"

"I saw him take an ice pick out of his dress and put it in the icebox."

"Do you know what time it was when you first saw him that morning, that is, what time it was when you saw him take the ice pick out of his shirt?"

"It was about ten o'clock in the morning when he came home. I was at his house because his wife was crying and I went to see why she was crying. I saw him take his—take an ice pick out of his dress and put it in the icebox."

"You say 'dress.' He wasn't wearing a dress, was he?"

"He took it from his pants, the bib of his overall. He put it in the ice chest."

"Was he putting ice in the chest?"

"I don't remember if he brought any ice."

"Did he seem upset? Was he hurt or anything like that?"

"I don't remember if he was bleeding or not. I don't remember if he was limping or not."

"You said that before he got there, his wife was crying. Did she tell you why she was crying?"

"Before Leandro got there, she knew that her brother-in-law had been killed because she came ahead."

"What do you mean, she came ahead?"

"She came ahead, she was there, at the place where Ignacio was killed. She saw it and she was crying because of the killing."

"Your Honor, I have no further questions," David Chavez said, and looked at the defense table to see which of them would dare cross-examine this remarkable young witness. He should have guessed.

John Simms knew better than to take the unstated dare. He rose and said: "Your Honor, I don't think we need trouble this young lady any further. We have no questions."

While her testimony was quite incriminating, it would be lost soon enough. What would linger on the minds of the jurors was the demure way she left the stand and the soft glance she cast at the long bench on the other side of the room.

I had a law practice to worry about, so I drove down to Gallup after the trial ended for the day and worked in my office till about ten. Then I went to the American Bar for a nightcap before turning in. The young men in the bar had heard about Inez and talked mostly about her; the old men talked mostly about ballistics. Measurements were involved in both discussions, but that was about all they had in common. It was the subject of ballistics that carried on till late that night. As it turned out, this was the night before J. Frank Powers was to take the witness stand. That was because he stayed in Gallup for two days before the trial, at El Navajo Hotel. Several of Gallup's finest citizens spent their lunch hours with him, talking about bullet caliber, muzzle velocity, and barrel rifling.

Of course, he was mum about his actual testimony since he knew the press was following the case real close and he couldn't be all that sure just who was sitting at his table. There was usually a crowd. Apparently he entertained the locals by giving a spontaneous lecture on the basics of ballistics. Everyone was interested but didn't know just how the so-called science of ballistic evidence was going to figure in the case.

Bullets are measured by caliber, which is the diameter of the bullet in 1/100ths of an inch. A .45 caliber is 45/100ths of an inch across. With other things being equal, the larger the caliber of the bullet, the greater the extent of damage. A .45-caliber bullet causes great damage to whatever it hits. If it hits a man, the stopping power is immediate. His skin, muscle, and bone are immediately destroyed, and he is likely to die. But it takes more than just bullet caliber to figure it all out.

Experts have to figure in muzzle velocity, bullet design, and marks on the bullet itself created by the "rifling" on the inside of the barrel of the weapon. The muzzle velocity of handguns can vary some. Muzzle velocity is the speed of the bullet as it exits the end of the barrel and can range anywhere from 600 feet per second to several thousand feet per second. The greater the velocity, the greater the transfer of energy and the greater the damage to the man it hits.

As for bullet design, old Frank Powers patiently explained that the bullet is the projectile part of a cartridge. There are three main types. There's your standard low-velocity lead bullet, your full-metal-jacket high-velocity bullet, and last of all, a semijacketed bullet. Bullets made of lead are alloyed with antimony, which makes them too soft for high velocities. Most bullets are metal jacketed. Brass or a copper-plated steel jacket covers the soft lead core. Bullets with a full metal jacket keep their shape when they strike a target or a man.

Folks wanted to know about two things: First off, could old Hoy's gun have gone off accidentally when it fell out from his waistband? Second, was it Hoy's gun that was used to kill Sheriff Mack? Powers answered the first and danced around the second.

Single-action revolvers can discharge just from being dropped. Semiautomatics and double-action revolvers will not discharge when dropped, although, as you surely know, pulling the trigger can "accidentally" fire them. As to whether it was Hoy's gun, well, that depends on the rifling marks scored on the bullet they took out of the sheriff's body. If those marks line up with Hoy's gun, then they'd have a match.

But how can you tell if you don't have Hoy's gun? Well, now, that's what Mr.

J. Frank Powers was about to tell that jury up there in Aztec. But first they had to hear some more boring testimony from Officer Martin.

"Judge, we will call Officer Martin of the New Mexico State Police as our next witness."

H. C. Martin was everything that Inez Lopez was not. No one thought him pretty, small, or young. He was a cop's cop—barrel chested, weather beaten, and stern.

"Officer Martin, will you give us a brief summary of your experience in law enforcement?"

Before he could answer, John Simms stood and interrupted: "Judge, we are all well acquainted with Officer Martin. As he is here to lay foundation for the admissibility of exhibits and not to give perceptive testimony, we offer to stipulate to his credentials and the fact that he is a sworn and respected officer of the law."

"Yes, that should make it quicker. The record will so reflect. Mr. Chavez, please proceed as though the witness had been fully qualified."

"Yes, Your Honor. Officer Martin, we need your assistance in the matter of several bullets that have been identified with exhibit tags by the court clerk. Let me start with . . ."

Although it took longer than it needed to, Mr. Martin established that he had been present at the autopsy of Sheriff Mack Carmichael. He took custody of the bullet taken from the body and properly secured it. Then he took custody of Carmichael's gun and properly secured it. Having accomplished that, he took custody of Deputy Wilson's gun and properly secured it. Only then were the prosecutors able to establish the chain of custody and enter into evidence Exhibit 26 (the Carmichael gun), Exhibit 27 (Dee Roberts's gun), and Exhibit 28 (Deputy Wilson's gun). At that point the prosecutor handed them to the jury for their inspection.

As the jury was looking over the three guns, Frank Patton rose and informed the judge that the next witness would be none other than J. Frank Powers, the famed ballistics expert from El Paso, Texas.

Hugh Woodward whispered to John Simms as Mr. Powers strode to the witness stand: "Here it comes. Hang on, John, this is their case."

"Maybe so, maybe not," Simms said as he looked for the exhibit list on the now paper-strewn tabletop.

Mr. Powers testified at some length as to his considerable credentials and experience in ballistics. He explained to the jury that he had been qualified as an expert witness in many courts and had testified in several prominent criminal cases around the country. It took some time, but finally Mr. Patton asked Mr. Powers about the guns, bombs, and bullets in this case.

Powers started with the tear gas bomb thrown by Hoy Boggess and explained the effects that the particular type of tear gas bomb would have had on the people in the alley that morning. The tear gas bomb used in this case produces sickness of the stomach. The actual release of the gas makes no noise; it's a nonexplosive. After the firing pin is released, there's a cap, a percussion cap, which ignites the powder, that is on the inside of the can. The purpose of that is to heat this can to such a great heat that it's impossible for anyone to pick it up and rethrow the bomb at the thrower. That powder makes a hissing noise. The cap makes a small noise very much like the sound of a .22 rifle.

Then Mr. Powers covered how he could ascertain the make and caliber of the gun from which a bullet has been fired by examining only the bullet. The bullet is placed under one part of a compound comparison bullet microscope for the purpose of measuring the angulation of the rifling marks. You also measure the width and depth for comparison of that bullet with a known standard that the bullet in question is suspected of matching.

He identified Exhibit 3 as a bullet that he examined under his compound comparison microscope and covered at some length the procedure and his machine. The short version was that his machine was actually two microscopes mounted on a common base and connected at the top by an eyepiece known as oculars, a connecting eyepiece. The oculars are an arrangement of prisms that permit the viewing of two objects, placed under different microscopes, at the same time in the same field. He said that in this manner it was possible to line these objects up for the purpose of the identification. This bullet, Exhibit 3, was placed under that microscope, compared against known standards, and identified in that manner.

"Excuse me for interrupting, Mr. Powers, but what do you mean by 'known standards'?"

"By that I mean that I have standards of bullets fired through all known types of pistols. We have been able to collect those over a number of years. A pistol barrel has rifling. The rifling within a barrel is produced by the drawing of the barrel through a cutting tool, which scrapes the metal from the center of the barrel. This scraping process cuts down and makes a groove. After that process has gone on until the correct depth of the groove has been obtained, it is then moved into the second position and on around until it has completed the turn."

Next Mr. Powers identified Exhibits 25, 26, and 27 as the three guns that were given to him for testing by Officer Martin. Exhibit 25 was the semiautomatic pistol used by Mr. Boggess at the scene. Powers was quick to explain that he was told it was actually Mr. Wilson's gun that Boggess secured from Mr. Wilson after he was wounded in the melee. Exhibit 26 was the gun removed from Sheriff Carmichael's body at the scene of the crime. Exhibit 27 was the gun used by Dee Roberts.

"What did you do with those three weapons, Mr. Powers?"

"I fired test shots through all three of them in my laboratory. The test shots fired through these three pistols were then compared with Exhibit 3, which is the evidence bullet taken from the body of Mr. Carmichael. I determined that this bullet, that is, Exhibit 3, was not fired through any of these state's exhibits, the pistols."

At that point Judge McGhee interrupted: "Hold up a second, Mr. Powers. Did you say *not?* Are you saying that none of the guns offered in evidence here fired the shot that killed the sheriff?"

"Yes, Judge, that is what my tests prove."

Frank Patton appeared somewhat irritated at the untimely interruption by the judge but went on with his examination. "Let me hand you Exhibit 4. Please identify this for the jury."

"Exhibit 4 is the bullet taken from the body of Deputy Bobcat Wilson."

"Did you examine it in your laboratory as well?"

"Yes, of course. It's possible with modern equipment to ascertain definitely from an examination of a bullet and a comparison with another bullet whether the gun that produced the comparison bullet fired it. I was most interested in comparing Exhibit 3, the bullet taken from the body of the sheriff, with Exhibit 4, the bullet taken from the body of the deputy. It is my opinion that these two bullets were fired from a Smith & Wesson .45 double-action army-type revolver, of a model of 1917."

"How sure are you of that identification?"

"I'm absolutely positive. You see, I ascertained that definitely from my examination."

"How can you be so sure, Mr. Powers? Is there no possibility that those two bullets came from some other type of weapon?"

"No, sir. You see, the gun used to fire these two bullets is the only type of firearm made in the United States that fires a .45 caliber in which the rifling has a right-hand twist. There's no other type of gun made that has a right-hand twist in that caliber. This type of gun, a .45 Smith & Wesson, was designed for use by the United States Army and was adapted to the use of rimless or automatic type of ammunition. That type of ammunition can't be fired in that revolver without a clip. And there's another reason I'm so sure. At first, the shells used in this special type of handgun stuck and weren't very functional. So later on, a clip was designed for holding three of these shells, which are placed into the magazine or into the revolving cylinder and discharged in that manner."

"Thank you, sir, that was most helpful—"

"Wait, I'm not quite finished answering your question. I have here in court a container that has all of the bullets of a .45-caliber type known to ballistic experts and criminal identification experts all over the world. It covers all of the .45 cartridges made, dating from 1878 to the present time. You can see there the shells that are in the middle, which are marked .45 automatic rim and are especially designed for use in that type of revolver without a clip. It's not necessary to use a clip with the rim-type ammunition. This type of ammunition marked .45 won't fire in the .45 Smith & Wesson double action. The cartridge case is approximately a quarter of an inch too long and won't fit. The .45 rimless can't be fired through Exhibits 26 and 27 in any manner—they're not adapted to this type of firearm. Those two are the weapons carried that morning by Sheriff Carmichael and Undersheriff Dee Roberts. They would slip through the chamber. There can be no question about it: Exhibits 3 and 4 were fired through a .45 Smith & Wesson double-action army-type revolver, of a model of 1917. And that, sir, is a very rare weapon indeed."

"Thank you, Mr. Powers. Your Honor, I turn the witness over to the defense for cross-examination."

As expected by everyone in the courtroom, John Simms rose for the cross. As he began his cross, his face seemed to have a puzzled look on it. He tilted his head and squinted at Mr. Powers, who waited patiently and confidently for the first question. "Do I have this straight, sir: You are saying that the bullets taken from Carmichael and Wilson did not come from any of the guns that *are* in evidence, but they were fired from the same gun, which is *not* in evidence?"

"Yes, sir. That is exactly what I'm saying. They were both fired from the same .45 Smith & Wesson. And that one was the extremely rare type I told Mr. Patton about. The one the deputy lost at the scene."

"I see. Now, sir, you also examined another bullet, did you not? One that was fired from a .45 Colt?"

"Yes, I did. That one was quite different. It was the bullet taken from the leg of the lady who was wounded at the scene, a Mrs. Soledad Sanchez. I carefully examined that bullet."

"And did you determine whether it was fired from one of the guns that is in evidence, or did it come from a different weapon that is also not in evidence?"

"No, sir. I determined that that bullet, I call it the Sanchez bullet, was fired from a gun that is in evidence, Exhibit 25."

"Exhibit 25 is a Colt automatic pistol. That is the gun carried by Deputy Bobcat Wilson, is it not?"

"Yes, you are correct."

"So you examined the bullets taken from the two lawmen, Sheriff Carmichael and Deputy Wilson, and a bullet taken from a bystander, Mrs. Sanchez. What other bullets did you examine?"

"I also made an examination of the bullet that was taken from the body of a Mr. Solomon L. Esquibel. That is an entirely different type of bullet. It was a 255-grain .45 caliber."

"Did you compare it to the guns given to you by Mr. Martin of the state police?"

"Yes, of course. It was fired through the pistol of Undersheriff Dee Roberts."

"Now, another man was killed there that day. His name was Ignacio Velarde. Did you examine the bullet removed from his body as well?"

"Well, I examined that bullet, but it wasn't removed directly from his body. That bullet was purported to have passed through the body of Velarde. It was picked up on a vacant lot and shows the effect of ricochet."

"And just so our record is clear, sir, the bullet that supposedly went through Ignacio Velarde, ricocheted off something, and ended up in your lab is marked here in this courtroom as Exhibit 27. Did you determine which gun fired it?"

"Yes, this particular bullet, State's Exhibit 27, was fired through the pistol of Undersheriff Dee Roberts."

"So you're saying that he shot both Esquibel and Velarde?"

"I'm saying that his weapon was the one that fired the bullets taken from them. I don't presume to know who actually fired the weapon, as I was not there at the time."

"And just so we are complete here, you examined one other bullet, did you not?"

"Yes, one more. The last bullet I examined came from the vacant lot. It was subjected to a benzidine test and it showed no trace of human tissue or blood."

"Thank you, Mr. Powers. That's all.

Well, there you have it. All the waiting was over, but the big question was still unanswered. The science of ballistics was more or less convincing on some things but more or less confusing on others. It looked like old Hoy's hog-leg shooter, as Bobcat called it, was the gun that somebody used to shoot Sheriff

Mack and wound Bobcat as well. It looked like Undersheriff Dee Roberts could take the credit for killing two of the rioters, in the line of duty, of course. It looked like Hoy shot the woman in the leg with Bobcat's gun. And it sure enough looked like none of the guns from the officers were implicated in the shooting of the sheriff. Unless, of course, one of them picked up Hoy's gun. Or unless Hoy never lost his gun and used that revolver to blast away while Bobcat fired his automatic, just as the two independent witnesses say he did.

As of this part of the trial, we had heard from everyone but Dee and Bobcat. Mary Ann and I wondered if the jury had figured out from the testimony that Dee never got close to Hoy's gun and Bobcat damn sure didn't shoot himself. So who shot the sheriff?

It seemed to us that the answer had to be that someone, somehow, got hold of that gun that shot the lawmen. Was it Esquibel or Velarde? If so, how could they have managed it when they themselves were killed by Dee at the time they fired at Sheriff Mack and Bobcat? To say that the evidence was confusing was the understatement of the day.

Later on I learned from a man in Gallup who had a dinner table with Mr. J. Frank Powers at El Navajo, the day before he testified, a bit more about the so-called rare Smith & Wesson .45 that Hoy lost in the shoot-out. As he explained it, the .45 ACP cartridge is a rimless cartridge. That means that there's nothing for the extractor star of a revolver to push against. Now, if your fingernails are real stout, you might stick those cartridges directly into the chamber of your weapon. After you were done shooting, you would have to pluck out the empties by brute force. But that's not a very good solution because this weapon was specifically designed as a sidearm for army officers in World War I. So what they came up with was something called the half-moon clip. It was a steel-stamped little plate that snapped into the extractor grooves of three rounds of .45 ACP, holding them firmly into place. What you did was load two of the three-shot clips into your weapon. Then after you fired 'em off, the cylinder could be swung outward and a quick stab of the ejector rod would jettison all six empties right down to the ground. That meant the special Army Model 1917 .45 Smith & Wesson that Hoy had (and lost) could be reloaded nearly as fast as the Model 1911 Smith & Wesson auto-loading pistol.

The main point the fellow made was that there were a lot of those guns made by Smith & Wesson. At least, that was how the dinner crowd heard it. That was very different from the impression Mr. J. Frank Powers left that Aztec jury with. He told 'em the gun was "very rare." For our part, Mary Ann and I couldn't resolve the conflict. If the gun wasn't all that rare, then maybe someone else in

Gallup had one besides Hoy. If that's the case, then why did all of Chihuahuaita get torn up while the lawmen looked for Hoy's gun?

I couldn't speak for the men on the jury, but I was sure of the feelings of the crowd in the back of the courtroom: We were all glad the end of the trial was at hand. The ballistics stuff was interesting, but what everyone really wanted was to hear from Dee and Bobcat.

But we weren't yet to that point. Chavez rose from the prosecution table and announced to the clerk: "We call Mr. Bob Roberts to the stand."

Bob Roberts was on the stand a half hour or so. He confirmed his age, sixty-five, that he was Dee's big brother, and that he had been the sheriff of McKinley County before his brother held the job. He said he didn't see the shooting in the alley but emptied all the bullets from Carmichael's gun, a .45 Colt revolver, right there in the alley.

Hugh Woodward started out the cross-exam with some softball questions and established that Bob Roberts was proud to have been a peace officer and the sheriff of McKinley for quite a number of years. He confirmed that he didn't see the actual trouble that morning and so didn't know anything on his own knowledge about who shot anybody.

"Tell the jury about the crowd that was still there when you arrived."

"I just saw the crowd there afterward. I saw Old Mexico Mexicans, and Spanish Americans and Anglos, Italians, Czechoslovakians, and other nationalities there."

Bob Roberts paused and then added gratuitously: "And nine of the defendants were still there at that time too. I walked up to the crowd and told them to go away, to disperse and go on about their business."

"Now, sir, let me change subjects on you a little bit. Isn't it true that you swore out an affidavit on the day of the shootings that related to the .45-caliber pistol lost by Hoy Boggess?"

"Yes, sir. I believe I did."

"And didn't you swear in that affidavit that the lost gun was in the house of several different citizens at the *same* time?"

"Well, yes, I guess so."

"And you swore in that affidavit that you had personal knowledge that a *larceny* had been committed in McKinley County, New Mexico? Namely that the ones named in the affidavit stole the gun?"

"Yes, that's what we were after."

"Now, it says in the affidavit that the stolen goods, to wit, one double-action

.45-caliber Smith & Wesson revolver, was concealed in the premises of Peter Grenko, 241 Maxwell Avenue, Gallup, New Mexico. That is what you swore to, right, sir?"

"I was positive it was there from what I heard."

"But you swore that it *was* there, not that you *heard* it was there. Now, which was it, did you hear it or did you know it?"

"I presumed it was there. All the officers were looking for the missing gun, the officer's gun."

Judge McGhee looked confused and said: "Isn't this the same one Carmichael was killed with?"

The witness nodded while the defense shook their heads. Up to this point in the trial, no witness had testified to this, not even Frank Powers. At best, the evidence established that a gun with a right-hand twist like that of Mr. Boggess was the likely murder weapon. Now the trial judge was essentially telling the jury it *was* the gun.

"Let's get back to the question, Mr. Roberts. Didn't you also swear on the same day that the missing gun was in the following houses: Manuel Montoya at 615 North Third Street; John Tomac, Gamerco Road; John Doe, 501 West Aztec?"

"Yes. Well, that's what we had that day. But I also swore out more search warrants on April 6 and 7, 1935. We were searching for the gun, and parties came in and told me the gun was in this place or that place, and so I would swear out a search warrant."

"How long have you been a peace officer?"

Woodward extracted a little more blood from Bob by forcing him to admit that his affidavits were flawed because he "took these men's word" on the facts. He rationalized the search in Chihuahuaita by saying, "We had to have some kind of paper to do that." He seemed surprised by the connection Woodward made between his conduct as a "peace officer" and the fact that he had been a mine guard for Gallup American Coal Company for the last seventeen years. Woodward dismissed the witness, and Chavez didn't offer anything in rebuttal.

Looking out at the audience, Judge McGhee said: "I am well aware that tomorrow is a Saturday, but the court and the lawyers have discussed this, and everyone is desirous of having a Saturday session of court since our jurors are sequestered for the trial. The jury has been advised and is willing to go along with this plan."

The audience started stirring and gathering up their things, but Judge McGhee banged his gavel and said: "I'm not through with you people yet. There is another matter that I want to bring to the attention of the spectators in this courtroom. You all have been orderly up to now, but I am told that tomorrow, while we are having a rare Saturday court session, there are some demonstrations planned around the state and here in Aztec. They concern the so-called Gallup Defense Day. Now, let me tell you all that I will not tolerate any questionable acts on the part of visitors to the San Juan County Courthouse. It has been brought to my attention, and in fact I have noticed myself, that there are a number of out-of-state licenses on automobiles around this courthouse. There is to be no contacting of these jurors in any way. There are to be no demonstrations of any kind where these jurors might see them. They are to be escorted back to their place of lodging and left alone throughout the remainder of this trial.

"Now, if any demonstrations are attempted here in this courtroom or if any signs or propaganda are shown, I will have the offenders brought to me immediately and they will, I assure you, be put in jail. For a long time.

"I have already had to deal with one demonstrator, a Mr. T. R. Montoya, and I have issued a contempt order on him. I have more of those just in case you all out there don't think I'm serious about maintaining order and protecting this jury from outside influence during this trial."

Turning back to the jury, he said: "Keep an open mind. I will see you at nine-thirty in the morning. Counsel, we are adjourned."

That evening over coffee, the lawyers met to consider the judge's suggestions regarding jury instructions. They pondered the dilemma of preparing jury instructions this far in advance of knowing just what the facts were. The state, of course, had a much better idea because they knew, more or less, what evidence their remaining witnesses would add to the case. For their part, the defense not only didn't know what the evidence would be at the end, but they couldn't plan their real defense—whether to have the defendants testify on their own behalf—until they heard all the state's case. To complicate it, the judge had refused to make the state narrow its case by electing among the various legal theories available which ones would be given to the jury at the end of the case. About all that both sides could agree on was that the legal theories of conspiracy and of aiding and abetting a felony were still in. But the theory that one of these men on trial was the *actual* shooter wasn't moving very high up on the list.

I stopped by Mary Ann's room after the lawyers' meeting. She also pondered a dilemma, but for her, it was different. Her coffee was cold and her hand tired from the frantic note taking all day. But she told me to scram because if she didn't write tonight, she would forget tomorrow.

Friday Evening, October 11, 1935

Dear Journal:

I described this morning's session as "interesting." Well, this afternoon was positively exciting. Maybe I *should* go to law school. But I love my students, and I would hate to be so wasteful of everybody's time as lawyers always are. But as I said, today was an exception. The lawyers had exciting testimony to put on, and both sides scored great points.

The afternoon began with one of the most poised and believable witnesses to grace the courtroom this week. Her name was Inez, and she was only sixteen. She was the picture of innocence and good manners, but that didn't stop half the men in the room from lusting after her. You should have seen them, with their jaws hanging open and their minds on her body instead of her words. But I think she was too pure to notice. It's just as well; she'll soon learn that her opinions will routinely take second place to her looks, at least in the presence of the men of Gallup.

Inez seemed saddened to have to tell that her neighbor, Leandro Velarde, brought home an ice pick and put it in the icebox right after the riot in the alley in which his brother was killed. While it wasn't an artifact, her testimony was one hundred percent believable because she said he took the ice pick from his "dress" and placed it in the icebox. At first, the word *dress* threw everyone in the courtroom—she repeated it twice. The lawyer asked her if Leandro was wearing a dress, and she calmly explained that he took it from the bib of his overalls. To her it must have looked like a dress. Anyhow, it served to make her testimony extremely believable because she could never have made that up; it must have happened just as she saw it. Now everyone in the courtroom is assuming that there's a connection between Velarde's ice pick and what happened in that alley an hour earlier.

But I'm wondering how it can be. That so-called newspaper, the *Gallup Independent,* reported last spring that Hoy Boggess was stabbed, but he didn't testify about that, and neither did anyone else so far. Surely they're not going to bring him back for a fourth time to the witness stand. So if Hoy wasn't stabbed, who was? And if no one was stabbed, what is the relevance of asking Inez about the ice pick?

Somehow this all ties in to the conversation that Mrs. Green overheard a week before the riot. Remember that she said that Leandro said we only need our "toothpicks." Then there was that big fight in the courtroom over whether the word was *ice pick* or *toothpick*. Now, we have testimony that the same man (Leandro Velarde) who *might* have said "ice pick" *did* have an ice pick. So what? Is this relevant evidence? The ultimate absurdity could be at work here—maybe he said "toothpick" and maybe no one was stabbed. Wow, think about it!

I asked Billy Wade, and he said relevant means "tending to prove a probative point in the case." What is the point here? That someone got stabbed or that someone had an ice pick? Don't they have to connect it up or something? I mean, it doesn't seem fair to put in the testimony about an ice pick, even in Spanish, and then not put in testimony about using the ice pick to hurt someone. Maybe the jury will miss it and assume that someone got stabbed even if they didn't.

Anyhow, Inez Lopez was a perfectly wonderful young woman and made me proud that I'm a teacher. I wonder why I haven't seen her around town before?

The other exciting thing that happened today was that Mr. Powers, the gun expert, testified. I'm not sure whether he's a gunsmith or not. Maybe he's a gunjones (a little journal humor can't hurt, can it?). In any event, he was most impressive about guns and bullets. And he sure did cause a stir on the bench.

He explained how he tests bullets and gave a very interesting lecture on ballistic science. Then he laid his own little bombshell right in the courtroom. He said the gun that killed Sheriff Mack and nearly killed Bobcat was not only the same gun, but it was definitely, positively, no doubt about it, the one that poor Mr. Boggess lost. I could hardly believe it. Neither could the judge—he asked Powers if that "was" the gun that killed the sheriff. Neither could Mr. Simms—he asked Powers if he was sure that it was Hoy's gun since the lawmen never found it and he never tested it. Powers was quite sure. I'm not. I wonder if the jury is more like me or more like Mr. Powers?

His testimony was very long, but his point was very short. Bullets don't lie. They prove, beyond a reasonable doubt, what none of the witnesses have said thus far. Whoever shot the sheriff to death did it with a deputy's gun. How could that be premeditated murder, I ask you?

The last witness of the day was Dee's older brother, Bob. He looked it too. This man was not well schooled, shall we say, in legal procedure. I don't think he was very schooled in the sanctity of a sworn oath, either. It appears that Deputy Bob swore out warrants for Hoy's gun by saying he knew that the gun was in over a hundred different homes all at the same time. Incredible! It made me so mad, I can hardly write about it. So I won't.

Tomorrow is supposed to be the last day of the trial for the prosecution. Tomorrow is also Gallup Defense Day, and they have rallies scheduled for everywhere in the state and several other places as well. The point seems to be to raise money for the defense, but the press hounds are all saying that none of the money is going to Mr. Simms or Mr. Woodward and none of it is going to the families of the men on trial. Pray tell, where is it going? Too bad I have to cover the trial. Otherwise I would go to the rally here in Aztec and ask someone about the money. But duty calls, even if it's a duty I made up for myself. Good night, Madam Journal.

Postscript. These little PSs are becoming fun. I'm actually looking forward to them because I can disappear them from sight if I want to. Knowing that, I'm free to be me. Not that I'm not free in what I write in the main part of this journal—I am. But I'm freer here. Billy Wade, you're smart, you're handsome, and you feel good. You're worth holding on to, and I must be nuts to even be wondering what I'm wondering. Here's what I'm wondering. Can I hold on to you? I can if I follow the plan—which was, until Gallup erupted with blood in that alleyway, to meld our lives and our ways and think about making little babies along with the love we make whenever we can. But this trial and what might happen here is forcing me to "review the plan," as my father would say. What if the plan gets changed and I move on—to another place or another profession? Will I change and hold on at the same time? I see you so happy in who and where you are. I thought I was happy with who and where I was. But what if I change? Are you strong enough to change with me? If not, I can't hold you, my love. Stop, I can't do this—I don't know whether to cry or spit. I guess I'll cry because ladies don't spit.

eleven

DEE SWEARS AND BOBCAT DOES NOT

Saturday, October 12, 1935

The prosecution had two more witnesses to call that Saturday morning before getting to the testimony of Dee Roberts and Bobcat Wilson. One of them was thirty-three years old, and the other was only fourteen.

Perfecto Garcia, the thirty-three-year-old, was another jailer who had been in court with the rest of them back in April. He identified Leandro Velarde, Rafael Gomez, Gregorio Correo, Victorio Correo, Manuel Avitia, and Juan Ochoa.

The fourteen-year-old witness was John Green, Jr. He would have been the youngest witness to testify except for one thing. The judge said no. It seems that the prosecutors brought him to Aztec because he had gone to the scene of the crime late in the afternoon, after school on April 4, 1935. The state called him to prove that he found a spike sharpened at one end with a curve or handle hold at the other end, about five or six inches long. He found it lying along the concrete wall toward the west end of the alley. He took it home and gave it to his father. The defense objected and the court sustained the objection, saying his testimony was "too remote."

Thus the stage was set for the last two witnesses for the prosecution. Dee and Bobcat, or Bobcat and Dee, depending on who they called first. That was the subject of some discussion at the morning coffee break.

"John, who do you figure they'll put on first, Dee or Bobcat?" Hugh Woodward asked.

"Hard to say. If it was me, I would want to close with my best witness, but I can't tell if that's Dee or Bobcat. Certainly Dee is strong, and he's the shooter. We know something of his testimony because he did give some information at the preliminary. But Bobcat hasn't said a word as far as I can tell. Maybe they're keeping him under wraps as their final star witness."

"Well, I don't think so," replied Hugh. "Dee did the shooting and, according to Frank Powers, shot straight and true. But Bobcat was himself shot, and next to calling the sheriff himself back from the grave, he's the genuine victim. It's always nice when you're prosecuting to have a victim to close out your case. It sort of puts the jury in the right frame of mind, if you know what I mean."

Simms said, "You could be right; we'll know soon enough."

"Tell you what, John, I'll cross-examine the next witness up. If I'm right, then that will be Dee Roberts. You need to handle that little banty rooster Bobcat anyhow, and I believe they're saving him for last. As for me, I'd like to take a crack at the man who arrested more than a hundred men and women for shooting the sheriff when he knows damn good and well that the man who shot the sheriff is one of the two he killed right there at the scene. Sort of burns me, if you get my drift."

When they got back into the court after the morning break, David Chavez announced that Sheriff Dee Roberts would be their next witness. Woodward leaned over to Simms and said: "I win."

"Good afternoon, sir. Please state your name, age, and occupation for the jury," said Dick Modrall as he faced Sheriff Dee Roberts in the witness box.

Dee Roberts looked every bit as old as he said he was, fifty-eight. It took the better part of an hour to cover the *prima facie* parts of his testimony. Somewhat reluctantly, he admitted that there was not much of a crowd in front of the justice court when they arrived with Navarro that day. He volunteered that they took five officers because they "looked for a little trouble that morning." He said the crowd started to gather after they got there and that during the hearing on the Indian boy, the crowd began "hollering, yelling, shaking their fists, and hammering on the glass windows and pounding on the door." He stared directly at the defendants' bench when he identified four of them as being out there in the crowd in front—Willie Gonzales, Leandro Velarde, Serapio Sosa, and Manuel Avitia. Mr. Modrall walked him through Navarro's "arm movement" to the crowd looking in the glass window just as the hearing ended and got Dee to say that the crowd rushed around from the front of the building to the alley in back.

"What did you do?"

"We hesitated for a minute, and Mr. Carmichael said to me, 'Now what?' Mr. Wilson said, 'Let's go.' Mr. Carmichael said, 'Let's go,' and I said, 'We'll all go.' And we did."

"Describe the rear door, if you will."

"The rear door was a double door, with a two-by-four for a bar across these doors, and they opened to the inside. As we went out, Mr. Carmichael was on the left and I was on the right; each had Mr. Navarro by the arm. We continued that position for about forty-five or fifty feet after we got into the alley to go east to the jail."

"Before you get too far down the alley, tell the gentlemen of the jury how many people you saw out there in the alley as you first came out the door."

"As soon as we opened the door, I saw about seventy-five people out there. Even before then, we could see through the glass in the door, and I recognized some of the defendants in this case."

"Will you name them, please?"

"I saw Willie Gonzales, Juan Ochoa, Joe Bartol, Manuel Avila, Leandro Velarde, Rafael Gomez, Serapio Sosa, and the two Correos. I don't remember seeing Agustin Calvillo at that time. They had formed what I would call a half circle in front of this door. When we came out, the crowd was all around us. We worked our way through the best we could, pushing them out of our way, and proceeded east with our prisoner. Bobcat Wilson came out behind us. Roy Boggess came out with him."

"What was the first sign of trouble?"

"After we went about forty feet up the alley, I heard a shot. They were all around us, hollering and talking, and our prisoner was pulling back. We had to push them out of the way. Our prisoner was giving us a lot of trouble."

"Let me ask you to be very precise here, sir. Did you see any one of the defendants commit an act of violence in that alley?"

"As we came out of the alley Juan Ochoa struck at me with a hammer."

"What else happened when you heard the first shot?"

"When I heard the shot, Mr. Carmichael turned his head and looked back at the west; then I heard another shot. That bullet struck him right in the face. I could see the blood pop out as he turned to fall and fell toward me, and I got him by his right arm as he fell and held to him until he went down."

"What did you do then?"

"I turned facing the crowd and saw two men shooting toward me. One was on my left at the corner of the *Independent* building. The other was down the alley about twenty feet to my right, also firing. He was right opposite the telegraph post. As I turned I saw Velarde; he was on my left, shooting. I pulled my gun and shot at him, and he fell. Then I fired at Solomon Esquibel, the one that was shooting down the alley to my right. I missed him the first shot; he went down on his hands and knees like he was struck. As he raised back up I shot at him again. That time he fell."

"Where were your other officers during this time?"

"At about the time I fired the last shot at Solomon Esquibel, I noticed four or five people on top of Hoy Boggess kicking him and beating him. I recognized two of them that were on him kicking him."

"Who were they?"

"Those two were Juan Ochoa and Manuel Avitia."

"All right, sir, then what happened?"

"After Mr. Carmichael had been killed and after the shooting practically—after I finished firing, Mr. Wilson backed up by Mr. Carmichael with his pistol in his hand, stooped over, and said, 'I'm shot.' That is the first time I had seen him since the battle started."

"The last time you had seen Mr. Wilson was when he was alongside of Mr. Boggess, is that right?"

"After I shot Esquibel, shot at him, these people that were on top of Boggess jumped off him. He got up and staggered up to where I was. He was bleeding and cut in two or three places, and I told him to take Mr. Wilson and get to the hospital as quick as he could. I reloaded my pistol, stood there for a few seconds, then left to get my machine gun. I had emptied my gun. I had five shells in it."

"Now, have you told the jury all you know about the actions of these particular defendants here?"

"Well, as I came out the door before the shooting, I saw Rafael Gomez. He was just in the front. I never saw him do anything, but he was there in the front with Victorio Correo."

"What happened to Navarro?"

"As we went up the alley the prisoner was pulling back, jerking back, trying to get away all the way up the alley. He finally got away. He has never been apprehended."

With that, Mr. Patton looked at the jury, paused for a few moments as if assessing their mood, and turned back to the judge. "Your Honor, that concludes our examination of this witness."

Hugh Woodward elected to start slowly. "Sheriff, I understand you have been in the business of enforcing the law for most of your adult life, is that right?"

"I have been a peace officer for about twenty-five years. I served four two-year terms as sheriff. I was the undersheriff for a long time. But I didn't draw a salary except for a few months while I was undersheriff to Mr. Carmichael."

"Yes, sir, and it is also true, is it not, that during most of those years you were also employed by the Gallup American Coal Company?"

"I worked at the mine at Gamerco. My brother was in charge of the camp out there while the mine was having trouble."

"You were a mine guard, were you not?"

"I was an officer for the mine, yes."

"Not a member of the union, I presume?"

"No."

"You are knowledgeable about the law that covers the power to make an arrest, are you not?"

"I've made arrests and have served a lot of warrants as a peace officer or a deputy sheriff."

"And you must have served many warrants signed by Judge Bickel, right, sir?"

"I had served warrants for Justice of the Peace Bickel. I know that except for first-degree murder, every man charged with a crime is entitled to bail. Is that what you're getting at?"

"Actually what I was getting at is the warrant regarding Mr. Navarro. Did you serve that one?"

"I did not serve the warrant on Navarro or on Campos or on Lovato."

"All right, I'm glad we've cleared that up. Now, I'd like to ask you a question or two about your relationship with Sheriff Carmichael. I'm sure that you and he were close and that you worked together for many years. Is that true, sir?"

"Sheriff Carmichael served under me as my deputy when I was the sheriff. He was a good deal younger than me."

"And you certainly respected him and thought he was a good officer, did you not?"

"I trained him as a peace officer."

"All right, sir. You have named several of the defendants who are on trial here as being at the scene on April 4, 1935. Let me ask you this: Did you know their names, or did you just know them by sight?"

"I didn't know any of the defendants that were there that day by name, but I knew them."

"And based on your experience, both in the sheriff's office and for Gallup American Coal Company, were others there who you knew, if not by name, then by sight?"

"Yes, there were. I saw Bill Cuton and his wife and daughter, and I saw Mrs. John Tomac, Mrs. Hernandez, Mrs. Gomez, Mrs. Mendoza, José Lopez. I also saw Mrs. Leandro Velarde there and a number of people whose faces I know, but I never learned their names."

"I mean no disrespect, sir, but will you tell me who was in charge the instant that Sheriff Carmichael died that morning?"

"Upon the death of the sheriff, I took charge."

"And in taking charge, I presume you directed the roundup of citizens that day and the following day?"

"We rounded up and brought in for investigation a lot of people after the killings."

"Do you know exactly how many people were rounded up?"

"There would have been in the neighborhood of a hundred people. They were picked up and held. We were trying to find some guns and people."

"And the method you selected to use to search and arrest was to round up anyone who you thought *might* have been anywhere near that alley that morning, right, sir?"

"We picked up those that we thought were at this gathering. We were holding the people that possibly were in this battle."

"How long did you hold those people, Sheriff?"

"Well, we had to turn a great number up there loose, but we held forty-eight out of the number we had picked up."

"Forty-eight, did I hear you right?"

"Yes, forty-eight. We turned the rest loose."

"I hand you Exhibit 4. You signed this, did you not?"

"Yes, it's the complaint that I signed charging the murder of M. R. Carmichael. I swore to it."

"And it names Doreto Andrade as one of the defendants, right, sir?"

"Yes, it does."

"And it names Juan Castro as one of the defendants, right, sir?"

"Yes."

"And it names Pedro Moreno as one of the defendants?"

"Yes, he was named."

"But since this is your own personal document, one that you *yourself* swore to, none of the men I just named were there that day, at least to your personal knowledge, were they? You swore out a murder warrant on them and they were not even there?"

"I did not personally see any of them there that day."

"All right, let me ask you about another one. Bonifacio Fernandez was named as a defendant. I think you recalled you did see him, am I right?"

"I did see him out in front that morning."

"But not in back where the shooting took place, right, Sheriff?"

"No, I don't recall he was in the back."

"Sheriff, I'm going to try to speed this up a little. Instead of reading all forty-eight names to you, I'm going to hand this list to you and let you read it to yourself." Woodward watched the jury as the witness slowly moved his finger down the list. Roberts seemed to take a long time, as though he was trying to remember which ones were there that morning and which were not. "Have you read it, Sheriff?"

"I have."

"And those are the names of the forty-eight men and women you swore under oath committed the murder of Sheriff W. R. Mack Carmichael, right, sir?"

"I already said that."

"But you will admit to these men on the jury, won't you, that you really do not know whether some of them were even there that morning, do you?"

Sheriff Roberts looked down at the list on the rail in front of him. "Don't remember seeing Doreto Andrade there or Juan Castro, but Jacobo Barreras was out front. I don't recollect Mike Starov; he's a Slav. Altagracia Gomez was there somewhere, and this one here, name of Albino Casias, he was in the courtroom that morning, so we named him too."

Roberts looked up from the list, and Woodward looked back at the jury. There was an awkward pause in the courtroom. I couldn't help but wonder if the men on the jury were thinking what I was thinking: Is it possible that the people not mentioned were charged with murder just because someone thought they *might* have been there?

Hugh Woodward broke the awkward silence with his next question. "Now here is a name I want to ask you a couple of questions about. Victor Campos. Mr. Campos was the main subject of the dispute that led up to this hearing, was he not?"

"He was."

"And you included him on the murder warrant, the one you swore to, right, sir?"

"Yes, he was in the courtroom. So he was included in the complaint."

"But sir, he was in the courtroom under guard, by you and your men. He was never in the front, he was never in the back; he was under guard at all times. Is that your only justification for swearing under oath and charging him with *murder,* that he was in the courtroom a few minutes before the shooting started?"

"Well, he was one of them, so he got added."

"*Them?* You accused him of murder just because he was one of *them?* Did I hear you right?"

"You heard me."

"And you included Mrs. Soledad Sanchez on the warrant as well?"

"She was the one that got shot in the leg. We included her."

"Let me ask you a question. I do not mean to sound disrespectful, but did you even read this complaint before you swore to the court that it was true?"

"I read the complaint before I signed it. I never investigated."

"You *never* investigated?"

"No, I never investigated; I just signed the complaint after the district attorney had drawn it up. Different people recognized different ones that were in the alley and in front in this mob, and their names were put on the complaint and I signed it. It was prepared by the district attorney."

"But sir, all together there were forty-eight defendants included in the complaint and you swore to it. You swore that you *believed* they were guilty, and that is the basis for charging them with the murder of the sheriff."

Dee Roberts didn't answer the question. He just sat there for a full minute and glared at Hugh Woodward. It was as though he was trying to decide whether to respond or to arrest this arrogant son of a bitch. He finally exploded: "Now, you just hold on a minute. Carmichael was a close friend of mine. I had served with him for years. I had the same relationship with Mr. Wilson, but not as much as I had with Mr. Carmichael. I resent the death of Mr. Carmichael and the shooting of Mr. Wilson. And I resent what you are trying to get me to say. We did what we had to do. That's all I'm going to say on the matter."

Hugh Woodward took the outburst quite calmly. He moved away from the witness box and said, more or less over his shoulder, "Very well. Let me change subjects. I am unclear about just who started this movement out the rear door of the court and into the alley. Can you clear that up for me?"

"Mr. Wilson and Mr. Montoya took the bar off the rear door before we opened it to go out. Both doors swung open. We walked right out and pushed the people away."

"Is that when you drew your gun?"

"I did not draw my gun at that time. I didn't see any other officer draw his gun at that time."

"You said that Juan Ochoa was about three or four feet away from you when he struck at you. Did he hit you?"

"It was a claw hammer, a regular carpenter's hammer. I put my hand on my gun then but didn't draw it. Then I put my back to the crowd and walked about forty-five feet from them."

"Excuse me, sir, my question was, Did he hit you?"

"He tried to. I didn't look back at them. As we walked they were all around us, moving up the alley with us."

"You said you saw Velarde shooting. That was Ignacio Velarde, right? Not the defendant on trial, but his brother, right?"

"That's right. When I saw Velarde shooting, he was about fifteen feet away; Esquibel was probably about twenty feet away when he was shooting. The Velarde who was shooting wasn't the one who's a defendant. It was his brother, Ignacio. Ignacio is dead now."

"And you shot them both; that is, the men you believe shot Sheriff Carmichael?"

"To my knowledge, both of those men were killed by bullets from my gun. In addition to shooting at them, I shot at Navarro. I tried to kill the little—well, I tried to kill him when I fired my last shot at him as he was running down the alley. I don't think I hit him."

Dee Roberts didn't seem fazed that he had almost used a profane word to describe Navarro, and no one on the jury seemed surprised at his attitude. It was more or less expected given the close relationship between Dee and Sheriff Mack. Hugh Woodward continued to grind away at Dee and extracted some other admissions. Dee said he didn't know why Hoy Boggess had the tear gas bomb with him that morning. He admitted that the sheriff's office used handcuffs routinely but no one had any with them that morning to use on Navarro. He admitted that no one was between him and Solomon Esquibel and that his direct testimony was that he hit Solomon as they were facing each other. He didn't know that Solomon was shot in the back. He denied seeing Bobcat fire his weapon and insisted that he saw Boggess fire Bobcat's gun, not his own. Woodward summarily dismissed him with a wave of his hand.

Mr. Patton knew he had to at least *try* to rehabilitate his star witness on redirect examination. He spent twenty minutes going over the testimony that Dee had given at the preliminary hearing up in Santa Fe last June. He established that Dee knew most of the defendants by sight and some by name. He said that he had known Velarde, Ochoa, Gómez, and Sosa for years. He said he saw Joe Bartol around Gallup almost every day for seven or eight years. The only defendant he didn't know was Agustin Calvillo. Incidentally, Calvillo was the only defendant who Dee didn't say was in the alley at the time of the shooting. He explained that he was afraid the crowd would try to free Navarro and that was why they kept the crowd out of the courtroom in the first place.

Turning to the judge, Patton said, "I have nothing further, Your Honor. May the witness be excused to return to his duties, Judge?"

Judge McGhee turned to the defense table and asked: "Any reason why this witness should not be excused, gentlemen?"

"No, Your Honor," replied Woodward.

With a display of confidence, Patton turned to the judge and said: "Your Honor, at this time, the prosecution *rests* its case."

At first I thought I had misheard him. Did he just say that the prosecution rests? How could that be? I looked over at Mary Ann, but she was busy scribbling her notes on Dee Roberts. The judge didn't change his stoic courtroom face, and the jury seemed relieved but not particularly surprised. Was it only me? I couldn't see the faces of the defense lawyers because I was three rows in back of them at the time. But I did see Hugh Woodward and John Simms look at each other and then quickly move their chairs closer so they could confer. Later I learned that they were as stunned as I was.

John Simms and Hugh Woodward could hardly believe their ears. They looked in disbelief at the prosecution table. What was this? How could they rest their case now? They hadn't called Bobcat. Where was Bobcat Wilson? Of course, I knew where he was. He was back at the hotel, packing his bag.

Why didn't he testify? That was the question du jour in Aztec. He was subpoenaed to Santa Fe and to Aztec and sent home from both without giving his side of it. Not that he was all that eager to tell his side of it. No, sir. He wasn't eager to tell you about anything that was personal to him, much less about getting shot. The prosecutors told him what happened to Hoy and Charlie and Dee and said it wasn't pretty. But that wasn't it. Bobcat wasn't afraid of anything, so it was damn unlikely that he'd be bothered by a lawyer yapping at him in court or out. He never knew for sure why they decided close their case without his testimony. He didn't know and didn't care. One thing for sure, it wasn't because of hard questions that might be put to him by the defense. Maybe Bobcat didn't care, but I sure did. What did they know about Bobcat that made them rest the case without putting him up there?

I didn't know it at the time, but later on I got the speculation from the American Bar—there were more explanations than beer drinkers, and that's saying something. One group, mostly the ones at the big round table in the back, said it was on account of Bobcat might just get up there and tell a whole different story than anyone else. Bobcat was up to that, they said. Nobody messed with Bobcat, not even the by-God attorney general of this whole state.

Around the room, that explanation got a lot of "yes, sirs, that's it for sure." But as soon as it was agreed to, it was undone. Just how was his story different from anybody else's? Did he see who shot the sheriff and not want to talk about it? That might be the case if the one he saw doing the shooting wasn't on that long bench in the courtroom. Did he see who shot the sheriff and refuse to talk about it? That was different from not wanting to talk about it. What would make Bobcat refuse was something that no one had any good speculation about. Bobcat was Bobcat, after all. That seemed to be explanation enough.

The boys who preferred to stand at the bar were of a slightly different mind than the ones at the big table in the back. That's partly because they didn't know Bobcat as well. These boys sort of liked the speculation that maybe Bobcat did more firing than he was being given credit for that day. Maybe he shot one or the other of those two strikers that most folks thought Dee hit. Maybe he knew something about what happened to Hoy's gun. He damn sure knew Hoy had it and was known to kid Hoy about packing that hog-leg shooter, as he called it. Maybe this. Maybe that. But one thing there was no maybe about—Bobcat wasn't going to testify unless the defense decided to call him as their witness.

Judge McGhee didn't focus on the fact that the prosecution had rested their case *without* calling Bobcat Wilson. In fact, he didn't realize that Bobcat was a key witness. He had the official witness list but wasn't keeping track. That was the lawyers' job, not his. He seemed pleased but not surprised that the state had rested after putting on the new sheriff of McKinley County. He looked over at the defense table and said: "Well, the state has rested. The defense has reserved its right to make an opening statement. We do have two more hours of daylight this afternoon. What is your pleasure, gentlemen? Do you want to present your opening now and start with your witnesses Monday or should we recess now so you can start fresh with everything Monday?"

John Simms turned to Hugh Woodward and got a slight shake of the head and a small frown. He turned to the bench and said: "Your Honor, we are pleased to see the state rest their case, but in all candor, we expected them to call at least one more witness. We would prefer to adjourn now for the afternoon and begin first thing Monday morning with our opening statement to the jury."

Judge McGhee paused and looked over at his jury. "Gentlemen of the jury, the state has rested their case, but that does not mean that you can discuss the case among yourselves yet. The defense will give you a short statement when the court reconvenes and then can call witnesses if they choose. Meanwhile, you must continue to follow my admonitions. Please do not read any newspaper coverage about this case and do not talk to anyone about the evidence or the issues in this case."

With that, Judge McGhee started to spin his chair around for his usual quick exit, but John Simms interjected: "Excuse me, Your Honor, but there is one other matter. We would like to have use of the courtroom after the jury leaves for a conference with our clients. It will be necessary for the bailiffs and court deputies to depart, as this will be an attorney-client privileged meeting."

"All right, Mr. Simms, the deputies will make your clients available for a private meeting in this courtroom for the remainder of the afternoon. Court's adjourned."

The jury filed out, the prosecution team and the deputies left, and the courtroom was cleared of spectators. When all was quiet, John Simms asked the official court interpreter to leave and relied on Juan Ochoa to interpret for the rest of the defendants. The only people left were the defense lawyers, the defendants, and me. I was about to get another education in real lawyering.

The meeting lasted several hours, but most of the time was spent on the critical issue of whether these men would take the witness stand or remain mute. It seems simple, but for a man charged with a capital crime, it wasn't simple: it could mean life or death.

John Simms stood and moved around to the other side of the table so he could face his clients. "Gentlemen, you all have a decision to make now, and we will advise you on it, but we cannot make the decision for you. Under the Constitution of the United States, you do not have to testify against yourself. No one can make you do that. It's your constitutional right.

"You do not have to prove anything.

"You do not have to take that witness stand over there. You don't have to deny anything or admit anything. In fact, they cannot even call out your name in the courtroom and force you to *refuse* to testify. If you do not voluntarily take the stand, they can't do anything about it. In short, you do not have to prove your innocence. They have to prove your guilt."

John Simms paused from time to time as Juan Ochoa translated for the group. Some of them knew enough English to get the gist of what he was saying without translation, but he wanted to make sure there was no question about giving them the advice they needed to make their decision.

"Now, this decision as to whether or not you testify in this case is one that must be made separately by each one of you. Some of you might think you have to get up there and tell those jurors your side of it. Some of you might not. It's an individual decision. As I said, none of us can make it for you."

As the men talked back and forth, one thing became clear: None of them really knew *how* to make the decision. They vigorously professed their innocence but had little trust in the system or the constitutional guarantees afforded to them. So they didn't have any real context in which to make the decision. After an hour of discussion it was clear that unless they really *knew* the risk, all of them might stand mute together or testify together just because one of them wanted to. It dawned on me that this was entirely consistent with what these men stood for. They were miners, and their safety in the mine depended on what the other man did just as much as what they did individually. They were union men, and their jobs and their futures depended on what they did collectively, not individually. They were Spanish speakers in an English-speaking courtroom; they heard the evidence from a translator, not whoever was on the stand at the time. They faced the electric chair because they were there in the alley together, not because they were there alone. So why shouldn't they make a decision that all would testify or none of them would?

John Simms could also see the dilemma. Of course he probably knew it all along, whereas I had only come to it as the afternoon wore on. "Gentlemen," John Simms began, "let me be frank with you. I can't make the decision for you, but I do have some strong beliefs on the matter. To start with, I believe it would be a mistake for all of you to make the same decision, whichever one it is. The evidence in this case is stronger against some of you than others. The evidence in this case might warrant some of you taking the risk of testifying, but not others. The evidence in this case needs rebuttal by some of you, but not all of you. So let me tell you how I see it for each of you, both as a group and as individual men.

"Mr. Ochoa, the prosecution has spent a lot of time trying to make their case against you. I suspect that is because you were pretty vocal over the last few years and several witnesses have placed you there in front of the court as well as back in the alley that morning. And some of the witnesses made statements about you that you ought to get up there and deny. Now, you and I have gone over that privately, but maybe it will be helpful if I mention some of it again.

"You were at the meeting at the Spanish-American Hall the day before the shooting; in fact, you were the chairman of that meeting. You went to see Carmichael the day before the shootings. You were there on the street the next morning, and you were part of the so-called semicircle around the back door of Bickel's court when they brought Navarro out into the alley.

"True or not, they have presented evidence that the jury could accept that connects you to the gun Deputy Boggess says he lost in the melee. In other words, they will most likely argue that you could have actually shot the sheriff yourself. That is in addition to their conspiracy argument and their argument that you aided and abetted whoever did shoot the sheriff. You are also the first one named in the indictment, and that is no accident on their part. I believe you should seriously think about getting up there in the morning and telling your side of it. I think that the jury might hold it against you if you don't.

"Now as to you, Mr. Avitia, they have pretty much the same and then some. You were at both meetings, you were at the scene the next day, and they put up witnesses to say you had a gun and you fired it in the alley that morning. They also have a witness saying you were beating on Hoy Boggess. Their witnesses, at least several of them, knew you for years and implied that you were a troublemaker. So you'd best think seriously about taking the stand along with Mr. Ochoa. You don't have to, as I said, but if I were you, I believe I would.

"Mr. Velarde, your case is different. I'm not saying that I think you ought to take the stand, but I do think you'll have to offer evidence on your behalf.

"Let me go over that for all of you. Tomorrow morning we will ask the judge to dismiss all the charges against you. That's called a motion to dismiss, and we have to make it before we start the defense of the case. This judge is not likely to give it one second's worth of thought. He'll deny it right from the bench. But when he does, you have the right to 'stand on your motion.' That means that if you don't offer any evidence on your own behalf, then whatever comes in evidence from that point on cannot be used against you.

"For example, I've told Juan that he probably needs to testify on his own behalf. When he does, he'll be subject to cross-examination, and then they could ask him about one of you who will not be testifying. That's permissible, but if you elect to stand on your motion, then what he says cannot be used against you. The judge will explain all that to the jury.

"Now, Leandro, to get back to your case. All in all, I believe you should not testify because there's a lot of risk for you. However, at the same time I don't think you can just stand on your motion to dismiss. You have to offer evidence even if you don't testify in person. It's your decision, of course, but here is what they have on you. To start with, your brother was killed in the affray. That shouldn't make any difference, but I'm afraid it might. Some might think you saw your brother die and then scooped up that missing gun and blasted away.

"And they put up some evidence that you were seen going through the crowd out in front that morning, motioning the bunch to head on out back. One witness said you led the pack into the alley. Others put you in the semicircle around the door in the alley. Deputy Montoya said you raised your fist at him and said something about being disgraced. You remember that testimony, don't you? Most of the officers said you were right there in the thick of things.

"Then there's that business about what went on at Mrs. Aurelio's home back in March, a week or so before the shootings. They tried to put the word *ice pick* in your mouth but ended up with *toothpick*. Either way, those are words that might need explaining by you. And to top it all off, they put up that pretty young lady to say that you took an ice pick out of the bib of your overalls an hour after the shooting. That would have been a whole lot more important if they had any testimony that someone had been stabbed with an ice pick. We thought Hoy Boggess would say that, but he didn't. If you take the stand, they might use it as an opportunity to cross-examine you about Hoy's alleged stab wounds. That's important and maybe ought to be dealt with by you on the stand. As I said, I do not believe you should take the stand. There is a risk either way, but you'd best think about it real carefully.

"Now as to the rest of you men, the case is different. No one took the stand and said you hit anyone, said anything, had a hammer or a gun, or led the charge, either that day or the day before. As to each of you, the real basis of the charge is that you either conspired with the actual shooters or that you aided and abetted them in their shooting of the sheriff. You really have nothing specific or concrete to rebut. You can't just get there up and deny conspiracy or aiding and abetting. Of course you can; I didn't mean that. But what I'm saying is that those kinds of denials are expected but not relied on.

"All things considered, if I were in your boots, I'd exercise my right to decline to testify. They've got all they can on you now, and in my opinion, it isn't much. I would hate to see you give them something on cross-examination that makes a stronger case against you. You can take the stand if you want to, each and every one of you, but you ought to think seriously about standing mute tomorrow."

The other defense lawyers chimed in, and they had some real healthy differences to work out. The meeting ended about suppertime, and the men were taken back to jail.

Avitia, Calvillo, and Ochoa decided to take the stand and testify on their own behalf. Leandro Velarde decided to call independent witnesses to the stand, but he wouldn't take the stand himself. The other defendants would stand on their constitutional rights. After that it would be up to the jury.

Saturday Night, October 12, 1935

Dear Journal:

As I drove down to Gallup from Aztec this afternoon, I drove through the little dusty area where they held the "Gallup Defense Rally," but there was nothing left but a small banner proclaiming "Free the Gallup Fourteen." I couldn't help but think about the impact of Mr. Modrall's astounding announcement that the state was going to rest its case—without calling Bobcat to the witness stand.

The most fascinating thing about watching this trial, up to now, has been the way the jury and the lawyers react to the testimony of the witnesses. The judge is pretty impassive no matter what is said, but the jury and the lawyers always react somehow. Of course, they try to hide it, but the little things give them away.

But today, Madam Journal, they reacted to something that did *not* happen. That's a first for this trial. Up to now things have gone along according to plan, even if the rest of us didn't know the plan. Today the state rested its case without putting on the testimony of Mr. L. E. "Bobcat" Wilson. Everybody reacted. Remember I told you about the man on the top row of the jury box, closest to the judge? Well, he nearly fell off his chair. He looked at Chavez with a sort of frown and then quickly moved his focused stare to Dee Roberts and that state policeman, Mr. Martin. It was as though he thought they were somehow involved in the decision not to call Bobcat to the stand. Bobcat wasn't hanging around the courtroom today, as he has been all week. Something happened. Billy Wade will know, but will he tell me?. He'd better; I have something he wants. But back to the scene in the courtroom.

The defense lawyers looked at one another, dumbfounded. I couldn't tell whether they were happy or not, but they sure did look surprised. Mr. Simms, ever the gentleman, looked as if he had just been tricked. Mr. Woodward, ever the slouch, actually sat up straight in his chair. The other three defense lawyers looked at one another, back and forth, back and forth, as though they were also dumbfounded about Bobcat not being called as a witness. But come to think of it, they're pretty dumbfounded about the whole trial.

Mr. Modrall, who announced the end of the prosecution's case, did it confidently, but his colleagues seemed less certain. I could see the puzzlement on their faces, as though the decision wasn't exactly unanimous.

Judge McGhee seemed to take it in stride and was even happy about it since it means the case might end earlier than he thought. But I couldn't help feeling he thought they shouldn't have rested until they put such an important witness up for the jury's consideration.

For their part, the jury was both happy and perplexed. Actually, I don't know whether farmers and ranchers get "perplexed" any more than other men do. They usually mask their feelings, at least when women are around. Being perplexed is probably a sign of weakness among strong men and is therefore an emotion to be avoided wherever possible.

But up there in Aztec this morning, the jury surely was "perplexed." I'm not sure they knew why they were perplexed because they've heard a lot about Bobcat and might think that the defense will call him as a witness, since it's now their turn to do that, call witnesses, I mean.

Well, Madam Journal, here's Billy Wade's take on all this. He seems to think the defense will *not* call Bobcat. But he thinks they sure as the dickens will comment on the failure of the state to produce him. As he put it, "They will pay the price."

That brings me to what did happen today: Mr. Dee Roberts himself.

I didn't know that he wasn't actually paid by the county for his work, but he told the jury that except for a few months as undersheriff to Sheriff Carmichael, he has never drawn a salary. I also didn't know that in his four terms as our elected sheriff, he was still paid by Gamerco American Coal Company as a guard for them. In fact, he and his brother, Bob, were in charge of the camp out at Gamerco "during the trouble out there." He didn't explain what trouble he was talking about, but one of the reporters for the *Albuquerque Journal* told me it was while martial law was declared here to protect the mining payroll. I'll have to look into that.

I found myself vacillating during Dee's testimony. He's widely respected in Gallup, and I think he's a basically honest man, like Bobcat. But unlike Bobcat, he seemed enraged about the killing of his friend. He seems to want to lash out at whoever "might" be responsible on a very personal basis. This could be a case where loyalty has overtaken objectivity.

Sheriff Dee started out his testimony by telling the jury what happened in the alley. I tried to write down exactly what he said on the important things because I have a feeling that his words are going to be crucial when the jury starts to deliberate on the case.

He said, "As soon as we opened the door, I saw about seventy-five people out there. Even before then, we could see through the glass in the door, and I recognized some of the defendants in this case."

Mr. Modrall asked him to name which defendants he saw, and he said: "I saw Willie Gonzales, Juan Ochoa, Joe Bartol, Manuel Avitia, Leandro Velarde, Rafael Gomez, Serapio Sosa, and the two Correos. I don't remember seeing Agustin Calvillo at that time."

I know I'm a skeptic and a cynical person and that I have been doubtful about just how these ten men came to be on trial, but that seems too pat to me. Is it just a coincidence that he saw nine of the ten men on trial the first time he looked out that door into the alley?

How could it be that not a single other witness saw them as a group? Remember, Madam Journal, that there have been twenty-four witnesses on that stand and most of them could not name *any* of the defendants. Of course Boggess did, but he was easily led. I think Dee Roberts is the only one to name them all (although he did give Agustin Calvillo a pass). I haven't made a chart yet of just exactly "who named who" yet, but I'm going to now. Maybe the chart will tell me what my memory cannot. Were these nine men named as being there just outside the door by anyone else in this case, or is it only Dee Roberts who the jury will have to rely on?

Sheriff Dee told the jury that one of those men, Juan Ochoa, "struck at me with a claw hammer," but he said it happened at different times depending on who was asking the question. He told Mr. Modrall that it happened *after* they walked their prisoner down the alley and *after* the first shots were fired. But he changed his story when Mr. Woodward asked him the same questions on cross-examination.

Mr. Woodward reminded him that his testimony was that Juan Ochoa was only three or four feet away when he struck at him with the claw hammer and then asked: "Did he hit you?" Dee was evasive. Here's Sheriff Dee's answer as I wrote it down this morning: "It was a claw hammer, a regular carpenter's hammer. I put my hand on my gun then, but didn't draw it. Then I put my back to the crowd and walked about forty-five feet from them."

Mr. Woodward wasn't satisfied with that answer and repeated his question about whether Sheriff Dee was hit or not. Sheriff Dee said, "He tried to. I didn't look back at them. As we walked they were all around us, moving up the alley with us."

Now, what's wrong with that picture? First he names Ochoa as the only one to commit an act of violence. Then he says that when he does it, namely, trying to strike him with a claw hammer from three feet away, he just turns his back on him and walks forty-five feet down the alley with the crowd all around him. He didn't even draw his gun. By God, talk about nerves of steel! He's either the bravest man ever to wear a badge or he's exaggerating his hero role in the case. I honestly don't know which. If the jury convicts Ochoa, he can blame it entirely on the fact that they must have believed Sheriff Dee. But I shouldn't judge so quickly. Maybe Juan Ochoa will take the stand on Monday and clear all this up.

Getting back to Sheriff Dee's testimony, he said he shot and killed the *two* men who he saw shoot the sheriff. I was a little surprised that he was that direct about it since this trial is supposed to be against the men who shot the sheriff. Besides, no one else saw *two* men shoot the sheriff!

He also said that happened after he saw Ochoa and Avitia beating on poor Mr. Boggess on the ground while Bobcat walked toward him with his gun in his hand. That was odd because he later said that Bobcat didn't shoot, or at least he didn't *see* him shoot. Dee said he saw Boggess fire twice "with Bobcat's gun." It seemed to me he was trying to support Boggess's testimony and that he must have known when he said it that Mr. Modrall had decided *not* to call Bobcat as a witness. This is a very curious thing. I really wish I knew why they didn't call Bobcat. Two independent witnesses saw Bobcat fire his gun. Why are Dee and Boggess both evasive about that? Why doesn't Bobcat step forward and clear that up? It's his reputation that's on the line here.

Maybe the cruelest thing was when Sheriff Dee said that he fired all five bullets in his gun but he saved the last bullet for Navarro when he was running down the alley. He said: "I tried to kill him as I saw him running away down the alley." I'm pretty sure I heard that right. I have to ask Billy Wade if the law allows a policeman to shoot to kill in that situation. That is, can you "try to kill" a man who was in your custody when he's running away from you? Don't you have to try to shoot and wound him, like shooting him in the legs or something? Sheriff Dee was quite emphatic when he said: "I tried to kill him." Maybe it's just me, but I would have felt better if he had said, "I tried to stop him," or simply, "I shot at him." Somehow it just struck me as vicious that he was actually trying to kill him for escaping. He's the guard, not the executioner, for God's sake.

Sheriff Dee is obviously a man of the law and a powerful one at that. He was the epitome of strength up there on the witness stand, but he didn't seem to have much compassion or much respect for the law itself. For example, he admitted to Mr. Woodward that he signed a complaint, under oath, naming scores of men and women as murderers just because the district attorney put their names on the list. In fact, he said he didn't "investigate" them; he just signed the document that Mr. Chavez gave him. I wonder what he thinks the oath means?

As another example, he admitted that Victor Campos was under guard at all times that day. Before, during, and after the riot. He was under guard by Sheriff Dee's men; yet he was still named on the murder complaint. When Woodward questioned him about this, he said: "Because he was one of them." Woodward said, "Did I hear you right—did you say you named him because he was one of *them?*" and Sheriff Dee said: "You heard right." There was no doubt in that courtroom when Woodward emphasized the word *them* that he was talking about the Spanish-American union members.

Actually, come to think of it, that was the first reference in open court to the biggest problem in this case: Were these men named on the murder complaint because of their allegiance to the union? And is it a communist union? Are those two things connected in this case? The newspapers and the rallies and the barrooms seem consumed with the possibilities, but the courtroom seems to ignore them.

None of the witnesses have talked about that, and I expect it's because the judge has told the lawyers not to mess up this trial with political issues. That's what Billy Wade thinks too. But maybe the defense will get into it when they start their case on Monday. I don't know whether I'm dreading it or looking forward to it.

If I were on the jury, I would have to think that the evidence so far isn't strong enough to convict *anyone* of first-degree murder. Maybe, just maybe, second degree if you believe Sheriff Dee and Hoy Boggess, but that's all. Maybe not even that if the men on trial are really only there because they were agitators for the union.

I don't care whether it's a communist union or not. The NMU has worked hard to get fair wages and safe working conditions. That ought not to be a crime, even in New Mexico.

So, Madam Journal, I'll sign off for now and go meet Billy Wade. No, I will not be writing anything about *that* in this journal. That's private and this is just semiprivate, at least so far.

Postscript. I intend to broach the bear tonight. After we finish our "private" stuff tonight, I'm going to ask Billy Wade whether he might, possibly, maybe, think about leaving Gallup. I'm thinking about it, so why can't he? After making love, we always talk about soft things—in more ways than one, actually—but what I mean is we talk about easy subjects. Leaving Gallup is not only not an easy subject, it will be frightening to Billy Wade. He's a secure man because it's easy to be secure in Gallup—

easy if you're white, educated, employed, and a man. What more is there? He will no doubt ask why I want to leave, so if I start this, I'd best have an answer. How about—there's more to life than the complacency of security? Even if it's not very philosophical, it has a catchy ring, don't you think? I think those ten men feel so insecure and so lacking in a future that maybe I ought to think *for* them. Maybe if I start to plan my future, a different future, that is, they can somehow find a way to face theirs.

The next morning, Sunday, October 13, 1935, the defense lawyers met again at a café a block from the courthouse to work out the other major problem facing the defense. They had defense witnesses to call and they had three of the defendants themselves to testify, but the troubling question was, Should they call Bobcat Wilson to the stand? He was under subpoena and, as far as anyone knew, available. He had been seen around town.

Hugh Woodward's position was somewhat compelling, but he didn't argue it; he just stated it: "John, if the state has decided not to call him, we should. There can be only one reason for their decision: he hurts their case. Anything that hurts their case helps ours, don't you think?"

Simms shrugged. "What you say is often the case but might not be in this one. Bobcat Wilson is thought by everyone who knows him to be a man of few words. They say he's truthful, and they say he's tough as a ten-cent steak. He was shot up pretty bad, and that might explain why he didn't testify at the prelim in Santa Fe.

"But he may be off the stand in our case for a reason that none of us can guess at. Maybe he disagrees with part of their case, but a part that isn't important to us. If we did call him, I'm sure he would name most of our defendants as being there, and he would damn sure be believed, being shot like he was. He would also be the most likely one to know who was beating on the man next to him, Hoy Boggess, and that can't help us. He can't help us on who actually shot the sheriff, and he's not likely to offer good character evidence for our men although he has the reputation of being a lot more friendly to the Mexican community than some in Gallup."

Hugh poured himself another cup of coffee and said, "I'm not sure I disagree with you, but I sure think we need to weigh the risk of putting him up there. We don't need any more coffin nails banged into our case than we already have. What do you say we postpone the decision for now? Let's make our opening, put up the defendants and our other witnesses, and then revisit this. Okay?"

twelve

THE DEFENSE

Monday, October 14, 1935

Well, now. Can you hear the auctioneer singing out the bids—how many have I got now for death, how many for life? What are you gonna say, boys? Biddin's going on—all done?—all in?—Going once, going twice . . .

The state was pretty much all done and all in on their case. Maybe that was why the so-called Gallup Defense Committee picked Saturday, October 12, 1935, for the observance of "Gallup Defense Day." They had a rally in Gallup in Kitchen's Opera House, another one up in Aztec, and a third one on the plaza in Santa Fe. The speakers at these rallies made a big point of saying they were also having rallies in Denver and all the way back to New York.

Part of Gallup Defense Day was to get folks to sign those little petitions that were being sent to Judge McGhee and Governor Tingley, urging them to "free the Gallup Ten." The talk in the bars was that the judge wasn't taking kindly to that up in Aztec. Rumor was that he was considering contempt citations on a whole bunch of folks who lived up in Santa Fe. The names being bandied about were José Rodriguez and his wife, Willie Martinez, and Alfredo Rodriguez. There were others too, but those were the ones who seemed to be gathering signatures on petitions and submitting them during the middle of the trial.

Some said, That just isn't right. Why can't they wait till it's over? Others said, They have a right to petition the government, don't they? No one seemed to know for sure. Some people were signing, and others were tearing the damn things up.

Down at the American Bar, the men spent some of that Saturday night mulling over the news from Aztec about Judge McGhee's speech to the spectators that Saturday morning. As usual, before anyone could get to the speech, they had to argue. The first point of contention was why in the hell were they having court on a Saturday? Some said that it wasn't fair to keep them jurors locked up, even if they were in a church. They ought to let 'em out to get the chores done, at least.

Others said, Hell, let's give him a cheer—he's moving this trial along. This way it's one day sooner to fry time for those red bastards. Anyhow, getting back to the judge's speech, it seems he gave them a real fire-and-brimstone warning about acting up in the courtroom. And not just there. He warned them about propaganda and signs and the like anywhere the jury might see them.

Down at the Angeles Pool Hall, they heard about the judge and they heard about the demonstration over in Old Town in Albuquerque, right there in the plaza. The Gallup Defense Day had rallies there and everywhere, but the one there was the one they talked about the most. What about Vincent Grofolo? No one knew him, but he was some kind of a hero, at least for the day. Did you hear he stood up and said the *gringo* judge had "no regard for the Constitution"? He even had a stenographer there who was taking down all the words: "I have every respect for the sacred American Constitution, but what happened to the constitutional rights of Montoya and what has happened to the constitutional rights of the workers in Gallup?"

Who is this Montoya he's talking about? Turned out it was Teleforio Montoya. Don't you know him? they said. He was saying things up there in Aztec around the courthouse and it pissed off the *gringo* judge and he locked his ass up. But do they have any room for more men in the jail up there? That was meant as a joke, but it didn't sound funny.

What else did this Grofolo say, and who the fuck is he, anyway? they asked. He's a student at the University of New Mexico, and he's speaking for us even if he doesn't know us, so don't speak ill of him, they said. He said that "basic rights of New Mexicans are on trial at Aztec, and when you're fighting for the lives of ten workers, you're fighting for the rights of all workers in New Mexico."

Back at the American Bar, they didn't know his name and didn't care to know it. They heard about the big rally in Old Town in Albuquerque and the one in Santa Fe and every other damn place, but what really pissed them off was why no one was holding rallies for the prosecution. How come just the reds have rallies? A tall man at the bar said, "We don't need rallies; we got juries. They'll do what they need to do. They'll give us our revenge."

On Monday morning, October 14, 1935, the defense dutifully and perfunctorily moved the court to dismiss all charges against their clients. The court dutifully and perfunctorily denied the motion. The defense then told the judge that some of the defendants would rely on their "motions" and not present a defense. This was sort of code for saying some of them would not risk cross-examination and would invoke their constitutional right not to give evidence against themselves.

Judge McGhee asked the court staff to summon the jury. When they were seated in the jury box, he said: "Gentlemen of the jury, you are instructed that the defendants Willie Gonzales, Rafael Gomez, Joe Bartol, Victorio Correo, Gregorio Correo, and Serapio Sosa, upon the advice of their counsel and having stood upon their motions, will not offer evidence. This means that any further testimony in this case adduced on behalf of the other four defendants will have no application nor effect whatsoever as to the six defendants who have rested their case, and as to them, the jury will not consider any further evidence."

The defense team had elected to reserve the opening statement based on the brevity of the statement made by the attorney general. Now was the time for the jury to hear the defense summarize its case. John Simms stood and faced the jury. He looked at them carefully for a full minute and then stepped toward them and said:

"May it please the court, learned counsel, and you, gentlemen of the jury. As you know by now, my name is John Simms. My colleagues, Mr. Woodward, Mr. Augur, Mr. La Follette, Mr. Thayer, and Mr. Brick represent these men who are on trial for their lives.

"You have heard the case for the state; you have seen their witnesses and their exhibits and listened to their theory of murder, conspiracy to commit murder, and aiding and abetting the commission of a murder. Now let me tell you about the case for the defense. I intend to be brief.

"All ten of these men are charged with first-degree murder, largely because of who they are and what they believe in. They are charged with first-degree murder because they went to the court to seek justice for Navarro but were denied entrance. They are charged with first-degree murder because some of them were there the day the sheriff was killed.

"Now, charging these men is the right of the state. They have the power to do that, and they exercised it. But having the power to do something and getting it done are two different things. In order to make their first-degree murder case against these ten men, the state must prove beyond a reasonable doubt that it was one or more of these men here who coldly and with premeditation shot and killed Sheriff Carmichael on the fourth day of April this year in Gallup, New Mexico.

"These ten men are protected by the same constitutional rights that protect you and me. They can stand mute before you and let you assess the evidence against them. If that evidence is compelling beyond a reasonable doubt, then you can convict them. If there is any doubt at all, no matter how small, you cannot convict them. That is their right and your duty.

"Three of these men have decided to take that witness stand and tell you what they did and give you the truth as they know it. They will do that today. The judge has given you their names. The rest of them will exercise their right to stand mute because they do not believe there is any, I say *any,* credible evidence against them.

"But whether they present evidence or not, they all stand charged with first-degree murder. And that is not all. As you know, the state has also charged these men with second-degree murder. This second-degree charge is based on the state's *theory* that even if these men did not actually shoot the sheriff, they aided whoever did that dastardly deed. But it is for you to assess their evidence on that point.

"I tell you that aiding in the commission of a crime, even murder, is not established by mere presence at the scene of the crime. To aid in the commission of a murder, the state must prove that a defendant assisted the murder by an outward manifestation of approval of the act. And most importantly, the state must prove beyond a reasonable doubt that the man knew and shared the killer's criminal intent before he can be guilty of a crime like this.

"The evidence we will produce for you today in this courtroom will be that these men were there in that alley because they believed they had a right to be there; because they believed in the law and because they had a political grievance that demanded justice. They were not there to do harm to the sheriff or any other man. They were not there to break the law. They were there because of the threat to their jobs and the threat to their homes.

"This small group of ten men was whittled down from a group of over a hundred men and women, and even a few children. The first cut into that group dropped the number down to forty-eight men and women. That first cut was because there was no compelling or convincing proof that anyone in the big group of more than one hundred or the second group of forty-eight actually shot the sheriff. But someone thought that maybe one or more of this group of ten men did shoot the sheriff. So they filed the case before you now.

"There is no proof that any one of these ten men shot the sheriff. To the contrary, the state has actually proved that none of these ten men did it. They did that by proving, with their own witnesses and their own forensic evidence, the bullets and the guns, that the men who killed Sheriff Carmichael were themselves killed by Sheriff Dee Roberts.

"It is now our opportunity to present evidence to you. We ask that you give our evidence and our witnesses the same close attention that you gave to those men and women called by the state. Thank you."

John Simms returned to the defense table. Hugh Woodward waited until John was seated and then announced: "Judge, we call Maria Livira Aurelio as our first witness."

"Give us your name and address, please, ma'am."

"I am Maria Livira Aurelio. I am married to Concepción Aurelio, and we live in Gallup at 803 West Logan."

"Is that address in Chihuahuaita?"

"Well, that's what they call it, but it's in the Gallup post office."

"Do you know Mrs. John Green?"

"Yes, she is my friend."

"Do you know the defendant Leandro Velarde?"

"Yes."

Mrs. Aurelio proceeded to calmly explain that Mrs. Green had come to her home to borrow some medicine and that she was there while "the men" talked about the eviction of Victor Campos. She said that Leandro told everyone that if they took the house away from Campos that they might take away the homes of everyone else in Chihuahuaita. She flatly denied that Leandro said anything about fighting the sheriff or the police or that he said anything about "toothpicks."

David Chavez briefly cross-examined this nice lady and got her to resolve the confusion about her name. Turns out that her full name is Maria Livira Gonzales de Aurelio and that is the name she used when she gave a statement to the police back in May 1935. This statement was given to Mr. Martin of the state police. Perfecto Garcia was the translator. The statement was read to the jury but didn't do much to contradict her direct testimony.

Woodward rose and addressed the court. "Your Honor, our next witness is Manuel Aurelio." Manuel Aurelio took a long time to walk to the witness stand. He passed his daughter-in-law in the aisle and stopped to hold her hand for a minute. She had left the stand nearly in tears, and it was clear that he was embarrassed at the way she was treated.

"Mr. Aurelio, we will need only a few minutes of your time. We want to talk to you about the meeting at your house in March of this year. It is our understanding that Leandro Velarde was there and was talking to Mrs. John Green and to your daughter-in-law and yourself. Is that right?"

"Those people were at our house and were speaking in Spanish. But now, some people are saying it different. I was there, and I know what everyone said."

"Did you hear Leandro say something about arms or toothpicks that day?"

"Leandro did not say that the people could throw away their arms and take care of the officers with toothpicks. He didn't say anything of that character. He said nothing, absolutely, about anyone fighting the officers."

Woodward thanked the witness and said to the judge: "That is all I have, Your Honor."

David Chavez had no interest in cross-examining another member of the Aurelio household. He said: "No questions, Your Honor."

John Simms then stood and said: "Your Honor, that completes the defense on behalf of Leandro Velarde. We rest his case."

"Very well, I will give the jury an instruction as to the defendant Velarde directly. But there is a matter I want to discuss with counsel. So I'm going to send the jury out for a little break so we can take this matter up on the record."

The jury filed out, and when they were gone, the judge addressed the lawyers. "I've been looking over my notes. I understood the prosecution would be making an application to call back the witness Hoy Boggess to the stand." Looking at David Chavez, he said: "Now, you told me, out of the presence of the jury, that he would testify as to receiving wounds with an ice pick, but no record was made of the statement. I don't know if the state is still going to go down that path, but they have rested their case, and now the defense has rested the case for Mr. Velarde. The testimony about ice picks and such is relevant only if someone, namely Mr. Boggess, was stuck with an ice pick. So here is my ruling: If the witness appears, I will then hear the application of the state to reopen. If they do, the defense can offer further testimony on behalf of Velarde. But for now I think we have to give the jury a cautionary instruction. Do you all agree?" Both sides nodded their acquiescence in the judge's position. Accordingly the judge called the jury back in and gave them the following instruction:

"Gentlemen of the jury, you have heard testimony to the effect that the defendant Velarde made certain statements regarding the officers at the home of this Mrs. Aurelio. I instruct you that this testimony is to be considered by you *only* as against Velarde and not as against any of the other defendants; likewise, you will *not* consider the testimony regarding the ice pick, which it is claimed the defendant Velarde took from the bib of his overalls or from his person, at his home after the trouble, except as against the defendant Velarde. You will not consider that as against the other defendants as this occurred after the crowd had dispersed and Velarde had gone to his home. Now, the defense may call its next witness."

"Thank you, Your Honor. At this time Manuel Avitia will take the witness stand and testify on his own behalf."

Avitia was the second from the end on the defendants' bench. Juan Ochoa got up to make room for him to get out, and the jury got its first look at any of the defendants on their feet. So far, every time the jury entered the room, the defendants were already seated, and they never moved while the jury was present. Every man on the jury was paying close attention as Manuel Avitia moved from the far side of the courtroom and walked to the clerk to take the oath.

The clerk administered the oath in English, which was translated into Spanish. After hearing the oath, Mr. Avitia said in a somewhat high-pitched voice: "*Sí,* I do promise." The fact that he mixed Spanish and English in his answer was not lost on the jury or on John Simms.

Avitia was a fairly short man with bad skin and narrow eyes. His eyes were deep set, making it hard to tell their color. The combination of a baby face, curly hair, and soft muscles made him look younger than he really was. His mouth had a petulant set to it, but his eyes, to the extent you could see them, looked bemused or belligerent, depending on your view of things. He had kept that look all through the trial and carried it with him to the witness stand.

His dark brown suit and tan work shirt made him look uncomfortable. Like the other defendants, he had worn the same clothes to trial for the last seven days. Unlike the others, he seemed to be restrained as much by the suit as by the deputies who sat behind that long defendants' bench.

"Now, Mr. Avitia, I will put my question to you in English, and our translator will put the question to you in Spanish. But just so the jury is clear, tell me how much of this question you understand in English before it's translated."

"I can get most of it. I learned English, but some words I might not know. And my answers will be more clear if I can give them in my native language, *español, por favor, señor.*"

"Let's start with some background information. Tell the jury your age and address, please."

I watched Avitia closely as he gave his testimony. Everyone but Mary Ann was staring directly at him. Mary Ann, of course, was trying to write everything down and so couldn't look at the witness. He explained in a halting but ultimately calm way that he lived on Wilson Avenue in Gallup with his wife and son and that he was a twenty-seven-year-old unemployed miner. He talked about the meeting at the Spanish-American Hall on April 3, 1935, but remembered it more as a meeting about forming a committee of some sort to go to Santa Fe to help all the employed men in Gallup. He emphasized that it wasn't just about the unemployed miners. He minimized the part about the meeting that concerned Campos or his eviction in Chihuahuaita. He said he didn't stay for the whole meeting and knew nothing about the visit to the sheriff's office to see Campos and Navarro.

"Let me move ahead to the next morning, the fourth of April, 1935. What did you do that day?"

"The next morning I left home at nine-thirty; I was working in a garage. I was going to get some rings for a car that I was fixing at home. I'm an automobile mechanic. I went into the Angeles Pool Hall, and then I went out on the street. I saw a crowd of women and children that were just turning up past the old post office. They were going south on Third Street."

"You said women and children. Were there any men?"

"There were men also. They weren't going fast; they were just walking. The people turned inside the alley, and so I went in with them. There were many people in there. Do you want me to go on or what?"

"Let me ask you some questions about what you saw. Could you see any sheriff's officers from where you were?"

"I saw some officers come out here with a prisoner," he said, pointing to the clay model on the table in front of the jury.

"What were they doing, if you could tell?"

"When I saw them, they were walking down the alley."

"Now, sir, this is important. Look at the jury and tell them whether or not you had a gun at this time. Did you?"

"No. I did not have a pistol or any arms of any kind."

"Who was there in the alley who you knew?"

"I knew the prisoner; he was Esiquel Navarro. I know Deputy Boggess. I know Bobcat Wilson."

"What did you see then?"

"Then the prisoner retarded like this a little. He pulled back. Then Mr. Wilson got his gun up to hit him. Then the people started to retire. Then—"

"Wait, slow down a little. What do you mean, the people started to retire?"

"They were backing up."

"Why?"

"Because a bomb exploded about here. Tear gas. The gas came into my eyes, the fumes came. Tears began to fall. I started wiping my eyes. Then I heard the shooting."

"How many shots did you hear?"

"About twelve or fifteen shots, something like that. When the shooting started, I ran back this way."

"Mr. Avitia, you know the sheriff was killed that day. Tell the jury what you saw that related to the sheriff."

"I didn't see the sheriff fall. I didn't see Mr. Boggess knocked down or who hit him. I didn't hit him."

"Did you do anything to harm the sheriff?"

"No."

"You also knew that a man named Ignacio Velarde was killed. What did you see about that?"

"I don't know who killed Ignacio Velarde. I did see Solomon Esquibel lying in the alley. But that's all I know."

"We've had lots of estimates of the number of people in the alley that morning. What is your best estimate?"

"I would say there were about one hundred twenty-five people in the alley. Some were walking, and some were standing still. When the shooting started, all of them ran."

"You know that you are accused of hitting a deputy by the name of Boggess. Did you do that?"

"I never did anything to Boggess."

"This jury has been told that you had a gun in the alley; did you?"

"I did see a child lying there in the alley—he was about six or seven years old. I picked him up because he was crying. Then I saw a gun lying in the alley. It was about six or seven feet away from Esquibel's body. I don't know whose gun it was. It wasn't mine. I picked it up. I saw it because I stepped on it. I don't know if it was loaded or not, but it was hot. I never shot it. I picked it up so that nobody else would pick it up and cause more disturbance than had happened there. I was a little excited. When I turned the corner out of the alley, two more shots were fired. They took the gun away from my hand."

"Who was that? Who took the gun away from you?"

"I don't know who took it from me. I was on the corner of the *Independent* building when they took the gun away from me."

"The jury has also been told that you yelled something out there in the alley. Did you?"

"I never yelled anything to Navarro when I was in the alley. I didn't use the gun because I had no intention of shooting anybody. Just as soon as I picked up the little boy, he ran outside the alley."

"Did you stay there by the alley after the shooting was all over? If you did that, can you explain why?"

"Probably about a half hour after it all happened, they arrested me there on that corner. I didn't go home because I had no reason to run home."

"And when they arrested you, where did they take you?"

"When they took me to the jail, it was full."

"Thank you, Mr. Avitia. I have no more questions for you, but I'm sure that the prosecutor will have some. Your witness, sir."

David Chavez stood and glared at Avitia for a moment before speaking. "You have not always been a mechanic, have you, sir?"

"I worked the mines until about February of this year."

"You attended those meetings because of your work in the mines, right?"

"I went because I was unemployed for a while, then I got a job in the garage. I was a mechanic."

"Let me turn to the morning of April 4, 1935. You were in the crowd out in front of Judge Bickel's court that morning, weren't you?"

"I wasn't in the crowd in front of the justice court. I don't know where the justice court is."

"But you saw the crowd; you have already admitted that."

"I didn't see them until they turned the corner and went down Third Street."

"Now, sir, your house is very close to Third Street, isn't it?"

"My house is on Wilson Avenue, but it has no number on it. It's not in Chihuahuaita."

"You're not from Gallup, are you?"

"I was born in Santo Diego de Papas Ciquiaro in the state of Durango."

Avitia turned out to be a difficult witness for Chavez even though he was allowed to lead him on cross-examination. I tried to explain this to Mary Ann and listen at the same time. Avitia admitted talking to Mr. Martin of the state police but denied saying anything incriminating. He admitted being at the meeting at the Spanish-American Hall on April 3, the day before the riot, but denied being involved in the effort to help move Victor Campos's furniture back into his house. He admitted knowing Dominica Hernandez but said he never heard anyone call her "little chief." He admitted being in the alley at the time of the shooting but denied taking part in it. He admitted having a gun but denied firing it in these words: "I didn't shoot through the crowd."

I happened to be looking at one of the jurors in the front row when Avitia said this. He narrowed his eyes and slowly shook his head as though he was thinking, "How could this guy be so stupid as to answer the question that way?" Avitia went on to try to explain away his presence downtown that day by saying he had to go to the toilet and the closest one was at the Angeles Pool Hall across the street from the justice court. He even denied knowing that the justice court was there. At this point he seemed to loose all credibility with the jury, and they avoided looking at him for the rest of his testimony.

Mr. Chavez seemed frustrated with Mr. Avitia. He angrily turned to the bench and said: "Your Honor, may we approach? I have a matter to bring to the attention of the court out of the hearing of the jury."

At the bench conference Chavez explained that he was trying to impeach the witness with statements Avitia made to the police. Simms argued that his client's constitutional rights had been violated since he was not told he had a right to a lawyer and had a right not to incriminate himself.

Judge McGhee overruled the defense objections and allowed Mr. Chavez to read to the jury the statements made by Avitia at the scene as recorded in the police notes.

Chavez turned to the jury with the police notes in his hand. He raised an accusatory finger at Avitia on the witness stand as he read the statements to the jury. "Here is what this man told the Gallup police the day of the shootings":

> The gun I found was the first one I had ever held in my hand in my life. I had never owned one, held one, or fired one. In fact, I had only seen one or two guns in my whole life.

With that dramatic ending, the prosecutor summarily dismissed Avitia with a contemptuous wave of his hand and a disgusted voice: "I am finished with you."

As Manuel Avitia left the witness stand, the jury watched him carefully. Up to now they had not had to really think about the differences in the testimony. Did he just find the gun, or did he have it with him? Did he shoot at someone, or was he just trying to protect a child? Now they had to face the problem squarely. Was this man to be believed?

Juan Ochoa stood and moved to the side to allow room for Manuel Avitia to sit back down on the defendants' bench. Before Ochoa could retake his seat, John Simms motioned for him to go to the clerk's table for the oath.

Simms announced: "Your Honor, the defendant Juan Ochoa will take the stand on his own behalf."

Mr. Ochoa took the oath in English, turned, and walked deliberately, almost defiantly, to the witness stand. The man who took the stand had a Spanish name and was believed by the jury to be either a Mexican or a Spanish American. But he looked more Indian than Spanish. His coal black hair was slicked down, combed straight back, and parted just off center.

His dark eyes, which never settled on one person for more than a moment or two, were wide and alert. That dark movement, combined with his high cheekbones, gave him a fierce look. The distinctive scar in the middle of his square jaw added to the look of a man to be reckoned with.

He settled lithely into the chair and turned to ready himself for the first question. Anticipating that it would be introductory, he slowly nodded as John Simms asked: "Mr. Ochoa, tell the jury whether or not you shot or hit or harmed in any way Sheriff Carmichael or any of his deputies on April 4, 1935, in Gallup, New Mexico."

Ochoa was a man of keen intelligence and recognized his inappropriate facial gesture as the question was moving from his ear to his brain. He stopped the slight nodding, turned to the jury, paused to make sure he had their attention, and said in a bold, strong voice without any hint of accent: "No, I did not. I swear that I did no harm to any man there."

"Did you plan to do harm to the sheriff or his deputies?"

"I swear that I did not."

"Were you aware that others were planning anything that might cause harm to the deputies?"

"I can't speak for everyone there, but I know that none of us charged with this crime planned it or carried it out. But when you mix injustice and guns and a show of force, sometimes this is what you get. No one wanted it. But it happened."

"Thank you. Now, sir, tell the jury something about your background."

Ochoa was relaxed as he answered the routine questions about him. The jury learned that he was thirty-five years old, was married with two kids, and had not worked as a coal miner since February 1934. He was born in Hillsboro, New Mexico, and went to work in the mines when he finished the seventh grade. He worked for a lot of different mining companies, including the Gallup American Coal Company at the Allison and Diamond mines as well as the main one at Metmore.

"Now, sir, let's turn to the meeting that took place the day before the shootings, the meeting of April 3, 1935. Tell the jury what you know about that meeting."

"I called the meeting at the Spanish-American Hall. We had different transactions to discuss. I posted the notices."

"What was the purpose of the meeting?"

"The main object was for the purpose of electing a committee to send a telegram to Santa Fe. It was to represent the local Unemployed Council in Santa Fe. I posted the notice early in the morning that day. I posted it on the bulletin board on the corner of the courthouse. The notice said what the meeting was for."

"When you called the meeting, did you intend to include the matter of the eviction of Mr. Campos or the arrest of Mr. Navarro?"

"No, that wasn't why we were having a meeting. When I posted the notice, I didn't even know that Mr. Campos, Mr. Navarro, and Mrs. Lovato had been arrested. I didn't learn that until the meeting was going."

"Why was it brought up at your meeting?"

"I'm not sure, but it was of interest because a lot of the people from Chihuahuaita belong to the Unemployed Local. Some people's homes were involved, and some knew other people from another part of town who were also interested. This was on account of the eviction proposition."

"Can you tell the jury what the focus of the discussion was on the Navarro matter?"

"From what I understood, Navarro was the one that was assisting people in preventing evictions in Chihuahuaita. There was a great number of them interested in that. There was talk there about Navarro having been arrested and Campos and Mrs. Lovato. They wanted some action to be taken. And so we did."

"What action was taken?"

Ochoa said that a committee was elected to go to the jail and talk to Sheriff Carmichael. They wanted to know if they could get Navarro an attorney and what the bond setting was. Ochoa said he wasn't on the committee but was there at the meeting hall when they came back and reported that Sheriff Carmichael wouldn't let them talk to Navarro and told them the trial would be the next day, April 4.

"All right, Mr. Ochoa, let me direct your attention to the following day, April 4, 1935. Were you present at Judge Bickel's court that morning?"

Mary Ann continued to scribble as fast as she could while Ochoa was on the stand. I decided to look at Judge McGhee and try to guess his reaction. He seemed impassive when Ochoa explained that he wasn't really interested in Navarro's trial itself, only in the result. He said that almost everyone in the crowd felt threatened by Vogel, and so they wanted to see if he was going to be successful in his criminal prosecution of Navarro. The judge seemed to perk up when Ochoa flatly denied being in the back alley at all that day. The judge took notes when he named the women he was talking to out in front when the shots went off—Mrs. Alfonso Ray, Mrs. Velarde, Mrs. Tomac, Mrs. Hernandez, and Mrs. Demertis. I wondered whether the judge was noting the fact that three of those women were defendants in the other case he had been assigned arising out of the riot.

Ochoa denied having a gun, but unlike Avitia didn't say anything stupid like he had never seen a gun before. Ochoa admitted that after the shots were fired, he went to the alley.

"As I turned into the alley I met a group of women who were crying. Someone made the remark that Navarro had been killed, and I passed the women—they were just about turning the corner in front of the post office. Right in back of them, about eight feet in back of these women I'm talking about, I met Rudolfo Fernandez. He was the one that told me Navarro had been killed. I said, 'How could they do that?' and I kept on walking down the alley until I came to about eight feet from the corner on this wall. There was a pool of blood on the sidewalk. José Lopez, my stepfather, was looking slantwise into the alley. I asked him if Navarro had been killed. He said that's what he had heard. As I was standing here, I looked in the same direction into the alley, and I noticed a man leaning against this wall in a stooping position as if he was holding somebody between his legs. Then I turned around. As I turned around, I saw Manuel Avitia crossing the street as if he was going to the opposite side of the street. Right in front of the alley I saw Vicente Guillén looking directly into the alley. I turned around and went north."

He made it clear to the jury that he never entered the alley itself and that he wasn't arrested until about three that afternoon. He looked the jury right in the eye and denied seeing anyone shoot anyone at any time that day. Simms passed the defendant to Mr. Chavez for cross-examination.

Chavez rose for the cross and skillfully led the witness. "You are fluent in English, are you not?"

"I speak Spanish and English fluently."

"When you chaired the meeting at the Spanish-American Hall, did you do so in English or Spanish?"

"Both."

"And you admit that you were the chairman of the meeting, do you not?"

"I was the chairman of the meeting at the hall, and I translated part of that meeting."

"There were other speakers at the meeting, were there not?"

"Yes. Carl Howe wasn't there, but Joe Bartol was. He spoke at the meeting."

"And planned or not, you did discuss the Navarro matter at the meeting?"

"One of the matters at the meeting was the Navarro matter."

"And did you have a personal interest in this meeting?"

"I was a local member of the Unemployed Council in Gallup at the time. I was there in front that morning because I was interested in the case of Navarro. But I didn't live in Chihuahuaita, and I wasn't being evicted. The only defendant in this case who did live in Chihuahuaita was Leandro Velarde."

"Even though you were not a resident of Chihuahuaita, you sympathized with them, did you not?"

"I was very much in sympathy with the case of Navarro."

At this point Mr. Woodward made an objection, and the judge said: "I want all counsel to approach the bench." When the lawyers had gathered around the bench for a private conference out of hearing of the jury, Judge McGhee said: "Mr. Woodward, I don't want to fine you, but if you don't rise when addressing the court, I will have to. You have done this several times. Now, I know you are here without pay and have little prospect for getting anything for your work, and I would hate to do it, but I will slap a fine on you if you don't rise."

Woodward looked chagrined, and Simms looked amused. In his best southern drawl, John Simms said: "May it please the court, you know Hugh won't have any money and he'll just lean over to me and ask me for the money, and then I'll be out the ten, so please be careful, Judge." They all returned to their tables and picked up the examination as if nothing had happened.

"You knew all of the other defendants before you were arrested, didn't you?"

"I knew these other nine defendants and had known them all for some time before April 4, 1935."

"And you met with them and talked about matters of common interest on a regular basis, didn't you?"

"I had discussed various matters with them."

"And some of these men were there with you that morning, weren't they?"

"Some of them were out there in front of the court that morning. I saw Joe Bartol there; Basilio Gutierrez wasn't there; I did see Serapio Sosa there that morning, but I didn't see him in front. I can't say that Serapio Sosa was in the back of the alley."

"Did you hear anyone there say they wanted to get Vogel or words to that effect?"

"I never heard anyone say, 'We want to get Vogel.' "

"Didn't you try to get into the trial that morning?"

"It was mostly the women who wanted to get into the trial, although I know that Gomez also tried to get in and Gregorio Correo tried to get in. One man did get in; his name was Rafael Gomez. Nobody told the women to get in the front while the men stayed in the back."

"And this crowd was made up of men who lived in Chihuahuaita, right, sir?"

"The crowd that was there that day was mostly the Unemployed Local."

"Now, you have mentioned that before. Tell the jury what this 'Unemployed Local' is."

"It was a local of the National Miners Union."

"And you and all these other men were members of the National Miners Union, weren't you?"

"Yes, we were."

"And that is why you were there, isn't it? Because of the union?"

"Sure, I was the chairman of that local."

Chavez paused for effect and looked at the jury as he posed his next question. "You are not a member of the Communist Party, of course?"

Before the witness answered, Woodward objected: "Your Honor, we object to that as incompetent, irrelevant, and immaterial."

Judge McGhee was quick to rule and frowned at Chavez as he said: "Sustained. Move on."

"Very well, Mr. Ochoa, which of the other defendants are officers in the National Miners Union?"

"None of the other defendants were officers."

"Not even Joe Bartol?"

"No, Joe Bartol was not an officer."

"Where did you live as of April 4, 1935?"

"On that day I was living at 221 West Firestone Avenue in Gallup."

"Are you claiming you not only did not participate in the shooting, you did not even see it happen? Is that what you are claiming?"

"I didn't see any of the shooting."

"And I suppose you never saw the two men who were killed there that day?"

"I didn't see Ignacio Velarde there or Solomon Esquibel in front or in back that day."

"And you deny that you saw the other defendants there that day?"

Chavez spent a long time going over the names of the defendants and their involvement in the case. Ochoa categorically denied seeing any of the defendants in the alley at any time that day. Chavez returned to the prosecution table and said: "No more questions, Your Honor."

The next witness called by the defense was Mr. R. C. Ritchey. Mr. Ritchey's testimony was very brief, and some on the jury wondered why he was called to the stand. He was a mortician in Gallup who operated Ritchey Funeral Home. His brief testimony related to the embalming of the body of Solomon Esquibel. He told the jury that he examined the entry wound made by the bullet that killed Mr. Esquibel. There was only one. It was two and one-half inches to the right side of his spinal column. It was in his back. There was no exit wound. He didn't do the autopsy. Dr. Travers and Dr. Pousma did it.

Funny, neither Dr. Travers nor Dr. Pousma mentioned that when they testified for the state.

Hugh Woodward, being careful to stand most of the time now before he addressed the court or examined a witness, said: "If it please the court, we call Mrs. John Tomac to the stand."

As she took the stand, it was clear that Mrs. Tomac was well known by the defendants. Some of them smiled at her, and all of them nodded respectfully when she settled in the chair and looked over at them. She was the kind of woman who not only looked ready to engage in a spirited debate about almost anything; she looked ready to win it.

She was well dressed by New Mexico standards, but there was nothing about her that suggested that how she looked was nearly as important as what she thought. This was a woman of principle, not style.

"Mrs. Tomac, please tell us your full name and address."

"I am Mary Tomac. We live out on Gamerco Road, just a few miles north of Gallup."

Mary Tomac was a forceful and persuasive witness. She explained that she was involved in several organizations in Gallup and in Santa Fe and that she spent a good deal of her time trying to help the unemployed power plant workers and the miners. She said she knew Juan Ochoa very well and that she and he were talking about the situation in Chihuahuaita when she heard the first two shots fired that morning. She looked at the jury when she said that Juan was right next to her in front of the justice court when the shots went off. After the first two, she heard several more. She and Mrs. Hernandez stayed there, and Juan Ochoa went down Coal Avenue to see what happened. Woodward said, "Thank you, Mrs. Tomac. Your witness, Counsel."

Frank Patton's cross-examination was brief. He established that Mrs. Tomac was of Slavic descent and that her husband owned a filling station. She admitted that Mrs. Alfonso Ray was also there that morning and that she talked to Joe Bartol before the hearing started. She remained steadfast that Juan Ochoa was there with her the whole time and that when the shots were fired back in the alley, Juan was right there with her—on Coal Avenue in front of the justice court.

Judge McGhee looked at his watch and said with a skeptical look, "Can we finish another witness today, or should we recess?"

John Simms answered: "Judge, we have three witnesses left, but it might be a stretch to finish the first one today. I'm confident that if we start fresh in the morning, we can finish up all the testimony tomorrow."

That was obviously just what the judge was fishing for, as he quickly said: "Well, mighty fine. Gentlemen of the jury, we will take our evening recess a bit early today, but we will start promptly at our usual time of nine-thirty in the morning. Now, you just heard Mr. Simms say they would most likely finish up their testimony tomorrow, but that doesn't mean you can start talking about the case today. You must wait until the evidence is all in and the arguments and instructions have been given to you at the end of the case. And keep on staying away from the newspapers too. I will see you all in the morning."

Monday Evening, October 14, 1935

Dear Journal:

I really must tell you that the language of the law could stand some updating, to say the least. This was the opening day for the defense, and it started out by the Honorable Judge James McGhee explaining to the jury that these men had constitutional rights without any effort to explain or make clear what those rights were. Then he, at least in my opinion, added to the confusion by telling the jury, in his most solemn voice, that six of the defendants "on the advice of counsel and having stood upon their motions" would not be offering any evidence in the case.

When was it that the language of the law and the language of the rest of us parted company? Just think about it (I have). "Having stood upon their motions." That's what he said, believe it or not.

In the first place, the lawyers, not the defendants, made the motions he was talking about. In the second place, the defendants just sat there through the whole thing. They never stood. So it seems to me, as an English teacher, that the judge got both parts wrong. The defendants made no motions and they never stood.

What is this curious language that only lawyers and judges speak? I could ask Billy Wade, but he would think I was being ridiculous and give me a typically evasive rebuttal in defense of the arcane language of the law.

It seems the main point of all this was that the defendants who were standing (even if they were seated the whole time) on their motions (that is, the ones asserted by their lawyers) couldn't have any further evidence considered against them. And that's where I really started to think about the whole process.

The judge made his point very clear to the jury: *Do not consider the rest of this case* (as against the six men he named, namely Messrs. Bartol, V. Correo, G. Correo, Gomez, Gonzales, and Sosa).

I asked myself as he was "instructing" the jury on this point of law, What if the evidence that is about to come in actually helps the six defendants who are declining to participate in the rest of the case? I can understand the Constitution protecting them from evidence *against* them, but why does it prohibit the jury from considering any further evidence *for* them? I mean, what if someone says something in favor of one of them, sort of by accident? Does the jury have to say, Never mind, that helps you, but we must ignore it because the judge (and the Constitution) says so? I don't think so. In fact, I think the jury will do what it pleases anyhow, no matter what the judge says on this antique point of law.

Enough of language and on to substance. The next thing to happen this morning was the opening argument of John Simms for the defense. Of course, they said it was an opening statement (as opposed to an opening argument), but it sounded like an argument to me. And a very good one at that. It was especially good compared to the bland little thing that Attorney General Patton had the audacity to *read* to the jury last week at the start of their case. I still can't get over it. Instead of delivering an oral statement in a persuasive fashion, he resorted to *reading* something that was most unpersuasive. No one can accuse John Simms of that.

Mr. Simms wasn't exactly dramatic, but he was very credible and spoke in soft, measured tones. It was almost as though he was sitting in a living room, discussing the case with the jurors. He told them that three of his clients would take the stand and tell the jury just what happened.

But more importantly, he put the case for the defense in context of the greater issue in this case. He said: "These men were there that morning because of the threat to their jobs and the threat to their lives."

I thought that was a very big point, but I can't say whether the jury got it or not. I watched them as closely as I could, particularly the man on the top row nearest to the judge. He was the only one who seemed moved by that statement, but I have to admit that I could be imagining his reaction. He, like the rest of them, was pretty stone faced all morning. But at least he nodded ever so slightly.

Mr. Simms calmly pointed out that not only was there no proof that any one of the ten men on trial shot the sheriff but, quite to the contrary, the proof by the state was just the opposite. He reminded the jury that the eyewitnesses, the bullets, and the expert testimony all confirmed that the men who shot Sheriff Carmichael were themselves shot by Sheriff Dee Roberts.

Now I understand why the defense lawyers elected not to present their opening statement last week. They wanted to wait and see just what evidence the state had to offer. Mr. Simms couldn't have made this point had he stood up and argued his case last week, but he sure could this morning. I called Billy Wade, and he said that was "wise policy, skillfully executed."

The first witness of the morning was a gracious woman with a lovely name. Maria Livira Gonzales de Aurelio. I don't speak Spanish, but I wish I could record the sound of her name as she softly spoke it to Mr. Simms. She rolled her *r*'s and sang out the vowels in a most beautiful way.

Speaking of names, there was some confusion over just who she was because of her husband's name. His name is Concepción Aurelio, and some were confused, apparently because they thought Concepción was a female name.

I suppose she might have been on the witness stand ten or fifteen minutes, but she really said only one thing: Leandro Velarde didn't say those things that Mrs. Green says he said. He never said a word about fighting the officers or toothpicks.

The next witness was her father-in-law, Mr. Manuel Aurelio, and he seemed out of place and maybe a little too strident in his denial of Mrs. Green's accusation against Leandro Velarde. In short, he doth protest too much.

But the judge seemed to get the point because after Maria and Manuel testified, he told the jury, in another of his little "instructions" to them, that the testimony about an ice pick was relevant only to Leandro Velarde. I wonder why it's relevant to anyone? I would understand it if someone had been stabbed with an ice pick or threatened with an ice pick, but so far, there's no testimony like that. Maybe the judge thinks one of the defendants is going to say someone was stabbed or that they saw Mr. Velarde threaten someone with it. I'm missing something here. I just can't figure it out.

After those two witnesses testified, the defense announced that Mr. Velarde would offer no further evidence. I suppose that means he won't be testifying in the case.

The next witness was Mr. Manuel Avitia. He was the first defendant to take the stand. I guess he thought he needed to because the evidence against him seems to be stronger than against any of the other defendants, except possibly Mr. Ochoa (if you believe Sheriff Dee). In any event, he did take the stand, but he didn't comport himself very well.

He's an elusive man. I know this sounds bad, and I almost feel terrible even to say it, but, well, he has such bad skin that it makes him look untrustworthy. I know that might sound shallow and unkind, not to mention illogical. But somehow, how a man looks when he testifies definitely affects his credibility. Funny, up until now I thought that looks were only important to men when they're thinking about women. This experience has made me realize that sometimes, how a man looks affects how others think of him.

Manuel Avitia admitted having the gun that Chief Presley and Mr. Porter talked about last week, but he offered the jury an explanation. Well, not exactly an explanation, more like an excuse. And a lame one at that. He said he saw a gun lying in the alley next to a small child and picked it up. He said it was "hot," meaning that it had just been fired.

He also said (although I don't think anyone will believe him) that he did this "so nobody else would pick it up and cause more *disturbance* than had happened there." I wrote it down just as he said it. It sounded contrived and made up when I heard it, but now that I'm looking at my notes, I wonder if something wasn't lost in the translation from his Spanish to the jury's English.

He said "cause more disturbance." Is that a literal translation of what he said in Spanish? If it is, then he either lacks vocabulary skills or he badly misunderstands just what happened there that morning. Three men were killed, five other people were shot and seriously wounded, and dozens of women and children must have been scared out of their wits. Armed policemen and armed rioters fired dozens of shots. Half of the fifty or so people there were gassed. Does he really think of that as a *disturbance?*

To top it all off, he said he was "a little excited." Can you believe it? It must be the language barrier. No one could be that benign about the bloodiest riot in the history of New Mexico.

When it came time for the cross-examination by Mr. Chavez, he really hit Avitia with his own words. It seems that Avitia gave a statement to the police right after the riot. When they asked him about the gun in his hand, he told them that not only was it not his gun but "this was the first gun that I had ever held in my hand in my life." No one is going for that one. This man is about to get convicted by his own words!

Juan Ochoa was next. He was very, very different. He gave his testimony in a way that was absolutely mesmerizing. Honestly, I'm not sure I believed him, but he's a powerful man. It's not so much his words but his obvious belief in the truth of what he's saying. This man is a leader, but he has such a dark look about him that some men will fear him. Not women. Women will, for the most part, either admire him or secretly lust after him. But as you know, there are no women on the jury. Too bad for Mr. Ochoa.

I gather that his defense will be based on the testimony of several women. He said he was standing on the street in front of the justice court when the shots rang out in the alley to the north of them. At that precise moment he was talking to five local women, Mrs. Ray, Mrs. Tomac, Mrs. Velarde, Mrs. Hernandez, and Mrs. Demertis. Wouldn't you know it, all women?

He emphatically, almost passionately, denied ever going into that alley, although he admitted following some of the crowd down Third Street to the entrance to the alley.

Mr. Ochoa looked the jury right in the eye and said with real conviction that Dee Roberts was wrong when he said he was in the alley and that he struck at him with a claw hammer. But as I listened to him say it, I couldn't help but think that I would hate to rest my life on who the jury is going to believe, *sheriff* Dee or *agitator* Juan.

You see, the prosecutor brought out on cross-examination that Juan

Ochoa was the chairman of the Unemployed Local Council and chairman of the National Miners Union in Gallup. He made him admit that all the defendants were members of that union and sarcastically challenged Ochoa with "and I suppose you are *not* a member of the Communist Party."

That's the first time anyone mentioned the word *communist* in front of the jury, although Billy Wade says lots of arguments about party membership have been made to the judge out of the jury's presence. In fact, that became clear to me when Judge McGhee immediately sustained an objection to Mr. Chavez's challenge and said, "Not relevant. Move on." As though that little "instruction" cured anything! You can't unring bells, and you can't cleanse the jurors' minds of the clear accusation (even if it was in the form of a sarcastic question) that Ochoa is a communist.

Of course, no one really knows what is in the minds or hearts of these jurors as they hear this case. But the papers and the street corners have been full of the so-called red menace ever since this case started. If all the men on the jury have been living under rocks on their farms and ranches for the last six months, then the reference to "communist" might slide by. But if they've been sitting up and taking nourishment for the last six months, then they came into the courtroom *suspecting* that some or all the defendants are communists. Now they *know* that Mr. Ochoa is a communist, even though the judge disallowed the question.

As I see it, the jury might think he's not only a communist, but a liar to boot. That's a dangerous combination for any defendant and might be enough to send him to the electric chair.

I can't say I believe him or that I don't. He's the most controversial defendant and the most likely one to be convicted *if* this jury believes Dee.

Postscript. I don't have the energy to write it all out. I also don't have the courage. The short version is that Billy Wade and I had a talk (more than one, actually) about my—our—future. I'm glad we did because his assumptions about the future (ours and his) were flattering and frustrating. Flattering because he seemed to think it unthinkable that I wouldn't be in his future. Frustrating because he just takes it for granted. He thinks of this trial as fascinating, but for the wrong reasons. I think of it as fascinating because it's a true watershed event for New Mexico and for me. It will change us both, no matter how it turns out. But it won't change Billy Wade. His life as a Gallup lawyer will go on no matter what happens here in Aztec. And no matter what happens to me. How sad. Damn, I hate that.

thirteen

CALVILLO TAKES THE STAND

Tuesday, October 15, 1935

The next day turned out to be the first heavy frost of the fall. It was overcast and seemed to set the mood of the courtroom. Judge McGhee had a stern look on his face as he took the bench. "All right," he said gruffly as he sat down, "call your next witness."

Simms rose and said to the clerk: "We call Dominica Hernandez."

"Please state your name and residence, ma'am."

"I am Dominica Hernandez, and I live with my husband in Gallup, New Mexico."

"Are you a native of Gallup?"

"I am a Spanish American. I live in Gallup. I was born in this country, in Socorro County. I went to college in New Mexico."

Dominica Hernandez was a defendant in the case that was to follow this one—she was charged with aiding in the escape of Navarro. But that seemed to have little effect on her focused direct testimony. She was a schoolteacher and was fluent in both English and Spanish. She told the jury without hesitation that Juan Ochoa was there out in front of the justice court the whole morning, including the time when the shots went off back in the alley behind the justice court. She was quite insistent that she, Mrs. Tomac, Mrs. Ortega, and Juan were talking next to a parked car on Coal Avenue when the riot erupted.

David Chavez handled the cross-examination. He started out trying to establish friendship as a possible motive for untruthfulness. "You have known Juan Ochoa for many years, have you not?"

"I have known Juan Ochoa for about three years."

"And you knew him better than anyone else there that day, isn't that true?"

"Well, I also know the acting sheriff, Mr. Dee Roberts."

"It was no accident that you were there on the street that morning, was it? I mean, you were there on purpose, not just shopping downtown?"

"Yes, there was something in particular that took me downtown that morning. I went down there because I knew the trial of Navarro was going on. I was interested, but I was not particularly interested in Navarro himself."

"What were the people in front of the court saying?"

"They said, 'We want to get in.' They said, 'We want to hear the trial.' A woman was already in front of the door when I got there, and she said that they wouldn't allow us in."

Mrs. Hernandez continued to deflect the cross-examination without any apparent motive or bias on her part. She described the shots from the alley as being quite close together, "quite rapid." When the prosecutor tried to establish evasion by refusing to talk to the state's investigator, the following exchange took place. "Now, Mrs. Hernandez, you went over your testimony with the defense lawyers, didn't you?"

"I told all this to one of the defense attorneys, Mr. Woodward. I also told it to another lawyer before that."

"I suppose that was Mr. Wirin or Mr. Lynch."

"No, not them. But I know who they are, and it wasn't Mr. Levinson either. It was Mr. Augur and some other man."

"Did they tell you what to say?"

"No. I told them the same thing I told to Mr. Patton for the prosecution, but I don't think they wanted to hear what I had to say."

Hugh Woodward had been looking agitated at the defense table at the suggestion that he had coached this witness into favorable testimony. From his chair he said: "Objection. He's trying to badger the witness."

As it turned out, he wasn't nearly as agitated as Judge McGhee was. He'd had enough of Mr. Woodward's bad habit of addressing the court without standing up. Instead of ruling on the objection, he said: "Ten dollars, Mr. Woodward. The fine imposed was for failing to stand when addressing the court, after having been warned many times."

It didn't seem to faze Woodward when John Simms reached for his wallet and gave him a ten-dollar bill. Both the lawyers at the prosecution table and the judge seemed to enjoy the touch of humor, and it lightened an otherwise heavy moment.

Judge McGhee's smile only lasted a moment; he turned to David Chavez and said: "Proceed, Counsel."

Chavez knew when to stop and said: "I have no more questions, Your Honor."

Hugh Woodward slowly rose, nodded respectfully to the judge, and said: "If it please the court, I meant no offense. It's just that where I practice, standing is not required. I do have a question or two on redirect, if I may?"

"Yes, of course," said Judge McGhee in a congenial tone.

"Mrs. Hernandez, did you know what Navarro was charged with; that is, why was he on trial that morning?"

"I didn't know what offense they were charged with that morning. I just wanted to hear about these people. I knew that Mr. Campos had been put out of his house in Chihuahuaita, but I didn't know that the people who were arrested had put his furniture back in the house. I thought it had something to do with the people being put out of their homes in Chihuahuaita. That's all I knew."

Hugh Woodward sat down, and David Chavez stood up and asked: "Judge, can I ask one more question on recross?"

"Just one, Counsel. Proceed."

"Mrs. Hernandez, you knew very well that Campos had been put out of his house, didn't you?"

Having apparently forgotten the ten-dollar fine he had to pay just two minutes before, Woodward said from his chair: "Objection, she has already denied that."

Judge McGhee was at the end of his patience and said: "Ten dollars more, Mr. Woodward. I think you have gone far enough now."

Chavez tried to ask her questions about Sheriff Carmichael and Clarence Vogel, but the judge sustained the objections Woodward made—all from a standing position.

As though it was an afterthought, Chavez closed his cross-examination with a damning point. "Mrs. Hernandez, you were arrested and jailed along with the rest of them that morning, weren't you?"

"Yes, I was."

Judge McGhee said, "Call your next witness, Mr. Simms."

Simms rose and announced: "We call Bernadine Ortega."

The jury watched a young woman walk from the back to the courtroom and take the oath. She wasn't as breathtaking as Inez Lopez but was pretty, young, and scared to death. She was dressed as if for a solemn occasion, like a funeral, but her testimony was about a dance.

"Miss Ortega, please tell the jury your full name and residence."

"My name is Bernadine Ortega."

"Do you live in Gallup?"

"Yes, we used to live in El Paso, but we live in Gallup now."

Miss Ortega went on to explain that she and some friends went to city hall that morning to get a license for a *baile*. Thinking that an Aztec jury of ranchers might not know what a *baile* was, she explained that it was like a dance. She was told at city hall that Dee Roberts was in charge of giving out licenses and that he was down at the justice court that morning. Her only real point was that she was standing next to Mrs. Tomac's car, talking with Juan Ochoa, when the shots went off in the alley behind the courthouse.

David Chavez began his cross-examination with: "How long did you say you knew the defendant Juan Ochoa?"

"I've only known Juan Ochoa for a few months. I only knew him casually. I had seen him at dances."

"Didn't you ever see him at a meeting, like at the Spanish-American Hall?"

"I never saw him at a meeting because I never went to any meetings."

"And you are not related to him?"

"No, I'm not related to him. Victorio Correo is my brother-in-law; maybe that's what you heard."

The rest of the cross-examination was just about as penetrating. Chavez managed to get Miss Ortega to admit Juan Ochoa was wearing overalls, a blue jacket, and a cap.

Simms rose and said: "Your Honor, at this time, Agustin Calvillo will take the stand and offer testimony on his own behalf."

The judge looked somewhat surprised, as he had thought that Avitia and Ochoa were the only two defendants who had elected to take the stand. He said: "All right, the record will show that the defendant Calvillo voluntarily takes the stand on his own behalf."

As he moved from his seat on the end of the defendants' bench, Agustin Calvillo looked hesitant and very frightened. He either had a slight limp or was stiff from sitting on the bench all morning. It seemed to take him a long time to get to the witness chair. He didn't look at the jury as he took the oath, and he looked down at the floor as he slowly walked to the witness stand.

His demeanor was inconsistent with his physical stature. He was a big man with drooping shoulders and a large mustache that drooped down the sides of his cheeks. The black mustache was the dominant feature of his face but couldn't mask the fear in his eyes.

He grasped the rail in front of the witness box and took a deep breath just as John Simms was putting the first question to him. "Mr. Calvillo, I will go slow so the interpreter can get my questions. Do you speak any English, sir?"

Calvillo looked at the interpreter and waited for the translation. He was to do that all morning and into the afternoon. He was very careful to listen to the

Spanish version of the question, and he typically paused before he answered. "No, *señor,* I have only Spanish."

In his methodical way, John Simms established both the personality and the history of the defendant through short direct-exam questions. The jury learned that Cavillo was forty-five years old and married with six children and that he had been in Gallup for eight years. He was a coal miner in Jalisco, Mexico, before he came to this country. Calvillo smiled respectfully and nodded politely to the jury at the end of most of his answer. He explained that he did not live in Chihuahuaita, but his parents did. Calvillo said he went to the meeting at the Spanish-American Hall the day before the shooting. Simms paused as though he was having trouble thinking about how to pose this next question to a very frightened witness who couldn't speak his language. "Mr. Calvillo, did you hear anyone at the meeting talk about doing violence to the sheriff or his men?"

"*Señor,* no one there talked about shooting the sheriff or about taking the prisoner Navarro away from the sheriff."

"All right, Mr. Calvillo, let me ask you about the next day, April 4, 1935. What did you do that day?"

"The next day I left from my home around nine-thirty."

"Where did you go?"

"I was going to the welfare office to get a check. I was working for the Federal Emergency Relief Administration."

"Where was their office?"

"On Coal Avenue. That's why I was going up the street on Coal Avenue."

"Is the FERA office close to the justice of the peace court there on Coal Avenue?"

"I didn't even know that was where the office of Judge Bickel was. But I saw many people coming over on this side."

Pointing to the clay model, Simms asked: "Which side?"

"I was walking along there by the old post office when I heard many shots. They were coming from the other street from where I was going."

"How many shots?"

"*Señor,* maybe there were twelve or thirteen. They came right away, all of them."

"What kind of shots?"

"It sounded like pistols."

"What were the people doing?"

"I could see people at the Cairo Theater, and they began to pass to the side where there were some more."

Calvillo explained to the jury that he saw the people running *out* of the alley as he walked toward it. He had heard the shots and that was why he walked down Third Street toward the alley. Simms asked him if he ran with the crowd when it came out of the alley. Calvillo said: "No, *señor.*"

"Why not?"

"I cannot run. I have not run for many, many years now. So whoever says I am running is seeing someone else. I cannot run because one of my legs is not right."

"Can you explain to the jury what you mean by 'not right'?"

"It is not right because of an operation."

"Did you go down the same street that they had gone?"

"When I got a little farther on, Martin Borasa spoke to me. He said not to get near because he was coming from there."

"So what did you do?"

"*Señor,* I went back."

"Had you reached the alley by the time you started back?"

"I did not go to that alley."

"Did you see anyone with a gun, a rifle, or a pistol or anything?"

"No, *señor.* I don't have a *pistola.*"

"How about a club?"

"*Nada,* no club either. I was going to get my check from the FERA."

"Mr. Calvillo, I hand you what is marked as state's Exhibit 24. Do you recognize this?"

"It's a club, but it's not mine. I have never seen it before."

"Mr. Calvillo, I will tell you that the chief of police in Gallup identified you as the man carrying this club that morning. Is that true?"

"I do not know the chief of police. I heard him on the witness stand say that he took it from me, but he did not. He did not take anything away from me. I just stayed there all the time. He must be thinking of another man."

"When were you arrested in this case?"

"Between one-thirty and two o'clock on the fifth."

"Who arrested you?"

"Jeremiah and Patricinio arrested me. There were five of them, but I only know those two."

"Why did they arrest you? What did they tell you?"

"They were looking for Anecito Ramos. They passed my house and asked me if I knew him. I told them I did. Then they got him and they said, 'You also.' "

Somehow that phrase "you also" rang true to me. I looked at the juror in the back row as I heard Calvillo, and he seemed to have the same thought I did. This Calvillo is a man without guile, without subterfuge, and probably incapable of real evasion. His simple life makes him a simple witness. I was to hear more of this remarkable answer to why he was arrested.

"Where did they take you?"

"They took me to the office where they take prisoners. Then they took me upstairs to the court."

"Who was there?"

"There I saw Mr. Dee Roberts and Mr. Bob Roberts and Mr. Molina and Mr. Vogel."

"What happened there?"

"They made me turn around. First with my hat on and then without my hat."

Calvillo stopped as though he had said too much. "Go on, sir, tell the jury everything that happened in that room."

Calvillo looked over at Dee Roberts, sitting behind the prosecution table, as though he might get into more trouble for talking. "When I turned around the last time, Dee Roberts was there and all those that accompanied him were there. Everybody said they didn't know me, and the young lady who came here to testify also said no. When they asked me if I was there, I told them no. Then they asked the sheriffs if I was in the alley, and they said no. Then when I had taken two or three steps down the hall, the brother of Dee Roberts said, 'Come here.' He said, 'What is your name?' 'Agustin Calvillo,' I said. 'Where do you live?' 'Lincoln Avenue,' I said. He said, 'And you also.' "

"You also. Is that all he said?"

"Yes, *señor;* 'you also.' "

"What did that mean?"

"I guess he wanted me to be in the prison. So I stayed there together with the rest that they were going to bring up."

"What do you mean, the rest they were going to bring up?"

"The rest of the men and women who were in trouble. They took forty-eight of us to the preliminary in Santa Fe. Ever since that day I have been a prisoner in Santa Fe, in the penitentiary. I never even went into the alley."

"Thank you, Mr. Calvillo. I have no more questions."

"You are welcome, *señor.*"

The attorney general elected to conduct the cross-examination. He may have mistaken the quiet, frightened voice of this big, powerful-looking man as a sign of guilt. He made several erroneous assumptions early in the cross. Actually, the cross-examination took about ten minutes, but the answers could have been given in ten seconds. Calvillo admitted to working in all the mines around Gallup. He admitted knowing Bill Cuton, Manuel Terrasas, and Albino Casias. He admitted that he was wearing a mustache in court and that it was the same one he wore on April 4, 1935, and the same one he had worn for all his adult life. Oh, he also admitted that he wore a hat on the day in question—the same one he always wore. At that point, having accomplished very little, Mr. Patton turned to the judge. "Your Honor, we have no further questions for Mr. Calvillo."

John Simms was quick to imply that the cross did nothing to weaken the testimony. "Your Honor, we have no redirect examination."

Judge McGhee looked relieved and said: "Well, mighty fine. Call your next witness."

John Simms rose and asked for a moment to confer with his co-counsel. A short whispered meeting took place at the defense table while the jury looked on expectantly. Simms then rose and looked straight at the jury while he addressed the court. He spoke in carefully measured tones. "Your Honor, the defense rests its case."

David Chavez rose and said: "If it please the court, we'll have a few rebuttal witnesses, but they will be brief."

The oldest man on the jury, the one on the end on the back row, let out an audible groan. Judge McGhee obviously heard it and said: "Gentlemen of the jury, it is the right of the state to offer any rebuttal testimony they feel is appropriate at this time. But as you have heard, it will be brief, and then you will get your chance to go to work on this case. We will put this testimony on by the state first thing in the morning. That is because I want to adjourn for the afternoon so the lawyers can meet with me to work out the final jury instructions in this case. Then after the testimony tomorrow, we will hear the closing arguments of the lawyers for both sides. I remind you to remember my admonitions about talking to folks and about keeping an open mind on the case. Court's adjourned."

Tuesday Afternoon, October 15, 1935

Dear Journal:

Judge McGhee let us out a little early today. The jury went back to the church basement, and I came here to the peaceful banks of the Animas River south of town. The last witness to testify yesterday and the first two today were a refreshing change of pace. They were all women. Smart, articulate women. The men on the jury seemed to listen to their words intently, but I'm not sure they will be believed. Rather, I should say, accepted. You see, Madam Journal, all three were there to give Juan Ochoa an alibi. So the men of the jury might well believe them and ignore them at the same time. What else is new?

Mary Tomac, Dominica Hernandez, and Bernadine Ortega are very different, although they had a common mission here in Aztec; that is, to save Juan Ochoa. All three come from very different parts of town, have different social and cultural backgrounds, and were there on the street that day for very different reasons.

Mary Tomac described herself as Slavic and was undoubtedly perceived as something of a busybody by the prosecutors. She was there because she was concerned about the men and women of Gallup who are out of work and becoming desperate over their homes.

Dominica Hernandez was herself arrested that morning because she is an activist and a fervent believer in the cause. She was much more than just an observer there that day. She is the type of woman who will accept nothing readily and who demands respect from everyone, even *gringa* women like me. I wish I knew her better.

Bernadine Ortega is not a believer or an activist. She's just a typical young girl more interested in dances than causes. But she will grow, and I feel she will become a woman of substance.

All three of these women are intertwined with their belief in, fascination for, and, perhaps, romantic feelings toward Juan Ochoa. A tall, dark man deeply troubled and deeply in trouble. It is to his rescue that these women of Gallup rode today. I fear the jury will disappoint them.

All three women categorically confirmed Juan's testimony that he was with them, out in front of the justice court, when the first shots were fired. All three swore that he was calm and collected and seemingly uninterested in the crowd gathered just a few feet from them at the front door to Judge Bickel's court. They didn't see where he went after they heard the first round of seven or eight shots.

No one mentioned it, but I was thinking as they testified that there's a way he could have been in two places at once. Remember the vacant lot just east of the Sutherland Building? Well, he could have gone through there because all three of them lost sight of him after the first shots were fired. He said he went west on Coal Avenue and then south on Third Street, but then again, his credibility is at issue in this case.

I suppose I could go on for pages about these women, but I better get on with this and tell you, Madam Journal, about Agustin Calvillo, the last defendant to testify on his own behalf. He's the oldest of the defendants and has something that is quite remarkable and may save him from the electric chair. He walks in a slow and painful manner. That's important. He walked to the stand in obvious pain, and all who saw him believed that it was real, not an act.

Remember that the main witnesses against him were Chief Presley and the merchants' policeman Massie. Both of them say he was *running* down Third Street with a club in has hand and that they (or at least Chief Presley) took away his club. No one else saw him; not even Dee Roberts.

As I looked at this man, I couldn't help but recall Sherman Porter's testimony about Mustache Man (at least that's what I call him). I'll bet you that Chief Presley is mixed up and misidentified Mr. Calvillo with the Mustache Man who Porter talked about.

Mr. Calvillo wasn't a coal miner. He wasn't an agitator, and he wasn't even going downtown that morning because of the Navarro hearing. He's an old man with six children to feed. He was on his way to pick up his FERA check. Most importantly, he could *not* run and has *not* run for many years because he has a bad leg. This was totally unchallenged by the prosecution. I think they might even be sorry they charged him. We'll see.

If the jury accepts the arguments by Mr. Simms that these defendants were charged mostly because someone saw them there that day, then Mr. Calvillo's testimony may help all of them. It just doesn't seem as if he was involved at all, and I think that the officers got him mixed up in the terrible confusion of men and women and children running every which way after that stupid tear gas bomb went off. If they're that mixed up about him, who else are they mixed up about?

Well, I guess that's enough for today. I want to review my notes and finish my chart that I'm making to sort out the testimony about who was where and who said so. You remember that I said I would do that; well, I've started on it and should finish it up tonight.

Tomorrow is likely to be the end of the trial. The state had some so-called rebuttal witnesses to call, which, by the way, made the jury groan out loud today when the lead prosecutor mentioned it. Anyway, they will be on the first thing tomorrow and then we'll get the closing arguments and the final instructions on the law from Judge McGhee. Billy Wade says the lawyers argue first and then the judge gets to overrule them with his "instructions" on the law. I'm not sure what he means, but I'll find out tomorrow.

This journal is getting a lot longer now that I'm used to talking to it (actually, it's not an "it"; I mean no offense, Madam Journal). I guess I'm getting to know and like you. I think I'll call Billy Wade on the telephone. Talking back is sometimes a good thing. Good evening to you, Madam Journal.

Postscript. Nope, no postscript this evening. The future be damned. I like the present just fine, thank you very much!

You know the old saying about the winners smiling and the losers saying "deal the cards again"? Well, that's what it was like in Gallup the night the defense rested its case. Down at the American Bar, the consensus was that whatever harm might have been done to the case by Mr. John Simms would get squared away by the attorney general and their rebuttal witnesses.

On the other hand, actually on the other side of the street at the Angeles Pool Hall, they were finally feeling like maybe, just maybe, the men on trial might get a fair shake after all.

"No hagas cosas buenas que parezcan malas porque la gente es muy juzgona." That pretty much says it all. "Don't do good deeds that may appear suspect, because people often misjudge." You see, the men shooting pool and drinking beer (and maybe a little tequila) didn't know the intricacies of the Fifth Amendment to the Constitution, but they knew that only three of the defendants took the stand up there in Aztec. They thought it was probably a wise thing. If you give those *gringo* jurors a chance, they might put it to you. If you stood on your motion (whatever that meant), maybe they would think you were so innocent that you didn't have to say nothing. So they were starting to think there was a chance that the men who stayed silent might escape the electric chair. *"Asaco, non cincho"*—a chance, not a certainty.

From what they heard, the three women who testified were very good witnesses for Juan. And they knew he would need some really good witnesses. It was known he was the organizer of the National Miners Union, and it was known that he didn't think the *cabrón* mine owners gave a damn about the workingman. So it goes to show they would arrest him even if he was only out in front, right there across from the Angeles Pool Hall the whole time. He had to stand up there and look at them and tell them no way it was him. Even then, they'll probably get him.

Poor Manuel. He was a different case. So angry, but not very good for himself on the witness stand. It was his story against theirs, and he had no one to say he was out in front the whole time, like Juan. And besides, he was the only one who had a gun. They caught it on him, and his story about picking it up wasn't a very good one. As the smoky room passed on what they heard about his testimony, the men said he was probably *"finado, muerto."*

The man who lifted their spirits the most was Calvillo. No English, no motive, no bad feelings. Everyone who saw him said he was a most believable man. Of course, they didn't know why he wanted to testify when the others didn't. He's a proud man but full of fear, and so it was a surprise that he took the stand. Nobody thought that Bob Roberts had it in for him, but why did he say, "You also"? They had heard that some big man with a big mustache led the run down Third Street to the alley, and some even claimed to be that man. But that's whiskey talking. It sure wasn't Agustin Calvillo. He has a bad leg, but did they believe him?

And so in time they got around to talking about Leandro Velarde. It wasn't easy to talk about him because of his brother dying and all. It was also hard because he has lots of family and lots of friends, on both sides of the tracks. But the men of the law weren't his friends, except maybe for Bobcat. Leandro is a man of conviction. It's those convictions that might get him convicted, no matter that he didn't stab anyone with a *"pica diente."* That brought a good laugh in the bar. *Gringos.* There's no telling how they can fuck things up just because they can't understand Spanish. But the thought running through the heads of most of the men in the Angeles Pool Hall that night was: It's not our language they screw up, man; it's us.

fourteen

CLOSING ARGUMENTS

Wednesday, October 16, 1935

"Good morning, gentlemen. My bailiff tells me the state has only two rebuttal witnesses to call before we begin the final arguments, is that correct?" Judge McGhee asked.

"Yes, Your Honor," Modrall said. "We call John Green to the stand."

"Mr. Green, we are calling you here for a limited purpose. We will limit your testimony to the translation services you provided to Mr. H. C. Martin of the New Mexico State Police regarding the case at bar."

Mr. Green explained to the jury in a dry monotone that he was the translator at the meeting between State Policeman H. C. Martin and Mrs. Maria Livira Aurelio in the sheriff's office on April 14, 1935. He said that Mr. Aurelio reported that Mr. Leandro said everyone was supposed to help Campos with his furniture after he was evicted. It took a little over five minutes, but that's all he said, believe me.

The next rebuttal witness called by the state was H. C. Martin. He had already given his direct examination and so was not sworn in again by the clerk. Officer Martin was called to support the testimony of John Green, the translator, and to rebut the testimony of Mr. Ritchey, the mortician. The defense stipulated that his testimony would be the same as that just given by Mr. John Green regarding the statement of Mrs. Aurelio. The state accepted the stipulation and proceeded to rebut the testimony offered by Mr. Ritchey. Martin said that he had been a state police detective for ten years and had attended numerous autopsies. He was present at the autopsy of Solomon Esquibel and was certain that the entrance wound was on the left side of Mr. Esquibel's back and that it went in at an upward direction. He said it as if that was somehow helpful to the state's case.

Simms sat there, wondering what he missed and wondering why Martin was ever recalled. He said, "Your Honor, I don't believe this witness rebutted anything that Mr. Ritchey said and so have no questions for him."

Judge McGhee seemed to be in agreement as he nodded at Simms. He turned to Dick Modrall and said: "Is that it, or do you have something else?"

"No, Your Honor, we have nothing else."

"Then do you rest?"

"We do, Your Honor."

"Does the defense have anything further?"

"No, Your Honor."

"All right, mighty fine. Gentlemen of the jury, both sides have rested and they will present their final arguments to you this afternoon. Now, I'm sure these gentlemen will be brief, but even so, I expect it will take a good part of the afternoon. As soon as that is finished, I will give you my instructions on the law and then you will have the case to decide. I will see counsel in my chambers now, and we will finish up the instructions. Court is adjourned."

As had become his habit after the first week of trial, the bailiff waited until the judge was up and scooting out his little invisible door before he even attempted to gavel him out with the traditional, "All rise . . ."

So that was it. The barroom crowds on Coal Avenue allowed that the "evidence was all done and all in." All, that is, except for the arguments. But as it turned out, there was one more burr under Gallup's saddle. Most folks assumed that the lawyers spent Sunday afternoon preparing their final arguments. That didn't turn out to be the case. Three of them, Hugh Woodward and those boys from back east, Thayer and Brick, were embarrassed by an automobile accident on the outskirts of Aztec. Another man by the name of G. P. Winkler was with them when it happened. G. P. Winkler was the stringer for the Associated Press. Eight kids in a roadster came up on Woodward's car real sudden like, couldn't stop, and rammed them right in the rear. Seems most of the kids got bruised and cut up, but the lawyers got out of it without a scratch. Wouldn't you know it?

The *Aztec Times* reported that the defense lawyers were on their way to a fried turkey dinner sponsored for them by the state counsel. The boys in the American Bar wondered why the state was entertaining the defense just before the final arguments. Down the street at the Angeles Pool Hall, they wondered why anyone would want to fry a turkey. *Que no?* Maybe that's how they eat turkey up there in Aztec. Throughout town, the consensus was: If the trial had been held down here in Gallup like it should have been, well, there would be no fraternizing just before the arguments in the case, and even if there were, the turkey would be baked, by God, just like it's supposed to be.

That afternoon David Chavez gave the first closing argument for the state. Since the state had the burden of proof, they got to make two arguments—or, as lawyers put it, "open and close" the arguments. Dick Modrall was slated to give the second closing argument after John Simms summed up the case for the defense.

Mr. Chavez gave a journeyman-like argument. That is, he repeated the facts that the state relied on to prove its case. That was mostly the process of identifying each witness who identified each defendant as having been at the scene. He wisely elected not to go through the case of each defendant separately, because the theory of the state had always been grounded in the mob mentality that prevailed in Gallup on the morning of April 4, 1935.

Chavez also wisely elected to place most of the emphasis on the character of Dee Roberts and, to a lesser extent, his brother Bob. He stressed the clear, unequivocal testimony of Dee Roberts and called him an American hero for blasting away at the men who would tear down our system of justice and our treasured institutions.

Chavez didn't spend much time recalling the testimony of Hoy Boggess and spent even less on the testimony of the other officers. He completely ignored the fact that Bobcat Wilson was never called to the stand.

He spent a great deal of time extolling the virtues of ballistic science and the expert testimony of Mr. J. Frank Powers. He argued long and hard that the evidence could lead to no other conclusion other than it was Hoy's gun that was used to kill the sheriff and wound the deputy.

His argument was factual, but not emotional. He accused the defendants of a capital case, but not on a personal basis. He praised the bravery of the sheriff's men, but ignored the fact that they most likely killed the only men known to have actually fired a gun in the Gallup's most famous gun battle.

He didn't think he needed to appeal to the emotional aspects of the case or to seek sympathy to sway a jury made up of conservative farmers and ranchers. Chavez assumed that the men on his jury believed in the law and would take the word of the men who served the law.

Since Chavez was a Hispanic himself, as were some of the officers who testified, he didn't want them to convict the defendants because of their ethnic background. He never mentioned the word *communist,* but he did describe the defendants as agitators and instigators. He didn't ask them to look to matters outside the evidence, but he reminded them that they shouldn't leave their common sense outside the jury room when they deliberated.

Although he didn't say so, I thought he was hoping that the jury would remember just what kind of a communist conspiracy the law in New Mexico was up against. He wanted them to see this case as a chance to stop the red menace right here. He closed his argument with thanks to the jury for their attention and careful consideration of the evidence.

John Simms listened patiently and respectfully to the somewhat dry but comprehensive argument of David Chavez. He knew as he watched the faces of the jurors that the evidence in this case wasn't very strong for the state. He also knew that the strength of the case might not make a whit of difference to this jury. This case wasn't really about evidence; it was about justice under the most difficult of circumstances. One or more men in a crowd had shot down a much respected sheriff in cold blood. The sheriff was only doing his duty in a reasonable way. The crowd of men included at least some of his clients. It was quite possible that some of his clients did "conspire" to commit a lesser crime that day. He knew that even though the hard evidence against his clients was thin, it might be enough to put some or all of them in the electric chair. His thoughts and his analysis were calm and deliberate. But he knew he couldn't argue the case that way.

He stood and addressed the court. "May it please the court." Simms moved close to the jury rail and looked for a moment at each juror separately, without speaking. After making sure he had their collective attention, he said:

"We have done all we can. Now it is up to you. You are about to take the lives of these men in your hands. You are about to make the most important decision of their lives, not to mention yours. You all swore to do a duty that is honored in all the courts of this land: to justly and fairly try the case and render a verdict on the evidence presented to you, so help you God. We have done all we can to help you understand the evidence. Now it is your job to see if it rises to the level of a capital case. With all due respect to the men who represent the state, this case is more than just one bubble off plumb.

"His Honor told you many times during this trial to avoid reading about the case or talking about the case to people outside the courtroom. That is because they cannot know what you know. That is because only you know the evidence. You know it better than I do. You know it better than my learned opponents at the table for the state.

"Why do I say you know the evidence better than I? Better than the attorney general, better than the judge, better than anyone here? Because you, we all trust, did what the judge asked you to do many times these last weeks: You kept an open mind. I did not. The prosecutors did not. No one on their side or on our side came in here and listened to the evidence in the case with an open mind except the twelve of you. That openness, that impartiality, that attention, is what makes you know this case like none of the rest of us can.

"You can see this case for what it is. Look at your hearts and think with your minds. You will see and feel its flawed truths, its warts, its failures of conscience and the base politics that brought us all here.

"Now, I give my friends at the prosecution table credit for a mighty battle. They have tried to convince you that the evidence spells out a case of murder, and they are right. They offered evidence to prove that a good man, Sheriff M. R. Carmichael, was murdered in cold blood. And he was. They offered evidence to prove that two deputies were beaten and shot. And they were. They offered evidence that a mob of men lost control of themselves when a tear gas bomb went off. That, too, happened in Gallup on the fourth of April.

"I ask you to ask yourselves this question: Why did this happen? None of us would be here today if William Bickel had done his job as a justice of the peace in Gallup, New Mexico, last March. As a judicial officer, it was his job to endorse bail on the record for the prisoner Navarro. Had he done that, the man could have been bailed out and there would have been no hearing, no tear gas bomb by a lawman, no riot, no shooting, no death, and no charges against these men. They are here because 'Bail-less' Bickel lived up to his name.

"Actually, Justice of the Peace Bickel had three chances to set bail for Navarro: once before he was jailed, again while he was in jail, and once again at his hearing on the morning of April 5, 1935. Because Bickel failed three times to do his job, the sheriff had to take the prisoner back to jail. The justice of the peace did no justice to Navarro, and there was no peace in Gallup because of it. He failed to set bail, and he caused a riot. That's why we're here.

"Where is the proof that anyone on that long bench over there did these dastardly and cowardly acts? The best proof of their *innocence* came from the best witness the state had in this case. That was Dee Roberts himself. Dee Roberts took that witness stand and swore that he shot and killed the only two men known to be shooting at Sheriff Carmichael. And you know what? On that matter, he told the absolute truth. You all know that because no one else fired at those two men *and* because their expert witness, Mr. J. Frank Powers, confirmed that for you. He proved beyond a reasonable doubt that Dee Roberts was the hero they said he was.

"The bullets the doctors pulled out of Solomon Esquibel and Ignacio Velarde came from Dee Roberts's gun. He shot and killed the men who shot and killed the sheriff.

"I don't mean to suggest to you that Dee Roberts is all that perfect. You know he is not. He is just a man. He can be proud for what he did to protect his men in that alley in Gallup and for shooting the men that attacked their party. But he ought to be ashamed of his roundup of hundreds of men and women and his ransacking of hundreds of homes in the days that followed. He overreacted in a way that the law should not condone. After the roundup he caused forty-eight of those people to be imprisoned in Santa Fe at the state penitentiary for what they believed, not for what they did.

"He caused hundreds of homes to be searched, looking for a gun that his deputy lost in the battle. No one blames him for looking for it or even for not finding it. But they are trying to carry that shameless time right into this courtroom. They are trying to talk you into putting that missing gun in the hands of one of those ten men sitting over there."

Simms moved close to the jury rail and looked intently at the man in the middle of the first row. When he had the man's focused attention, he said:

"These men can do nothing but watch.

"They are not the law.

"They have no badges.

"All they have is you."

Simms moved away from the jury rail to the clay model of the alley and the buildings. He paused to let his last words dwell in the minds of the jury and then continued:

"I want you to think about why the evidence in this case was so convoluted. Why did they try so hard to create a conspiracy? Why did they argue that these men 'aided and abetted'?

"I will tell you why. They do not have *the* gun. Without it, they have no case. They know it, and so do you.

"Who knows where that gun is?

"Who knows where Navarro is?

"Who knows just how Solomon Esquibel or Ignacio Velarde got that gun? Who knows which one of them did?

"The state wants you to speculate on that. Guess on that. Come to your best hunch on that. Their hunch, their guess, is that one of these ten men scooped it up and shot the sheriff. Of course, they first said that over a hundred men scooped it up and shot the sheriff. Then they said it was only forty-eight of them who did it. Now they are down to ten. But it's only their guess.

"The law will not allow you to guess.

"Would you want a man to judge you on the basis of a guess?

"Well, you do not have to guess. Trust your judgment, and test it against what you know for sure.

"Here is what you *do* know, based on the evidence given to you by the state:

"One, the gun is gone.

"Two, Navarro is gone.

"Three, Esquibel and Velarde are dead.

"One. Two. Three. That is their case, gentlemen.

"The gun that killed the sheriff cannot be found any more than you can find guilt based on it.

"The prisoner who escaped cannot be found any more than you can find that these men conspired to free him.

"Esquibel and Velarde are dead and gone. You cannot find them guilty, and you must not find these ten men here guilty for what those dead men did.

"The law will be read to you by the judge. He will tell you that the burden of proving these ten men guilty rests entirely with the state. Our judge has already told you that these men are *presumed,* under the law, to be innocent until proven guilty by the state."

Simms stopped and moved away from the jury rail to the far side of the courtroom. He wanted them to see him as distant from the prosecutors, who sat right next to the jury box. He also wanted them to settle on the pivotal question that he was about to ask. His deep baritone voice carried clear across the courtroom. "What does 'presume' mean?

"Think about that word, *presume.*

"It's a word you use every day, even if you don't say it out loud or think on it very hard. When you get up and say to yourself over breakfast, 'I think I'd best get that tractor blade fixed today,' or 'I think I'll work the south forty today,' or 'I think I'll go to town and get those supplies today,' you are presuming something. To presume and to think are the same thing.

"When you *presume* a man to be innocent until proven guilty, you have to *think* he is innocent until proven guilty.

"So if your oath means anything to you, you came in here and looked at those ten men sitting on that bench over there and said, at least silently to yourselves, 'I think they are innocent.'

"Now, what has changed? Has the state proved them all and each one of them guilty in your eyes? I mean guilty beyond *any* reasonable doubt. That is the standard of justice in this country. If there is any reasonable doubt, however small it rests in your mind, it is your sworn duty to acquit these men and send them back to their families.

"You came in here thinking they were innocent. The law requires that, and you all swore to it. Then you heard the evidence put up by the state. Maybe the evidence really got you to thinking these men just might have done it. They were there. The gun was never found. Maybe they did scoop it up. You might even think now that they did it, but that is not enough. You have to believe it, not just think it. You have to believe it beyond a reasonable doubt. If you don't, you must acquit these men.

"I want you to do something for me. Actually, I want you to do it for yourselves. You are the ones who are about to make a life or death decision. I am going to make it easy for you. I am going to go over there, and I am going to put my hand on the shoulder of each man accused of killing the sheriff. When I do that, I want you to imagine that it is your hand on each shoulder. Imagine that it is you in touch with them as I recall for you what evidence the state gave you."

John Simms walked back to the defense table. He stopped first to pour a drink of water from the small glass pitcher on the table. He was thirsty, but he also wanted the jury to think about what was about to happen.

The lawyers at the prosecution table were squirming around, trying to think of an objection to stop this. This wasn't legally objectionable, but it sure was something that none of them had ever seen done in a courtroom before. Men just didn't go around touching one another except to shake hands. What was he up to here?

John Simms went behind the long bench and stopped in the middle, right behind Rafael Gomez. Slowly he placed his right hand on the silent defendant's shoulder and kept his left hand at his side. "Look at this man, please. Look not just at him, but try to look into him. As you look at him and listen to me, try to remember each and every fact that the state proved about this man.

"He is an out-of-work miner, he speaks no English, he was there in front on Coal Avenue, and according to Dee Roberts, he was there in the alley, too. No gun, no club, no physical act, no violence, nothing turned up on the search warrant. My God, they didn't even prove this man was at the meeting the day before. Look into his eyes and ask yourselves this question: Can I vote to put this man to death because Dee and Hoy *think* he was in the alley?

Simms picked out six more men and did the same thing with each of them. The facts varied slightly, as others in addition to Dee and Hoy had identified some of them. Some of them were at the meeting on April 3, 1935, and as to them he asked an additional question: "Does the exercise of your political right of assembly put you at risk of the death penalty in this country? In New Mexico?"

After he laid his hand on the shoulders of the Correo brothers, Willie Gonzales, Joe Bartol, Serapio Sosa, and Agustin Calvillo, Simms turned his attention to the three men on the end.

"These three men"—he briefly stopped by Juan Ochoa, Leandro Velarde, and Manuel Avitia—"stand in a slightly different legal position."

As he talked about them he moved back forth and touched the shoulder of each man several times. He recounted the evidence against them and sprinkled in the evidence produced in their favor. Among the things he emphasized for each was: "All three went to the meeting at the Spanish-American Hall. All three went to the street the next morning. The sheriff and his men have known all three for years. All three felt that what Senator Vogel did was unjust and that Victor Campos should not have been evicted from his home. Trouble was, Senator Vogel had the law on his side and Victor Campos didn't.

"Neither did Navarro.

"But all three of these men are targets of the state, either because they spoke out against injustice or because they were disrespectful of the law. But this is not enough. Look at these men and remember this about them: They put on a case for you. The other men did not need to, although Agustin Calvillo did take the stand."

"These three men either took the stand and withstood the cross-examination of Mr. Chavez or they called witnesses who directly rebutted the state's witnesses."

Simms paused and walked slowly back to the jury rail. When he got there, he looked at each juror again, slowly and silently. "Did I bring these men into your heads just now? That was my intention. To make you think about them as men, as being no different than any man who wants to protect his family, do his job, and enjoy a modest life in rural New Mexico, just like each of you.

"I did not place my hand on their shoulders to seek your sympathy. They do not need that. They need you to think through what you are about to do. They need you to think like rational men and make a decision based on the hard evidence, not the assumed theory of a missing gun, a shadowy organization, a labor union, a panic by a lawman that resulted in tragic consequences.

"And perhaps most tragic of all: a mistake by a justice of the peace who should have set bail for Navarro but did not do his job. You see, it wasn't just a good man of the law who died that day; it was the law itself.

"That crowd would never have been there if JP Bickel had done his job. But he didn't, and those people gathered to see what was going to happen to them next. Then the crowd ran amok because a lawman panicked. Then the law itself ran amok because the man in charge panicked."

"I say to you: Do not panic. Do not allow yourselves to be caught up in the emotion of someone *has got to pay.* We have all paid a bitter price for the lawlessness in Gallup, New Mexico, on April 4, 1935. Now we have a chance to return the law to its rightful place, a place of justice and fairness. You swore that you would justly and fairly try this case. I urge you to do that now.

"I told you when I started my argument that I was going to entrust the defendants' lives to you. I have tried to bridge the gap between that long bench over there and your comfortable chairs here in this box. I have tried to make you see that they are defendants, not for what they did, but for what they thought.

"That, gentlemen, is no crime.

"That is a right of every citizen, whether freeborn here or not. That is a right of every alien who is legally in our country, as all of these men are. I urge you, gentlemen, do your duty and stand by your oath. Give these men your just and fair judgment and return them to their families.

"I am about to sit down now. I have entrusted the lives of these men to you, but I must tell you one more thing. You are not just the representatives of Aztec, New Mexico. Today you are the representatives of the American justice system. You have a chance to make Aztec the capital of American liberty.

"In the name of God and our country, do your duty."

John Simms paused to ensure the solemnity of the moment and then turned and walked to the defense table.

The courtroom was still. The only sound was the scraping of Simms's chair as he pulled it out to sit down. As if to break the silence, Judge McGhee turned to the jury and said: "Gentlemen of the jury, given the number of defendants in this case, I have decided to allow Mr. Woodward and Mr. La Follette to address you as well. They will be brief, I'm sure. Mr. Woodward, you may address the jury."

As Hugh Woodward gathered up his notes and made his way from the back of the defense table to the middle of the courtroom, Dick Modrall studied the jury. He didn't like what he saw. Those men had sat here for nine days with a deadpan look that defied his usual uncanny ability to predict how a case would come out. But now they were animated and anxious to hear more from the defense. The tall juror on the seat on the end, the one closest to the prosecution table, wouldn't look over at the prosecutors at all. The man next to him had turned his chair away from the prosecution table as though that would give him some distance from their position as well as their location. Modrall scribbled a few notes while Woodward cleared his throat to get the jury's attention.

Woodward took his position in the middle of the courtroom and pointed at the defendants seated on the long bench behind the defense table. "These men are poor, ignorant people trying their best to comply with American ways. Imagine their feeling when Navarro wasn't released on bail and they couldn't see him. Naturally, they were curious about the hearing to which they were not admitted. But there was no intent of violence among that crowd when they gathered outside Bickel's office on the morning of April 4. There has been no evidence of bricks thrown, no stones, no sticks.

"Just as there has been no evidence by Mr. Bickel himself. Why was not Bickel produced as a witness by the state? I'll tell you why. Because the prosecutors were afraid of what would happen to him on cross-examination. They didn't want you to hear his answer when we asked him why he didn't set bail for Navarro. So as you deliberate on this case, ask this as question number one: Where is Bickel?

"You should have the greatest admiration for Sheriff Carmichael and his men there that day. They did their duty. Bickel did not do his. They went out into that alley because he did not set bail for Navarro. They went out into that alley where Ignacio 'Sena' Velarde fired on them. They did as they should have done—they returned his fire and they killed him, as was their duty and their right.

"But because of that, the state asks that you convict six of these defendants who by their own proof were merely there standing in the crowd. But you must remember, if you do convict them, what are you to do about the hundred or more other persons there that day? Are they equally guilty for having shown their curiosity at what was happening to their friends and neighbors?

"Bickel was not the only man the state failed to produce for you. Perhaps even more importantly, they did not put on the witness stand L. E. "Bobcat" Wilson. You have a right to question that. You must ask why they failed to call him as a witness. He was here in this courtroom; you saw him. You saw him sworn in as a witness by the court at the beginning of the trial. So why was he not called?

"They didn't call him because the story he would have told you wasn't the same as was told by the others. You must ask yourselves: What are they trying to hide by hiding this important witness from you? Why don't you make that question number two: Where is Bobcat?

"And what are you to make of Navarro himself? He was a man who only tried to help his neighbor. He moved that old cookstove, the old chair, and the little table back inside the home of Victor Campos after Senator Vogel had the furniture moved out into the street in his eviction action. Also handled by Bickel. Let's make that question number three: Where is Navarro?

"You men of Aztec are privileged to live in a special place. Your town is named after the prehistoric Aztec Indian dwellings on the outskirts of town. I visited them just this last Sunday. I went down into the kiva. I sat in the ceremonial chamber. I saw the seats around the wall and the great stone slab where captives used to be put to death. If the Aztec Indians had lost a chief of comparatively little renown in battle, maybe they would put only one of their prisoners to death—lay one man on the slab, where a stone knife would be plunged into his breast and his bleeding heart removed.

"But if a great chief had been killed, the prisoners then became the object of a greater vengeance and perhaps ten would be placed on the slab. I direct your attention to these ten men sitting here. They are not to be sacrificed by the sentiment against mob violence.

"I knew Carmichael well. He was a man of great courage and loyalty and was well bound in his duty. It would not be Carmichael who would call for vengeance against these defendants. He would ask for a fair, impartial trial at which those defendants sitting there would be availed of their constitutional rights. And if they were adjudged guilty, he would say, Let the law take its course.

"But if these men are guilty, in my opinion, there are between one hundred and one hundred fifty other members of that crowd who are equally guilty.

"Just because a great chief is gone, there is no reason to make these ten men pay the sacrifice."

Hugh Woodward returned to his table, where Robert La Follette gave his brief statement on behalf of Joe Bartol. In less than five minutes he covered what little evidence there was of Bartol's presence at the scene of the Gallup Riot. He loudly proclaimed that there was no evidence, not one ounce, not one drop, not even a whisper of evidence of actual *involvement* in the Gallup Riot. He argued forcefully that the state had not connected Mr. Bartol to any violence or knowledge of any violence. He described Mr. Bartol as a man with strong political beliefs, but nevertheless a mere onlooker in this case.

La Follette's brief argument was made even more brief when he suggested that the real defendants in this case ought to be the owners of the Gallup American Coal Company. Judge McGhee sustained the state's objection, "Since such references are not in the testimony before the jury."

That closed the arguments for the defense. Because the state had the burden of proof in the case, they got the last word.

When John Simms sat down, Dick Modrall knew that any chance of a first-degree murder conviction was gone. The Simms argument was eloquent, forcefully given, and sobering. More important, it rang true and struck at the heart of the prosecution's biggest error, the blind insistence on a premeditated first-degree murder charge so that the death penalty would apply. The power of John Simms had eliminated that, at least in the mind of Dick Modrall.

When Hugh Woodward gave his dramatic analogy to the Aztec Indian ritual slayings, Modrall feared that his backup charge, second-degree murder, might also be in jeopardy. He stood and asked the court: "Your Honor, may we have a brief recess to confer before I make the final argument for the prosecution?"

"Well, yes, I suppose we could all do with a short break about now. Twenty minutes, gentlemen. Court's recessed."

The prosecution team gathered in the small anteroom just off the front entrance to the courtroom. There were no windows and no ceiling fan, and the air was close. The tension in the room made things worse. Dick Modrall spoke in measured tones to his colleagues. "Men, I believe that the argument John Simms just made will carry the day. I would surely appreciate your counsel on how best to deal with it. As I see it, the defense has pretty well summed up the case as though it was first-degree murder or nothing. He didn't pick away at our evidence like I figured him to. He attacked it with a broad brush and painted it an unfair color.

"Now, these men on this jury are country folk. That means they are, for the most part, fair and square with one another. They will want to be fair and square with the men on trial even if they are different in their politics and how they live their lives. My fear is that we gave a good opening argument that pretty much focused on first degree and then Judge Simms took away our first degree with a damn fine argument that I believe that jury bought hook, line, and sinker. What do you men think?"

Frank Patton, David Chavez, and D. W. Carmody all began to talk at once. Patton was the senior government officer and, arguably, felt that the major strategic decisions belonged to him. David Chavez was the elected official in McKinley County and, but for the presence of the attorney general in the case, would normally make the major strategic decisions in a case where McKinley County was the charging jurisdiction. Carmody sided as usual with Chavez. All of the men had played a role in putting the case together, and none of them wanted to think that it might fail after all this effort. More importantly, none of them wanted to face the harsh fact that maybe they had put too many eggs in one basket.

In particular, Chavez and Carmody had the town of Gallup to answer to, and by and large, those people wanted a first-degree murder conviction against somebody. They wouldn't care if one or even several of the defendants were acquitted as long as somebody was convicted and got the electric chair for the lawlessness and killing of a man they both liked and respected.

Modrall listened to the give-and-take of the debate and let the men state their positions. In the end, they somewhat reluctantly accepted his view that they had to close the case with an argument that put forth the second-degree murder charge as an alternative to a straight-out acquittal.

The conundrum was this: Was it better to try for second degree by softly accepting Simms's argument and get a conviction on second degree, or was it better to stick with the first-degree argument already before the jury by Mr. Chavez and risk an acquittal?

These men were all experienced trial lawyers and knew that in a hard case if you gave the jury a way out, they usually took it. Arguing second degree was giving the jury a way out. Was second degree enough?

Modrall more or less convinced his colleagues by reminding them of the forceful analogy Hugh Woodward used by comparing this courtroom to the Aztec Indian kiva. "Men, what John Simms *did* to our first-degree murder case Hugh Woodward *tried* to do to our second-degree murder case. I believe we have to reestablish our position with the jury or we might see all ten defendants walk out of here in a day or two."

They returned to the courtroom not of one mind but at least aware of the tremendous risk posed to the prosecution by the trial strategy of the defense and the eloquence of John Simms. They all hoped that Dick Modrall could rise to the challenge and bring this jury back to their side of the case, at least on second-degree murder.

"May it please the court, counsel, and may it please you gentlemen of the jury." Like Simms, Modrall used silence as a forensic weapon in the courtroom. He knew that no jury listened to you until they were focused on you. He also knew that no jury stayed with you if your first few sentences were small talk or legal babble. He waited until the jury settled and looked squarely at him.

Then he gathered them up with a wave of his arms and said: "You are the law.

"You are the representatives of a society that is founded on the rule of law.

You have a sworn duty to judge this case on the law. You must not be swayed by the eloquence of one of New Mexico's finest lawyers from applying the law to the facts you got from that witness stand right there.

"You cannot be swayed by the thought that you do not know everything you want to know about the case. You never will. No case ever goes to a jury with each and every fact in evidence. The law does not require that, and neither should you."

He paused to let his opening salvo sink in. He moved from the jury rail back to the prosecution table and stood near the acting sheriff of McKinley County, Dee Roberts.

He placed his hand on the shoulder of Dee Roberts and said: "This man is not on trial here.

"He risked his life to save the lives of others. He acted in accordance with the law under circumstances that appeared to pose great danger to the citizens of Gallup, New Mexico.

"He acted swiftly and under the supervision of a respected judge and a duly elected county attorney. He acted to protect his town. For doing what he did, John Simms would have you believe that those men over there were illegally persecuted for their political beliefs. They were not; they were legally prosecuted for their conduct in the riot that left three men dead, five others wounded, and an entire town paralyzed with fear."

Modrall paused again and moved back to face the jury. He tried to place his body so that the jury looked at him and not at the defendants. This was the time to focus them on the choice he was about to give them. He was going to give them the "out" they needed to convict these men *even if* they bought Simms's argument. Of course, he couldn't be blunt or obvious on this. They had to come to it of their own accord.

"Gentlemen, let me remind you that His Honor, Judge McGhee, will be speaking to you after the lawyers are done. He will give you the law as it has been established by the legislature and the courts of this state. He is the final lawgiver, and you are the final decision makers. You must take the law as he gives it to you and apply it to the facts as you see them.

"Now, some of the facts in this case are in dispute. That is natural and normal. No one expected this case to be one where both sides agreed on what happened. Mr. Chavez has carefully laid out for you exactly who was in that alley and what we believe they did that day. He laid out for you the evidence that connects each of them to the deliberate killing of Sheriff Carmichael. I will not insult your intelligence by repeating that evidence. What I want to do is give you a short summary of the evidence that the state contends demands a conviction of murder in the second degree.

"In other words, Mr. Chavez has given you our position on first-degree murder. Now I will give you our position on second-degree murder. I do this because Mr. Simms spent a great deal of his time trying to convince you that it was first degree or nothing. It is not.

"Second-degree murder is well within the evidence of this case. Here is why: I believe you will find from the evidence that the pistols that Ignacio Velarde and Solomon Esquibel were seen firing were never located after the gunfight. Deputy Boggess's pistol was lost on the ground when he was beaten into unconsciousness. It was never located. Sheriff Carmichael's pistol was removed from its scabbard on his body after his death. It was not fired that day. The bullet that entered the body of Sheriff Carmichael under his left armpit was later removed from his right shoulder. The bullet that gravely wounded Deputy Bobcat Wilson was later removed from his body.

"Now, the pistol that Deputy Boggess lost during the affray and never fired that day was a very rare .45 Smith & Wesson double-action revolver. That gun was made in 1917. Very few were made, and there was only one in Gallup that anyone knows of. That was the one carried by Deputy Boggess that day. The bullet removed from Sheriff Carmichael and the bullet removed from Deputy Wilson were both fired from the same pistol. That pistol was of the exact same make, model, type, and caliber as the one Deputy Boggess had taken from him in the alley that morning.

"So the question for you gentlemen of the jury is: What does this evidence add up to? Well, as you now know, the state had the right to put forward to you different legal theories for you to consider as you evaluate the evidence in a case. John Simms in his summation for the defense dealt primarily with our theory of first-degree murder. As I said, he is a powerful lawyer and has the ability to persuade. But you should not let that get you off the track here. Even if you were to disregard our theory of the evidence that supports first-degree murder, we still have two theories, shown by the evidence, that clearly support a verdict of second-degree murder.

"First, the evidence has established that someone shot the sheriff with the gun we have been talking about. Even if that man didn't think about it beforehand or plan it, that is second-degree murder. If that man is on that bench over there, he is guilty of second-degree murder." Modrall paused for effect, stared at Manuel Avitia, and said: "It's still second-degree even if he shot *wildly* into the crowd and hit Sheriff Carmichael by accident."

"Second, some or all of the defendants aided and abetted the man who actually shot the sheriff. So even if someone unknown to you or us actually shot the sheriff and one of these men aided that cowardly act, that's second-degree murder."

"If the evidence, in your minds, supports either one of these two theories, then you must return a verdict of second-degree murder. That's the law.

"As I told you when I started my argument, today you are the law.

"We are a civilized nation, and we, all of us, are subject to the rule of law. Mr. Woodward talked to you about his visit to the Aztec Indian ruins and their ceremonial kiva, where the Aztec Indians put their captives to death. Well, I say to you this is not a kiva, those men over there are not captives, and you are not involved in a ritual rite of vengeance.

"You are sworn to uphold the law of this nation. We ask not for vengeance; we ask for justice.

"On behalf of the people of the State of New Mexico, I will say to you that we tried our level best to put the evidence before you." Modrall moved his gaze to the stoic John Simms, sitting at the defense table. Simms seemed to be uninterested but nevertheless respectful. Modrall wanted to balance his argument and said: "This case is not one bubble off plumb; it is level, square, and right on the mark. I want to join Mr. Simms in telling you that we have done all we can. Now it's up to you. He reminded you of the importance of your oath as jurors. I, too, must remind you of that oath. You raised your hands and swore that this case would be fairly tried and justly resolved. That means fair to those accused of this crime *and* fair to those who are accusing them.

"The people of New Mexico are the accusers, as is our custom and practice under the rule of law. You must be as fair to them as you are to the men who are defendants in this case.

"You will find that your job is one of the hardest things that has ever been asked of you as a citizen. The state believes these men are guilty of a crime, and that crime has been proved for you beyond a reasonable doubt. I leave you now with this one last request on behalf of the State of New Mexico: Do your duty under the law."

Dick Modrall paused then as if he had more to say. He looked at each juror in turn and then at the bench. After what seemed a long time, he said: "Your Honor, that completes our case."

Wednesday, October 16, 1935

Dear Journal:

I am drained by the events of the day. I started this journal because I wanted to record the facts of the trial. But now I want to write of the poetry, the philosophy, and the goodness that flowered today in the courtroom. Today I learned that the most powerful, the most frightening, the most wrenching thing that can happen to a human being is to face a jury of ordinary citizens who have the power to take your life. Today I gained an appreciation for the power of the English language that I have so casually taught but never really "felt" until I heard what I heard today. For today I heard three very fine lawyers argue to those twelve silent men on the jury in a way that you don't see in books or hear at the theater. Goodness knows you don't ever "feel" this kind of an argument in a drawing room or a kitchen. This could have only happened in a courtroom.

"Closing argument." That is what the judge called it, and that is what all of us expected. But it was my first time. So I wasn't prepared to be *moved.* I thought I would be informed and maybe even convinced one way or the other. But instead I was moved. Madam Journal, do you know the difference? Being informed or even convinced is an intellectual result based on rational thought. But being *moved* is an emotional experience based on what your soul and your heart and your conscience demand of you. I wish I were a lawyer myself. Then I could move you as they moved me.

The day started routinely enough with the first argument by Mr. Chavez. He was factual and informative. He was even argumentative, but he did not move me. I mean him no disrespect because I know he tried his best. Billy Wade says he's a good lawyer, and I'm sure that's true.

Mr. Chavez went over the evidence that the state produced in a matter-of-fact way. I think he made a mistake in not talking about the things they left out. Like, he made no attempt to explain Bobcat's absence from the witness stand. He didn't even try to apologize for the massive roundup of innocent people after the riot, and he made no attempt to reconcile the differences in the testimony regarding who was where and what they did that tragic day.

You will remember I told you I was doing a chart of witnesses. Well, it's done. It shows some pretty amazing things. I hope someone on the jury has done one because without it, it's hard to remember who's on first. I love baseball, but this is really more like an intellectual scorecard.

I used a ten-column accounting ledger sheet to make my chart. I listed all of the witnesses in the order they testified down the left side of the chart. Across the top I arrayed the ten defendants. It gives me a graphical picture of exactly who was identified by whom and whether they were out there on Coal Avenue or back behind the court in the alley. It doesn't just give me the raw numbers; it gives me the sequence of identification. By comparing eyewitness testimony from objective witnesses to the more subjective recollections of the officers who were either engaged in a gun battle or enraged because of the death of one of their own, I can gain an appreciation of the likelihood of conviction. At least that's my theory. If the law can have theories, why can't I?

Ochoa, Avitia, and Velarde are all at risk of conviction. That's because the chart says so. Here's what it shows:

Ochoa was identified as being in front by six witnesses (three of whom were called in his case). Five witnesses said he was in back, and one of them (Dee Roberts) said he tried to hit him with a claw hammer. He admits part of it (being in front) and is obviously an agitator (not a good thing in the minds of these jurors). So it boils down to credibility. If they believe Dee, then Ochoa will be convicted of something.

Nine different witnesses identified Avitia as being in back in the alley. He admits it. Two saw him with a gun. He admits that, too. Two said he was beating on poor Mr. Boggess. He denies that. In his case, credibility is likely to go the other way. He was just not believable. That's not on the chart, mind you, but the chart shows him with more *x*'s than any other defendant.

Velarde also has eight people naming him as being in the alley. Sherman Porter is one of those eight (and he also named Avitia as being there). Besides that, Velarde was involved in lots of things, and there was all that testimony about the toothpicks and fighting the officers and having it in for Carmichael, or was it Roberts? Anyhow, just on the chart alone, he's at risk. But I don't think first degree. No, he's at risk for something else, but I'm not sure of the charges yet. Billy Wade said that would come at the end, when the judge gets his final say on the matter.

If my chart is any good at all, it ought to let Willie Gonzales walk free from the courtroom tomorrow, or whenever they come in with their verdict. Do you realize that not one single independent witness says he was in the alley? The only two people to even mention him were Bob and Dee Roberts, and even they were lukewarm on him. No gun, no club, no violence, no agitation, and no leadership. He's like an invisible defendant, even though he's there in the courtroom. He's so far down on the defendants' bench that half the jury can't even see him. He never moves or looks at them. I bet he takes a very happy walk soon.

Joe Bartol is obviously different, if only because he's Slavic and not Spanish American. I thought he was some kind of union leader, but the only testimony about that was from Juan Ochoa, who said he wasn't an officer. Four witnesses placed him in the alley, but all four were deputies or policemen. I'm not saying they were wrong, but there were five ordinary citizens called by the state who saw almost everything that happened in the alley. None of them identified Bartol as even being there. The three defendants who testified didn't say he was back there. The chart says he will be acquitted.

Agustin Calvillo stands out for lots of reasons. First of all, only Presley and Massie identified him; even Dee Roberts doesn't place him in the alley. Presley described the club allegedly carried by Calvillo differently than does Mr. Massie. And he can't run. He ought to get a walk, right out of the courtroom and back to his six children in Gallup.

That leaves the Correo brothers, Mr. Sosa and Mr. Gomez. Same theory. Weak identification by the lawmen and no identification by the independent eyewitnesses. Interestingly, each defendant got a slightly different count from the police officers. The Roberts brothers had their acts coordinated and were consistent, but the other lawmen were all over the place on these five men. Looks like a fair chance for acquittal.

But I'm spending too much time on this chart. Maybe that's because I spent so much time preparing it. I do detest wasted effort.

What I really want to do is to memorialize my feelings during Mr. Simms's closing argument. I knew he was good, and I accepted Billy Wade's notion that he was one of the best. But today I felt it. I wish Billy Wade had been there.

Judge Simms isn't just a lawyer; he's a poet. He's not a mere advocate; he's a philosopher. Most importantly, he's not a man who is there only to do a job; he's a man who is there to save us from ourselves.

As a society, we seek revenge when we feel wronged. Sometimes we seek it from those whose ways we reject or detest and who seem likely to have caused us the pain for which we seek revenge. Men like John Simms can help us to recognize the difference between rational judgment and striking out at those who are different and therefore suspect.

I wouldn't even try to reproduce his argument here, but I scribbled as fast as I could to record his eloquence. He stood first behind his clients and then slowly moved, without talking, to the middle of the courtroom. When he was sure he had the undivided attention of both groups of men, he said: "You are about to make the most important decision of their lives, not to mention yours."

As I said, he wasn't there merely to do a job. With those words, the jury knew that more was at stake here than revenge or politics.

He spent quite a while explaining how partial he was and how partial the prosecutors were. He admitted to having a closed mind on the case based on his job as the advocate for the defense. He almost complimented the prosecution for a vigorous prosecution based on their belief in their case. I couldn't see the point of this until he said: "You, gentlemen of the jury, can see this case for what it is. You have an open mind. Look at your hearts and think with your minds. Do you see this case? Can you feel its flawed truths, its warts, its failures of conscience, and the base politics that brought us all here today?" As I listened, I thought, Here is a man who sees the big picture and knows the importance of this case to all New Mexicans, not just the ten men on trial.

I still remember his words: "Bail-less Bickel lived up to his name."

His philosophical understanding of the importance of trial by jury came through when he stood behind his clients and spoke simultaneously to them and the jury: "These men can do nothing but watch. They are not the law. They have no badges. All they have is you."

But above all, I was moved by John Simms's studied explanation of one of the most fundamental concepts in America. You don't have to be a lawyer to know that all of us are presumed innocent until we are proven guilty in a court of law. I teach that at Gallup High. Every teacher, every writer, every politician, and every waitress in America knows that. But until today, no one made me think about just *exactly* what it means. He reminded the jurors of their oath and how that oath binds them to the presumption of innocence. That was pretty standard.

What was different was that he then equated the idea that when one "presumes" something, one "thinks" it. He forcefully made that jury accept the concept that because the law requires them to presume the innocence of the ten men on the bench behind him, they must, under the law, *think* of them as innocent unless and until the state proves them guilty beyond any reasonable doubt.

For me the difference was profound. Presumption sounds more like theory than reality. Thinking sounds more like certainty, not possibility. If the law requires me to *think* something is true, that is different than requiring me to merely *presume* that it is true.

Let me put it this way, Madam Journal: If I think something is true, then it probably is. On the other hand, if I merely presume something to be true, then it may or may not be. One is more demanding than the other is. Put in bridge terms, thinking trumps presuming.

After getting the jury in the right frame of mind by his "presuming means thinking" argument, Mr. Simms then did something no ordinary man ever seems to do in public or to someone not a close relative. He placed his hand, for a long time, on the shoulder of each one of his clients. By showing the jury that he *felt* for his clients, he showed his *belief* in them. A lesser man would have shrunk from the task.

I know some might have seen that as a forensic trick, but for me, it was a way to bridge the gap between the jury box and the defendants' bench. By that simple device, he put his clients right there in the box with the jury and made them look eyeball to eyeball at one another.

Simms closed his argument with this: "You are not just the representatives of Aztec, New Mexico. Today you are the representatives of the American justice system. You have a chance to make Aztec the capital of American liberty. In the name of God and country, do your duty."

I can remember my father saying that the way to get something you want is to make the giver bigger than you are. He will then see it as his privilege to reward you rather than his burden. I believe that is what Mr. Simms did. By telling the jury of their importance and their significance to our entire system of justice, he put them in the position of acquitting, as a grand gesture of benevolence, whereas convicting might be a local act of malevolence. Brilliant!

The next man to argue was Hugh Woodward. He was no John Simms, but he was forceful and entertaining. It was clear that he was used to arguing for the prosecution, not the defense, as he was quite dogmatic about reviewing the minutiae of the evidence. But he did rise to the occasion and pose rhetorical questions to the jury. He blamed most of what happened on the combination of Senator Vogel and Judge Bickel.

He forced the jury to wonder why the prosecutors didn't produce Bickel or even defend his actions. He asked: "Where is Bickel?" in a booming voice that was more condemnation than question.

I watched the jury closely during the "Where is Bobcat?" argument. Several of them nodded and let it be known that they agreed. It's clear to me that Bobcat's absence from the witness stand is no accident. I suspect that Mr. Modrall orchestrated that. He's a smart one. I don't know what Bobcat might have said, but it couldn't have helped the state, or else they would have put him on. Woodward argued it, and the jury seemed to be in complete agreement.

Mr. La Follette was allowed to give an argument for Mr. Bartol. It was a rare event; that is, Mr. La Follette doing anything in the case. He described Mr. Bartol as a "man with strong political beliefs but a mere onlooker in the case." Actually that was as true of Mr. La Follette as it was of his client. Mere onlookers, both of them.

Mr. Modrall seemed to me to be the strategist on the prosecution side. He wasn't as eloquent as Mr. Simms but was clearly very thoughtful and resourceful.

For example, he took a page from the Simms book when he walked over to Sheriff Dee and put his hand on his shoulder and said: "This man is not on trial here. He risked his life, he followed orders, etc., etc."

What came through the clearest in his argument is the notion that the state had lost its first-degree murder case. Modrall was there to salvage what he could from the surgical knife of Simms and the wrecking ball wielded by Woodward. He even prefaced his argument by saying that Mr. Chavez had presented their arguments on first-degree murder and he was there to present the arguments on second-degree murder. Bosh. He was there to save the case for the state.

He gave a clear, cogent account of the evidence that supported second degree but was careful not to tie in all the defendants by name. It was as though he had seen my chart. More likely, he has one of his own. If a simple high school English teacher like me can make one, surely he can.

He closed by using another of John Simms's eloquent comments. Simms had closed with the emotional appeal for the jury "in the name of God and our country, do your duty." Modrall added something: "Do your duty, *under the law.*" He seemed to be telling them that the judge had something to say about this case and they should not decide guilt or innocence until they heard from him.

Tomorrow we hear from the judge. Then someday soon we hear from the jury. I'm anxious but apprehensive. I want to see justice done. I just am having a hard time deciding whom to believe. I strongly suspect that some of these men played a role in the death of the sheriff, and I want to see someone convicted. But I have doubts about the case. I have a strong emotional reaction to what happened after the riot. Is that a reasonable doubt? Thank God, I do not have to decide.

Before I bid you good night, Madam Journal, I think I will vary from my habit of the last few entries. Rather than postscript my rambling discourse about *my* future, I will put it right here, where it belongs. Those men are sitting in a makeshift jail, thinking about dying in the electric chair. They are thinking about their families and about who will care for them. They are thinking about the unclear road that brought them here. They are thinking about tomorrow—that is, their future.

I, on the other hand, am selfishly thinking about moving from a place I like to somewhere I might like more. I am musing about bettering a good life and about who will care for me if I do. My road to Aztec was a voluntary one. I am thinking about the next fifty years (I will be young for at least that long). It's unfair to them for me to think about *my* future. I feel guilty because I have a future.

So good night, Madam Journal—tomorrow is not just another day. It's the most important day of their lives, and I am going to think of it as equally important to mine.

fifteen

LEFT OUT: WITH MERCY OF THE COURT

Thursday, October 17, 1936

The men in the American Bar were no longer talking like it was all over but the shoutin'. That was their mood two weeks ago, but no longer. The men in the Angeles Pool Hall weren't as gloomy as they were two weeks ago. What these last two weeks proved, at least so far, was that the courts of New Mexico were great levelers. The courts were places were things became level even if they started out heavy on one side. I don't mean to say that one side lost all hope and the other side gained it. No, sir. The killing that took place in the alley behind Coal Avenue caused an uproar that no one will ever forget. That uproar was a scream for more blood. More blood than was spilled in the alley and more than would ever be spilled up in quiet places like Aztec. The men who were responsible for all that blood in the alley must be brought to justice, tried, convicted, and, most of all, put to death for what they did. That was what Gallup wanted. At least that was what the businessmen wanted and what the elected officials wanted, and, for the most part, what the ordinary citizens wanted. Anglo, Slav, Mexican, Spanish American, all of them—first a trial and then the electric chair—that was the mantra. All of them wanted the men severely punished. No one really gave much thought to a "lesser charge."

Had they thought about it all, it would have been a fleeting one. A "lesser charge" wouldn't have seemed much of a solution to what most believed was a cold-blooded murder. But that was then. Now six months have passed, and order is restored. Martial law has been lifted; the troops are gone. The radical lawyers from Philadelphia and Los Angeles are gone, and real New Mexico lawyers are defending the men on trial. All in all, it's starting to look like maybe, just maybe, second degree was the right thing to do after all. That sort of started in the American Bar when the men at the big round table in the back more or less agreed that the trial evidence showed that more than likely, Esquibel and Sena Velarde were the shooters. If you accepted that, then it came down to old Hoy's gun. Maybe someone did scoop up that gun, but how in God's name did Esquibel or Sena Velarde get it? It seemed, from most accounts, that they shot the sheriff pretty much at the same time as Hoy was going down to the ground. If that was the case, then *they* didn't use the gun. Who did? Was it one of the ten men who made the final cut and got themselves up there before the jury? Could be. But what if they scooped up the gun and blasted away at Dee Roberts or Hoy or maybe even Bobcat in a sort of self-defense fashion? Was that possible? If it was, then what they did was flat-ass wrong, but maybe it wasn't first-degree murder. The law was damned confusing, but it seemed to say that if you fired a gun, not intending to kill but in the heat of the moment, then you ought to be convicted of second-degree murder. Now, that wasn't a death penalty affair, but maybe, just maybe, there had been enough killing.

Across the street at the Angeles Pool Hall, things had also changed. Not that anyone felt their *amigos* should be imprisoned but maybe, just maybe, some of those men acted *"no tener pensado,"* you know, without thinking about it. Maybe the *gringo* justice, which talks of premeditation, was the same thing. If you shot in haste or anger or without thinking, maybe you should pay for that. *Que no?*

In both bars, the argument raged over which side had the better man to stand up and give the closing argument. From what they heard, John Simms carried the day until Dick Modrall got up there and argued *for* second-degree murder. No one really knew how much weight the good farmers who were on the jury would give to the words of the lawyers.

The men in the American Bar speculated that the deciding factor was the evidence. But the men in the Angeles Pool Hall thought the jury decided the case based on what they knew outside the courtroom—that is, the fact that the defendants were radicals, and mostly Mexican at that.

But the lawyers about town and anyone who really knew about courtrooms and hard trials knew there was one other very important factor. The judge. Of course, the judge was supposed to be impartial. Neutrality was the name of the judicial game. Judges were referees; they didn't put on evidence or ask questions of witnesses. They didn't give closing arguments—or did they?

I tried to explain it to the bar crowd. New Mexico was a little unusual because our law allowed a judge to give the jury an opinion or a comment on the evidence if the comment was "fair." Now, that's a pretty ambiguous term when it comes to looking at what a judge can say to a jury. Seeing as he has to be fair, meaning impartial and neutral, who is to say that any comment he might choose to make to the jury is either fair or unfair?

The evidence in this case was hotly contested, and the witnesses in this case disagreed a lot. Could the judge comment on who was telling the truth and who was lying? Could he comment on who offered up the best evidence? Could he comment on what the jury ought to do in the case? If he could, then that might just well be the biggest thing in the case—a damn sight more important than either the evidence or the lawyers. That jury had no reason to trust either side, since both sides had a motive for wanting their side to win. But the judge, now that was another matter altogether. If he was to comment, the jury would more than likely side with him, seeing as he was "impartial" and all. And so the men and women of Gallup waited for the judge to have his say, and for the jury to have theirs.

"Good morning, gentlemen," Judge McGhee greeted the lawyers in his chambers. "I trust you are all well rested after your heavy day of arguments to our jury yesterday. I asked you to come in a little early this morning so we could go over my charge to the jury before they come in. I have carefully reviewed the proposed instructions offered by both sides. I have also given some thought to the arguments both sides have made on just how this jury ought to be instructed on the law; that is, whether an election of remedies or theories has to be made by the state and whether multiple degrees of murder should be charged against the defendants.

"It is my view that this case should be submitted to the jury on the issue of whether or not the defendants were engaged in the commission of a felony; that is, aiding and assisting a prisoner to escape, as well as ordinary murder. And under the testimony in the case, I think the jury might find that the defendants, or at least some of them, were not engaged in assisting a prisoner to escape or attempting to escape, but on the contrary either shot and killed Carmichael under such circumstances as to constitute murder or aided and abetted others in so doing. Perhaps the intent to kill Carmichael might have been formed out in front of the justice of the peace office or even after they reached the alley, when they might not have had time to reflect sufficiently, which would make them guilty in the second degree. At any rate, I think there is ample evidence, and it is up to the court to submit both first and second degree. I think, from all the facts and circumstances, it is a matter for the jury to determine under the instructions of the court. You all can make your record if you think my ruling is erroneous. I do not mean to foreclose any further argument you care to present, but on this issue my mind is set. What other matters do you have pertaining to my instructions to the jury?"

Even though they were in chambers, Hugh Woodward was careful to stand before he addressed the court this time. He didn't need any more contempt fines. "Your Honor, the defendants respectfully ask you to require the state to elect upon which of the theories set out in the bill of particulars the state will further proceed in this case."

Before the prosecution could answer, the judge waved them off. "No, Mr. Woodward that is not how I have decided to handle the multiple theories. The court will limit the theories upon which the case is submitted in its instructions. But there is no need to make them pick out one theory over another one now that the arguments are all in."

"Very well, Your Honor, but may the record show my exception to your ruling."

"Overruled, Mr. Woodward. You can appeal me if you want. But you do have a point I want to address at this time. In the early part of this trial, testimony was admitted at the request of the state showing that a meeting was held at the Spanish-American Hall in Gallup, New Mexico, at which a committee was appointed to wait upon the sheriff to ascertain the date of the trial. When this testimony was admitted, the defendants objected to its admission. I thought at the time it would be followed up by actual proof of a conspiracy to kill the sheriff or liberate the prisoner. No evidence was offered by the state to show anything improper was done or said at this meeting. Now, do the defendants desire to move or strike this testimony from the record? I am prepared to do that and to instruct the jury to disregard it. It's up to the defense. What do you say?"

John Simms responded: "Judge, you will recall we objected when the testimony was originally offered and we renewed those objections several times. You overruled us. Now the testimony in the case both for the state and the defense conclusively shows that the meeting at the Spanish-American Hall not only was *not* unlawful, but was merely the first of several steps taken by some of the defendants to obtain and ascertain the lawful rights of the parties in the Navarro case. Now, if the court, after the state has failed to connect up the meeting at the Spanish-American Hall as an unlawful act of any kind, were to take the issue from the jury, we would be greatly harmed. The meeting was lawful, it was peaceful, and it was proper on the part of the men and women who were involved in it."

Dick Modrall seemed perplexed. "Do I understand that the defendants object to having the testimony stricken and the jury admonished to disregard it?"

Simms said: "Yes, Dick, your understanding is quite correct."

Judge McGhee, who seemed mildly embarrassed at not having dealt with this issue before the closing arguments, said: "Gentlemen, being overwhelmed by the forcefulness of counsel for the defendants, I will not strike it, but I will tell the jury that nothing wrongful occurred at the hall. Now, what is your next issue?"

"Judge, we also object to all the instructions dealing with the testimony of certain of the prosecution's witnesses, particularly Dee Roberts, Hoy Boggess, and Sherman Porter. Your comment in those instructions isn't fair and tends to prejudice the jury against the defendants. If you give those instructions, you are giving the jury to understand that the court is not entirely leaving to the jury questions of fact involved in this case. To put it plainly, you are endeavoring to influence the jury's verdict, and we respectfully object."

"Overruled. What else have you?"

Hugh Woodward took the next one "Judge, the defendants are now aware that the state has abandoned its theory of conspiracy as set forth in the bill of particulars. So we move for a mistrial and a grant of severance to the defendants so that each of them may be separately tried. Your Honor, the joinder of all the defendants under one charge was extremely detrimental and prejudicial to the rights of the individual defendants. The scope of the testimony admissible in the trial of ten defendants is greatly beyond that which would be competent or permissible were the defendants to be tried separately and severally. By joining them, you deprive them of the due process of law, contrary to the provisions of the state constitution of New Mexico. As long as they were charging and relying on conspiracy law, maybe you could justify a joint trial. Now they have abandoned it because they had no proof. We request a mistrial."

"Overruled. Now, that appears to be it. So let's call the jury into the room and get them instructed."

The courtroom was packed when Judge McGhee took the bench. The lawyers seemed bored as Judge McGhee read his instructions, but the jury paid close attention. They heard them only once and were not allowed to take a written copy of them into the jury room for their deliberations. Judge McGhee told them, *inter alia,* that the state had the burden of proof to establish guilt of the defendants beyond a reasonable doubt. He told them the defendants were presumed innocent until the evidence beyond a reasonable doubt established guilt. He instructed them on the exact charge of first-degree murder. It was a long and difficult instruction, in part because it seemed to repeat the words *unlawful, felonious, willful, malicious, deliberate,* etc., etc., over and over.

As usual, the jury's eyes started to glass over at about thirty minutes into the reading of the formal instructions on the law. They listened patiently and intently, but the words of the law, careful as they were, sounded awfully redundant. Why was it that the law seemed so complicated? Of course, since the prosecution had fought so hard to get a second-degree murder charge, Judge McGhee also instructed the jury on the difference between first and second degree. He told them the difference in complicated language, but they seemed to get it when he said one was deliberate and premeditated and the other was not.

Judge McGhee didn't want to take any chance that this jury might misunderstand their role in a case such as this. He told them the state did not have to establish that any one of the defendants actually fired the shot that killed Carmichael. Guilt could be found in that a defendant aided in the killing of said Carmichael or assisted the prisoner to escape if that assistance caused Carmichael's death.

The evidence in the case against Manuel Avitia established that he had a gun. He admitted it, but said he picked it up to protect a child in the alley. As to this, the judge reminded the jury that testimony had been introduced in this case tending to show that the defendant Avitia was at the scene of the killing with a pistol in his hand. If the jury believed that Avitia did not kill Carmichael or help effect the escape of Navarro and was there merely as a spectator, then they should acquit him.

As to the evidence against Juan Ochoa, Judge McGhee said:

> The defendant Ochoa has introduced testimony to show that he was not present at the scene of the killing of Sheriff Carmichael, and unless you believe from the evidence beyond a reasonable doubt that he was so present and that he aided or abetted in the killing of Carmichael by some other person, or killed Carmichael, or aided or abetted in the escape or attempted escape of Navarro, out of which the killing of Carmichael resulted, then you must acquit the defendant Ochoa.

Judge McGhee did not want the jury to confuse some "general" agreement with the meeting at the Spanish-American Hall the day before the shootings. Judge McGhee had assured the defense lawyers he would clear this up in his jury instructions. He told the jury that testimony had been introduced showing that there was a meeting held in the Spanish-American Hall at Gallup on the afternoon preceding the homicide, which some of the defendants attended. There was no testimony in the record showing that anything improper was said or done at the meeting, and the only relevance of the testimony about this meeting was to show that the defendants present at the meeting had knowledge of the time and place of the proposed trial.

Agustin Calvillo's testimony to the jury about the club that he was accused of having was the subject of a separate instruction by the judge:

> The witnesses Presley and Massie testified that Presley took a club from the defendant Calvillo on Third Street near the scene of the killing. Calvillo denies that this testimony is true. I instruct you that if you believe from the evidence in this case or have a reasonable doubt thereof that Presley and Massie were mistaken in their identification of Calvillo, and if you believe from the evidence or have a reasonable doubt thereof that the defendant Calvillo did not know of or participate in any plan to kill Carmichael, or assist in the escape or attempted escape of Navarro, but was merely there as a spectator, and did not aid or abet in the killing of Carmichael or assist in the escape or attempted escape of Navarro, then you should acquit him.

Recalling the testimony about the dispute over whether Leandro Velarde was in the alley, and if so, what he did there, Judge McGhee reminded the jury that there was evidence to the effect that Velarde was present in the alley and he clenched his fist or raised his arms and told the crowd they were about to see a disgraceful thing or a disgrace, or words to that effect. He told the jury that it was up to them to determine whether Velarde's words were reasonably calculated to arouse others and cause them to kill Carmichael or assist in the escape or attempted escape of the prisoner Navarro. If he was not there or did not do what the lawmen said he did, then they should find him not guilty.

Both the state and the defense had offered evidence about the conduct of the two men Dee Roberts killed that day, Solomon Esquibel and Ignacio Velarde. As to that evidence, Judge McGhee instructed:

> You are instructed that none of the defendants are criminally responsible for any unlawful act of Ignacio Velarde or Solomon

> Esquibel, nor the criminal act of any other person unless the evidence establishes beyond a reasonable doubt that such defendant personally committed the unlawful act or aided or abetted in its commission.

Judge McGhee gave the standard instruction about the jury being the sole judges of the credibility of any witness. He said that whatever weight was to be given to any particular witness was strictly up to them. But he added to that standard instruction the following special language:

> As I have heretofore told you in these instructions, you are the sole judges of the credibility of the witnesses who have testified in this case and of the weight to be given to their testimony. Without expressing any opinion as to other witnesses who have testified, I feel it proper to call your attention to what I considered the fair and frank testimony of Dee Roberts, Sherman Porter, and Hoy Boggess. It seemed to me that these witnesses were endeavoring to tell only what they saw and heard, and I was strongly impressed by their testimony.

And so it ended. The jury took the exhibits and retired to deliberate. The last thing they heard in the courtroom was a man they all assumed they could trust telling them they should trust in the testimony of Dee Roberts, Sherman Porter, and Hoy Boggess because "he was strongly impressed by their testimony."

The bailiff was given a special oath to take charge of the jury during their deliberations, and the courtroom was cleared at 4:30 P.M. on the 17th day of October 1935. The jury began what all agreed would be a long and difficult process.

Mary Ann couldn't wait until we were outside on the courthouse porch to start on me about that last jury instruction of the judge. She was livid, and I was startled, but I inexplicably began by trying to defend the judge. "What do you mean, he had no right to do that? Of course he did. Judges in New Mexico are allowed to comment on the evidence, although I must admit it's rarely done."

"Billy Wade, you must be getting old or soft or both. I'm only an English teacher, but even I know a lynching when I see it. Those men have no more chance than a pea in a thunderstorm. Things were getting pretty even because of the strong defense put up by Mr. Simms and Mr. Woodward, but the judge just took that away from them. That jury doesn't know which side to trust or whether they can trust either side, but the judge is a very different thing. The honorable James McGhee looks like a judge, sounds like a judge, and, until just a few minutes ago, seemed neutral and impartial. So what do you think the jury is going to do with the contested evidence in this case? Do you think they're going to accept the arguments of defense lawyers when the judge goes out on a limb and tells them that he thinks the two lawmen and the most persuasive eyewitness told the truth? By exclusion, and not a very subtle one at that, he might as well have told them that Avitia, Ochoa, and Velarde are liars. How can you justify that? It makes me sick."

I took her arm. "Darling, I'm as surprised as you, but all I'm defending is the law that allows judges to comment on the witnesses. I admit that this case is so close, McGhee is risking these men's lives by inserting himself into disputed facts. Usually a judge will stick to the law and let the jury sort out the disputed facts. I can't imagine why he did that. The rumors about him are that he's a strong anti-Communist, but I never thought that would put him in a position where he actively tried to get a jury to convict a man just because of his politics."

"Well, you just saw it, and you might as well get used to it." Mary Ann shrugged me off. "Now more than ever, I wished your friend Bobcat had taken the stand. Maybe his story was different, and if so, then the judge wouldn't have dared pick out two lawmen and vouch for them without mentioning the third. If Bobcat's story contradicted either Dee or Hoy Boggess, then the judge might have been forced to let the jury decide the case. Isn't that why we have juries, after all?"

We were still discussing this amazing turn of events when we got a big surprise. At precisely 7:02 P.M. the bailiff reported to the judge that the jury had a verdict and was ready to deliver it to the court. Everyone thought the jury would be out a day or two. I had the terrible feeling that Mary Ann was right. The judge's comment about how impressed he was with Dee, Hoy, and Sherman Porter must have carried the day. If they believed those three, then these ten men were about to get the death penalty.

The bailiff was hastily instructed to summon the lawyers from their lodgings, the deputies were instructed to bring the defendants up from the jail, and the court staff put out the word to all the newspaper reporters and others interested in the case.

The courtroom was packed when the bailiff gaveled Judge McGhee in. This was the first time that everyone was present *except* the jury. Usually the jury was brought in and then everyone waited to rise when the judge entered. Now the spotlight was on the jury.

Before he ordered the bailiff to get them, Judge McGhee looked out over the expanse of the large courtroom and warned: "I understand the jury is ready to report. We don't know what the verdict is, but regardless of the result, there must be no demonstration of any kind or character. Nor will there be any visiting with the jurors after they have announced their verdict. I want to warn those here, particularly the press, that even after the jury is discharged, they are still under the protection of the court. These men have been chosen as jurors, had the protection of the court since they have been on the case, and will continue to receive the protection of the court after they are discharged. When this verdict is received, the audience will pass out in an orderly manner. Bring in the jury."

It took no more than two minutes for the jury to file in through the side door and take their seats. They looked a lot different than at any previous time in the case. They looked down at the floor and carefully avoided the piercing gaze of the lawyers on both sides of the room. It was as if their secret verdict might be revealed if they dared look at one side or the other. As soon as they were all seated, Judge McGhee said in their general direction: "Gentlemen of the jury, have you agreed upon a verdict?"

The foreman, a tall man in the first row, stood and said: "We have, yes, sir."

"Pass it up, please."

The bailiff took the paper from the foreman and gave it to the clerk, who in turn gave it to the judge. Judge McGhee looked at it for what seemed a long time, as though it was somehow deficient or confusing. His facial gesture was one of concern but not surprise. He then turned to the courtroom and, like the jurors, did not focus either on the defense or the prosecution side of the courtroom. Rather, he faced the jury and said: "Gentlemen, your foreman has handed up a verdict reading:

> We, the jury, find the defendants *not guilty* of murder in the first degree in manner and form as charged in the Information; the defendants *Juan Ochoa, Manuel Avitia, Leandro Velarde guilty* of murder in the second degree in manner and form as charged in the information; and the defendants *Agustin Calvillo, Victorio Correo, Gregorio Correo, Willie Gonzales, Serapio Sosa, Rafael Gomez, Joe Bartol not guilty.* D. C. HAMBLIN, FOREMAN."

"Is that the verdict of the jury?" Judge McGhee said as he frowned at the jury. Mr. Hamblin, the foreman, rose and said: "Yes, sir." As he sat down, a juror in the back row stood and said in a firm, almost angry voice: "Left out '*with mercy of the court.*' "

Judge McGhee seemed embarrassed and turned again to the foreman. "Is that the verdict?"

Before the foreman could answer, Hugh Woodward jumped to his feet and shouted: "Wait, we want to poll the jury to ask whether they intended—"

Judge McGhee cut him off and turned again to the jury foreman. "Did the jury intend to make a recommendation for clemency?"

A different juror, this one in the front row, glared at the foreman and said: "Yes, we did."

Now the judge looked at the two jurors who had so impertinently spoken up. He addressed his question to them collectively. "So say you all?"

To a man each one of them said yes, in unison, including the foreman.

"Well, write it on the bottom there," Judge McGhee said as he handed the verdict back to the bailiff, who handed it to the foreman.

The crowded courtroom held its collective breath as the foreman took out a fountain pen and wrote something on the bottom of the jury verdict. He replaced the cap and handed the verdict to the bailiff, who took it directly to the judge. The judge looked at it again and then directed that it be shown to the defense lawyers.

After looking at it, Mr. Woodward said: "The defendants waive the right to poll the jury."

Judge McGhee turned to the jury again and said: "Gentlemen of the jury, your recommendation of clemency will receive due consideration, and I want to express thanks to this jury for your patient manner and careful attention to this case; it has been long and it has been a trying case to all of us. I want at this time to express the appreciation of myself, the attorneys, and those connected with the case for the wonderful hospitality of the people of San Juan County. They have opened their homes to us and taken care of us very handsomely. And I want at this time to publicly thank all the attorneys in the case for the manner in which they have conducted themselves, and especially to thank Mr. Augur, Mr. Simms, and Mr. Woodward for their defense. These men would not ordinarily be found in a case of this kind; would not have been if they had not been appointed."

Turning again to the jury, he said: "You gentlemen are now excused, and if you go to the clerk's office they will give you your mileage and per diem." Returning his focus to the defense side of the courtroom, he said: "The jury has acquitted the defendants Agustin Calvillo, Victorio Correo, Gregorio Correo, Willie Gonzales, Serapio Sosa, Rafael Gomez, and Joe Bartol of all charges.

"As to two of you, you are discharged. Those two are Willie Gonzales and Joe Bartol. You are free to go once the deputies have taken care of the administrative matters at the jail. I do want to caution you two to mend your ways; you need to learn the ways of America and avoid communism. As to Serapio Sosa, Victorio Correo, Gregorio Correo, Rafael Gomez, and Agustin Calvillo, you have been acquitted and are discharged from the custody of the sheriff's office, but I am remanding you to the custody of Señor Fidencio Soria, the Mexican consular agent from El Paso. He will take charge of you. You are going to be deported from this country.

"As to the defendants Juan Ochoa, Manuel Avitia, and Leandro Velarde, the jury has acquitted you of first-degree murder but found you guilty of murder in the second degree. It is therefore ordered that you remain in the custody of the deputies. I am prepared to sentence you for your crimes at this time."

Before Judge McGhee could proceed with sentencing, Joe Bartol stood and started to address the court. "Judge, I am an American citizen and I want to—"

Before he could finish his sentence, Judge McGhee, interrupted. "Mr. Bartol, you are still represented by counsel. Perhaps you should discuss whatever is on your mind with him before addressing the court."

"Your Honor, with respect, can I ask you a question?"

"Yes, of course you can, Mr. Bartol, provided your counsel has no objection. You have been acquitted of all charges and are free to go, but you may certainly ask me whatever you want."

"Judge, I just wanted to make sure that I am free to return to Gallup."

"Well, sir, since you ask, I have to tell you that I think that is unwise. You have been a ringleader and an agitator there. I suggest you keep away; you'd better leave communism, radicalism, and bolshevism alone. You haven't any business in that sort of thing. Now, does any one else have anything for me before I sentence these men?" Not hearing anything, he said: "We'll take a short break so the acquitted defendants can leave the courtroom."

The judge didn't witness the bedlam that followed in the courtroom. As usual, he darted out the small door before anyone could realize he was gone.

An hour later, as the crowd gathered for the last time in the courtroom in Aztec, they faced an entirely different room. The clay model was gone, the exhibits were gone, the lawyers' tables were clear of papers, and, most noticeably, the long bench that served the Gallup 10 for the last two weeks was gone. So were seven of the Gallup 10. Now the three remaining defendants were seated at the defense table with their two primary lawyers, Simms and Woodward.

The bailiff gaveled in Judge McGhee, who wasted no time with preliminaries. "Manuel Avitia, Leandro Velarde, and Juan Ochoa, stand up. You and each of you have been convicted of murder in the second degree. Have you anything to say why judgment should not be passed upon you?"

The silence in the courtroom was deafening. Judge McGhee barely paused and went on: "It is the judgment and sentence of the court that you be confined in the state penitentiary at Santa Fe, New Mexico, at hard labor for not less than forty-five years or more than sixty years, and that you pay the costs of this prosecution. It is further ordered that you be remanded to the custody of the sheriff of San Juan County, New Mexico, and by him safely kept pending the appeal of your case. Then he can transport and deliver you to the superintendent of the penitentiary at Santa Fe, New Mexico."

Hugh Woodward rose and addressed the court. "May the record show in open court that the defendants now pray an appeal to the Supreme Court of the State of New Mexico and ask Your Honor to fix bond pending appeal."

Without hesitation, Judge McGhee responded: "The appeal is allowed and bond set at twenty-five thousand each."

Mr. Simms rose and advised the court that Mr. Velarde requested to address the court himself.

"Fine, Mr. Simms, I will be happy to assist your client if I can. What is the subject matter?"

With that, Leandro Velarde rose and addressed the court for the first time. "Judge, I would ask you to contact the warden at the prison and ask that they not shave my head. My eyesight is failing, and they are telling me that if they shave my head, it will be bad for me."

"Mr. Velarde, I do not know about that, but I can tell you that there is some time yet before you will be transferred to Santa Fe. There will be time for proper communications with the warden because your lawyers have already notified me they wish to appeal and bail has been set. You will be in jail unless you post bond pending the outcome of the case by the Supreme Court. You will not be remanded to the prison until your appeal is resolved."

It appeared to most that he was getting ready to adjourn. But instead, he seemed to take in a deep breath and looked out into the amassed members of the local and national press and said:

"I have something *more* to say now that this case is over." He looked down at the three defendants he had just sentenced to a long prison term and said: "Judge Otero appointed Mr. Augur to represent you men early in this case. Later, attorneys sent from New York did not join in the case and I appointed

Hugh B. Woodward and John F. Simms to defend you. I appointed these men because I knew their standing in New Mexico and standing in San Juan County.

"These are men who had the respect and confidence of the people of the county. These are not men who have been identified with the communist movement and have no sympathy with it. I notice that one of your former attorneys filed an affidavit in the case stating that most, if not all of, the defendants in this case were communists. According to reports, there has been a large amount of money raised for the defense of you men. These two attorneys from Mr. Donovan's office in New York state that they have not received any of it. Mr. Augur, Mr. Woodward, and Mr. Simms have not received any of it, so somebody must have plenty of money to finance your appeal.

"I am not going to require these three lawyers appointed by the court to further represent you. Check up on the books, and I think you will find somebody has plenty of money. If necessary, you can show the Supreme Court that you don't have the money and can't get hold of this money that has been raised for you, and they will appoint someone to represent you. I hope the members of the Supreme Court may be spared the abuse, the threats, and the attempted intimidation that has been practiced on me since my designation to sit in this case and that was heaped upon Judge Otero from the time of his decision in the preliminary hearing until he was disqualified in the case. It seems that after that, he became a good man again.

"The courts of the United States stand as a protection for the poor. Certainly only a small portion of the citizens of our country have any sympathy with the communist cause. The majority of the people are against such a movement. The communists and those reds, agitators, and anarchists who demand your release would demand your execution without trial. We don't operate our courts in New Mexico and the United States by mob rule.

"You prisoners have received as able a defense as I have seen practiced in any court, and I have been around courts since I was ten years old. It was because of this able defense that you and your co-defendants escaped the electric chair. Had it not been for the recommendation of the jury, I would have imposed the maximum sentence upon you men.

"I hope that future governors, in the event that this case is affirmed on appeal, will have the courage to do their duty and not release you unless they are convinced that an injustice was done in your conviction or that subsequent events justify executive clemency."

Judge McGhee turned to the bailiff and said: "Now, call the related case, please."

The courtroom cleared out as the bailiff left to call the next case on the calendar. Mary Ann watched as Teresa Avitia, Altagracia Gomez, Mrs. Dominica Hernandez, and José C. Lopez stepped forward for their case.

Thursday, October 17, 1935

Dear Journal:

I was the last person to leave the courtroom today. How do I tell you about my intellectual dissatisfaction with what I just saw? Where do I start? At the end? The end was so unsatisfactory and so unfair. Was it just a few hours ago that the twelve brave men on the jury risked the wrath of officialdom by acquitting *all ten* of those morose men of capital murder and urging clemency for the three they believed aided in the tragic death of Sheriff Mack?

Madam Journal, I have finally decided that you are mine; you are not to be shared with the world. That means I can write in you anytime I want or not at all, if that's my mood. My mood a few hours ago in that wonderful, warm courtroom was one of exhilaration. I wanted just to sit there and absorb how wonderful it was to *know* justice (it's very intellectual) and *feel* fairness (that's very emotional). The verdict was both just and fair. Now I understand as I never did before that those words are not redundant. Justice is very different than fairness. Last night's verdict was a bushel basket full of both.

The three women sitting in my row just one row from the jury held hands and prayed during the eternity it took for the bailiff to go get the verdict, hand it to the judge, and then wait while the judge studied it. I watched them out of the corner of my eye as the judge read the "not guilty" verdict. Two of them (the two closest to me) jumped up and then immediately sat down with their hands over their mouths. The third woman must be a wife or sister of Velarde because she sobbed when they took him away. So did I, but not right then.

You can't write and cry at the same time. I cried because I was happy and I cried because she did. I didn't feel her pain because I didn't know which convicted man was hers. Was it Velarde? I'm not sure, but I still cried for her and for whomever she was crying for.

For seven men, today was the most wonderful day of their lives. For three others it was a time to rejoice for their brothers and to wait for their fate to be told to them by Judge McGhee. Since the jury unanimously urged clemency, everyone, I mean *everyone,* thought the sentence would be short. What an utter shock!

I was not prepared to hear the anger in the judge's voice. I was not ready to listen to his diatribe about communists and radicals. Now I feel so let down by his incredibly harsh sentence that it's hard to recall the euphoria I felt when I heard the verdict.

By their verdict, the jury proved that New Mexico is a just state. We do not arrest, imprison, charge, and convict men just because they express their outrage at injustice.

Lest you think all was deadly serious today, I want to record, even if it's only for my own posterity, something the judge said that was absolutely hilarious, except he *meant* it. He admonished the audience against outbursts or demonstrations in the courtroom just before the verdict was brought in. He solemnly instructed us on our demeanor in his precious court of etiquette. He said (I swear he did; I wrote it down): "When this verdict is received, the audience will all pass *out* in an orderly manner." Come to think of it, maybe it wasn't a boo-boo on his part. Maybe he mistakenly used the word *audience* when he meant *prosecutors.* They looked like they were about to pass out when their handpicked all-white, all-conservative, all-stony-faced jury rejected all six of their legal "theories" about the case. So much for theory.

I had so many thoughts about the judge's instructions that I wanted to tell you about. But now it seems pointless to regurgitate the banal, redundant way the judge explained the law to those wise men on the jury. They did justice, despite the best efforts of the judge. At the risk of contradicting myself, I will say his instruction to believe Sheriff Dee and Sherman Porter backfired on him.

Remember that it was Mr. Porter who clearly identified Mustache Man as the leader of the crowd and as the man who struck out at Dee Roberts in the alley. He also made it clear, at least to me, that Mustache Man was free as a bird after being released at the preliminary hearing in Santa Fe. The jury must have taken the judge at his word. If they believed Porter, then Dee was wrong. That alone could explain why none of the men were convicted of first-degree murder. The only men who could have been convicted are dead; Dee shot them. He said he did. So by telling the jury to believe Dee *and* Porter, he was really telling them that none of these men led the charge or killed the sheriff. That explains the acquittal of all ten of them. Or does it?

Aztec is quite beautiful and serene this afternoon. The fall is in full bloom, and the Animas River is a calming influence. I am parked beside the river, eating another apple. Even if I can't write and cry at the same time, I can write and eat. I feel like today is a birthday for everyone who cares about New Mexico. Happy birthday, New Mexicans! We should all remember this day and celebrate it. It wasn't just the "Gallup 10" who were acquitted today; *it was Gallup itself.*

Postscript. Speaking of acquittal, I've decided to acquit myself of the notion that Gallup and I ought to part company. At least for the time being. This verdict is refreshingly reassuring. I don't think Gallup is where I will live forever, but for now, it'll do. Billy Wade is good for me, and I can make him a better wife than anyone else in town. Not that he's actually asked me, of course. He probably thinks he has, in his own way, but he hasn't. Good. I don't want him to, at least not now. I might say yes. That might be wrong. For now, I want to savor the moment, as seven of my fellow citizens are. We shall see about the other three. As to at least one of them, I now believe that his verdict was a just one—but I am so unsure about the other two. I am anxious to talk to Billy Wade about the possibility of an appeal. Theirs, and mine. *Buena suerte,* Madam Journal.

"Court's adjourned." Those were Judge McGhee's parting words to the jury, the lawyers, and to Gallup. The men in the American Bar took solace in it. It wasn't the death penalty they expected and it wasn't a conviction of every last one of those red bastards. But by God, that judge was a man to stand up for, wasn't he? He'd get free drinks in this bar anytime.

There was a lot of talk about how Judge McGhee had finally come out and said right there on the record that this whole damn thing was a communist plot. He as much as said that the Gallup 10 should have got the death penalty and that they missed it *only* because of John Simms and Hugh Woodward.

Down the street at the Angeles Pool Hall, the mood was a damn sight different. The judge's blast at communism was misguided because for them, communism was never important. For them this was about dignity, their homes, and their jobs. Communism was about politics. What they were offended by was his sentence, not his words.

Forty-five to sixty years at hard labor? That's *with* clemency? And what about him trying to tie the governor's hands? They said, He's only the judge, not God. The governor should be able to do justice even if the judge won't.

sixteen

APPEALS AND DEALS

1937 to 1939

It took about a month for the court reporter in Aztec to type up the trial transcript and ship it off to the Supreme Court up in Santa Fe. A week later I was in Albuquerque at a bar association meeting and saw John Simms. I was thrilled when he asked me to join him and Hugh for lunch to help figure out how best to write the appeal brief for Velarde, Ochoa, and Avitia. We met at The Alvarado. I learned for the first time in my career as a lawyer that a successful appeal had to focus on the law but also had to present the facts in a "favorable position."

Hugh said: "John, none of your former colleagues on the Supreme Court will overturn Jim McGhee on the law. Our only chance is to convince them that the jury didn't have enough evidence to warrant a conviction. We can't afford to make our argument for reversal dependent on the jury instructions; it has to be on the factual evidence."

John sipped his coffee. "I take your point about the level of confidence that Jim McGhee will generate in the men up in Santa Fe on our high court, but we have to put the appeal forward in the real context in which Sheriff Carmichael was killed. That means we have to start with Chihuahuaita, not Aztec. It also means we have to give them a real strong reason to free those three men. You know most of the bar thinks they got off easy since they avoided the death penalty. Our best arguments will be in the facts, not the law."

Hugh thought a moment and said: "You're right as usual, but what about McGhee's strong comment to the jury? He flat out told them they should believe Sherman Porter, Hoy Boggess, and Dee Roberts. Don't you think he overstepped his bounds there?"

"Yes, I do." John leaned across the lunch table to make his point. "But I don't think the Supreme Court will reverse this case on that ground. He did try to help the prosecution a lot more than he should have by that comment to the jury. But I've thought it over some, and I believe he knew the prosecution was in trouble and needed all the help they could get at that point. His comments might have made the difference between acquittal and second-degree murder, but they had no effect at all on the main charge; that is, the first-degree murder conviction."

"So where does that leave us? Do we stand a chance, or are just wasting our time and theirs?"

John looked at Hugh and said: "Hugh, you've tried a lot of cases; how many of your convictions as U.S. Attorney got overturned on appeal?"

"Not many, but the ones that were involved legal errors, not factual disagreements. You know as well as I do that no appellate court likes to reverse a jury if the facts are in dispute. That's why I think we have to concentrate on Jim McGhee's jury instructions and stay away from the facts."

John steepled his fingers and stared at the ceiling. "You might be right, Hugh, but let me just spell out my theory on why, if we give the facts in context, they might reverse in this case. It all starts in Chihuahuaita. It ends with Vogel, Bickel, and Boggess. Vogel and Bickel are the men who were supposed to uphold the law: one a state senator, charged with making the law, and the other a justice of the peace, charged with applying the law. It was their combined pressure that caused the lid to be clamped down so tight that morning.

"Then another officer of the law, Deputy Boggess, causes the lid to blow clean off when he throws a tear gas bomb out into that crowd that had run around to the back of the alley. The main point here that we have to argue is the crowd wouldn't have been at the rear door if the sheriff had let them in the front door in the first place."

Hugh Woodward and I sat there patiently and listened to this remarkably articulate man spell out in four minutes what it had taken them hours to argue to the jury. "But John, true as all that is, how can we ever get the Supreme Court to blame a state senator, a justice of the peace, a sheriff, and a deputy sheriff? That sounds a lot more like sour grapes than placing the blame where it ought to be."

"We can't make an argument based on blame." John frowned. "Our argument is about *why* that riot happened. It's not that these officers and upholders of the law are to blame. But we can't ignore the fact that they played a much bigger role in what happened that day than whatever hotheaded fool in that crowd who started blazing way like it was the O.K. Corral. The damn fool who did that is dead. And Dee Roberts dispatched him right and proper."

Hugh could never resist a chance to argue the obvious. "Well, I'm not so sure about that. I still believe that there's a connection between Bobcat Wilson's late absence from the case and Dee Roberts's testimony about just who shot whom that morning. Those boys up in Aztec ran Bobcat off just before they put Dee on the stand. That told me they had something to hide."

"Hugh, you don't have to reconvince me of that. I argued it, remember? But it's beside the point I want to make on appeal. We have to put the case forward on appeal with a real big picture. We have to show them just what happened there in that alley and how little the crowd had to do with it. Without that, our three defendants are going to do forty-five years in the pen. The real key here is the state's theory of the case. That theory is based on the assumption that the panicked deputy made a second mistake and lost his gun. Someone picked up that gun and blasted away at the sheriff and at Deputy Wilson. There wasn't enough time for *two* men to pick up that gun; what I mean is, not enough time for one to pick it up, shoot it, and then pass it off to someone else. So one man shot them both with the same gun and then he got killed himself. That man was Ignacio Velarde. The irony is that his brother stands convicted of what he did and there is no proof whatsoever that he helped in any way or even knew his brother was there that morning. That's all supposition on the part of the jury."

"Yes, that might do it for Leandro, but what about our other two clients, Juan Ochoa and Avitia?" Now it was Hugh's turn. He had given this part of the case a lot of thought while John was up on the Pecos River after the trial, pretending to fish. "We can make a good argument for Juan because he had strong evidence that placed him out in front, not in the alley, when the shooting started. But it's much harder for Avitia. He took the stand. He put his credibility on the line. He looked them in the eye, more or less. I do wish he hadn't been so meek with them. In any event, he wasn't able to convince the jury that the gun in his hand in the alley was one that had been dropped there by someone else. In essence, he told that jury that he was just keeping that gun safe until they arrested him with it. For Manuel Avitia, we'll have to limit our arguments to the legal errors, not the factual inconsistencies.

"The main area we can argue a legal mistake on is the charge to the jury on second-degree murder," said John. "This was tried as a first-degree murder case all the way. All the evidence they put up was focused on first degree. Hell, they didn't really argue second degree until you made your closing argument and blasted their first-degree case all to bits."

Hugh looked at him thoughtfully. "Dick Modrall figured it out quick enough.

He argued for and won a second-degree jury instruction from McGhee, and then he argued for and won a second-degree conviction from the jury. Without him and his arguments, the jury would have acquitted every last man. Well, damn—do we have any really good arguments on the law?"

"Yes." John gave him a tight smile. "I was saving our best argument for last. Judge McGhee overstepped his bounds and the statute in New Mexico when he told that jury that he believed Sherman Porter, Dee Roberts, and Hoy Boggess. It put the jury in an impossible position. If they rejected that testimony, it would have been interpreted as meaning they thought the judge was biased, and they didn't want that. If they accepted the testimony, it had to mean that Avitia, and maybe Ochoa and Velarde along with him, had to be convicted of something.

"Those are the three witnesses with the strongest direct evidence against the three men they convicted. There's no coincidence here. Judge McGhee as much as told them he thought the three were guilty, but it was okay to let the rest go. And that's exactly what they did."

Hugh looked straight at John. "So our strongest legal argument is the unfair and improper comment on the evidence by the trial judge."

"Right." John slapped his palm on the table. "Why don't you write up the legal errors, and I'll write the statement of facts and the factual insufficiencies. Then we'll blend them together and ship them to you, Billy Wade, for a look-see."

"Fine, Mr. Simms," I said, "although I'll probably say 'no comment.' "

"Billy Wade," he replied, "no comment is a comment."

It didn't take a legal genius to figure out that the district attorney's office was just as intent on keeping its conviction as the defense was on taking it away. The prosecutors had been relieved of the burden of trying to convict ten men of first-degree capital murder. They no longer had to push for the death penalty—in short, their workload was a damn sight lighter. All they had to do was convince the Supreme by-God Court that Avitia and Velarde and Ochoa ought to do their time for doing their part in getting Sheriff Carmichael killed.

The men in the American Bar had their own view about the legal brief filed by the prosecutors—not that any of them had actually read it, much less claimed to understand the legal jargon. As they heard it, Modrall wrote a more or less *new* version of the facts. Instead of starting in Chihuahuaita and talking about Vogel and Bickel, Dick Modrall's brief started in the Spanish-American Hall and put Avitia, Velarde, and Ochoa right in the middle of the discussion about what to do about Navarro. Then he moved that same crowd down to the street in front of

Judge Bickel's court and positioned the law on the side of the righteous by saying it took several deputies to keep the peace since the mob was so large that morning.

The state's legal brief told the Supreme Court that the first man identified out in the alley that morning was Leandro Velarde. Velarde shook his fist at the deputy and told him that he and the others were about to see who was "disgraced." He also told that first deputy to leave Navarro "to us alone."

Boggess threw his tear gas bomb because *those* two men (Avitia and Ochoa) were trying to free the prisoner. At that *same time* gunshots went off and the sheriff suffered two mortal wounds; one of them came from a bullet fired from Hoy Boggess's gun. That same gun was used to mow down Bobcat. The deputy attorney general reminded the Court that the defense lawyers didn't dispute this evidence—they didn't call their own expert, and they didn't impeach the state's expert. Modrall argued in his brief that the defense accepted the state's theory as to which gun actually killed the sheriff.

Modrall highlighted the state's evidence that no lawman ever fired a shot until after the firing commenced from the crowd at the sheriff and at his deputy. He argued that Avitia was seen running through the crowd with a gun in his hand. Both Avitia and Ochoa were seen beating and kicking Hoy Boggess. Avitia admitted having a gun in his hand although "his" gun was never found. In fact, none of the many guns that *must have been there* were ever found.

He didn't entirely forget Leandro Velarde, but he didn't focus his appeal on him, just as he didn't focus his closing argument on first-degree murder. Dick Modrall knew where his strong points were. About all he said about Leandro Velarde was that he was the man agitating the crowd and was the man who led them from Coal Avenue to the alley down Third Street.

That's it. That's plenty enough to uphold the convictions of men who got off light. Modrall closed his brief with the essence of the state's position in the case—the only shame is that all the court can do is sustain; they cannot convict the Gallup Ten of a new charge, one that stills carries the death penalty.

Mary Ann was furious. She looked at Billy Wade, sitting there so smug and knowledgeable. As much to herself as to him she said: "I have come a long way toward an understanding of that arcane world you lawyers live in. But the thought that the Supreme Court of this state cannot reverse a jury verdict is ridiculous. Of course, I believe in the sanctity of the jury and all that, but what if the jury is just plain wrong? Why can't the Supreme Court fix that? Isn't that what they're supposed to do, fix legal wrongs?"

Billy Wade sipped the strong black coffee and took a deep breath. He needed both after last night's bout of drinking and arguing at the American Bar. He had been over this and found it frustrating that laymen, and laywomen too, always wanted the end result of any litigation to match their personal expectations of what the law should accomplish. "Yes, I know. You've come a long way; of that there's no doubt. But somewhere along the way you forgot some basic high school civics. Juries decide the facts and make the decisions about guilt or innocence. Appellate courts can't change the facts or the outcome unless there's a legal error. You may see what the jury in Aztec did as right or wrong, and the Supreme Court may even agree with you. The difference is that you would change it if you could; they know they can't. All they can do is review the law and make sure it was applied correctly in the case. As to the facts, if there are sufficient facts to support the verdict, then they have to sustain the jury's verdict. That's what you teach your students in civics class, isn't it?"

"No, sir, I do not. I teach them about justice, and I teach them about right and wrong. The jury may have enough evidence to convict Avitia, but how in the world did they ever reach a conclusion that Velarde and Ochoa were guilty? Velarde had almost no connection except for that ridiculous comment about toothpicks, and Ochoa had an ironclad alibi from three disinterested citizens. Isn't that enough? Can't the court up there in Santa Fe see that?"

"They might, but the odds are against it. There were disputed facts about all three men, and the court can't take one side or the other. That's the jury's job. As to the alibi, the jury rejected it. That's their choice. As long as there was no error in admitting the evidence in the first place, the Supreme Court won't upset the applecart on disputed facts. But you might be right on Velarde—the evidence did seem a little thin on him. If the court sees it that way, he might take a walk."

Back in Gallup—February 22, 1936

Dear Madam Journal,

Billy Wade just left, and I didn't have the heart to tell him what needs to be said. I'm not even sure how to tell you. I haven't written to you out of a mixture of lethargy, fear, and indecision. Actually, being lethargic isn't a reason—it's more of an excuse. Fear is a reason. I've been afraid to tell you what I was, at first, afraid to tell myself. I've outgrown Gallup. Children outgrow their rooms and their things and their fears. Adults can too. Take me, for example. I have outgrown a town where change is fought unless it means a change in business. I have outgrown my students, especially those who yearn for change—because they have moved on. Those who resist new thoughts see no need to move. Most importantly, I have outgrown my fear of losing Billy Wade. I know he won't come with me now, but I know he'll visit and, in time, maybe he'll find the courage to give up something good for something better. I don't mean to sound too negative about Gallup. It's wonderful in its own way. It's just that it's more inclusive than I am. It includes those who have a history here and those who will thrive here. But by definition, that excludes the downtrodden, the foreign born (if they tend to the radical view), and those, like me, who want more from life than just teaching. I can't change much by teaching, and that's what I feel I am called on to do. Effect change—hopefully for the betterment of everyone, including the people of Gallup. The only place to do that in New Mexico is Santa Fe. So I gulped, stuck out my chest, and walked into the grand front office of the *Santa Fe New Mexican* and asked for a job.

It surprised me, although it shouldn't have, to find the front office of New Mexico's only relatively liberal newspaper something less than grand. I don't know what I expected, but it wasn't the disorder and disarray that seemed the order of the day at the *Santa Fe New Mexican*. What kind of a job? the business manager asked. As an editor, I think I mumbled. Are you an editor? he said. No, I mumbled, but I could be. And so, after a hour of give-and-take on the nuances of the English language and the politics of my father, I got an offer as an editorial assistant. They will pay me less and work me more, but I know I'm going to love it. I will love it as much as I love Billy Wade, and I will hate it as much as I hate leaving Billy Wade. But like everything else I have ever done, I seem not to have a choice. I can't stay and stay happy, so I'll go even if it makes me miserable. Stupid, isn't it?

For months after the legal briefs were filed, nothing happened in the case. Eventually the Supreme Court heard oral arguments, and that started a new round of speculation in the American Bar. The consensus was that they were "at it again, ain't they?" First off, it's our riot and our sheriff that gets killed, and what do they do? They move the trial from here up to Aztec. Now that the defense has appealed the trial, what do they do? They say the appeal will be up there in Santa Fe. When will Gallup get its chance?

It stood to reason that the court that was the last resort for the Gallup Three would be anyplace but Gallup. The state capital seemed a logical choice. It also stood to reason that the Supreme Court of the State of New Mexico sat in someplace other than Gallup. Gallup, in those days, wasn't exactly "supreme" at much of anything.

The bar crowd didn't cotton much to an "appeal" in this case. What is there to appeal? And just what are they appealing for, anyhow? Mercy? Justice? Well, the jury in Aztec gave them more mercy than most folks around Gallup would have. They let seven of 'em go off scot-free and gave the other three "clemency."

Seems more merciful than just. Where, the crowd in the back of the bar wanted to know, is the justice for the men that killed a good man like Mack Carmichael?

I tried to explain this to the crowd by reminding them that an appeal was more or less automatic these days. Sending three men to the state pen for forty-five years at hard labor was nothing to laugh about, and all cases like that were appealed. I explained that maybe it was the word *appeal* that the boys in the American Bar found objectionable.

What really happened was that another court, a higher one, would review the evidence and the law to make sure that justice was served. So if it makes you happy, just think of it as a "review" rather than an "appeal." Now, there was a word that fit. Review was what the men and women of Gallup did every day of their lives. They reviewed local politics, local scandals, the stores on Coal Avenue, the number of Indian traders, high school sports, and, of course, the Lobos and the Aggies.

They reviewed who was cheating and who was preaching and who was just exactly where on the social ladder. They reviewed one another and they reviewed the trial and that fair/terrible result up there in Aztec (fair or terrible depending on where you sat on the matter of justice for killing a sheriff).

So while they were at reviewing everything else, they might just as well review the case as though they were members of the New Mexico Supreme Court.

It took several sessions, but at some point the men in the American Bar got it straight that the Supreme Court was set up to look at the evidence *on the record.* That is, they read what the court reporters typed up as the transcript of the evidence and they read what the trial judge wrote down as his instructions to the jury. They also looked at the indictment. If the indictment was okay, then they would look at the evidence in the case, according to the written transcript.

They wouldn't call witnesses or try to decide the facts of the case. That's a goddamn relief. At least it was to old Hoy. He was mighty afraid he would have to go back to Santa Fe and tell it all again.

David Chavez, Wheaton Augur, and I all agreed on one thing, finally. The only thing the Supreme Court would look for was to see if there was enough evidence in the case to make the jury verdict fit the crime that was set out in the indictment. If the evidence was strong enough for that purpose, then they wouldn't second-guess the jury. But if it wasn't, then they might have to give some relief.

If the evidence was strong enough to support the verdict, then they would look at the instructions on the law. If they were right; that is, if the judge wrote down the law correctly, then they wouldn't mess with his part of the case. So if the facts were proved up and if the law was given straight, the Supreme Court would "affirm."

That means let it stand. Do not reverse it. Let those boys serve their terms.

But if the evidence just wasn't there or there was a legal mistake in the indictment or in the jury instructions, then they might reverse the verdict. If that happened, they could order another trial or an acquittal. But they wouldn't do that over some piddley-ass mistake. It would have to be some big-ass mistake to reverse in this case.

I put it more lawyer like. I explained that it would have to be a "fundamental" error. Not wanting to sound too stupid on the matter, they pressed me for an example of just what might be "fundamental" enough to cause a reversal.

Well, say that the Supreme Court found that the indictment was legally defective because it had all six of those damn theories in it, some of which were never proved. That might be fundamental enough.

Or say they found that the evidence against some of the men convicted just wasn't strong enough to support a guilty verdict. Let's say they didn't really prove that one of the men was there in the alley; they just assumed he was. That might be fundamental enough.

Or say they thought that the judge made a mistake in how he defined the law to them. Like, for example, what he told them about which witnesses were the most believable. That was close, but it might be fundamental enough.

Here's what it comes down to. Are the five men who sit up there on the highest court in the State of New Mexico likely to find fault with the biggest case ever tried in New Mexico? Are they likely to want to put Gallup through another trial (even if it was physically held up there in Aztec)?

It came down to the fact that it all depended on how good a brief the defense lawyers filed and whether the prosecution wrote a good one in reply. Then, the cynics said, you got to look at how the five men on the Supreme Court felt on the day they decided the case. If they felt good, they usually affirmed; if they felt cranky, they usually reversed. Get it?

More than likely they would decide that enough was enough and those boys could now take their chances in the political arena. After all, the governor would have a shot after the Supreme Court had theirs. He couldn't change anything like guilt or innocence, but he did have the power to commute a sentence. Any sentence. Even one laid on the Gallup Three. Got it.

August 25, 1937

State of New Mexico v. Juan Ochoa, et al. 41 N.M. 589, 72 P.2d 609 (1937)

The appellate review of an important criminal case is rarely quick and never wrong. That is because the appellate court is, at least in New Mexico, the court of last resort. Assuming there are no federal constitutional issues in the case, the New Mexico Supreme Court cannot be said to be wrong because there is no one to say it. They have the last word. It took them about twenty-two months to decide the case of *State v. Ochoa, et al.* Not bad, considering the length of the transcript, the complexity of the legal issues, and the fundamental dispute in the evidence.

"Supreme" courts, wherever they sit, are unerringly alike in one respect. They want their decisions to be both understood and accepted. Courts, unlike the other two branches of government, have no military or police power. They rely solely on judicial rhetoric to garner the necessary support for the decisions they hand down. They cannot make the law. That's the function of the legislature, but they interpret the statutes passed by legislatures and they decide matters of "common law." Their force *de jure* is the written opinion they hand down.

Justice Sadler signed the Formal Opinion of the Court. The court was unanimous, and the opinion itself was concurred in by Chief Justice Hudspeth, by Justices Bickley and Brice, and by District Judge Irwin S. Moise. As was the fashion of appellate courts for almost two hundred years, they announced their decision in the first paragraph on the first page of the opinion and then spent twenty pages explaining and establishing a basis for their opinion.

In some ways, it was as though Justice Sadler somehow knew about the pivotal meeting that Dick Modrall had with the other prosecutors just before he made the final closing argument in the case. Reading the opinion also makes you think that Justice Sadler was there when John Simms argued with his co-counsel about giving the second-degree murder instruction. And it was as though he was there in the secret jury room when that jury resoundingly rejected first-degree murder for all ten defendants but found three of them guilty of the lesser charge. In order to answer the question of whether the facts supported a second-degree-murder conviction, the Court observed that the state's brief on appeal set forth:

> two theories presented by the evidence shown [under] which the jury might find the appellants guilty of second-degree murder. First, that one of the appellants actually shot and killed Sheriff Carmichael. Second, that the appellants or any of them aided and abetted the person or persons who actually shot and killed Sheriff Carmichael.

The defense response was set out in the opinion of the Court:

> The defense says, without contradiction by the state, that the trial court eliminated any conspiracy theory by refusing to submit that issue to the jury. . . . The same may be said of the theory that the murder was perpetrated in the commission or attempt to commit a felony.
>
> The return of verdicts of second degree against some defendants had the important effect of acquitting them of the charge of first degree upon the theory of a homicide committed in the perpetration of a felony, to wit, the aiding of the prisoner, Navarro, to escape. So as the matter rests before us, the State must defend the verdict as one finding the defendants of common-law murder, either as principals or as aiders and abettors. This greatly narrows the issue under defendants' contentions that second degree was not properly submitted to the jury.
>
> We do not understand counsel to contend that the unexplained killing of Sheriff Carmichael with a deadly weapon would not warrant submission of second degree. But rather, that there is not sufficient evidence to connect them to the slaying, either as the actual slayers or as aiders and abettors.

The Supreme Court thus set up the basis for its opinion. If the facts were sufficient to support the charge and if the jury's verdict of not guilty for all defendants on first-degree murder charges acted as a rejection of the theory that they were trying to accomplish the escape of Navarro, then the only remaining matter was whether the law would permit a finding of second-degree murder. As to this the court held:

> Before an accused may become liable as an aider and abettor, he must share the criminal intent of the principal. There must be a community of purpose, partnership in the unlawful undertaking.

Thus, in the opinion of New Mexico's highest court, the question came down to whether there was sufficient evidence to connect these three men with the unlawful criminal intent of *whoever* shot the sheriff. In other words:

> As to the defendant Leandro Velarde there is no evidence that sufficiently connects him with the unlawful design of the slayer of Sheriff Carmichael. The last time he was seen prior to the hurling of the tear gas bomb and the firing of the first shot, he was in the crowd a few feet removed from Deputy Boggess. There was apparently nothing about his actions when then seen to excite suspicion. . . . He is not shown to have taken part in the assault on Deputy Boggess, as were Avitia and Ochoa. . . . The suggested testimony about an ice pick being used to wound Boggess was never admitted. If Velarde had on his person at the affray the ice pick that he removed from the bib of his overalls and placed in an ice chest at his home half an hour later, no proof of any display of same and of an effort to use was presented at the trial. Mere suspicion does not furnish the required support.

And with that, the Supreme Court freed Leandro Velarde. In their view, his conviction couldn't stand because he was acquitted of the conspiracy charge (as were all of the defendants by reason of the acquittal on first-degree murder charges). So if he didn't conspire to kill the sheriff, he could only be guilty as a principal or as an aider or abettor. Because no proof of his actual participation in the actual shooting was offered, he was set free. But the same reasoning didn't apply to his fellow defendants Manuel Avitia and Juan Ochoa. As to them, Justice Sadler said:

> The defendants Avitia and Ochoa are differently situated. . . . Even if it be assumed that these two defendants were without knowledge of the purpose of the slayer or slayers of the deceased to

> make an attempt on his life, the evidence abundantly supports an inference that with the firing of the first shot they become appraised of that purpose. The intent to kill, or to aid and abet in the commission thereof, may be formed at the scene of the crime, even though the accused may have gone there without such intention. . . . Both Avitia and Ochoa are identified in the testimony as being still engaged in an assault upon the fallen Boggess after two bullets had entered the body of the sheriff. . . . The fact that they were thus engaged in a vicious assault upon him (Boggess) after firing upon the sheriff's party commenced left it within the jury's province to infer, if it saw fit, not only that these defendants shared the intent of the slayer, but also that they aided and abetted him in his unlawful undertaking.

The rationale was that even if the killer of the sheriff was himself killed, what Avitia and Ochoa did after the firing of the first shot was enough to put them in prison for the next forty-five years. Maybe for sixty years. At hard labor. The court's mandate was:

> It follows from what has been said that the judgment of the district court must stand affirmed as to the defendants Avitia and Ochoa. As to the defendant Velarde, it is reversed, with a direction to the trial court to set aside the judgment of conviction pronounced upon him and to discharge the prisoner. *It is so ordered.*

And so the Gallup 14 became the Gallup 2. One hundred and eighty were arrested. Forty-eight red rascals were put in the pen. Fourteen were brought to a preliminary hearing. Ten were bound over for trial. Three were convicted. Two were affirmed. Do I have that right? The usual crowd was gathered in the American Bar, and the usual questions moved up and down the bar. Just what the hell's going on here? It wasn't just that a man escaped a long prison term; it was the ignominy of it all. Dropping from forty-eight to two is downright embarrassing. It's worse than being a railroad town with "slow" in your name.

There was no whoopin' and hollerin' in either the American Bar *or* in the Angeles Pool Hall. It didn't "make no never mind" to the men at the American Bar that Velarde's ice pick in his bib overalls wasn't "connected." It seemed downright silly to let him go on account of that. There was all that talk at the trial about *pica diente,* and he damn sure had the ice pick, didn't he? What difference did it make that the dumb shit prosecutors didn't get the evidence in about Hoy getting stabbed by an ice pick?

And he was damn sure there, just like Avitia and Ochoa, so what's the big deal? Convicting two just wasn't enough. But, so said the boys at the back table, at least it was over. The governor wasn't about to touch this case. Was he? Would he?

The gloom was about the same at the Angeles Pool Hall. Getting one off just wasn't enough. What about Avitia and Ochoa? The proof on them wasn't much different than for Velarde. Was it? Why couldn't the court see that the men who killed the sheriff were dead? Dee Roberts shot them, didn't he? What good did it do to lock up Juan Ochoa and Manuel Avitia for the rest of their lives? That's what forty-five to sixty at hard labor meant. The rest of their goddamn lives. The governor was a *gringo.* He wouldn't touch this case. Would he?

The opinion of the Supreme Court was the last *legal* word that could be taken in the case of *State vs. Ochoa.* But the governor has the last *political* word. Governor Miles was a little better off than his three predecessors were; he didn't have the National Miners Union to deal with. The NMU was more or less out of the picture after its members merged into the UMW. The UMW, that is, John L. Lewis himself, still had men to take care of. So the UMW petitioned Governor Miles to commute the sentences of the Gallup Two. Their petition was *to* a politician, based solely on *political* grounds to achieve a *political* end. Some said they didn't care about the two men at all but only wanted to prove their "sincerity." The way to do that was to remove any resentment over their fight with the NMU, and the way to accomplish that was to join the effort to free Ochoa and Avitia.

UMW district president Frank Hefferly and UMW organizer Earl Stucker led the negotiations. They pled the case succinctly. The charges were political, and the solution was political. Set them free, and the union would see to it that these two men caused no more trouble in Gallup.

It worked. In July 1939 Governor John E. Miles granted conditional pardons for the two men. The condition was that they get the hell out of New Mexico. They did. Ochoa went to Denver, Colorado. Avitia went to Bisbee, Arizona.

The American Bar nearly erupted—now how do you suppose that just four years after these men were sentenced to forty-five to sixty years at hard labor, a New Mexico governor turned 'em loose? And how come it was just two years after the Supreme Court affirmed their convictions? Well, to start off, he didn't do it by himself. I explained to the restless boys in the American Bar that New Mexico had a parole board that reviewed all cases. In both cases, Avitia's and Ochoa's, the vote was unanimous in favor of a conditional pardon. In both cases the chairman of the parole board, Mr. John F. Simms, recused himself from the vote. Naturally.

After he granted the pardons, Governor Miles got a few telegrams of his own. For example, the Committee for the New Mexican People sent him a telegram from their offices in New York that said:

> HEARTY CONGRATULATIONS ON YOUR PARDON OF JUAN OCHOA AND MANUEL AVITIA. YOUR RECOGNITION OF THEIR INNOCENCE INDICATES A NEW RESPECT FOR JUSTICE, CIVIL LIBERTIES, AND SOCIAL DECENCY IN NEW MEXICO AND THE BEGINNING OF EQUAL OPPORTUNITY FOR HER SPLENDID PEOPLE TO SHARE THE ADVANTAGES OF LIVING UNDER A DEMOCRACY.

That one pissed off a lot of folks in Gallup. Just why the so-called Committee for the New Mexican People had an office in New York (of all places) was a plain mystery to most of the town. Hardly anyone in Gallup had ever even been to New York. So who was on that so-called committee, anyhow?

The Formal Orders of the governor that granted the conditional pardons to Ochoa and Avitia were typed up on the same typewriter on the same day and contained the same single condition of granting the pardon:

> *A pardon from further service of said sentence* UPON THE CONDITION *that he immediately leave the State of New Mexico and remain away therefrom.*

But as it turned out, there was still one more New Mexico governor who would hear from Ochoa and Avitia. Governor J. J. Dempsey got a letter from Manuel Avitia dated June 15, 1943. I'm going to spell it out for you just like he did, misspellings and all:

> *Hon. J. J. Dempsey*
> *Governor of New Mexico*
> *Santa Fe, New Mexico*
>
> Dear Governor;
>
> I am an ex-convict. I was convicted of the crime of murder, in San Juan County, in 1935 and sentenced by Judge McGee to serve from 45 to 50

years in prison; I was taken to Santa Fe to the State Prison to serve my time.

I was immediately made a trusty of and allowed my liberty in and about the prison and was employed as a berber by trade in the Guard House for about a year or more, and was paid for my services during most of this time.

I was granted a conditional pardon, by Governor Miles, in 1939, and was required by such pardon to leave the State of New Mexico, so I immediately came to Bisbee, Arizona where I have been engaged every since in my garage and repair shop, and have worked ever since I have been here, and saved and accumulated several hundred dollars from my labor, and my business is now worth probalt $2000.00 counting tools and equipments, and I am gaining nicely and behaving myself in a manner becoming a good citizen.

I am a married man with a wife and two minor children to support, one of my children was born in New Mexico and one in Bisbee, and they are living with me now here in Bisbee.

Last September, I went across the International Line, to Naco, Sonora, Mexico to see an aunt of mine who was sick and only stayed about one hour, and then returned to Bisbee. I had a pass port and showed it to the Officers at the line and they allowed me to pass unmolested, and just here lately I have been arrested by the Immigration Officers as being unlawfully in the United States, and I expect that my hearing before the Immigration Inspector in Charge at Naco Arizona will be held probably on Monday, June 21st at 10 o'clock am of that day.

I will have Mr. Jacob Ramsower, the Chief of Police in Bisbee and Mr. I. V. Pruitt, the Sheriff of this county as character witnesses in my behalf who will swear that my conduct and deportment has been good ever since I have resided in Bisbee, which is over three years, and about a year ago I made application to become a citizen of the U.S. and filed the same with the Immigration and Naturalization in El Paso, Texas and was getting ready to attend my hearing on my petition in our Superior Court here when I was arrested by the Immigration Officers from Naco, and they have put me to a great deal of trpuble and worry and expense by so doing, but I am in hopes that I can make such a showing that the Department at Washington D.C. will decide that I may be permitted to remain and carry out my intentions to become a citizen.

If you will kindly grant me a full pardon it will help me greatly, before the Immigration Hearing, next Monday, and it will be hard to predict results of their inquiry if I don't get this pardon from you.

So, governor, upon receipt of this letter I would thank you to wire me, Western Union, at my expense, the results of your conclusions in this matter and if you will grant me a full pardon please so state in your telegram so that I may present it at the hearing, or if you can get the pardon here to me by that time it will be great help to me, as I can present it at the hearing.

Kindly send your telegram in care of S. K. Williams, my attorney at Bisbee, Arizona.

Trusting that you will do me this great favor for which I will forever be obligated and thanking you in anticipation of receiving the same, I am,

Most respectfully yours,

Manuel Avitia

Governor Dempsey wrote back to Mr. Avitia and told him he would present his request to the parole board. While they were considering the matter, the immigration authorities told Avitia that they would not deport him if New Mexico decided to give him a full pardon. On September 3, 1943, the governor wrote to Mr. Avitia and told him that the parole board had denied the petition for a pardon. And that's the last we heard from Mr. Avitia here in New Mexico. Likely he was sent to Old Mexico.

As for Mr. Ochoa, he wrote a letter to Governor Miles from his home in Denver, Colorado, on December 7, 1942. Most other folks were mindful of the one-year anniversary of Pearl Harbor on that day—maybe that's why Ochoa decided to ask Govenor Miles for permission to visit his mother during the week of Christmas here in Gallup. He explained to Governor Miles that his mother is "now up in years and has been more or less sick for the past period of months." Governor Miles passed the request off to the superintendent of the state pen, and he authorized a visit to Mr. Ochoa's mother for three days at Christmas but advised:

> . . . We think it would be to the best interest of all concerned if you would not put too much time around Gallup.

Two years later, in January 1944, Ochoa again wrote to the governor and asked for permission to visit his mother in Gallup. This time the governor said no. Far as anyone in Gallup ever heard, Ochoa stayed in Denver.

Oh, as far as the man they tried to free, Esiquel Navarro, he has yet to be heard from. Some said he might be in Bisbee. They're pretty tolerant down there.

Speaking of tolerant, I saw Mary Ann up in Santa Fe last week. We're friends again. We went from being in love to just loving to just barely talking. Her move was dumbfounding. I still don't understand why she couldn't change the world from here in Gallup. She hasn't changed all that much in Santa Fe, either personally or figuratively. New Mexico is as it was when she was here—tolerant of history, resistant to change, and fair. Gallup hasn't changed all that much either—course, that's her point.

epilogue

BOBCAT SPEAKS

May 15, 1987

The weather was crisp and the ground hard at the Rock Springs Ranch on May 15, 1987. Fifty-two years have passed since the riot in the alley down in Gallup, but not much has changed out on the Rock Springs. As I drove out there, I thought back on the enigma of silence, its importance and its irrelevance. Bobcat, as far as I know, never told anyone what happened in that alley back in 1935. That was important to me as his lawyer but irrelevant to me as his friend. But something told me that maybe, just maybe, Bobcat was ready to talk. It wasn't the passage of time; it was the mission I was on. His health, like mine, was good, but we were both living in our eighth decade of life in Gallup and, well, you know, you just never know.

It wasn't yet summer, and the cold air lingered here in the high desert twenty miles north of Gallup. Inside the massive living room of the ranch, Bobcat worked with his son, Larry, to sort out and catalog the large collection of guns stored at the ranch. Revolvers, rifles, shotguns, holsters, ammo belts, and cleaning tools covered the two large tables in the little room behind the massive bar on the south wall of the living room. More guns were hung on the log walls, and even more were waiting their turn in boxes and crates piled up in the corners. This room was initially the only room in the old Rock Springs Trading Post, an outpost on the border of the Navajo Reservation, which virtually surrounds Gallup.

Larry had finally talked Bobcat into letting me come out and prepare a detailed list of the gun collection for estate tax purposes. Joe Atkinson was there and had his video camera set up. Joe was in the insurance business and wrote the policies for the ranch and the gun collection.

"Billy Wade, there's chili on the stove and sliced ham in the cold box if you want some," Larry offered.

"Thanks, but I'm real anxious to get on with this. I mean to get your dad to talking today. It's about time, you know," I answered.

"Talking is something Bobcat is against, but you're welcome to try," Larry said.

We pulled the guns out one by one and set them on the old trading post counter in front of the new strobe light for good camera coverage. Gun after gun was placed in front of the camera while Joe and I described them by model, type, caliber, and value. Bobcat came in and sat in the old rocker by the woodstove, still warm from the morning fire. He watched and occasionally grunted when either Joe or I stumbled on the exact make and model of one of the guns in the massive collection. Guns were a way of life for the Wilson clan, and the years of trading and using guns had made both Bobcat and Larry widely recognized experts.

Bobcat knew every weapon in the room by heart. Larry knew them by sight. I knew them by description. Joe knew their monetary value.

Larry lifted the most special gun in the collection out of its special cherrywood, leather-lined box. The .45 revolver gleamed from gun oil and smelled of history. Larry laid it carefully on the trading post bar. The gun was unlike any other in the collection. In the box with it were an old newspaper article and a beat-up photograph of a bunch of people in a dark hall with their right fists raised up in the air, as though they were proclaiming something.

I said softly: "Larry, it's time." Larry looked at Bobcat but spoke into the microphone. "I'm led to believe that this here pistol is one that was, you might say, instrumental in New Mexico's most famous gunfight. Dad, seeing as how you were there and all, I'd sure be obliged if you'd speak up and tell us, once and for all, about this famous gun."

To Larry's surprise and my utter astonishment, Bobcat squinted at the gun and then just started talking, slow and serious like. "This pistol belonged to the McKinley County sheriff's office and old Mack Carmichael." And with that he stopped, just like always.

Larry held his breath and tried another tack. "Dad, Billy Wade and I were looking at this newspaper, that is, the front page of it, which has some of the story about this gun and your part in the famous gunfight in the alley down from the old jail. Look here at this old newspaper. By God, this picture shows three real handsome young men here. Which one is you?"

Bobcat looked at the old, yellowed newspaper as though it were brand new.

His eyes softened, and his voice dropped to a low whisper. "That newspaper there is the *Denver Post*. You can see the date on it is April the sixth, nineteen and thirty-five. The man in the photograph on the left is Hoy Boggess. The man in the center, Sheriff M. R. Carmichael. That's me there on the right."

I couldn't stay silent any longer. "Bobcat, this would be a mighty fine time to hear you tell the story of the riot and all that took place down in Gallup, what is it now, some fifty years ago? I read this article, and of course I lived through part of it with you, but I still don't know your side of it. What happened?"

"What happened was that Sheriff Mac was killed, and Hoy was near beat to death, and I got shot. That's what happened. You were there, you old fool; you ought to remember as well as me."

"Well, as one old fool to another, I'd best remind you that you never did tell your side of it, not to me or anyone else. So here's your chance." Larry aimed the camera and zoomed in a bit.

Bobcat answered just as though he'd told the story many times before, in his mind. There was no hesitating, no frowning for memory; he told it just like it had happened yesterday. "Mr. Carmichael was killed when he come out the door. I walked east about twenty feet, when I was shot under the right arm. I turned back and shot one fella, then I went on back and rescued Hoy Boggess. Two fellas had ahold of him. He was bleedin' from the head, and his eye was stickin' straight up blue. He says, 'Bobcat, I can hear your voice, but I can't see you.' So I shot one of 'em loose from him and got him by the arm and took him back to the sheriff's office."

As though that were all there was to it, Bobcat stopped. Larry knew better than to probe, but I was willing to risk Bobcat's well-known wrath at those who appeared to be sticking their noses into his private business. I gritted my teeth and said, "Well, damn, Bobcat. You can't just stop talking. Who started it?"

"When we opened the door and started out with the prisoner, I had him by the left arm. He reached over and grabbed Carmichael by the shirt collar, and when he did, I hit him so hard over the head with my pistol that it knocked his thumbnail off. Knocked him right down. Then I no more than got up against the wall, there was a telephone post, I went in back of the telephone post and come around and faced 'em, and that's about the time the shootin' started."

I interrupted, much to the dismay of Larry, who muttered, "Goddamn it; let him talk." "Bobcat, had they already shot Carmichael, or—"

"They shot him before they did me, because we was shot with the same gun. And this first fella I shot, I shot him right in the belly. He was right after me with an ice pick. Oh, he was a big fella. He weighed 250. And his eyes popped out there about an inch, but he never said a word. He went draggin' his ass back up against the *Gallup Independent.* And then this other one come out, and I said, 'Well, I better not shoot him. They say I shoot everybody.' So I shot in the street, and that time he hit me, and that was the time I got loose and I just started after all of them down there. And that was when I shot that fella that had ahold of Boggess. And Presley came around into the alley and started asking us—and I took Hoy Boggess back up to the sheriff's office. And by that time the Gamerco deputy sheriffs, they all come down, and I said, 'Get that machine gun and go down there and clean 'em out and get them shotguns, too.' And they said, 'It's locked.' And I said, 'Tear the damn door down.' So they did. And after they went down there, then Hoy Boggess and me went to get it over with."

"Bobcat, what do you mean, get it over with? Get what over with?"

"Well, they gave me about one chance in a thousand."

"You mean to live?"

"Damn straight to live. They hit me right between the backbone and that blood vessel that comes down there. They reached in there and pulled the bullet out, all except a piece about the size of a .22, and it's still in there. And I don't know whether it's causin' me trouble or been causin' me any trouble. The doctor wouldn't tell me. And then a bunch of them lawyers come in to help them fellas. So they went over to the Harvey House and got some rooms over there, as they claim. Now, I don't know. They got some rooms, then they come down there to get in their cars, as I've been told, I don't know. So when they got started to get in their cars, some of the boys grabbed 'em, as they claim, whupped 'em pretty good, and then took 'em out there in Tohatchi Flats and whupped 'em some more and turned 'em loose. And the next day they walked on the road and somebody picked 'em up in a wagon and took 'em to Tohatchi. At Tohatchi somebody come and got 'em and took 'em to Gallup, took 'em to Dr. Travers. And he said, 'Ah, they're not skinned up much. They don't look like they're hurt at all.' But they were goin' to sue the paper and they was goin' to sue everything, everybody. But it finally cooled off."

Sensing that Bobcat had said about all he was going to say on the shooting, I tried changing the subject. "How come you didn't testify at the trial?"

"They called me for the trial at Aztec, and ol' Dee Roberts told me before the trial, he said, 'I want to talk to you, Bobcat, and see what happened.' And so I said, 'All right, Dee.' So we went to the sheriff's office, and I told him word for word. When I got through talkin', he just reached over and patted me on the shoulder and said, 'Bobcat, you're right.' Then when we went up there to Aztec, they was havin' a little meeting. Chavez was district attorney. Carmody was the assistant. Eva Ella Sabin, she was the girl that wrote everything down. And so Chavez started talkin' to me, and he said, 'You can't say you shot anybody.' He said, 'You seen 'em go down.' Well, I didn't feel too good with that remark. And I said, 'Well, the bastard went down, if that's what you want to know.' So they dismissed it pretty quick. We stayed there from Monday until Saturday morning, and Saturday morning they come to Hoy Boggess and me and said, 'You can go on home.' And they said, 'We don't even want you to testify,' so I didn't testify. And Hoy Boggess told me, he says, 'If you testify, Bobcat, I'm goin' to Old Mexico.' So we come on back here, but the paper, or the lawyers, raised the devil wantin' to know why Bobcat Wilson didn't testify. But I had to stay with my right story. I couldn't change it. There was no way I could change my story. They all thought I was goin' to die. I thought I was goin' to die. So they just went ahead and told what they done and all this and what I'd done. And they was goin' to bring it up again, but they didn't. Judge's name was McGhee. He was the one they brought in up there."

Larry said, "Dad, now that trial up there in Aztec, why was it up there?"

Bobcat seemed equally puzzled by the question. He said: "Do you mean goin' to Aztec?"

"Uh-huh."

"That was for getting it out of the county where it happened. See, there were too many people here that knew what happened in Gallup, and one thing and another, you know, just change the scenery, get away from here; that's all. Well, you see, they figured there would be a lot more people from Gallup up there to fill the courthouse to see what was goin' on. If we get up there to get away from Gallup, we would get away from 'em all and have a fair trial up there. In Gallup, why, they didn't even think they could have the trial. If they had it here, there would been a courthouse full of different nationalities of people. And when it was over, they took 'em down and put 'em on a railroad car and shipped a lot of 'em back to Old Mexico."

"Did they ever convict anybody?"

"Yeah, they sent some of them to the penitentiary. I think they got about eight, but I don't remember now how many they did."

"What started it?"

"Well, when I went down there, I didn't know they was goin' to take this fella to court that day. And when we got down there, Carmichael acted pretty mad because his face was red as could be, and he says, 'Come on, Bobcat, and go with me.' And I didn't even have a gun on. So they unlocked the locker, and I reached up there and got ahold of a pistol and took it. We headed down Second

Street with me on one side of the prisoner and Mack on the other, and after we took him in there we went in the back room to go out to the alley. Carmichael had him. I said, 'Well, give him to me, Mack.' So he turned him over to me."

Larry said: "You just had him down there because he was going to have his trial, that eviction trial or whatever it was?"

"Yeah, that's right. But by God, they formed right in front on the street. There were women, kids, men, all a hollerin'. Hell, there was a street full of 'em. There was two hundred of 'em or more."

"There were two hundred of them and eighteen of you?"

"There wasn't eighteen officers. Some of them boys come from the mine down there. But when I went down there, there was Hoy Boggess, Carmichael, Dee Roberts, and Allie Aldrich and me. That's all that went down there."

"Just five of you?"

"Yeah."

"Everything was happening at the back door?"

"And there was one Mexican boy in there by the name of Freddie Montoya. He later killed a Navajo up there in front of the cigar store, Smith's Cigar Store. And when I went to court in Aztec, we was outside and he come over and told me, he said, 'Bobcat, any way you go, I'm goin' 100 percent with you because you're the only one that's got it right.' I never changed my story. You can't, you know."

Larry looked at me and said: "The truth is the truth. Right, Dad?"

"That's right. You got to remember we had all the mines a goin'. There were a lot of people in town. There was very good people and some very rough people."

That's how old Bobcat ended his telling of the tale the one and only time he ever told it. And he couldn't have ended it on a truer note. Gallup did have the mines and it had the people, the good ones and the rough ones. Together they put Gallup on the map, but not in a way that anyone ever figured on or ever wanted, except maybe Bobcat. Not that he wanted a shooting or getting shot himself. I just mean that he wanted things to be straight out. If you behaved yourself, you had no reason to fear him. If you messed with him, he would shoot you. That's what he did fifty-two years ago in that alley behind Bail-less Bickel's courtroom.

Or did he? Just who was it who shot Solomon Esquibel and Ignacio Velarde? Dee or Bobcat? Dee said he did it. At the time Bobcat didn't say one way or the other. Of course, at that time the dust had hardly settled and Bobcat was more or less dead. The fact that Doc Pousma pulled him through out there at Rehoboth, much to his surprise as well as Dee's, bears on why Bobcat held his tongue from April 1935 until May 1987.

Fifty-two years of silence. Fifty-two years of folks in Gallup wondering what Bobcat would say and wondering if he would ever say anything at all. All in all, it's now been sixty-four years since the shootout and the telling of this story. I started this tale off by telling you that nobody ever messed with Bobcat. No one did then, and I'm not about to start now. I believe I'll leave it at that.

The question most folks asked for years after the riot was: Whatever happened to Navarro? After all, he was the man the Gallup 14 tried to set free. What did he do after he ran down the alley and disappeared into history? Well, that's another story. I'll tell you about it someday.

ACKNOWLEDGMENTS AND BIBLIOGRAPHY

I could never name all the people from Gallup who played a part in bringing this book about—there are too many—but I hope all of you know how much I appreciate your time and your input. There are a few who I must name, although I could never thank them enough for making a real difference in how this book turned out—but I'll try. Thanks, Dad, Kath, Dean, Barbara, Karen, Larry, Octavia, Margaret, and Herbert.

My dad, Lester Stuart, gave me the idea. My wife, Kathleen, gave me the courage to try and propped me up along the way. My first editor, Dean Smith, taught me more than he'll ever know. My editor at the University of New Mexico Press, Barbara Guth, gently led me into the publishing world and provided the grit to sandpaper a rough draft into a novel. My other editor, Karen Taschek, polished and cut my blurred and ponderous manuscript. My friend Larry Wilson gave me his time, his memories, and his father's videotape—all of which were invaluable. And last but most assuredly not least, Octavia Fellin gave me her insight, her critical comments, and her vast knowledge about life in Gallup over the last sixty years.

I read a great deal in preparation for the writing of this book. For those whose appetites have been whetted by the Gallup 14, I offer the following short bibliography:

El Balderrama, Francisco, and Raymond Rodriguez. *"Decade of Betrayal: Mexican Repatriation in the 1930's.* Albuquerque, New Mexico: UNM Press, 1995.

Fergusson, Erna. *Murder & Mystery in New Mexico.* Albuquerque, New Mexico: Merle Armitage Editions, 1948.

Gomez-Quinones, Juan. *Mexican American Labor, 1790–1990.* Albuquerque, New Mexico: UNM Press, 1994.

Hannett, Arthur Thomas. *Sagebrush Lawyer.* New York: Pageant Press, 1964.

Long, Haniel. *Piñon Country.* Santa Fe, New Mexico: The Sunstone Press, 1975.

Nickelson, Howard B. "One Hundred Years of Coal Mining in the San Juan Basin, New Mexico." Bulletin 111, New Mexico Bureau of Mines & Mineral Resources, New Mexico Institute of Mining & Technology, Socorro, New Mexico, 1988.

Noe, Sally. *"Gallup, Six Decades of Route 66."* Gallup, New Mexico: Gallup Downtown Development Group, 1991.

O'Neil, Bill. "Gallup's Worst Day—April 4, 1935." Unpublished master's thesis, New Mexico State University, Las Cruces, New Mexico, 1978.

Rubenstein, Harry R. "Destruction of the National Miners' Union." Chapter 3 in *Labor in New Mexico: Unions, Strikes and Social History Since 1881,* edited by Robert Kern. Albuquerque: UNM Press, 1977.

State of New Mexico v. Ochoa (complete trial court transcript). Microfilm S208–209. University of New Mexico College of Law Library, Albuquerque, New Mexico, October 1935.

State of New Mexico v. Ochoa, et al. (New Mexico Supreme Court Docket No. 4220), 41 N.M. 589, 72 P2d 609 (1937).